Phantom Frost

Phantom Frost

A Novel

Alfred Wurr

A Wurreal Games Book

For my wife, Lorelei, and my parents, Bev and Alfred, Sr.

Contents

Welcome

Welcome and thanks very much for your purchase of *Phantom Frost*. *Phantom Frost* is a first-in-series novel written in Canadian English and professionally edited using the *Canadian Oxford Dictionary* and *Editing Canadian English* as primary resources. I really hope you enjoy reading it.

I've greatly enjoyed writing it and reliving the '80s when doing research to confirm my memories of the time. Some locations or businesses I've written about are entirely fictional, for purposes of the story. Those that are not fictional are, of course, used in a fictitious manner.

Shivurr's adventures will continue in the next novel in the series, which is in progress as of this writing. You can subscribe to my mailing list to get news, updates and more at: www.alfredwurr.com/subscribe.

Play as Shivurr in the upcoming video game coming to PC, Mac, and Linux. Stay up to date on the game's development progress by subscribing to the Wurreal Games newsletter at: www.wurrealgames.com/subscribe.

Phantom Frost

Chapter 1

Lunar Crater

No matter how cool you are, everyone melts, eventually. Those words echoed through my head as I raced across the desert floor, heading northeast toward Lunar Crater, under the Nevada sun. Where I had heard them before, I couldn't recall. My memory wasn't what it used to be, but I would hear those words spoken to me in my dreams sometimes, stepping out of the inky black fog of my damaged memory. I think someone close to me had said them ages ago. They were strange words since the only person I knew of for whom melting was a concern was me. Regardless, seldom before was that fate as likely to occur for *someone*—that being me—as it was today.

I'd been gulping dry air and daydreaming of cold cans of soda pop, muttering product slogans to myself to keep my spirits up for several miles now. Steam rose from my icy shoulders, trailing me in wisps, disappearing into the dry desert air a few feet back. My cold feet left wet footprints on the sandy ground that soon evaporated into nothingness. I kicked a loose rock, stumbled, but caught myself before falling.

Without more moisture, I'll soon be eating dust, I thought. *Just a hot mess for the agents to find. Scratch that—my corpse won't be around long enough. I'll melt away, leaving only a trail of faint roundish footprints leading nowhere. They'll think I flew away, picked up by Soviet agents in a helicopter. I'd love to see Dixon's face, thinking the Reds got me.*

Nineteen hours earlier, I'd escaped a prison—the labs of a top-secret research facility called the Bodhi Institute. For about a decade, I'd been an unwilling participant in more experiments than I care to remember. I'd slipped out a side door in the middle of the night with a small cache of supplies provided by my best friend, Scott. It was easier than expected, but I guess I didn't seem suicidal to the Bodhi Group watchmen. The weak part of me wished I were back there: trapped but cool, a glass of ice water in hand, watching TV, reading a book, or taking a nap. But my nightmares made that impossible. I'd ignored them for months, while they haunted only my sleep. But when they'd invaded my waking hours, I had to go. I had to find answers. I had to find the ancient chamber that stood at their epicentre and that some instinct told me lay ahead of me, in the desert waste.

I didn't know who I was or where I came from. Not really; not fully. Sure, I remembered most of the years of my detention with crystal clarity. I knew what I was: an organism of snow and ice, unique in all the world. A snowman, they called me; cold hands with a warm heart. I knew what I was capable of; even with no legs, my feet run like the wind and allow me to jump as high as I am tall. I can do other things—things that frighten and astonish people, people like those chasing me. So much so, they'd locked me up and studied me like a lab rat for the past decade. I remembered all that, but little to nothing further into my past than my capture and imprisonment. And I remembered my name, Shivurr, but it was a name, an identity, that lacked history or context, which was both freeing and frustrating.

I had bigger problems than amnesia, though. I'd messed up, big time—pushed too hard through the night instead of seeking shelter to wait out the heat of the day. When the sun rose in all its deadly glory, I gawked at its dangerous beauty like a Grand Canyon tourist instead of running for cover. Ten years stuck underground made me a sucker for a pleasant view and fresh air, I guess. By the time the view got old, only the open, unshaded desert encircled me. I had no choice but to keep on toward the crater. Hopefully I'd find shade there or water trapped near the bottom.

Right, I thought, *and there'll be a 7-Eleven selling Slurpees, too.*

I studied the red-and-white logo on the small glass bottle in my hand. A mouthful of dark sugary liquid sloshed around the bottom. *Black gold.* I drank the last swallow and scowled. Warm and sticky, the sugar crept to my extremities. My mind cleared as my body cooled. My frosty shell constricted, insulating my innards against the heat, delaying my inevitable demise for a while longer.

But for how long? I wondered.

Scott had once said, during one of our many conversations, "Life is just a car accident in progress. We twist and turn the wheel, following different paths—some hit the accelerator, some brake, some steer into others—but no one avoids that final fatal collision."

Looks like I hit a patch of black ice, Scott, but I'm not ready to stop twisting the wheel.

I'm only a kid when it comes to my memories; a frost child a mere decade old, too young to die. That thought and the soda pop renewed my resolve to fight against that final misfortune to the end, even against the scorching sun and scalding earth. Calamity or not, I had to believe that sometimes, for the lucky, enough joy and achievement occurs while the tragedy plays out to make the struggle worthwhile.

I'm already here, I might as well make the best of it, right?

I'd mapped out my journey before setting out using maps Scott had procured for me. Lunar Crater lay along that path, a short distance ahead. At my current speed, I would make it within an hour, so I raced on. I pushed my discomfort aside by focusing on the scenery and sounds of the desert insects and wind. I reeled back as a roadrunner burst from cover ahead of me, shot straight ahead, and veered off to my right. Its mottled black-and-brown feathers blended with the terrain before it disappeared as if it had never been there.

A sharp sensation—like I'd been stabbed with a two-pronged fork—rushed along my nervous system from my right foot to my brain. I snarled and looked down. A rattlesnake, snow dribbling from its mouth, glared at me and recoiled. I took several steps back, sat and rubbed my foot, keeping a watchful eye as it slithered into the desert underbrush and vanished from view. If not for the few drops of liquid left in its wake and my burning foot, I'd have thought I'd imagined it. I scrutinized the spot where I'd last seen it for a while after its rattle disappeared, then crawled over to rest a minute in the meagre shadow of a nearby bush. I lay there panting, feeling the venom course through my body.

My face felt sweaty and hot, and I sucked in quick, shallow breaths like I'd done the hundred-yard dash. This was my first rattlesnake bite. *At least that I remember*, I thought. *Is this how I go out? Bitten by a freaking rattlesnake? There's something I hadn't thought to worry about while planning my escape. I guess I was too focused on the sun and heat.*

"Remember," Scott said as I left the Institute, "the sun doesn't hate you, but it'll kill you anyway. Take this hat, it'll protect your head. I know you're excited, man, but you don't know what it's like out there."

"Don't worry," I said. "I'm tougher than I look."

"Shivurr, my body's seventy percent water. Its normal temperature is ninety-eight Fahrenheit; that's about thirty-seven Celsius. I've seen your files. Your body's water content is much higher, and your core body temperature is way below zero. You might as well be walking on Mars out there. If you didn't regenerate like you do, it'd be a suicide mission. It might be anyway."

"I should be all right as long as I've got enough water."

"Yeah, I saw the files," Scott said. "They're still losing their shit over it."

"I told you. It's the Underfrost. I still can't believe you can't see it. It's everywhere."

Based on the files Scott hacked into, all that water mixes with crystalline particles composed of elements not found on the periodic table. By interacting, they form my lifeblood, internal structures and snowy form. These grains of elemental sand interact with each other at the quantum level. They arrange, rearrange, and alter themselves in a process that can only operate at sub-zero temperatures. The colder the better. In so doing, they cool and alter and shape the water into—well, into me. Like warm bloods, I sleep, but I can go a long time without it. I eat and drink too, to replenish lost elements and fluids.

Most warm bloods I've met think I'm magic. I get it, sort of;

they've never seen anything like me. Then again, we're a lot alike: machines that operate by chemical processes. They're flesh and blood composed of cells and bacteria, grown out of a chemical reaction. I'm crystals and ice, but we're both thinking, breathing, living organisms. Either one is miraculous to me.

I rubbed my throbbing foot a final time as the sting faded, then clambered back to my feet and limped onward. *I guess I'm immune. Well, that's something.* I wobbled as a wave of nausea rolled through me. *Okay, maybe not completely immune.*

Aside from melting to death, I had other reasons to avoid sunshine; it's a lot harder to go unseen. Bodhi Group agents would soon be on my trail, if they weren't already. I also couldn't afford to be seen by anyone, as they'd no doubt report it—I am quite memorable, I'm told—giving my pursuers a trail to follow. Buying water at a gas station was not an option, even if one could be found in the middle of the Great Basin Desert and I had money to pay for it.

Delirious from snake venom, the sun, or the heat, I saw another vision of my destination flash through my mind's eye: a large cavern, steeped in darkness, decorated with statues encircling a Greek- or Roman-style temple-like structure, opposite a dais, inscribed with esoteric symbols, over which sat a floating globe of bright white light. I felt confident I'd been captured there but didn't know why I was having nightmares and now waking visions about it or feeling an increasing sense of peril associated with it.

The Bodhi Group had messed up my long-term memories to the point that I could recall little about my life before I came to the Institute. What remained were just disconnected fragments, without context. I could not remember who I was, what my origins were, or how I was able to do many of the things that I could do. Some of what I knew about myself had been told to me by my captors. They'd acquired extensive knowledge of my physiology during my time at the Institute, as they studied me and my abilities. What they'd told me seemed to be true for the most part. Then again, the best falsehoods have a lot of truth in them in my more recent experience. Even if they hadn't lied about anything, they might simply have been wrong.

As I staggered toward the crater from the southwest, I spotted a light blue Volkswagen Bus atop a hill in the distance. Scanning for people, I drew closer, intersecting with a dirt track, which I followed to the van at the top. The vehicle sat by the crater's edge, a short distance from the gravel path. The windows were down, and its fold-out awning extended toward the crater. Two tents were pitched nearby.

No one was visible in the vicinity, but it seemed a sure bet someone couldn't be far off—probably in the tents. I tiptoed closer to look for something to drink. Shuffling from bush to bush—a trail of steam in my wake—I made my way up to the side of the vehicle, keeping it between me and the vast crater on the other side. I stood still next to the van, held my breath, and listened. The sounds of laughter and playful shouts emanated from deep within the maar.

Chancing a look, I could see a group of people, their backs to me, as they walked a meandering path down to the crater's floor. They were too far away to make out faces or ages, but one rode another piggyback, while the other two walked hand in hand a short distance away.

Tourists or locals out for a hike to enjoy the scenery, I guessed.

The coast clear, I crept around the vehicle, skulking forward in a low hunch. Seeing no one on the other side, I took shelter in the shade of the van's awning, where I spotted a red cooler with a white lid, set between two lawn chairs. With a glance toward the crater to confirm the hikers weren't looking, I opened the lid and gasped.

Within lay a treasure trove of soda pop, kept cool by large bags of clear ice. I ripped one open and shovelled ice cubes down my throat, smiling like a kid in a marshmallow-eating contest. My trembling hands grabbed one of the cans of pop and cracked it wide. Salivating at the hiss of escaping carbonation, I threw my head back and dumped it all in, moaning. Watery, life-preserving coolness swept through me like quicksilver. Sighing, I took in the view with liquescent eyes and belched the first few letters of the alphabet, holding in a laugh.

"Hey, guys," said a voice from inside the van. "Back already?"

Footsteps and the rustling of fabric followed as a young man appeared in the van's open doorway. He looked about sixteen years old. He had a long face, with thin lips stretched over a slight overbite. Dirty-blond hair, too long in the back, as if he aspired to one day tie it into a ponytail, fell a little past his shoulders. A faded black AC/DC T-shirt shielded his gaunt torso from the wind. Either it had shrunk from too many cycles in a clothes dryer or he'd bought it second-hand from a shorter person, judging by how it failed to make the distance to his garish board shorts, exposing a fuzzy, pale white abdomen beneath its bottom fringe. The smell of marijuana hung in a cloud about him.

With no time to do anything else, I froze in place, head back, eyes to the sky, with a can of soda held upended in my hand above my gaping mouth. A single drop of dark cola dropped from the can's aluminum rim, even as the barefoot teen straightened to his full five feet seven inches and walked over.

"What the hell?" he asked, his voice trailing to a whisper as he studied my lightly steaming, frosty form. He glanced to his left in the direction of the crater, then back to me, blinking eyes still bleary with sleep. I still didn't move an inch as he rubbed his eyes and took two steps to stand before me. The corners of his mouth lifted, making his faint moustache curl like a caterpillar, revealing the slightly yellowed teeth of a smoker.

"Good one, dudes," he muttered, reaching a hand slowly toward me. His pointed fingers stopped an inch from me, as if he imagined touching me would make me disappear or pop like a balloon. Then, as if deciding, he completed the motion, poking me in the chest. The tips of his fingers left slight impressions before they faded away as he pulled back his hand. "Still ice-cold," he said, licking his fingers. I stifled the urge to gag.

He turned away and called to his friends. "Nice one, dudes," he shouted, flapping his arms. "You got me. Come on back." They were now almost a quarter mile away, nearing the bottom of the crater, hundreds of feet below. They looked back and waved in return before continuing their hike.

Save your breath, kid, they're too far away to hear, I thought.

Apparently drawing the same conclusion, he turned back to me and extended his hand once more.

"At least buy me a drink first, Slim," I said, grabbing his outstretched hand before he could touch me again.

He snatched his hand away like it burned, stumbling backward and knocking over a lawn chair. He continued to backpedal, hands raised high. His face contorted and his eyes widened before he turned and fled into the crater at a full sprint. Dust kicked up behind him as he ran, sneakers pounding the earth, arms pumping. "Holy shit, holy shit, holy shit," he shouted.

I tore the cooler lid off and tossed it to the side. It clunked against the ground. I stacked soda cans like firewood in the crook of my arm, then ran for it, arms full. The one I tucked under my chin fell, and I stopped to go back as footsteps thumped my way. "Hey, wait," the kid said as he returned.

Leave it, I thought, doing a one-eighty.

A half mile later, I looked back, but the kid hadn't followed. I slipped off the small backpack Scott had given me for the trip and secured my stolen booty.

Great, just freaking great, I thought. *I should have kept my mouth shut and waited for a chance to slip away when he wasn't looking.* At least then, I reasoned, there would have been a chance that he would have explained away my appearance as an elaborate prank, that being the most plausible explanation. Now he had seen me move and heard me speak. He'd tell his friends; word of my appearance might get back to the Bodhi Group. *Well*, I told myself, *maybe they won't believe him, or they'll consider it a marijuana-induced hallucination.*

Whatever happened now, it was time for me to go. If I guessed right, the hikers wouldn't make it back up the crater for a half hour or more. Adding time for the kid to get to them, I'd have an hour's head start or so, and that was assuming they believed his story and came back right away. I skirted the perimeter of the crater, keeping an eye out for any other people, but I saw none. Isolated and hostile to life, the region was visited only by geologists and tourists with any regularity. Tourists kept to the roads, but geologists did not, so I still needed to be careful. At least that's what Scott had told me during our preparations.

Fifteen minutes later I left the crater behind and turned northeast. I strode over miles of rocky terrain, covered with sagebrush, grass, and wildflowers that somehow survived the dry heat. The rugged landscape consisted of a lot of low hills and shallow valleys formed out of volcanic maars and cinder cones left behind by ancient conflagrations. I trudged up and down them for a while before the peaks and dales gave way to flatter, sandier terrain with far less foliage.

I walked north from there, toward a distant rise in the earth a few miles off.

That must be Easy Chair, I thought, thinking of the crater formed out of a two-million-year-old cinder cone volcano. From where I stood, it looked like any other hill. The crater and the sloping arms that had led to its name must have lain on the other side, beyond my view.

I thanked Scott in my thoughts for supplying me with satellite photos of the region. Although my visions and inner sense pointed me in the direction of my goal like a compass knows magnetic north, I still needed to navigate the difficult topography and wouldn't have known what to expect without them. Going in a straight line was fine for crows, but not for terrestrial beings.

My mind wandered again after a while, returning to my earliest memories, just before I'd first encountered the Bodhi Group, just before they'd taken me.

Sometime a day or two before that fateful meeting, I remembered waking up from a deep sleep, surrounded by ice and fog. Clusters of crystals glimmered and gleamed, illuminating the haze, reflecting in a kaleidoscope of colours off the clear ice walls of a massive cavern.

I'd awakened with a sense of urgency, alarmed by some threat I could no longer remember. I had the vague sense that I needed to protect something that had been taken from me or that was threatened.

To do that, I remembered leaving the ice cave, in a vortex of blues and whites, and arriving in a large cavern, surrounded by alien people and equipment. It was the Bodhi Group, a secret US-led multinational collaboration of Western countries, corporations, universities, and other organizations established with the primary mission of researching and developing tools and technologies capable of quelling any threats to democracy, freedom, and peace.

I didn't know that then as I stood before their representatives and researchers within a large circular structure. The building's high ceiling towered over my head, supported by thick stone columns, squatting within another large cavern as big as the one from which I'd just travelled. This one was lit by strings of lightbulbs arrayed on temporary metal stands, rather than whatever magical light had illuminated the previous one, but with most of it lost in deep shadow.

A blinking audience stared at me from the steps leading up to the platform on which I stood. I took a few steps forward and spoke. They looked at each other, then at me, with wrinkled brows and shaking heads. One of them shouted orders—gibberish to me—and a man in a yellow hard hat ran off. The one who had shouted approached me like I was a bomb ready to go off, speaking soft-toned words that I didn't understand. From that, everything else followed.

The next few weeks were a lot of gesticulation, drawing patterns in the dust, and fruitless vocalization, working out a basic vocabulary for communication. After several days of shouting and more than a little swearing, I finally succeeded in communicating my fears and they agreed to help, inviting me to go with them to what I later came to know as the Bodhi Institute: a secret underground facility that housed research and development laboratories focused on the development of weapons to combat those threats I mentioned earlier—chief among them the Soviet threat. There, they told me, I could live in cold comfort, drinking more of the wondrous libations of dark sugar water they offered as gifts during our initial meetings. They were happy to help, they said, but they needed my help too: just a bit of research to help in the fight against the Red Menace, then we'll help with your problem.

The liars…

Chapter 2

I Was Detained

I got my own supercooled room to live in, which was sweet. A few days in, technicians brought in a TV, I guess to help me learn English; hand signs and arm waving only get you so far. They didn't seem interested in learning my language, but I didn't mind. I enjoyed the shows, especially the action ones. They X-rayed and poked and prodded me for the first while, trying to figure out my physiology, while I watched *Sesame Street* and cartoons. They gave me video games too, testing my reaction time and hand-eye coordination, I suppose, or just keeping me distracted. I'm a quick study; within a month I knew enough to convey simple concepts in the heavily accented, stilted speech of a recent immigrant to a new country.

It took years for them to gain a rudimentary understanding of my biology and abilities. Even today, they don't really know how or why I can do the things I can do. My friend Scott says what I can do, even that I am alive at all, defies everything currently understood about biology, physics and the relationship between energy and mass.

"It's like you can draw energy, literally, from nothing," Scott said. "Like there's a field of energy beyond our ability, or that of our best instrumentation, to perceive. Best they can tell, it's pervasive and effectively limitless. Not only can you perceive what we can't, Shivurr, you seem to be able to draw on this at will and shape it, consciously. It sustains you somehow."

The eggheads said that I'm quantumly linked in some way with another dimension. This relationship, they postulated, allows me to touch and manipulate that other space to *manifest effects* in this reality. Effects like warping and shaping the relationship between realities to create temporary, targeted temperature alterations, bending the energy to my will and desires. Sort of like Einstein's "spooky action at a distance," but across dimensions.

No duh, I thought at the time. I've always called it the Underfrost: a place of infinite ice, cold, and snow that lies just *under* everything. It took a while for me to believe that they couldn't see it—like trying to fathom colour-blindness when you can see the full spectrum. By the time they'd figured out that much, I spoke like a native but no longer trusted them, so I kept the other things that I knew about the Underfrost to myself. Things like sometimes when the air is cold enough here, the boundary between the two vanishes spontaneously. Other times, areas of the Underfrost itself become cold enough to affect this reality, causing temperature drops in this one, even making it snow and storm. The opposite is also true, to a much lesser extent; if it gets too hot here, it gets warmer in the Underfrost.

Practically speaking, the Underfrost gives me the power to make it snow, cool the air around me, or conjure balls of frost energy, just by thinking about it. I can even make snow rise out of the earth or, with a lot more effort, appear out of thin air. I can't really explain *how* I do it. It's like walking or breathing or throwing a baseball; I just know how to do it without thinking about it. As Scott put it, it's sub-symbolic.

Working the Underfrost gets harder to do the warmer and drier the air, requiring deeper concentration and tiring me out much faster, if I succeed at all. Under my current circumstances, trying to do that would be like a mountain climber trying to sprint up a hillside near thirty thousand feet; in reality, the sprint would be a fast walk and the climber would soon be flat on his face, gasping for air. The opposite is also true; the colder and wetter it is, the easier accessing the Underfrost becomes.

While my captors figured out a lot of this during my stay, I managed to keep some of the stuff I can do to myself. I was counting on those secrets keeping me a step or two ahead of them in my quest. I had an inkling there were more things I'd forgotten or lost because of the mistreatment I'd suffered at the

Bodhi Group's hands. I'd see flashes of them in my dreams, then wake up sometimes unable to recall what they were, or other times unable to imagine how to do them, like someone who's never done a cartwheel dreaming of doing backflips.

Things turned nasty several months in. It's fuzzy, but I guess I got impatient with the excuses and delays and left. They picked me up as I staggered back to the facility, dehydrated suffering from exposure. I went on strike after that and they stopped playing nice. After that, my participation stopped being voluntary, if it ever was. From then on, many of the experiments were cruel, torture really. The more sociopathic among them finally got their wish, and they subjected me to stress tests involving exposure to varying levels of heat, cold, and water. Under some of these adverse conditions, I reacted instinctively, attempting to escape, exhibiting powers that fired their curiosity. While the scientists were initially interested in me as a phenomenon—a living, sentient being of ice and snow—their primary goal became to study the limits of my abilities and search for new ones, all the while monitoring me with instrumentation that they hoped would unlock the mysteries of the Underfrost.

Those experiments taught me a lot about my limitations. As you might expect, melting is a big issue for me. Losing too much water reduces my body's ability to cool itself. As my core temperature rises, I lose water faster, and then I get warmer faster, and so on in a vicious cycle. Eventually my entire system collapses—based on experiments that took me close to that point. If they'd taken it any further, I'd just be a residue of crystalline powder dusting the floor of a Bodhi Institute laboratory.

It was during those times that I started to forget things. I'd go to sleep and wake up feeling normal, then realize I'd forgotten stuff like where I'd lived before, where I'd come from. It was like I was dying in slow motion. It was terrifying and demoralizing. Eventually I stopped eating and drinking entirely, falling into a deep depression. *Better dead than a slave*, I thought.

I guess they were pretty freaked out, since the experiments stopped abruptly. Delirious, incoherent, I was beyond caring and barely noticed. A few days later, they brought in a head shrink,

Dr. Emmett Feldman, to get me back on my feet. It turned out that he was a cool old guy—for a shrink—about sixty, balding, with tufts of grey-and-white hair above big ears with hair growing out of them like moss and a ready smile. It took weeks for him to break through the protective shell that I'd drawn about myself, to build enough trust that I'd speak to him. Eventually, he did, and we'd chat for an hour or two every day about all sorts of things. Well, our early conversations were limited, but they got more interesting as my vocabulary improved. I'd listen raptly as he shared stories of his family, life, and travels, indulging my curiosity before returning to me. I'd catch him staring at me with curious eyes now and then, hanging on my every word.

"You're weirding me out, Emmett," I said once. "Take a picture, it'll last longer."

His face reddened then. "Forgive my rudeness. Even after all this time, I'm still overwhelmed to be sitting here talking to you. In all the history of the planet there's never been any living creature like you, as far as we know. No trace exists in the fossil record either. This begs so many questions. Where did you come from? Where did you all go?"

I wished that I had those answers.

Emmett figured my memory loss was my mind protecting itself, somehow. Maybe, he'd suggest, the memories were being locked away for safekeeping and we just had to find the combination to the safe where'd they'd been secured. It sounded like a lot of shrink mumbo-jumbo to me; my gut told me the Bodhi Group had stolen them and they weren't coming back. I started to feel better anyway thanks to having a friend. Plus, my memories before the Institute had vanished so thoroughly by then that it became hard to miss them. I knew, intellectually, that I'd lost something, but not knowing what it was made me care a little less, for a while. Even the problem for which I'd sought their help faded out of mind for a time.

At Emmett's suggestion, in exchange for my full cooperation, I bargained for better living conditions and perquisites. I don't need to sleep much unless I'm injured or heavily drained. With lots of time to kill, I insisted that they supply me with more of the books, movies, games, and VHS tapes of the TV shows that I'd clung to in my early days at the Institute. Relieved, I suppose, to have me back on my feet, they eagerly acquiesced. From then on, I lived comfortably, learning English, participating in experiments that tested my abilities but no longer exceeded them. When I wasn't doing that, I watched TV, read fantasy and sci-fi books, played video games on full-scale arcade machines and home game consoles, and drank soda pop. If TV is awesome, video games are the best. And the books. I read like a starving man eats hot dogs, escaping into new worlds from the comfort of my ice-cold room. I might be wrong, but something told me my people, whoever and wherever they were, weren't readers or writers. Then there were the snacks, of course. I've got a sweet tooth, and the soda pop was free and limitless.

Things were good, but I still felt like a pariah for a long time. Most of the scientists and security kept their distance—literally—hugging the walls when I'd pass by. In retrospect, I suppose biologists don't get too chummy with their lab rats, but their fearful expressions implied more than just clinical detachment. The food service personnel flatly refused to enter my room to stock the fridge when I was there.

"Try not to take it personally," Emmett said, seeing my face. "They're simply scared. There's a rumour you're a god...or demon, making its way through the kitchen staff."

I snorted. "Right, an amnesic god with a tendency to melt at temperatures above zero." I looked at the can in my hand. "As for demon, does caffeine fiend count?"

In 1978—five years before my current journey across the desert—things changed when I met Scott, while hunting Klingons. Installed a few weeks earlier, a mainframe terminal gave me access to research material, books, and text-based computer games. Super Star Trek was one of the latter. It was fun, even with no graphics.

I'd been playing just a few minutes when the screen went black. Text characters appeared on the screen one by one, as they were typed.

'Hey, man, how's it going?'

"What the heck?" I said, squinting at the white characters on the black screen. After several seconds, I typed a reply.

'Who is this?'

'Scott.'

Scott? Who do I know named Scott? None of the scientists or security guards, as far as I knew, had that name.

'Who?' I typed after several seconds.

'A friend.'

Over the next few hours, Scott revealed himself to be a part of the team responsible for maintaining the Bodhi Institute's computer systems. A few weeks earlier, while I was in another part of the base, he'd installed the terminal that I'd requested. As a Bodhi Group computer systems administrator and programmer, Scott routinely set up and networked computers as a part of his job. His interest was piqued by my ice-cold home, game systems and books. Unable to contain his curiosity, he began a mission to uncover who or what was living there.

Much of the data on me was on microfilm and in paper files in the restricted archives, but there was enough information in the mainframe computer to send him reeling. His mind was blown—his words—when he finally gained access to the camera feeds. He quickly decided that he had to meet me, or at least talk to me. As a science fiction fan, he'd always dreamed of and hoped for confirmation of the existence of extraterrestrials. While he wasn't sure if I was an alien, I was close enough as far as he was concerned. *I guess alien is better than demon*, I thought when he told me that. To him, meeting me was like meeting Elvis or Bigfoot, and a small thing like going to prison for espionage, or whatever, wasn't standing in the way. He always was a bit of a rebel. Besides, he was sure that he wouldn't be caught, being confident in his ability to cover his tracks.

There was no way he could just walk in with security guards watching the cameras around the clock, so he reached out via computer, and our friendship was born. With his root admin access and deep computer systems knowledge, it wasn't long before he set up secure network communication channels that allowed us to converse regularly with no one the wiser. For endless hours, we discussed comics, movies, books, and computer games. With his guidance, I soon had an extensive list of must-see, must-read, and must-play items, which I requested of Bodhi Institute Executive Director Jeffrey Wallace, PhD, in payment for my ongoing cooperation. I just told him that I'd seen, heard, or read about whatever I was asking him for in the content that they'd already given to me. I don't think that he cared all that much anyway as long as I was cooperative.

Once a promising scientist himself, Wallace had traded that in for a career as an administrator, and for the past thirty years he had managed numerous researchers in innumerable highly classified research and development projects. In his early sixties now, he was nearing retirement. Five foot two, grey-haired and balding, he, and by association those around him, suffered from a serious Napoleon complex. If I was cooperative, he denied me nothing, providing Security Director Harland Dixon had no concerns.

Dixon, as far as I could tell, managed a team of fifty to sixty well-trained security officers. Many of the members of his team, Scott told me, were ex-military; others were poached from the CIA, the FBI, and other covert US government organizations. Harland was in his early fifties, five foot nine and fit, and he still had all his hair, which, once deep brown judging by the photographs that decorated his office, had turned mostly grey. He was a former CIA spook who had served in that capacity during the early years of the Vietnam War before joining the Bodhi Group several years before the war's official end. He kept his hair cut short and his face always clean-shaven. Scott figured this was Dixon's way of ensuring he was never confused for one of the *hippie bums* that the security chief blamed for the war's outcome.

As luck would have it, or more likely Scott arranged, they sent my friend shopping for a lot of my requests. They even let him hand deliver them. As a result, my room was soon cluttered with VHS tapes, books, game consoles, a film projector, and other paraphernalia. After repeated appeals, film reels for *Star Wars* and similar movies were, somehow, located. I watched them for weeks, memorizing every scene, and for a while almost forgot I was being held against my will. With all the reading and movies, my grasp of English, my second language, got better too. Scott got himself assigned to the night shift and would sneak in to hang out and watch movies, replacing the security camera video feed that recorded my every move with pre-recorded footage of me sleeping.

After a while, he set things up so that I could join his favourite computer bulletin board system and meet some of his friends, virtually. I chose the online handle Cool Hand after a movie that I had seen once. It seemed to fit. I didn't share my true identity with the BBS's other denizens, of course; they wouldn't have believed me if I'd told them, I suspect.

Though we communicated solely by text, interacting with other like-minded people became a favourite part of my day. Behind the anonymity of the keyboard, it doesn't matter what you look like or sound like or where you come from—just what you type. On the BBS, we were connected by common interests and were able to be, in some ways, more our true selves.

Until recently, life had been as good as it could be without my freedom. I'd been having dreams since just before arriving in the cavern all those years ago, but they'd stopped after the experiments that took my memories. Then, six months earlier, in February 1983, they'd started up again with no warning.

Flashes of frost and fire, blackened earth and clouds of steam on a lifeless, scorched desert plain left me moaning and sweating for weeks. They weren't all doom and gloom; others presented images of glittering crystals, radiant, crackling with power, giving off light in all the colours of the rainbow. Some were mammoth, the height of three-storey buildings, yet others as small as marbles. Next, a swirling sphere, white as snow, translucent, surrounded in a veil of fog.

At first, I tried to ignore them all as random flights of fancy of an overwrought mind. The experiments were taxing, requiring me to channel and manipulate the Underfrost for hours on end. *I must be cracking under the strain*, I thought. Then I started to see myself flying over the desert floor, on a journey somewhere, and suspected my mind was trying to tell me something—

something it had forgotten or could not integrate into a conscious thought. I knew I had amnesia, that my long-term memories were damaged, jumbled, or locked in my subconscious. Maybe this was my wounded mind struggling to repair itself. Whatever the source, they didn't go away.

Instead they continued to grow more frequent and urgent as time passed. In the past month, they'd become so intense I feared going to sleep, so I'd just stay awake for weeks on end, but it was an unsustainable solution. I don't need to slumber every sixteen hours like warm bloods, but I still need to do so periodically. More than a week without it and I'll suffer from sleep deprivation like anyone else.

After trashing my quarters during a particularly intense hallucination, I consulted my small circle of friends—Scott and Emmett—desperate for a solution.

"Too many movies, maybe?" Scott suggested when I finally told him of the visions. "Have you watched anything with a desert in it lately? After watching *King Kong*, I once dreamed I was running from a creature on a tropical island in a dress, wearing high heels."

Laughing at Scott's jokes and staying conscious helped, for a while—then I started hallucinating even while wide awake.

Eventually we concluded that the visions were drawing me back to the cavern of crystals where I'd first arrived. Whatever I had once known about the cavern had disappeared along with my memories, so I had nothing to go on except what my friends could find out.

"When you see the desert, are there identifiable landmarks, anything that stands out?" Scott asked, when quizzing me for details.

There wasn't much to distinguish one part of the desert from another, but a few large craters did catch my eye. To aid in the search, Scott secured classified satellite photos of the Nevada desert and I pored over them, but most were too high-altitude to match what I saw in my visions. With no other alternatives, we both put out the word on the BBS, describing the two most notable craters. A day later, Boreas, the BBS SysOp, suggested

Lunar Crater as a possible match. "It's a volcanic maar," Boreas wrote. "Astronauts trained there for the moon landings. It's a bit of a tourist spot these days." Scott located some photos; it matched my visions. Easy Chair Crater came quickly afterward, lying roughly northeast of Lunar Crater.

Scott solved the mystery of the crystals, using his root computer systems access to find out what he could. "They've been studying them since before you showed up, Shivurr," Scott said as we played Ms. Pac-Man. "Apparently the crystals contain chemical elements not found on the periodic table. Even a single unknown element would be incredible, but these crystals are made of *several* new elements." He pushed his eyeglasses back up his nose, shaking his head. "No wonder they're so interested."

I shrugged. "What's that got to do with me? They're still just a bunch of rocks, right?"

Scott shook his head slowly and pursed his lips. "More than you'd think, man. You're made of this stuff, too."

"You're kidding."

"Uh-uh, no joke," Scott said. "Seems the crystals react to you too. It's been part of their experimental protocols for a while now. There's some connection they don't really understand there. I don't know, man. Maybe the crystals are calling you or something."

Whatever the case, I realized that I needed to get wherever the dreams wanted me to go, find out more and hopefully put an end to the visions and my compulsion to find the chamber at their centre. Leaving my few friends and the safety and comfort of the Institute wasn't easy. I had no real choice, though; staying meant losing my mind, eventually.

Chapter 3

Unto the Allfrost

A quarter mile from Easy Chair, I veered to the right and followed a shallow valley between it and another shorter rise to my right, treading on a bed of volcanic bombs and scoria. Six miles later, the blacktop of a two-lane highway lay across my path, bisected down its centre by twin lines of yellow. *US Route 6*, I thought, smiling. *Right where it should be.* No vehicles were visible in either direction, coming from neither California on the left, nor Utah on the right.

I walked across without stopping and up the rise on the other side. Loose stones and gravel rolled down behind me as I climbed. After a few more miles of similar countryside, the ground turned black and rougher, stained dark with volcanic ash, evidence of an ancient conflagration of brimstone and fire, lava and steam, too terrible to imagine.

I ascended gradually, making for the peak of a hill a few hundred feet high and a mile or so distant, an island surrounded by a sea of black. I glanced to my left at the sun, now descending into the western horizon, spreading an orange-and-yellow glow across the sky above the mountains in the west, almost appearing to set them alight. Shadows, cast by rocks, boulders, and rises in the terrain, lengthened and stretched across the ground, often indistinct and indistinguishable among and upon the blackened earth, until darkness swallowed them fully. I tripped now and then, but there was still enough ambient light to make my way—barely.

I'd been walking for about five hours since leaving Lunar Crater. I'd sucked down a few more sodas on the way, staving off dehydration in the intense heat and sunlight of the afternoon. Now that the skies were dark, I felt like a 7-Eleven Slurpee put back in the fridge after being left out in the sun too long.

I paused in my trek and took another small sip from my dwindling supplies. The fresh moisture spread through me with a rush. I shivered as my digestive system worked to cool and crystallize the water, restoring the snow that I'd lost to the sun and warmth and dry wind, a process fuelled and fanned by sugar and caffeine. It made me light-headed, drained as I was. I stopped short of drinking all of it, lowering my hand like helium balloons were tied to my wrist. Not knowing when I'd be able to resupply, I knew that rationing now might mean the difference between life and death.

Finding the drinks at Lunar Crater saved my life, I realized. Any lingering regrets about exposing myself to the long-haired kid vanished. I resumed walking, feeling better.

The crystals were close, buried somewhere in front of me under tons of volcanic rock, giving off a chill like a campfire radiates heat. The ground continued to rise, and the blackened earth gave way to the rusty reds and browns, mixed with grey, of the slope of the hillside. I trudged steadily to the northeast, then turned due east and at last made it to the plateau at the top. I spent the next thirty minutes exploring the summit, looking for a way down into the rock but finding none. The faint whup-whup of helicopter blades, carried on the wind, drew my gaze to the east. A few miles away, a black helicopter rose from behind a hill. I crouched down, held still, and watched as it flew southwest.

Curious, and with no better alternatives, I began walking east, toward the helicopter's point of origin. Stars grew visible in the sky overhead as I marched, shining bright in the dry, clear air. The relatively flat ground made the going much easier. About a mile farther along, I found myself at the bottom of another volcanic maar, partially filled with volcanic residue, ash, scoria, and sand that spilled out to the west. To the east, the massive bowl was still intact, forming a sloped wall of rock four hundred feet high, from behind which the helicopter had first appeared. I walked to the top, scrambling over rocks and sliding on gravel. An aura of light reflected off motes of dust hanging in the air at the top of the hillside.

The far side was all murky shadows, except for the lights of a large camp at the base of the hill. Unable to see much, I descended for a closer look. As I neared, inchoate rectangles coalesced into an encampment of windowless trailers, trucks, tractors and other excavation equipment. Off to my left, I could see a collection of portable toilets, bookended by large blue dumpsters. Beyond the trailers lay a helicopter landing pad, currently unoccupied, next to a collection of large fuel tanks. Heavy-duty construction lights on stands stood sentry, illuminating the grounds. To the right, several chairs ringed an unlit firepit. Stacks of wood—trucked in from elsewhere, I presumed—lay ready for the cool nights and recreational gatherings of the camp's inhabitants.

I drifted closer, hugging the ground, hoping that the glare from the floodlights would blind anyone in the camp to anything that lay beyond. No people were visible. The loud hum of gasoline generators washed away the sounds of my approach in a sea of white noise. Electric cabling snaked from the generators across the desert floor into the nearby trailers to the east and into the hillside beneath my feet, running alongside thick hoses and ductwork attached to large portable air-conditioning units.

No way this is a coincidence, I thought. *I've got to get in there.*

I remained still, above it all, and listened. Hearing no voices or footsteps, I moved down into the camp and raced over to the closest generator. Discarded bottles, cans, and cigarette butts littered the area. Keeping low, I glanced left, taking note of an opening in the side of the maar, leading down into the earth to the west, from where I'd come—from where I still felt the crystals' pull.

The sound of a radio playing hard rock rose above the generator's hum as a trailer door opened to my right. A man stepped out, lighting a cigarette. He leaned against the wall.

"Close the damn door, Larry," shouted a voice from within. "You're letting in the heat."

Without reply, the smoker, Larry, kicked the door shut, taking a long pull on his cancer stick, the tip glowing red in the near darkness. He wore military fatigues, a battle dress hat over a buzz cut, and a sidearm in a holster on his hip. I judged the fresh-faced soldier to be in his early twenties.

The trailer lacked windows; more men than just the one who had complained about the open door might be inside. Looking around, I spotted two sentries I had missed before as they walked the perimeter of the encampment and another standing guard a hundred feet away, down the faint trail that led off into the desert. That made at least five soldiers that I had to worry about.

The door of another trailer, crowned with multiple satellite dishes and antennae, banged open. A woman and two men, all wearing white lab coats, exited, engaged in conversation. Though I didn't know them personally, I'd seen enough egg-heads to recognize their type at a glance. The woman had dark hair, cut short. She appeared to be in her early forties. One man was balding, with a trim beard, wearing thick glasses with heavy black rims, and of similar age. The other appeared to be mid-fifties, judging by his shock of grey hair.

Oh, shit, I thought as they moved my way. I hugged the generator and looked for an escape. *Lights to right of me; lights to the left of me.* If I moved, with my white complexion, I would be as visible as a lighthouse on a dark night.

"It's unchanged," said the woman as they approached my hiding spot. "Particle bombardment has, at best, minimal effect."

"Electron diffraction interference patterns still fluctuate chaotically as temperature rises," the younger man added as they walked past, heading for the tunnel entrance. "Eventually the crystalline structure collapses and disintegrates."

I let out a breath I hadn't realized I was holding as they strode by my hiding spot.

"With no trace?" said the older man, raising his eyebrows.

"Not so much as an atom. Thermal reduction, applied quickly, reverses degradation in some cases; statistical analysis shows the function is sigmoidal rather than thresh...," the woman said before moving out of earshot as the trio descended into the maar. I counted to sixty in my head, watching the soldier smoking by the trailer before he flicked the cigarette butt to the ground, crushed it with his boot, and walked toward the distant toilets. With his back to me, I burst from my hiding spot, running on tiptoe for the tunnel entrance.

To the right and left, large black, red, and white signs announced "Danger, Risk of Cave-In" next to even larger red-and-white "No Trespassing" signs. A few steps past them lay an even scarier yellow-and-black sign warning of radiation danger, behind which sat tightly spaced traffic barricades: a last effort to discourage, but not physically prevent, intruders from going any deeper. *Must be for trespassers that can't read,* I thought as I strode past, slipping between the barricades without hesitation. It was all bogus—lies and fabrications left to keep away anyone who might somehow wander or sneak past the security outside.

Undeterred, I slipped inside. Within, my way was lit by a string of lights stretched along the ceiling above. Like the scrawling of an overly enthusiastic child, the tunnel floor was criss-crossed by countless tractor treads. A few hundred feet within the twelve-foot-wide, twenty-foot-high passageway, large boulders and rocks had been piled to seal it tight around a concrete tube, the end capped by a metal wall with a single door.

As I approached, the three scientists were zipping up heavy winter coats taken from a wall of nearby lockers. I hugged the wall behind large metal canisters lining the right side and waited as they placed yellow hard hats on their heads and pulled on gloves. The woman punched a code into the keypad near the door, her body blocking my view, and the trio entered. The door slammed shut moments later, and I advanced, on tiptoe, once more.

The door was thick, metal—like a square door to a vault. I tried it anyway. It clunked but refused to budge.

I didn't try entering a code in case invalid entries raised an alarm. *Besides, what are the odds I'd guess right?*

Waiting by the door for the scientists to return, or for more to enter, and slipping in after them was an option, but risky. If soldiers came in behind me, I'd be trapped, and the longer I waited, the greater the chance of discovery. Not to mention, I had a rendezvous to make. Scott had arranged a ride for me on the back of an ice truck heading north from Las Vegas tomorrow morning. The sooner I could find what I had come for and get on my way, the better. I needed to find another way in.

Five minutes of searching revealed that no opening existed through which I could fit. Electrical cables, ventilation ductwork and other equipment ran along the wall into a narrow tube that led straight into the piled rock. The machinery piping was crowded; a snake might squeeze through its hoses and cables, but not me.

I grabbed one of the boulders, roughly three feet in diameter, and pulled and pushed and muttered curses under my breath. It jiggled slightly as if tickled by my efforts to move it. I tried budging some of the smaller rocks, but other stones, about the size of a fast-pitch softball, rolled from atop the pile, nearly hitting me on the way down.

I scurried back and looked upward, in case more rubble followed, and watched as a few more pebbles bounced their way to the tunnel floor and the rock pile settled into a new configuration, still blocking my way.

I sat down at the base and pondered my options.

"All right, just give me a minute. Got to finish my rounds," said a voice, coming from the direction of the tunnel entrance.

The shuffling of footsteps followed.

I burst to my feet, scanning for somewhere to hide. The nearby lockers were too small for me to fit. The row of canisters where I had hidden on my way in was too far away and a poor hiding spot at best.

I'm blown.

I clambered up the rock pile to where it met the ceiling, cloaking myself in thick shadows. I looked for a snowman-sized crevice. I found a cat-sized one instead. The gap in the barrier, presumably caused by erosion and gravity, wasn't large enough for me to fit through.

Cool air emanated from the hole, but I didn't have time to enjoy it. An idea was forming in my head, though it meant using up more, maybe all, of my water reserves; there wasn't enough latent moisture in the earth to accomplish what I had in mind. I pulled out my last water bottle and splashed its contents into and around the opening, soaking the area. I reached inside as far as I could and splattered the rest.

The footsteps stopped abruptly. "Hello," said the voice I'd heard earlier. "Is someone there?"

I looked back. The soldier, Larry, skulked toward me, weapon half-raised, squinting into the dim light. He stopped, patting his jacket with his free hand.

I slipped the empty bottle into my backpack, straightened my hat, and reached out, focusing my energy, shaping and directing it, manipulating the moisture I'd splashed on the bone-dry ground. Snowflakes materialized out of thin air, crystalized from the evaporate that had not yet drifted away on the faint breeze, and fell slowly down upon the damp rocks and cinders. Moments later, pure white snow bloomed from the ground, spreading like moss down the side of the scree and forward into the gap.

As the light of Larry's flashlight lit the wall next to me, I stepped forward, gasping with pleasure at the feel of the cold snow on my weary, hot feet. With a stomp, I sank into the inch of fresh snow up to my neck, unable to get lower in such a thin layer. I moved forward into the tiny aperture, pushing my backpack ahead of me for a few feet before emerging on the other side.

My hat had brushed against the tunnel's ceiling and fell from my head as I'd pushed my way through. Looping an arm through a strap of my pack, I popped up out of the snow and reached back to retrieve it, hearing the sounds of sliding rocks and scrabbling footsteps growing in volume on the far side.

On my side, large fans hummed and rattled somewhere in the distance, blowing a cool breeze across my sunburned exterior.

Out of the fire, into the frying pan.

I blinked, peering into its murky depths. Faint light from a portable light stand ten feet ahead glowed softly, then died, leaving me in a closet of darkness, save for a fading afterimage. It occurred to me that they must shut off the lights in the passageway when not needed. *Got to save power, and fuel for the electrical generators*, I mused.

I hadn't brought a flashlight, but fortunately I didn't need one. I can light up a room with more than just my magnetic personality when I want to—bioluminescence, the scientists called it. Basically, I'm a bit like a firefly, except my entire body lights up when I do it, not just my tail. Well, I don't have a tail, but you know what I mean.

The scientists theorized that I'm from one of the Earth's poles and that I have this ability for that reason. It made sense. I can't see in the dark any better than they can, and being able to glow on demand *would* be useful when you're living in months of darkness. Then again, another theory is that my people use it to communicate or for defense, to confuse and deter predators. Either way, it comes in handy.

With a thought, I became luminous, bathing the area in dim light, casting shadows that rose like inky black monsters on the rocky walls as I moved. I opened the lab coat that I'd worn since my escape, casting more light to my front, making it easier to see the path before me. Two people could walk abreast with their arms outstretched and their fingertips would've just touched the walls. Heavy boot prints in the dust snaked ahead of me, doubtless made by soldiers and scientists that regularly travelled this path—who had come here years ago and stayed to pilfer the secrets entombed within. My lip curled at the sight of the discarded candy bar wrappers and aluminum cans that littered the floor.

I moved deeper into the cave and turned sideways as the walls closed in a short distance ahead. I ran my hands over the rough, heavily textured volcanic rock on either side. The two sides looked like adjoining pieces of the same puzzle, suggesting the rock had been torn apart by great seismic forces.

This tunnel's recent, geologically speaking, I thought, stepping over the broken fragments littering the floor at my feet.

I squeezed along the passageway until it widened again. The air cooled to an almost tolerable level, and the tunnel appeared to brighten ahead. I stopped luminescing and confirmed that a light source lay in the distance. The first rule of covert infiltration is do not skulk about, when possible, lit up like a Christmas tree, so I resumed my trek with my own light off.

The widening walls of the tunnel stopped at a large white curtain, attached to iron pitons driven into the rock. I drew it aside and slipped through a slit in the plastic that served as the only doorway.

Floodlights, some atop light stands, others attached to scaffolding, revealed a giant amphitheatre carved out of volcanic rock, with five-foot-wide concentric rings of stone dropping with each level toward the room's centre. At four points on the circle, stairs ran from top to bottom. The highest level, where I stood, was twenty feet wide, ringed by great sculptures that had also been carved out of the volcanic rock. The room crackled with frost energy, directionless like fog. Everywhere, yet coming, it seemed, from nowhere in particular.

The ceiling was a rounded dome upon which carvings depicted an open sky, the sun on one side, moon and stars the other. Landscapes around the circumference showed varying terrain: mountains, prairies, forests and stormy seas. Upon these two-dimensional lands, great creatures battled, telling a story, or stories, of ancient quarrels.

At the theatre's centre stood an immense circular green-domed structure just like I'd seen in my dreams, nearly the height of a three-storey building, supported by thick fluted columns, on a raised platform at the centre of a mirror-calm pool of water. Graduated steps led up to the building from the amphitheatre floor. Its architectural style was suggestive of the ancient Greek or Roman temples I'd read about in books, though not quite a match to either.

Are those marble pillars? I asked myself. *Where'd they get marble around here? And how did it survive whatever tremors opened the passageway in?*

Sixty feet from the temple lay a raised circular dais, accessed by steps leading up to it from the floor of the amphitheatre, surrounded by shadows, and brightly lit by several floodlights aimed at its surface. Behind it, massive crystal pillars rose from the floor to the ceiling, sparking like Tesla coils. Hovering above the dais as if by magic was a pulsating sphere of white light, spinning on its axis. Arcane symbols and glyphs decorated the floor of the platform, glowing with blue light, just visible beneath the brightness of the energy sphere and overhead lamps. Much of it was indecipherable to me, but I could read some of the text, even though it wasn't English. In carved letters, one sentence read: *Unto the Allfrost, Underfrost Come, and the Frostchild Keep the Earth.*

Across the room, metal scaffolding supported a large, flat wooden platform, reachable by a timber walkway that lay off to my right, upon which several people moved and worked. Among them stood the threesome that had passed me outside in the camp, still gabbing, their words visible as puffs of fog in the cool air, as they pointed to the complex equipment arrayed around the chamber.

I recognized the video cameras resting on tripods aimed at the dais, but not much else. Above them, long rectangular boxes, each with a short round tube protruding from one side, pointed at the ball of energy and the large crystals behind it, held in place by articulating robotic arms. They resembled the video cameras below them but lacked the telltale lens.

After a moment, I realized some of the robotic arms held canisters with long hoses leading to nozzles also aimed at the sphere and crystal pillars. The labels on the fat white containers were too far away to read, but something about the way they were poised made me think of fire extinguishers.

These were the primary focus for the three scientists, and their colleagues who sat behind a clear polycarbonate viewscreen that lay between the dais and the viewing platform. A soft glow tinged their faces green as their heads bobbed up and down between the floating energy sphere and whatever their monitors showed them. Only the two soldiers that stood in the back showed no interest; one looked bored, the other spoke briefly into a handheld radio and checked his watch.

I slipped deeper into the room, keeping to the shadows, and stifled a swear as I bumped into something hard and metallic. My hand shot forward, grabbing the edge of a shiny steel container as it tipped, catching it inches before it banged against the stone floor. A work of art itself, the floor was a mosaic of interlocking stones, depicting themes like those of the wall and ceiling reliefs surrounding me. I moved it back into position like it held nitroglycerin and bent down to read the label. *Liquid nitrogen.* I gave the container a light shake. *Empty.* More of them, identical to those suspended above the dais at the room's centre, extended into the darkness ahead.

The cavern hummed with the sound of air-conditioning vents exhaling their cold breath into the room like sleeping ice dragons, cooling the massive void in the earth. The temperature in the cavern felt just above freezing, making me more alert and clearer-headed than I had felt since leaving the facility. The air felt thicker too, almost damp, perhaps the result of humidifiers.

Cooling such a large area must have taken weeks, I thought. *I guess tons of rock help keep it that way, but why go to the trouble?* I could only guess that this somehow involved the thermal reduction that the scientists had discussed on their way into the chamber. Seeking answers, my feet padded along, as silent on the stone floor as on plush carpet. *Huh, no echo from the machinery either*, I thought. *It's like the walls absorb sound instead of reflecting it.*

As I circled the upper level at a glacial pace, I could see that the sculptors had hewn large sections of volcanic rock from the outer walls, leaving portions behind, out of which they had chipped and chiselled massive statues of wondrous and terrible creatures in fearsome poses. Behind them, the walls themselves displayed figures posed as if they were leaping from solid rock into thin air, entombed prisoners struggling to escape.

The pool encircling the building was my first goal. I circled around behind it so that the stone edifice of the temple-like structure lay between me and the viewing platform, hiding me from sight.

I hoped.

Keeping to the gloom, I descended the steps to the pool's edge. Near the centre, symbols glowed beneath the surface, distorted by the water's refraction.

I stuck my hand in, going in to nearly my elbow before my fingertips brushed the cold stone floor, checking the depth. I yanked an empty water bottle from my backpack, screwed off the lid, and refilled it, then did the same for the rest. The pool did not appear to miss it. Resupplied, I waded carefully out to the centre to get a better look, soaking up moisture like a sponge. As I did so, ripples radiated outward, splashing against the pool's rim, the lip of which lay just a few inches higher than the swells.

As the liquid coursed through me, my eyesight improved, bringing the world into sharp focus. My other senses, too, became hyperacute; the smell of wet stone, dust, and people tickled my nose and the hum and whir of machinery boomed in my head. Time itself appeared to slow as a roiling wave of ice-cold energy, electric, rose like quicksilver from my core to my tips. I shimmered briefly with a palette of iridescent whites as my watery exterior crystalized in an instant, restored to a hard, frosty shell. I shivered with delight as the wind of the AC fans blew over my snowy flesh, now tumescent with renewed moisture, tingling and turgid.

I resisted the temptation to draw upon it to freeze and frost the earth, summon snow from the air around me, and call forth a blizzard that would make this cavern a wintry paradise. As much as I'd have enjoyed it, the people nearby would've surely noticed, so I held back.

The water sank lower, half its original height now. Thin ice had begun to form at the periphery of the pool as my presence cooled its dwindling waters. The symbols on the pool's bottom glowed brighter in the shallowed water but still meant nothing to me. I knelt, reaching out a hand to touch them.

As my fingers traced their letters, the word *tholos* popped into my head, then the word *akontia*. Their meanings drifted to the surface of my mind from the depths of my amnesia. Tholos referred to a circular building, a temple, just like the one in which

I now stood, while akontia were javelins used by soldiers—pel-
tasts—of Ancient Greece. I had to wonder what a temple of
Ancient Greece was doing in the middle of the Nevada desert
and what any of it had to do with me.

I stumbled and put a hand over my mouth, trying not to hurl.
My tissues were dissolving like a sugar cube in warm tea. When
I'd first entered, my outer shell had hardened, forming a protective layer of ice that regulated the absorption of water, giving
my body time to transform and integrate it, but I'd stayed too
long. The excess water ate at that barrier like a horde of starving
piranhas, breaking it down, allowing too much water to pass
through.

Drained by my desert trek, my bone-dry frame had had more
room to spare than usual, but the extra time that had bought me
had just run out. I needed to get out of the water immediately.
As my vision blurred, I lumbered to the side of the pool, then
staggered and fell. My arms broke my fall, smacking hard against
the pool's stone border.

I should have stayed closer to the edge, not waded out into the middle, I
realized, in perfect hindsight.

Then, in my delirium, I heard Scott's voice in my head saying,
"Beat yourself up later, Shivurr. Get out now."

My arms felt like they belonged to someone else as I dragged
myself onto the stone shore and collapsed with a wet squish.

Sorry, Scott. Looks like I may not make that rendezvous after all, I
thought as I lost consciousness.

Chapter 4

Stay Frosty

My eyeballs throbbed in their sockets, as if pushed outward from the inside, as the hiss of a nitrogen dispenser nudged me awake, and I fluttered my eyelids. The last time I'd felt this way—during a bout of depression—I'd drunk every soda in the fridge and hadn't slept for a week.

Reluctantly, I staggered to my feet and looked around, my eyes slits. Flashes of light strobed near the room's centre, illuminating statuary and casting shadow monsters on the distant walls. I peered around one of the tholos's pillars. The scientists stared at the dais, where the energy sphere still hovered like football fans watching the Super Bowl during overtime.

I slogged my way around the edge of the chamber, shedding water like a wet dishcloth dragged across the floor, and hoped the blare of equipment and voices buried the sound of my footsteps. Taking no chances, I stayed in the deep shadows, beyond the range of the floodlights, and hid behind whatever objects I could find.

I circled the room until the wooden stage lay between me and the dais, so I could approach it from the rear. I snuck closer, keeping a twenty-foot statue of a monstrous creature between me and the people, then crouched behind it. Peering around its edge, I had an unobstructed view of the scene.

"Oscillating photon bombardment now," said a man seated by the computer terminals, his voice raised over the hum of machinery. I recognized him as the balding bearded scientist that I'd encountered on the way in. The gathered group watched, holding their breath, then smiled, gesticulating excitedly at the monitors. "Thermal equilibrium is holding."

"Cut the cryogenic applicator," said the woman from the same trio of scientists that I'd seen outside. "Let's see how it reacts."

"I'm seeing harmonic perturbation at the higher end. Temperatures are rising, but no disintegration."

"Okay, fantastic. Let's not push our luck; disengage, shut it down."

Cheers erupted from the group as the technician typed in the commands at the terminal. The scientists shook hands and slapped backs, overjoyed by the apparent success of whatever they were doing.

"Wait, something's wrong," the seated man said, worry in his voice. "It's not stopping."

"What do you mean?" the woman asked, still shaking a fellow scientist's hand. "Stop the bombardment."

"I did, Harriet," he said, glaring at her. "The reaction is continuing on its own. It's self-reinforcing." His chair swivelled as he checked another screen. "Crystal temperature is still rising," he continued. His fingers danced and keys clicked in a short burst. "It's accelerating."

"Bring the applicator online," Harriet said, walking to the terminal. "Give it a ten-second blast."

A robotic arm whined audibly, moving into position, followed by the hiss of the applicator. A cloud of steam billowed from the energy sphere like fog on a disco dance floor as the technician sprayed it with liquid nitrogen.

"Terminating application cycle," the technician announced after ten seconds, stopping the stream with a few clicks of the keyboard. He dragged a finger across the green screen, then tapped it hard. "Minimal effect." He shook his head. "It halted during application, but it's increasing again."

"Hit it again," said the grey-haired scientist, the third member of the trio, walking over to the railing to stare at the orb now obscured by fog. "Fifteen seconds this time."

"I've got this, Marcus," Harriet said. "Please, don't interfere."

Marcus held up his hands and took a step back. "By all means."

"Thank you," Harriet said, nodding. "All right, Andreas, give it another blast. Fifteen seconds this time."

The technician, Andreas, moved to obey, and the sizzle of steam resumed. The cavern air was heavily clouded now. The energy sphere faded from view, lost in the cloud of vapour, its position betrayed only by an electric crackle and flashes of light, now tinged orange and yellow. The air felt noticeably warmer; the air conditioning, still blowing cool air into the room, thumped and rumbled like an old jalopy.

The hiss of the cryogenic applicator died.

"Anything?" Harriet asked, keeping her eyes on the fog.

Andreas shook his head. "Still rising. It dipped slightly but started again. Infrared shows surface temp approaching five hundred Kelvin." He poised his fingers over the keyboard and looked at Harriet. "Again?"

"How much is left in that tank?" Harriet asked.

"Enough for another twenty to thirty seconds, maybe," Andreas replied, tapping the computer screen.

"We should wait until the ventilation has cleared the air," Marcus said, turning away from the railing. "Oxygen condensation is a concern. We don't want to pass out in here."

"Good thinking," Harriet said, nodding. "In fact, let's clear the chamber of everyone non-essential."

Chairs squeaked across plywood and pens and clipboards crashed as everyone except Harriet, Andreas, Marcus, and one guard rushed for the exit.

"Temperature is now seven hundred and fifty-five Kelvin," Andreas exclaimed.

"The rate of change is decreasing," Harriet noted, pointing at something on another computer screen. She paused, studying the readout. "Yes, it's equalized at seven hundred and eighty."

Marcus removed his parka, laying it across the folding chair next to him. "Am I imagining it or is the entire chamber heating up?"

"The AC can't keep up," Andreas said, tossing his own coat onto an empty chair. He loosened his tie and unbuttoned the top two buttons of his shirt. "The sphere and crystal pillars are giving off too much heat."

Harriet's jaw dropped and she pointed. "Look, the crystals, they're—"

"The gazebo!" Andreas shouted, bursting from his chair.

The crystal pillars—now columns of sunlight—and other structures flickered in and out of existence, one moment there, the next gone, then back again. The entire chamber wavered and warped, as if reflected by a funhouse mirror. The white orb transformed into a roiling ball of flame in an instant, burning away the fog around the dais as it expanded outwards to several feet in diameter.

"That's it; this is getting too dangerous," Harriet said, shaking her head and waving a hand at the door. "Everyone out. Quickly!"

"We can't miss this," Marcus said, stepping toward her. "This is incredible."

"The instruments will keep recording. We can observe the footage from the command centre," she countered as Andreas and the guard raced for the exit.

"Until the heat melts them," he replied.

"You'll be dead before that happens." Her shoes pounded against the wooden walkway as she moved to leave. "Come on, Marcus," she said, beckoning to him from the exit.

A flash of electric light crashed against the polycarbonate barrier.

Blocking the glare with his hand, he nodded. His shoes tapped a rapid drumbeat toward the tunnel, and he slipped through the plastic doorway after his colleague.

Now sweltering, the room was a deathtrap for me, with only one way out. Whatever the scientists had set in motion, it seemed to be getting worse, and I hadn't found the answers for which I'd come looking. Far from it—I now had more questions than I'd had before arriving. My origin and my identity remained mysteries to me.

I've got to stop whatever they started.

I jumped onto the wooden platform and grabbed one of the discarded parkas from a nearby chair. I pulled it on, after shrugging off my backpack, like an astronaut getting into a spacesuit in an airlock that was about to be opened to the vacuum of space.

I cursed as the zipper caught halfway up. Taking a deep breath, I backed it up, freeing it, and tried again, then drew it up to my neck before tugging the hood over my head. Protected from the heat, I loosened my backpack's straps as far as they could go, so I could slip it over the thick coat, before snugging them tightly against my shoulders.

Fiery wraiths, translucent, as if only partly in this world, materialized near the sphere, solidifying like a TV tuning in to the right signal as I looked on. Some floated up into the ceiling like sparks from a fire, disappearing into the rock. Others rocketed across the room and disappeared into the walls.

Cooling the energy sphere had failed, but maybe it was too little, too late. My hands flew over the keyboard. Fortunately, the technician, Andreas, hadn't locked his terminal and had left the nitrogen dispenser control program running. Entering a question mark brought up the help menu, allowing me to locate the right command. I typed it, and the liquid nitrogen hissed, fogging the platform once more.

I left it activated and jumped the side railing, heading for the spot where the tholos used to be, before it had faded from existence. I kept low, dodging fiery will-o'-the-wisps as I moved. I didn't want to find out what getting hit by one of them felt like—maybe nothing, or maybe they'd rematerialize inside of me. I took an indirect path, using the deeper fog to try to reduce the risk of being caught on camera. If I survived, I didn't want the Bodhi Group to know I'd been here.

The cryogenic applicator sputtered and stopped as I re-entered the pool of water—which was all that remained to mark the tholos's former location. The ball of fire appeared nearly quenched but swelled again moments later.

With no time to lose, I moved deeper into the pond. The bottom edge of my new coat brushed lightly against the no-longer-icy surface as I neared the centre. Still cool, the water contrasted sharply with the scorching air. It soothed my flesh, but I felt queasy again from the excess water soaking through my outer shell of ice.

Time to use it, I thought.

I swirled my hands in a circle, materializing a ball of frost out of thin air. Born of the Underfrost, it crackled with power, engulfed in a nimbus of churning white vapour. I bounced it back and forth from hand to hand, then launched it at the ball of fire that still floated, impossibly, above the platform.

The fiery globe sizzled angrily as the frost bolt struck it and exploded on impact, intense heat meeting absolute cold. Three more balls of frost energy chased the first. The ball of flame continued to hiss and buzz and shrink slightly with each collision, a stubborn spike thrust into stone by a hammer of frost. A barrage of dozens of frost balls later, the pool of water dwindled at my feet. The fireball was half of its former self, perhaps five feet across, but still radiating heat like an old steam boiler.

Chest heaving, I slumped over, resting my hands on my hips. *Getting there, but not fast enough.*

Narrowing my eyes, I conjured more frost and rolled it across the floor. Waves of cryogenic energy rippled outward from it as it travelled, slicing holes in the barrier between this world and the Underfrost, raising a trail of snow as wide as a pickup truck. I did this a dozen more times. I sent most in the direction of the orb of fire, with a few others in a ninety-degree arc to either side of it. A minute later, a blanket of snow buried the entire area, and the pool was just a thin layer of ice at my feet.

While I'd been rolling snowballs, the molten sphere had grown to eight feet in diameter. A thick, soupy fog clouded everything except the sphere's bright red-hot glow, which burned off the vapour in its vicinity, creating a void of clear air around itself. Before it could grow larger still, I stepped onto the thick snow and advanced, pelting the fire with a hail of frost and stepping closer with each salvo. It shrank with each impact, even as the snow melted around me, and water dripped from my face, and another fiery will-o'-the-wisp swept past me to my left.

I cowered and grabbed my face as the blaze ballooned in size in an instant, flash-melting my exposed flesh like I'd just opened the Ark of the Covenant. Peeking between my fingers, I watched it shrink back to its former volume a moment later. I rubbed my nose, then moved forward again, windmilling frost at fire as fast as I could.

Hissing and spitting, the ball shrank again to a few feet in diameter. Unfortunately, my throwing arm felt like dead weight hanging from my shoulder, giving me serious doubts about my ability to maintain the assault. Growing desperate, I scrunched my eyes and turned my face into my shoulder as I ran up to the orb's side, screaming at the scalding heat. As my exposed flesh melted, I thrust both of my hands out as if to warm them at a campfire and channelled frost energy from my fingertips like fire retardant onto a grease fire. The globe hissed, raging against the onslaught, and the earth quaked, nearly knocking me off my feet. Then, mercifully, the fire shrivelled to the size of a golf ball and went silent. For several seconds after, I kept up my attack, then lowered my hands, sagging into the melting snow.

The sphere was gone. The cameras, floodlights and equipment surrounding the dais sagged toward the floor, blackened and melted by the intense heat, but I could still hear the hum of the air conditioning, and lights still glowed somewhere in the haze. Between the AC and the cooling effect of the snow, the room was returning to its former self, minus the tholos.

I raised my hands to my face. My nose felt a few inches shorter and my left eye seemed to bulge as if the socket's depth were diminished. I tried to close my eyes, but my left eyelid wasn't there anymore. I moaned, feeling a rush of nausea, as my fingers probed a hole in my face where my cheek should be. Huge chunks of my lower half, that not protected by the burnt and blackened parka, were missing too.

A noise to my left drew my eye. I flinched as a ball of fire rocketed through the air in my direction. The warmth from it singed my already-ruined face as it flew past.

I sank to my waist in the snow. The winter jacket bunched up under my arms, slowing my descent, as a vaguely humanoid creature of molten rock and fire emerged from the mist. Broad-shouldered, thin-waisted, it floated over the ground on a carpet of flame. *Fire elemental*, I thought, the name coming to mind unbidden.

Its left hand blurred, sending another globe of fire in my direction. With half my body buried in snow, I dodged to the right, then rose to the surface and hurled frost in return. It sailed through the mist as if thrown by a toddler playing catch with his dad, falling short of its target. I shook feeling back into my arm as two more of the creatures emerged from the vapour. The leader shrieked and shrank back, its gaze snapping to the snow at its feet.

Fatigue from my desert trek and struggle with the orb of fire threatened to overwhelm me. Fighting these things was a boxing match, after a wrestling match, after a marathon. I needed to escape or take them out fast. Taking three of them down, in my condition, wasn't likely, but my options were limited. I needed to punch through them, so I spazzed a few more frost balls their way, then stormed at them. As one moved to meet me, I deked right, then to the left, like a quarterback avoiding a sack. With my speed enhanced by the snow, I managed to slip by, though the one on the right got in a hot slap to the back of my head that blossomed stars in my eyes.

I tossed a few frost balls over my shoulder as parting gifts. They missed but discouraged pursuit long enough for me to get a bit of a lead.

Fireballs whizzed past my ears as I barrelled for the tunnel. I flew over the ground until I reached the snow's edge and leaped onto the stairs, pulling myself along by the wooden railing. Fire pummelled my back as I left the steps. The thick winter coat took the brunt of it, but I stumbled and fell, banging my face and palms on the hard rock before pushing myself upright.

Another ball of flame caught me in the head as I stood. Heat radiated through the hood of my jacket, but the thick material insulated my head like an oven mitt. I reached up to brush away the residue as I slipped through the plastic curtain and entered the passageway.

I dashed down the corridor twenty feet, then whirled a hundred and eighty degrees and walked backwards. As the first fire elemental pushed through the flap, the material melted beneath its touch but did not ignite.

My recovering throwing arm blurred, sending frost at the thing as it came through. The ball sailed to the left and crashed against the curtain. I'd already conjured a second one, though, and sent it after its predecessor. I pumped my fist as it hit the monster in the chest. It wailed and retreated behind the curtain, giving me the stink eye.

Balls of fire pounded the curtain from the far side moments later, melting away large sections.

I turned and ran.

They still hadn't turned off the tunnel lights after the emergency evacuation. The lights were spaced far apart, so it wasn't exactly bright, but I could see my way, more or less. Even so, I stumbled and bumped into the sides of the walls in my hurry to escape, muttering curses.

When I got to the narrowest section, I rolled frost along the path in front of me, ran over the resulting snow bloom, then turned and did the same back the way I came, creating a thick layer of snow. *Let's see you cross that, freaks*, I thought.

"Hey, you," said a man's voice from behind me. "Why didn't you evacuate with the others?"

I froze in place, watching my last frost ball roll across the snow, which was now a few feet deep. Someone must have been sent in to check on the situation in the cavern, I realized. In the dim light, backlit, with the winter coat I'd stolen, I must have looked like another researcher.

"Hello? You deaf?" he said in a southern accent when I didn't turn around. "Identify yourself."

"Sorry, just give me a second," I said. "Having trouble with my zipper." I quietly readied a frost ball and swung around, keeping the swirling mass behind me. As I turned, the lights went out, plunging the tunnel into darkness. Only the glow of the frost behind my back provided any light with which to see.

"Ah, damn it to hell," said the voice. "Generator quit again."

I heard him fumbling with his hands before something clicked. A beam of light illuminated the tunnel floor at the newcomer's feet. The guard I'd seen before, Larry, stood about fifteen feet down the tunnel, flashlight in one hand, assault rifle—hanging from a strap over his shoulder—in the other.

I held my free hand in front of my face, blocking the light of his torch as he raised it. As I expected, his expression changed from annoyed to puzzled, then his eyes widened as he looked over my shoulder.

"Watch your six," he said, raising his weapon and waving me to the side.

I hugged the wall and turned as a fireball streaked past me, catching Larry in the midsection. Bullets whizzed by as he fell, firing down the tunnel at the approaching enemy. The noise was deafening in the confined space.

I threw the frost that I conjured for the soldier at them instead. It struck home, and I followed it up with more. The lead elemental went down, but his pals moved up to the snow's edge and the tunnel flashed with firelight. I yelped and patted out flames as one hit my shoulder, setting the winter jacket alight. I threw myself against the wall, hiding in its curve, just out of my enemies' sightline. An angry howl followed an instant later. I poked my head out to see one of the fire elementals backing away from the snow trail that I'd laid down as a cloud of vapour rose from the floor.

I glanced back to where Larry lay holding his blackened and smoking midsection, groaning. "Oh, damn, it hurts," he wheezed, pulling himself awkwardly back down the tunnel with his other arm. "The hell's going on?"

Steeling myself, I burst from cover and dashed over to the fallen soldier. He leaned against the wall, holding his stomach, wincing. I held out a hand for him to take and pulled him upright.

"The fuck are those things?" he asked as he regained his feet. His eyes widened as he met my gaze. "What are *you?*"

"No time," I said, looking back at our mutual enemies as they bombed the snow trail with fireballs. "The snow won't keep them much longer." I grabbed his arm and began pulling him down the tunnel.

"Hold up," he said, tugging free of my grasp. He took a few steps and stooped, snatching his still-lit flashlight from where it had fallen. "Going to need this."

As we left the fire creatures behind, the tunnel grew dark, and we relied on the soldier's hand torch to guide our way. I was glad for it; I could forego fluorescing to generate light and avoid freaking him out more.

The young soldier groaned, nearly dropping his light as we reached the security door leading to the camp.

I grabbed his elbow to support him. "Hey, easy, Larry. Take a seat."

He sank to the ground, wincing. "How'd you know my name, sir?" He looked up, shining the flashlight at my chest. "You're him, aren't you? Subject Winterboy?"

"My friends call me Shivurr," I said, checking his wound. "How are you doing?"

"Jacket caught the worst of it," he replied, pulling the material taut to reveal the impact point. The fireball had burned through the outer shell, insulation and military jacket he wore beneath it, leaving red and blistered skin exposed in places. "Knocked the wind out of me. Skin's burning like a sumbitch." He let the jacket fall. "Think I'll be all right after a spell."

"Glad to hear it."

"Why'd you come here, sir?" he asked, patting his jacket with his free hand.

"Trying to get home," I replied, watching his hand, expecting him to pull a gun.

"Oh, shit," he said, scanning the ground around him. "My smokes! I must have dropped 'em. Now I'm pissed! Fuck it."

Satisfied he was okay and apparently not about to shoot me, I tried pushing on the door. It didn't budge. "What's the code?"

The soldier pulled himself to his feet, grimacing, and punched in the numbers. As the door opened, a roar from one of the pursuing infernos goaded us through. I pulled the door shut behind us and ran down the tube to join Larry at the second door. He pushed the bar that latched it from our side and shoved the door wide, and we burst through into the wider tunnel beyond.

The lights were out on this side, too, but faint illumination beckoned to us from the camp outside.

"Powerful warm out here," Larry said as a blast of warm air washed over us. He shrugged off his coat and tossed it aside as I made for the nearby lockers.

Finding what I was looking for, I dropped my burned and blackened parka onto the ground and pulled on an undamaged one. Slipping my arms through the straps of my backpack, I turned to find the young soldier had waited, though he looked near ready to bolt. Seeing me geared up, he did just that, and we ran toward the light and open air.

The camp was a shambles, like a grassy plain after a brushfire. Several trailers, vehicles, and a few electrical generators burned, throwing black smoke high into the sky. Flames from spilled gasoline drums sputtered and died as their fuel sources burned and dwindled. A strong wind blew over the carnage, fanning the fires, and the sounds of gunfire chattered softly somewhere in the distance.

As we moved onto the battleground, a light rain began to fall from thick clouds that raced and roiled overhead, blocking out the moon and stars, as the lightning flashed and the thunder rumbled.

"Je-sus," Larry hissed. "It's an invasion." He raised his weapon, eyes wide, pointing it into the camp, scanning for targets.

I followed, glad he wasn't pointing it at me—at least not yet. Saving him in the tunnel, I felt obliged to keep an eye on him. Seeing no immediate targets, he crossed to the trailer where I'd first encountered him. The door stood ajar; no one was inside.

"Sounds like gunfire," he said, emerging from within. He walked to the side of the trailer and looked east out over the desert. Vortices of fire swirled near the horizon, soaring to heights of more than sixty feet, among which smaller flickers of flame could be seen. Flashes of gunfire and streaks of flame appeared intermittently in the distance. "Boys must be in the shit over there."

"It sure looks like it," I said.

"Too far away to get to in time without transport," he said, looking at the burning vehicles in the vicinity. "More of those fire critters?" he asked, walking in a half crouch to the trailer from which the scientists had appeared earlier this evening.

"Maybe." I shrugged.

The door to the other trailer was pulled tight. Larry banged on the door and shouted, "Anyone in there?"

"Yes," came the muffled voice of the scientist Harriet from within. "Who's there, please?"

"Private Donner," Larry shouted back. "That you, Dr. Huggins, ma'am?"

"Oh, thank God!" Harriet replied. "Is it safe to come out?"

"Sit tight for now, ma'am," Larry responded. "The area is not secure." He leaned sideways, looking east toward the sounds of fighting. "Has Command been notified?"

"I called it in a few minutes ago on the sat phone," said a voice I recognized as belonging to the older scientist, Marcus. "They tell me help is on the way."

"Where's the lieutenant, sir?" Larry asked, speaking into the door.

"Pursuing the entities that attacked us," Marcus said. "We lost radio contact with him a few minutes ago, but I hear gunfire, so they may be too busy to respond to our hails. Those beings manifested out of thin air, hurling fire. The soldiers fired back. Lightning struck one of the generators. It was chaos."

"All right," he said, rubbing the stubble on the back of his shaved head. "Y'all stay put. I'm fixing to search the camp, see if anyone is hurt."

He turned back to me and shooed me away from the trailer. We walked to the edge of the encampment, out of earshot of the occupants, as the thunder and lightning subsided and the wind slowed, and the camp burned around us. The air was much cooler now, the rain changing to sleet.

"Look, Win…uh, Shivurr," he said. "Team's on its way. You best get Oscar Mike before they get here. I won't say nothing 'bout seeing you here; wouldn't be right seeing as you saved my ass in there. I nearabout lost my mind."

"Who're they?" I asked. "I don't know anyone named Oscar or Mike."

He grinned. "I mean you should get moving. On the move. Skedaddle."

"Oh, got it," I said, snorting. "Thanks, Larry. Bit surprised you didn't turn that gun on me."

"Nah, I've heard stories," he said, waving a hand. "I hear you're a good fella; not right what they been doing to you."

"Appreciate it," I replied, extending my hand. "See you around."

"Stay frosty, sir." Larry smiled back, pumping my hand.

"I don't know how to be anything else," I replied, taking my hand back.

I turned and slipped away into the darkness, leaving the devastation behind, as the sleet turned to welcome snow.

Chapter 5

Ain't Near Enough

A few hundred feet south, I headed west and continued until the hillside that lay over top of the cavern of crystals was directly to my right, still encircled by a sea of black ash, then moved south again, retracing my steps from earlier in the day. Several helicopters travelled across the night sky toward the encampment as I walked—the help of which the scientist Marcus had spoken, I presumed.

The snow kept falling for the first few miles that I travelled. I felt my face, afraid of what I'd find. My cheek felt normal, whole. I closed my eyes and sighed with relief. I couldn't see out of either one. *Just like it's supposed to be.* Like my cheek, my missing eyelid had grown back. I felt my nose and smiled as my fingers traversed its full and proper length. I looked down at my ruined bottom half. It too had regenerated back to its normal roundness. I slapped it like a beachball, laughing aloud. *I'm still gorgeous,* I thought, walking with a lighter step.

As I approached US Route 6, the snowfall diminished before fading away entirely. Looking back, I could see clouds, dark and thick, still hanging low over the hills behind me. To my front, in contrast, stars dotted the clear desert sky with their brilliance. Absent any light pollution, the Milky Way was radiant, casting enough ghostly light onto the desert floor that I imagined I could have read a book by it.

As I hiked, I realized that the compulsion to seek out the chamber had left me. Whatever need pulled me there had, it seemed, passed. Either I had done what I needed to do, or it just didn't matter anymore. It was time to move to phase two, getting to the pickup spot to catch my ride.

Before I left, Scott had arranged a ride with a trucker friend to take me north to another friend's cabin. The pickup spot was on the outskirts of Las Vegas, which lay nearly two hundred miles away as the crow flies, longer following the roads.

It might as well be on the moon, I thought. Despite my most grievous wounds being healed, I still felt like crushed ice in a saucepan. I needed somewhere to rest and recuperate. I'd replenished my supplies in the chamber's pool, but they wouldn't last long; I'd already dipped into them since leaving Larry at the encampment.

After some consideration, I decided to head back to Lunar Crater, gambling that the kids with the cooler of soda pop were still camped there. I knew that what I left behind in that treasure chest would be enough liquid to make the trek to Tonopah. I figured that I could make it there by morning. Tonopah was the wrong direction, but a lot closer than Las Vegas. I'd have the chance to pilfer more supplies in the small town and find a phone booth. Scott had given me a number to call if I needed help, so once there, I could call to delay my Las Vegas pickup, buying myself more time to make the longer journey to Sin City. *At least I know the terrain and the dangers on the way to Lunar Crater*, I reasoned. Who knew what I'd find—enemies, possibly—or not find—supplies or shelter—on my way to Las Vegas?

Having made that choice, I picked up my pace. In the cool of the night, the journey seemed a lot shorter than it had during the day. Before too long, I approached the crater for the second time in twenty-four hours and sighed with relief.

The Volkswagen van sat parked as it had been when I'd last visited, next to the two tents. A dark-coloured Ford Bronco pickup was parked a short distance away, its engine still running and headlights on. The light revealed several people clustered between the vehicles, behind which a small campfire burned.

Must have brought the firewood with them, I thought, *considering the lack of wood out here*. I'd seen enough fire for the day, so I almost kept walking, but curiosity and thirst overcame that impulse.

I circled behind the Bronco, keeping the truck's headlights in front of me. Hard rock blared from the radio inside the truck, mixing with pop music coming from the vicinity of the van, as I skulked closer.

"Well, this ain't near enough for our troubles," said a voice. The man who spoke stood in front of the pickup, holding a wad of cash in one hand and a burning cigarette in the other. At his feet lay discarded wallets. Another man leaned against the hood of the truck and looked on, holding a pistol carelessly, aimed in no direction. Five people knelt in the gravel before them, their hands behind their heads, panicked expressions on their faces. I recognized the kid that I'd encountered during my last visit, the one who I thought of as Slim, among them. The other four must be his friends—the hikers I'd seen at the bottom of the crater.

"That's all we have," replied one of the boys, who knelt a foot or so ahead of his friends. "Please, just take it and leave us alone."

The bandits were late twenties to early thirties. The one in front had the start of a potbelly on a slight build, brown hair, dirty white T-shirt, denim jacket and jeans. The other leaning against the truck was thicker, heavyset, with longish black hair and beard. He wore a black-and-red lumberjack shirt with a green trucker's cap pulled down over his eyes.

Potbelly took a puff of his cigarette, then left it dangling from the corner of his mouth so his hands were free to stuff the money into the front of his trousers. He pulled a gun from his waistband and pointed it at the group.

"How are you going to make this worth our while? Hmm? How about you, sugar tits?" he asked, leering at one of the women. The raven-haired teen cringed and began to shake. "You got any ideas?" One of the boys scowled at that, but Potbelly's eyes were focused on the girl. "Ahh, now, now, no call for that. Come on over here," he said, making a come-hither gesture with the gun.

The girl quailed but didn't move.

"Now," he snarled, aiming the gun at her.

The scowling boy gritted his teeth and started to lower his hands. *Don't do it, kid,* I thought, knowing that if he rushed the gunman, there was no way he'd make it from a kneeling position.

He'd be shot dead and bleed out on the desert floor.

I flinched as a gunshot ripped through the night and someone screamed. In the seclusion of the desert, there was little chance its sound would disturb anyone but those gathered here.

"I said, get over here," repeated the lead thug, lowering his pistol as a thin wisp of smoke drifted away on the breeze.

His head snapped to the side as my curveball pelted his ear, sending his cigarette flying. The gun hit the earth, and he followed it to the dirt an instant later and lay unmoving. His head steamed as the snow and ice melted, and his ear blazed an angry red.

Damn, is he dead? I'd tried to softball him, but his neck looked fragile as he lay there, limp as a wet dishrag. They'd not yet harmed anyone, aside from psychologically, as far as I could tell, so I wasn't trying to take them out permanently. *No time to worry about it now*, I thought. *So much for keeping a low profile.*

My feet, still tired from my run here, felt heavy as I skirted the truck, changing my direction of approach, but keeping myself hidden in darkness. Four of the five captives scattered, some scrambling away on hands and knees; others leaped to their feet and ran. The teen brunette, however, remained huddled in the truck's headlights. Her friends motioned frantically to her from the cover of the nearby van.

The other gunman's head whipped around. He aimed his weapon where I used to be. I threw a frost ball at him as I moved to my right, but it went wide. He backpedalled, firing in my direction. I was still moving, so his shots hit only air. He retreated behind the truck, peering over the hood into the desert.

"You liars! Just the five of you, my ass," he snarled, glancing at the van. "Who's out there?" He pointed his weapon at the girl, who still sobbed, collapsed into a ball. "Come on out," he yelled. "Show yourself or I shoot your friend here. What d'you think of that, asshole?" After a moment's thought, I drifted into view. "What the hell?" said the bearded thug.

His right eye narrowed and his left flared wide, and his mouth opened and closed like a guppy feeding. The barrel of his gun rose, turning in my direction, and I exploded into motion, running at him like a six-foot avalanche.

The gun spat twice as I hurtled at him. Hot lead tore into my abdomen, leaving holes in their wake. I winced at the burning sensation but kept coming. Ten feet from him, I pelted him with a wad of molten frost.

Wheezing like a forty-year smoker, he fell on his ass, holding his chest as the frost energy coursed through his body, sucking the heat from his flesh. An eyeblink later, I was on him, throwing wild punches. Hunched over as he was, my first few blows hit him square on the crown of his head, bruising my hands but doing slight damage to my opponent. Realizing that, I channelled frost energy to my knuckles, sending flashes of frost into his thick skull with each blow. His cap offered minor protection, and he fell to the ground, out cold, soon after.

No, he's still moving, I realized as I stood up. Gulping air, I conjured more frost and brought it down on his head like a coconut against rock. "Take a chill pill, asshole," I muttered, kicking his weapon to the side.

One of the young men crouched next to the crying girl, his hands on her shoulders. The other tourists slowly appeared from the darkness like wraiths, blinking, mouths ajar, as their eyes bored holes in me. I walked over to the still-burning cigarette of the first gunman and snuffed it out with my foot. "Remember, only you can prevent forest fires," I said with a tired grin.

I glanced at the smoker. He lay in the dirt on his side, with one arm trapped beneath his body and the other extended to his front. I stooped next to him and placed the palm of my hand against his chest as it swelled and then contracted. *Good, still breathing.*

It had all happened in a few frantic moments and, happily, amazingly, five gunshots later, no one was dead. The lead thug's handgun was nowhere to be seen. *Must have been thrown when he fell,* I thought, finding nothing under his body. Satisfied the guns were out of easy reach of the two unconscious goons, I felt my chest, afraid of what I'd find; snow and ice had rushed to close the gaps. While narrowing, I could still feel the paths the bullets had torn through me. *I guess the bullets didn't hit anything vital, if there is such a thing in my insides*, I thought.

"Anybody got a drink?" I asked, slumping—a slowly deflating balloon now that the danger and excitement had passed.

Slim walked to their cooler, rummaged around inside, and returned with a can of Coca-Cola, holding it out to me like he was feeding a tiger at the zoo from the wrong side of the bars. "H… he…here you go," he stammered before clearing his throat.

I nodded, taking the can. "Thanks, Slim."

"All good, dude," he said, shrugging. "It's the one you dropped." After a moment, he added, "I'm Caleb, by the way."

"S'up," I said, before taking a swig. The chemicals thundered through me almost immediately. I stood taller as my vision cleared.

The boom box was still playing, now halfway into a song about an echo at a beach, as one of the girls appeared at Caleb's side, blinking like she had dust in her eyes.

"This is Lucy," Caleb said. "That's Brad," he continued, pointing to the young man standing next to him, hands held to the sides of his head as he stared at me. Then, more softly, "And Alan and Lilith," referring to the two crouched teens.

"This is unreal," said Brad, lowering his hands as he stepped closer. In his early twenties, clean-shaven, Brad stood about five foot eight. His straight brown hair was cut short on the sides and back; long, feathered bangs hung down almost into his eyes. Of medium build, he had the air of an athlete and the tanned skin of an avid outdoorsman. He wore faded blue bell-bottom jeans with a black leather belt, and blue Nike running shoes with a yellow swoosh. A pair of dark sunglasses hung from the front of his white T-shirt with black sleeves that read The Police. "Are you…? Wha…what are you?"

"Uh, duh. He's a snowman, obviously," Caleb said, smiling broadly and puffing out his chest. "Just like I told you guys."

"Not sure what I am," I said. "Pretty sure 'snowman' doesn't quite cover it."

"But," he said, snorting, "you *are* a snowman."

"I guess you're right…meatman," I said.

They chuckled.

"He's got you there, Caleb," Lucy said. She smiled, flashing perfect white teeth. Curvaceous, a few inches shorter than Brad, and of similar age, she looked like a cheerleader on her day off with wavy blond hair pulled back in a loose ponytail. She wore tan shorts and a blue halter top, with knee-high white socks and running shoes.

Lilith stood, rubbing tears from her face. Alan put his arm around her, but she shrugged him off impatiently. "I'm all right. Just give me a second."

She was young, perhaps fifteen or sixteen years old. Long, straight raven-black hair reached well past her shoulders. Wavy at the ends, it framed a pale, pretty pixieish face and bright, intelligent blue eyes. The glint of silver earrings peeked between the strands as her head moved. The left side of her nose was pierced as well, with a simple nose stud gleaming silver in the flickering light. She approached me slowly, craning her head as she looked up at me. Small-framed, just a few inches over five feet, she wore cut-off blue jean shorts and a grey sweatshirt several sizes too large for her with large black letters that read "Surfer Dude."

"This can't be real," Lilith said. She crossed her arms over her chest as if chilled. "Are you real?"

I shrugged.

"If this isn't a dream, thank you for saving us," she said, looking me directly in the eyes. "Seriously."

"Fuckin' A to that," Caleb said, nodding. "What's your name?"

"Shivurr."

"Awesome to meet you, dude," Brad said, thrusting a hand toward me.

I glanced down at the gun and soda. "Just a sec," I said, slipping the weapon under my armpit before shaking his hand. "Good grip."

He rubbed his hands together and blew into his palms. "Icy."

The thug at our feet groaned and we all looked down.

"Guys, find something to tie up these dickweeds," Brad said, looking around, "before they wake up."

"Whoa, Alan, what are you doing?" Lucy said.

Alan, the tallest of the group, aimed the other handgun at the unconscious thug with shaking hands. The teen's thick, shaggy brown hair, bleached blond by the sun, spilled about his broad shoulders like a lion's mane, blending with a sparse three-day beard. Lean and muscular, he looked like a cross between a football quarterback and gymnast.

"Relax, dude," Caleb said, furrowing his brow. "Ease up."

"He's got it coming," Alan said, red-faced, waving the pistol to emphasize each word. "They both do."

"No doubt, dude, but you don't want this heat," Caleb said. The shorter teen made a down motion with his hands. "Just take it easy…please."

"Alan, stop it," Lilith said, glaring daggers at him.

"Brad, do something," Lucy said.

Brad walked over and held out his hand. "Don't be a dork, Alan," he said quietly, seemingly unconcerned. For a few tense moments, the two stared at each other. Alan's face twisted, re-laxed, twisted again, then smoothed for the last time. He lowered the weapon, letting it twirl around his finger by the trigger guard, and held it out so that Brad could take it. Brad slipped it into his waistband at the small of his back, then slapped Alan on the shoulder and pulled him into an embrace, pounding his back. "Let it go, bro. How would I explain you shooting them to Mom and Dad?"

"That was harsh," Caleb said, eyes wide, looking around as if for a bucket into which to throw up. "Totally looked like you were going to waste 'em."

"Not even," Alan said, waving his hand dismissively. "Seri-ously," he added, seeing skeptical expressions on the faces around him.

"Whatever," Brad said. "Come on, find something to tie 'em up. I'll keep an eye on them."

"I'll search their truck," Alan said, heading for the Bronco. A few moments later, the radio went silent as he shut off the en-gine.

"Caleb, I swear, don't light that shit," Brad said, sneering. "I need you sharp."

"Just a short puff to calm my nerves," Caleb muttered, tossing a match to the ground. A cloud of marijuana smoke drifted away on the wind. He looked at me, avoiding Brad's gaze. "You going to keep that?"

I glanced down and pulled the gun from my armpit by the barrel.

"Wait, don't touch it," Lucy said, running to the van. She returned a moment later, opening a paper bag. "Put it in here. Fingerprints," she explained, rolling it closed, "for the police."

"Shivurr touched it already," Caleb said, taking another puff.

"No fingerprints," I said, holding up my free hand.

"Lil, hon, get my camera." Lucy pointed to the van.

"What for?"

"So I can take pictures of them and the scene," Lucy said. "Evidence, people."

The girl returned holding a large Nikon camera. Lucy peeled off the case and snapped on the flash, and the camera whirred and clicked as she moved about. I followed, keeping out of the camera's eye.

"How do you know to do all this?" I asked as she laid the guns next to each other and snapped more photos.

"Lucy loves detective shows," Lilith said, walking to the van. "Cop shows, mystery novels. Especially girl detectives."

"She's my Angel," Brad said, walking past, holding a coil of rope that he'd pulled from the roof of the van. He smiled at her. "Looks like one, too."

A smile blossomed on Lucy's face, but she kept taking pictures without responding.

"Get a room," Lilith said, rolling her eyes. A moment later, the pop music died as she hit the stop button on the ghetto blaster.

The wind, crickets, and crackle of the fire mixed with the sounds of the group hustling about, securing the robbers. Now and again one of them would glance in my direction, as if expecting me to be gone like a mirage or figment of their collective imagination. I pretended not to notice and looked out over the crater, its depths lost in the inky void of the night's shadows.

Occasionally, flashes from Lucy's camera disturbed the darkness as she finished documenting the scene. I half expected to see monsters in those flashes of light, skittering from the abyss to drag me and my companions back down to their lair to be devoured.

I snorted to myself, appreciating in that moment the shock my companions must have felt when I'd first appeared, and maybe still did. I was something completely unheard of by most of humanity. Their only points of reference for me were crude, unliving idols—snowmen—sculpted seasonally by children in colder climes. The resemblance seemed weak to me, but I'd heard the comparison enough to accept that that was how they'd see me.

I wasn't sure whether these snow sculptures were just a coincidence or something more. Had my kind encountered primitive man ages ago? Were these snow sculptures some sort of vestigial cultural practice, or a deliberate attempt to remind their descendants of something? Whatever the answers, I didn't know if their familiarity with snowmen allowed the kids to better cope with the seeming impossibility of my appearance or made it worse and more improbable. Whatever the case, pooled with humanity's widely held belief that they are the only intelligent, sentient life in the universe, my appearing, walking and talking must have threatened to unravel their minds. I could only guess at what they were thinking or how their brains were working to find an explanation that they could accept.

I thought about leaving the group now that the situation was under control. Maybe they'd explain my appearance away as some sort of collective hallucination, brought on by marijuana and the stress of being mugged. *Keep dreaming*, I thought, shaking my head ruefully. *Leaving isn't going to help*. Besides, I was still in big trouble, and I really needed their assistance. Extra water or other beverages or a ride closer to my next destination could make all the difference in surviving the next few days, so I sipped my soda and waited while they worked. For the time being, I said nothing and hoped that they'd get used to me in time, as my former captors had after years of regular contact. I just hoped that it wouldn't take that long this time around.

For those at the research lab, once I had spoken English and become an expert in pop culture, I'd seemed a lot less alien and a lot more approachable. How you speak and act and what you value tends to either set you apart from or connect you to others, even more than what you look like. Sharing culture and ideas and speaking like a native diffused and confused any prejudices they had—it wasn't enough to make them let me go, but enough to convince them to treat me better, and even for me to make a few friends like Scott, eventually allowing me to escape. Even when a new scientist rotated in, they warmed to me faster after chatting about baseball or something. A guy who shares your interests can't be all bad, right?

Until today, I hadn't met anyone new in years. Seeing the kids' astonished and bewildered expressions reminded me of what I wanted to forget: to the average person, I'm a freak that's going to scare the shit out of them. Scared people are dangerous people—if I showed up in a public place, I knew many would either run from or attack me, not stop to chat about their favourite movie—so I needed to stay out of sight. Still, these five hadn't done either. Instead, they'd shaken my hand and introduced themselves. *Maybe we can be friends.* In the few years that I could recall being alive, I'd learned that you didn't get far without a friend or two.

Fifteen minutes later, the two thugs were tied up with rope scavenged from the van's roof rack. Lucy had lit a Coleman lantern, which hissed like water on a low boil, casting long shadows across the area. Alan and Caleb dragged the robbers over the dirt and leaned the goons up against the front bumper of the Bronco.

Our captives woke up a short while later, shouting threats and insults until I stepped into view, tossing frost from hand to hand. They pressed themselves against the truck, staring at me with bulging eyes, as Alan pulled out their pockets. After a few moments of struggle, he stood holding two wallets, out of which he yanked wads of the group's stolen cash. Lucy took the empty wallets as Alan counted the money. The pictures on their driver's licenses identified the bearded assailant's name as Dale Simmons and the other's as Jack Esterhazy. We moved just out of earshot but kept a watchful eye on the duo.

"Now what do we do?" asked Lucy, shining one of the large red flashlights that she'd recovered from the van at the ground near the two.

"Break camp and book it back to Cali," Brad said, shrugging. "Or do you still want to go to Vegas?"

"We've got to turn them in, don't we?" Lucy said, frowning. "They've probably done this before, maybe even murdered people."

"No duh," Lilith said. She glanced at the highwaymen, flaring her nostrils and curling her lips.

"There's a sheriff's office in Tonopah," Lucy said. "It's the closest. We can take them there."

"Forget that. I'm not getting in the same car with them," Lilith said, biting her nails. "What if they get loose?"

"You're right," Brad said, nodding. He puffed his cheeks, looking at the bound men. "We've got their wallets and ID. We can leave them here, tied up—send the police back to get them."

"Any chance of a ride?" I asked, coughing and holding up a hand. "I need to get to Las Vegas, if you're going."

Brad looked at his friends, shining his flashlight at each of them in turn. After a brief pause, Lucy nodded, almost imperceptibly. Lilith looked dubious but said nothing.

"Tonopah first," Lucy said. "It's a lot closer."

"Radical," Alan said, grinning.

"Awesome," Caleb agreed.

"Uh, sure," Brad said, looking back to me. "Why not?" He strode for the nearest tent. "Okay, dudes. Let's pack up and jet."

Chapter 6

Tonopah

We travelled northwest, headed for US Route 6, over rough backcountry roads, more dirt track than formal road. Turning left onto the highway, we continued southwest to Warm Springs, then west, heading for Tonopah, looking to find the sheriff's office, turn in the highwaymen, and then drive south on State Highway 95 to Las Vegas.

The van lumbered down the lonely highway as the sun rose behind us. The enclosed space was a welcome relief, trapping the icy chill that I naturally exude and creating a microclimate several degrees cooler than the desert air outside. Still a bit too warm for comfort, it was far better than being outdoors—for me, at least. The rest of our party pulled on jackets and knitted hats shortly after we got underway, once they noticed the chilling effect of my presence.

My companions were Californians, on a three-week road trip to visit several national parks and landmarks in California, Nevada, Arizona, and Utah, and were therefore equipped for camping in the cool nights of the mountains or the warm weather of lower altitudes.

Brad, the van's owner, drove while his girlfriend Lucy rode shotgun. Alan, who I now knew to be Brad's kid brother, sat in the back seat with his arm around his high school sweetheart, Lilith. His best friend, Caleb, sat next to them while I stood in the middle and leaned against the wall of the van, opposite the sliding door, and watched the desert roll past.

"So, what happened back there?" I asked. "With those guys?"

"They drove up about ten minutes before you showed up, while we were roasting marshmallows," Brad said. "They acted friendly at first, but I had a bad feeling right away. The first guy, Jack, asked us where we were from, where we were going. Once they knew it was just us, they became total dicks, pulling guns, stealing our—"

"Are you a government experiment or what?" Caleb interjected.

"Jesus, Caleb," Alan said, glancing at the ceiling. "Subtle much?"

"A subject, not a creation," I said, shaking my head. "They captured me, held me against my will, for several years."

"Holy shit," Caleb replied, bobbing his head vigorously. "Seriously? I was just kidding."

"The less you know, the better," I said, looking out the window as several large trucks flashed by heading east.

"Oh, come on, dude," Caleb said, throwing out his hands in supplication.

"Well, I suppose I can tell you a bit," I said, stroking my chin.

For the next few miles, I shared enough of my story to give them an idea of the risks they were taking. I left out names and the details of my quest, saying only that I had been held in a secret facility, had escaped, and was on the run.

Alan seemed doubtful about my claims of amnesia. "Sure, dude," he said, snorting softly. "Don't tell us if you don't want to."

"I think that's super sad," Lucy said, reaching over her seat to pat my shoulder.

"Sad, but true," I assured her. "It's okay, though. I'm free now and not going back, ever."

"Are we in danger?" Lilith asked, biting her lower lip.

"I don't know." I paused, considering. "I doubt it. They'd probably question you, then let you go with some bullshit story."

"But we've seen you," Caleb said. "Won't they need to silence us?"

"Once they caught me, no one would believe anything you say about me, not without me as proof. I'd pretty much have to go on network news and answer questions for an hour, and there'd still be people that would say it was a hoax. Anyway, they've no idea where I am now. If I keep low, it should stay that way."

"It's the freaking Man," Caleb said loudly, snarling. He pulled a joint from the pocket of his jeans. "Just like I've always been saying. Men in freaking black."

"Caleb, I told you, don't smoke that shit in the van," Brad said, glaring at his younger friend in the rear-view mirror, then looking back at the road. "You should probably ditch it all before we get there. I don't want the cops finding it."

"What about your beer, dude?" Caleb muttered, slipping the joint back into his jeans.

"I'm over twenty-one, smartass."

"Lucy, pass me that roll you took of those men," Brad said. She rummaged around in her bag and passed it to him. "Is there anything else on it?"

"No," Lucy replied. "I put in a fresh roll. I'm not giving them my photos. Not sure about the ones I took of the stars tonight, but I got some nice ones of the crater, I think." She looked at me. "There's basically no light pollution out here. It's perfect for time-lapse shots of the stars."

"Astronauts trained there, you know," Lilith said knowingly, turning her head to me. "For the moon landings."

"Cool, I didn't know that," I said, even though I did.

Smiling, Lilith blew a pink bubble with her chewing gum, popping it loudly, and hit play on her boom box. Her long hair swayed gently as she bobbed her head to the beat.

Despite the early hour, Tonopah was bustling with activity as we drove through. Brad, the group's apparent academic, explained that the price of silver and gold had risen a few years ago, causing old mines to be reopened. Combined with increased activity at Tonopah Test Range—near which the Bodhi Institute was located—the town boomed with activity. Automobile and foot traffic seemed heavy as the town started its day, especially after the solitude of the desert. The town had the general feel and appearance of an Old West mining camp, which, as Brad explained, was no surprise given that was how it had started out. There was an actual old mine right in town, in fact.

"Hey, is that a bakery?" Lilith said, pointing with a hand lost in the sleeve of Alan's too-large sweatshirt. "Can we stop there?"

"Bakery, eh?" Caleb smirked. "Makes you think—donut?"

Alan chuckled as Lilith rolled her eyes.

"Later, after the sheriff's," Brad said, looking at Lucy.

"Right, the sooner we report those men, the better," Lucy added, pressing her lips together.

"I've got to piss like a racehorse," Caleb moaned.

"Careful, Brad," Alan said. "Caleb's going to piss his pants again."

"Dick," Caleb said, shoving his friend. "That was ten years ago. I was five years old."

"All right, fine," Brad said, shrugging. "We need gas anyway."

We stopped at a gas station, just past the old Mizpah Hotel, a five-storey salmon-coloured building with a large rooftop sign identifying it in large red letters. Brad gassed up the van while the others went inside to ask for directions to the sheriff's office, use the restrooms, and stock up on drinks, snacks, and ice. I waited in the van and peeked between the drawn curtains to people watch.

Caleb returned first, holding a full grocery bag in the crook of his elbow and a drink in the other hand. Brad, having finished pumping gas, gave him a friendly slap on the shoulder as he passed him on his way inside to pay.

The teen slipped in the front passenger door, letting in a blast of heat. Putting the bag on the seat, he slid between it and the driver's seat to get to the back.

"Try one of these," he said, tossing me a cold soda can with Dr Pepper written on the side, the outside of which was moist with slight condensation. "It cures what ails you," he quipped with a goofy grin.

"Nice one," I replied with a nod as he sat down beside me. The can cracked open with a hiss, and I guzzled from it, moaning.

Caleb ripped open a bag of chips and started digging in. Mouth full, he held out the bag in wordless offer.

"Sure, why not." I grabbed a handful, popped them into my

mouth and chomped the chips to dust. "Not bad."

"Put these Pop Rocks in your mouth," Caleb suggested, grinning. "Then take a sip of your drink. Gnarly, right?" he said, winking at the look of surprise on my face as the candy buzzed in my mouth. "Where's my jacket?" he mumbled through a paste of potato chips. "It's downright chilly in here."

"Yeah, right." I plucked at the fabric of my winter jacket. "I'm freezing my nipples off here."

Bits of chips flew across the van as Caleb chortled appreciatively. "Man, these chips are good," he muttered, stuffing more into his mouth.

A moment later, the side door slid open a crack. I hugged the wall as Lucy and Lilith slipped inside, also carrying grocery bags. Alan jumped into the front seconds after.

"All right," Lucy began, "the sheriff's office is on the edge of town, apparently. Caleb, if you're holding, now's the time to ditch it. We don't know what's going to happen when we get there," she added in a motherly tone.

"Maybe I should hang out here and you can go without me," Caleb said, looking pained. "What am I going to do for the rest of the trip?"

"Give it to Shivurr to hold," Alan suggested. "He can stay in the van."

"You shouldn't do drugs, Caleb," Lucy said, wagging a finger at him. "It's not good for you."

"Just say no," Alan said, smirking.

"Okay, *Mom*. I'll give it to Shivurr," he said, looking defeated. He dug around in his jacket and produced a transparent plastic bag with several joints in it. "Hang on to this herb for me, will you? Just don't smoke it, okay?"

"Sure, but who's Herb?" I asked, squinting my eyes. "Why are you laughing?"

"Here comes Brad," Alan said. The van wobbled slightly as the last member of our party jumped into the driver's seat.

He looked in the rear-view mirror at the group. "Let's get this over with and then get a few hotel rooms. I could use a shower and some sleep. I'm bonking."

It had been a sleepless night for all of them, with the attack on their camp. I knew that people need to sleep regularly, or fatigue clouds their minds and abilities. Las Vegas lay more than a three-hour drive away. I don't need to sleep as much as humans do so I hadn't considered how tired they must be until that moment. I can go weeks without it, but I do need to regenerate my mind to process experiences and allow my body to repair and rejuvenate. After the ordeal of my flight from the Institute, the battle with the fire elementals, and the desert heat, a rest would be welcome, even critical to surviving whatever lay before me. *Sleep is also a weapon*, I'd heard somewhere before.

"What about Shivurr?" Lucy asked. "He can't just walk into the hotel lobby with us."

"Dunno," Brad said, turning the key to start the vehicle. "We'll figure it out. Give it some thought."

"I need to make a phone call before we leave town," I said.

"No problemo," Brad replied. "Alan can take you after we check in."

Brad put the van in gear, and it lurched forward, heading for the sheriff's office.

"Just keep driving straight, then turn right on Radar Road," Alan said, pointing.

We soon passed a pale blue-and-white two-storey building with a sign out front identifying it as the Clown Motel on our left, then the Old Tonopah Cemetery, which lay well back from the road. The drive was short; within five minutes we pulled into the parking lot surrounding the Nye County Justice Court, Jail, and Sheriff's Office. We drove through once, getting the lay of the land, then circled back around. The lot was almost empty, but Brad still parked at a distant corner, as far away from the door as possible.

"No one should bother you here, Shivurr," he said, pulling the keys from the ignition.

"Let's go get this done," Alan said grimly.

The group exited the vehicle and made their way inside. I sat and waited, hoping no one would pass too closely, notice the frosty windows, and get curious. Then waited some more. Two and a half hours later, they re-emerged.

Everyone hopped back into the vehicle. "Hey, Shivurr, any trouble while we were gone?" Lucy asked, taking a seat beside me in the back.

"Glad that's over," Alan declared, leaning back in his seat, and running his hands through his hair.

"Hell, yeah," agreed Caleb as the others nodded their heads.

"All quiet here," I responded. "How did it go?"

"They sent a few deputies to the crater. Made us wait while they did, but the bastards were gone," Brad said, scowling.

"Even the truck," Lilith said. "They must have had another key."

"Or hotwired it," Caleb said, looking at Alan.

"Maybe," Alan said. "I heard it's not hard."

Lucy turned in her seat to face me. "The sheriff issued an arrest warrant. We gave them the guns, vehicle description, plates, and driver's licenses. They're getting the photos developed for evidence, but we already picked them out of a book of mug shots."

The van rumbled to life. I braced myself as it lurched backward, and we pulled away. Brad turned left onto Radar Road to take us back to town.

"They'll get them," Alan said reassuringly. "It's just a matter of time."

"I hope so," Lilith said, frowning.

"Anyway, they told us we were free to go," Lucy said. "They'll call us if we need to testify."

Brad turned left again onto Main. "So, Mizpah Hotel?" The others nodded agreement.

"Can we find a phone after?" I asked. "I need to call a friend."

A short while later, the company secured two rooms at the historic old hotel, one for the girls, another for the guys, while I waited in the van. They unloaded the luggage and transferred their bags to the rooms. While the others showered and tried to get some sleep, Alan returned to the van to drive me to find a secluded phone. He had managed to sleep some while waiting in the sheriff's office and claimed to be more wired than tired.

"Who's this friend?" Alan said, glancing at me from the driver's seat, then back at the road.

"A friend of a friend," I said, reluctant to give a name. "It's safer if I don't tell you more."

"Need to know," Alan replied with an exaggerated wink. "Understood."

We found a dusty phone booth near the Clown Motel that we'd passed earlier. Vehicles were parked in front of some rooms, curtains drawn, while window-mounted air conditioners rattled and hummed, fighting to cool the guests within. Alan parked near the motel office, over which a large sign with yellow-and-red lettering welcomed visitors. He parked at an angle, using the van as a curtain, ensuring we couldn't be seen from the office or parking lot.

The glass booth provided an unobstructed view of the graves of the Old Tonopah Cemetery, which neighboured the motel on its west side. It squatted in a shallow valley between the motel's asphalt parking lot and some mounds of earth a quarter mile away—detritus of an ancient rock quarry, I presumed.

"Here," Alan said, dumping a handful of change into my cupped palms.

"Appreciate it." I scanned the vicinity, making sure we weren't being watched, then picked up the receiver, dropped in some change, and dialed the number.

A woman answered on the third ring. "Hello?"

"Hi. Is Boreas there?" I asked, giving Alan a thumbs-up. The long-haired teen leaned against the van, muscled arms crossed, and pulled his shades down over his eyes.

"One moment, please," the woman replied with a snort. "Wil," she shouted, her voice muffled but not fully muted by, I presumed, a hand over the receiver, "one of your Dungeons and Dragons pals is on the phone."

A short while later, I heard footsteps, then fumbling sounds as the phone changed hands.

"Thanks, I've got it," I heard him say. Then again, "I said,

I've got it," followed by footsteps fading into the background.

"Hello?" said a man's voice.

"Uh, hi. Is this Boreas?" I asked, continuing to use his BBS SysOp handle. We had never met, except through text chats, arguing about *Star Trek* versus *Star Wars* mostly, so I didn't know his voice.

"Yup, that's me," replied the voice. "People call me Wilhelm in analog life. Who's this?"

"Cool Hand," I answered. "Scott's friend."

"Cool Hand?" Wilhelm replied. He paused. "Oh, hey, bud. What's up?"

A computer aficionado, Wilhelm Schmidt owned and operated a computer bulletin board system that I frequented, popular among geeks, nerds, and hackers such as himself. So much so, that he'd had a few extra phone lines installed at his home, allowing multiple users to connect simultaneously. People across the country regularly dialed into his computer to post messages, share files, play games, and, most importantly, chat about stuff, particularly movies, comic books, and computers. Scott was a member and a few years earlier had written and installed software that allowed me to join too, without the Bodhi Group being any the wiser.

Before I'd escaped, Scott had told me Wilhelm's real name—until then, I'd only known him as Boreas—and given me the SysOp's voice line phone number to call if I ran into trouble. "Just call him and tell him you need to reach me," Scott had explained. "I'm over at his house quite a bit to play D&D. He lives up the street from me. It won't raise any suspicions if he calls me at work."

"I need a favour," I said into the handset. "My computer is busted, so I can't get on Olympus, but I need to get a message to Scott. Can you help me out?"

"Uh, sure, no problem. What's the message?"

"One sec," I said. I opened the phone booth door. "What's your last name, Alan?"

The athletic teen lay parallel to the ground, doing push-ups next to the van. He'd tied his hair into a ponytail to keep it off the asphalt and dirt. "Davis," he shouted back, jumping to his feet and dusting off his hands. He began shadow boxing himself in the reflection of the van's side windows.

"I need him to call me at the Mizpah Hotel in Tonopah," I said into the handset. "Just ask for Brad Davis's room."

"For sure, man," Wilhelm replied. "Consider it done."

I hung up the phone. Alan had untied the ponytail and was combing his hair, using the passenger window as a mirror. "All good, dude?" he asked, tossing his hair back like a heavy metal rock star.

"Yep," I said, smirking. "We can head back, if you're done admiring yourself."

"Hey—this," he said, looking down at himself and striking a pose, "doesn't happen by accident."

"Okay," I said, chuckling. "All set, gorgeous?"

"Dick," he said without rancour.

"Why all the training?"

"Surfing, bro," Alan said. "Trying to be the best."

"Doesn't that sort of take the fun out of it? Taking it so seriously?"

He shrugged. "I want to be the best. Do something cool, not live some boring, sad life that's been lived a thousand times before."

"Be careful what you wish for," I said. "Being special can be lonely."

We hopped into the old van and drove back to the hotel. After some discussion, my new posse decided that I'd room with the guys. They'd rented a larger suite, so they had more room. Plus, if the call came, it would, as I'd instructed Wilhelm, be to Brad's room.

The midday crowds were eating lunch and rushing to and from work, making getting to the room a tense operation. We sat in the van by a back door to the hotel and debated a few different options. Finally, we just went for it. I pulled up the hood of my winter jacket, hiding my face, and jumped out of the van through the back door, which Caleb held open, rushing up the deserted stairwell. Lucy went first, scouting ahead to ensure the coast was clear, and Lilith brought up the rear, ready to run interference if we heard someone coming. Everyone was hungry after that, having missed breakfast. The snacks they'd had when we'd gassed up were long forgotten, so the group headed out, while I stayed behind. Caleb promised to bring back some drinks and snacks for me as I gave him back his stash.

With nothing else to do but wait, I turned on the television, put some towels down and lay down on the bed. The towels were just a precaution. I don't sweat much when calm and cool, unlike the snowmen decorating front yards at Christmas. Almost comfortable, for the first time in days, I watched TV for a while, tossing ice cubes into my mouth like popcorn from the bucket Lilith had brought me, and relaxed. Eventually I nodded off and napped while sounds of a detective show played in the background. After a time, the loud, insistent ring of the telephone woke me from a dream haunted by fiery monsters and flashing sirens.

I picked up the handset halfway through the third ring. "Hello?"

"Hey, bro, it's me, Scott," said the caller. "How're you doing, my man?"

"Surviving, so far, buddy," I said, rubbing my eyes. "I wasn't sure I was going to make it for a while."

"I'm looking forward to hearing all about it, but it'll have to wait. I can't talk long." I recognized the sounds of a loudspeaker in the background. "We've all been confined to the Institute since your escape. They're interviewing everyone. Dixon thinks you had help, so he's on the warpath."

I sat back down on the bed, taking the phone base with me in my other hand. "Should you be calling from there, then?"

"Don't worry," Scott said. "Wil's using one of the Olympus phone lines to patch me through. He's holding the handsets together as we speak. If Dixon checks the call logs, they'll show me making a call I make regularly. Besides, he won't check them himself; he'll ask me to do it."

"Smart."

"Thanks. Look, do you think you can make it to Las Vegas,

to Wilhelm's house, by tomorrow night?"

"Why's that? What about the ride north?"

"We've got to meet, in person, first," Scott said, lowering his voice. "After you left, security got a bit slack internally. Everyone was out searching for you, so I snuck into the restricted archives."

I whistled softly. "Are you nuts? I thought it was too risky."

"It was worth it," he said. "Believe me."

I quelled the urge to ask more, since our time was short. "I think that should work. I met some new friends; they said they'd be willing to give me a ride. If not, I'll go cross-country." My face broke into a sweat at the thought.

"I'm not sure when exactly I'll get there—so hang with Wilhelm until I do," Scott said. "Play some video games. Watch movies. Stay out of sight." He took a breath. "I should let you go before someone starts looking for me."

"Sure thing," I said. "Thanks for all your help, dude."

"Most def, my friend. See you soon." The line clicked as he ended the call.

My new friends returned about thirty minutes later, goodies in hand. As we sat snacking and relaxing, I told them about the phone call. Before I could even ask, Lucy said, "Of course we'll still take you. It's the least we can do after you helped us."

"Right on," Brad said. "Looks like we're going to Vegas after all. We'll head out tomorrow, first thing."

Chapter 7

May We Come In?

As planned, everyone woke at eight the next morning and went downstairs to eat. I stayed behind and watched cartoons and chugged sodas while I waited. I'd spent the night regenerating in the tub. It was surprisingly comfortable, with ready access to all the water I might need or want. With the door closed, bringing the temperature close to freezing in the enclosed space was no sweat.

An hour later, Caleb and Alan returned to shower and pack. Brad and Lucy, they told me, had left to gas up the van, and buy snacks for the road. After a long time blow-drying and teasing his long hair, Alan left the room soaked in cologne, saying he was going to check on Lilith. Caleb cleaned up next and sank into one of the suite's plush chairs to watch cartoons with me. I felt rested and refreshed, and positive about the future for a change. *By saving the gang at Lunar Crater*, I thought, *I may have saved myself.* I didn't want to think too closely about what might have happened if I hadn't come across them when I did.

A few cartoons later, curious about my new friends, I asked, "What brought you guys to Lunar Crater?"

Caleb shrugged his shoulders, continuing to watch the TV. "Lil begged us. She's a space geek; wanted to see where the astronauts trained. It was kind of on the way back home after Utah. Awesome parks there, dude. Zion is unbelievable."

"How long have Alan and Lilith been dating?" I asked, flipping to another channel on the TV.

"Long time, dude. Must be almost a year," Caleb said, looking thoughtful. "He asked her out last summer, after teaching her to surf. He gives lessons for extra cash."

"She's pretty pale for a surfer. I mean, not as pale as me, but you know."

"She's more a skater girl." Caleb nodded. "Picked up surfing fast, though. Guess they're kind of similar."

"You surf?"

"Chee-uh, since I was eight years old."

"Are you going pro too?"

"Nuh-uh, too serious for me. Gotta enjoy life."

A half hour later, Alan returned from Lilith's room and slammed the door. The bed rocked as he tossed himself onto it, saying nothing. I looked at Caleb, eyebrows raised. He looked back, shaking his head, almost imperceptibly.

"Everything cool, Alan?" Caleb said.

"Fine," Alan said, staring at the wall.

"Sure?"

"I said I'm fine. I'm going to the arcade." He shot to his feet and left the room.

"Chicks," Caleb said, sneering.

"What's going on?" I asked, looking at the door.

Caleb grimaced. "Dunno, but trust me, Lil's the reason."

"Aren't you friends?"

"Lil's cool, but moody," Caleb said. He swirled his finger in a circle next to his ear. "Queen of the friggin' mind game." He lowered his voice and leaned forward, holding the back of his hand to the side of his mouth. "He's got it bad, dude."

"It?" I asked, whispering back. "What's it?"

Caleb chuckled, sitting back in the plush chair. "Duh, he likes her bod, man." He waggled his eyebrows suggestively. "Anyway, they—" Caleb cut himself off as Alan walked back into the room. "Hey, man, forget something?"

"Quarters," Alan replied, glaring at his friend.

"Come on," Caleb said. "What's up?"

His friend shrugged. "Nothing."

"Spill, dude."

He pursed his lips, and huffed, then said, "She's mad about last night. That I didn't protect her." Alan sat down on the edge of the bed and rubbed his face. "She's right. I didn't do anything."

Caleb's jaw dropped. "She *said* that? Do what? Get shot in the face?"

"No, not exactly," Alan replied, collapsing into a nearby chair. "We were making out, she started crying, told me to leave." He rubbed his face, sighing. "I was gutless," he said, voice rising, fists pounding his knees.

"As if...," Caleb began, hesitating. "Let it go. Bullets beat fists. Shivurr, tell him, man."

"Most definitely," I said.

"You did something," Alan said, his voice barely audible.

"And got shot." I fingered my chest where the bullets entered. "Twi-ice," I finished, holding up two fingers on my other hand like a hippie making peace signs at a sit-in.

He looked up at me with a crooked smile, then nodded grudgingly. "Point taken."

"Lil knows it too," Caleb said. "She's just freaked. You know her."

Alan grabbed his wallet. "Whatevs. Want to hit the arcade?" he asked, looking at both of us. The hotel had an arcade with several popular games.

I squinted my eyes. "Whatcha talkin' about, Alan?"

He grabbed the winter jacket that I'd taken from the desert chamber and held it up by the hood. "It was empty when I was there just now. We can scout it out."

I pulled on the winter jacket once more.

"Do they have Dig Dug?" Caleb asked with a smirk. "Ready to get your ass kicked again?"

"As if, dude," Alan said. "Put some money on it."

Brad burst through the door as I pulled up my hood. "Van's fuelled up," Brad said. "Let's pack up and get going."

"Ah, nuts," Caleb said.

"Lucky," Alan said. "To be continued, dude."

The guys began to pack up. Alan finished first and did sit-ups while waiting, resuming his argument with Caleb over who was the better gamer.

"Bite me, Caleb," Alan said, switching to push-ups. "Least I carve waves better than you."

"Do they always argue like this?" I asked, looking at Brad.

"Only about surfing and video games," Brad answered, zipping up a gym bag. "Every frickin' day," he said, with a crooked grin.

A pounding on the door startled us all. The girls would have entered without knocking, so we all looked at each other like deer in headlights. Alan waved me towards the bathroom, mouthing the word *hide*. He raised his voice. "Just a second."

Brad approached the door and peered through the keyhole as I tiptoed like a ghost into the bathroom and closed the door softly behind me.

"Who is it?" Brad said as the bathroom door closed.

"FBI, sir. We would like to ask you a few questions," said a man's voice, muffled by the door. "Please, open up."

"Uh, sure," Brad responded. "Can I see some ID?"

"All right," he said after a pause. The sound of the door opening followed a moment later.

I stepped into the tub and drew the curtain closed. It was still damp from the boys' recent showers. Large wet towels hung from a chrome rack attached to the wall opposite the showerhead. I held still and listened.

"May we come in?" asked the man. The sound of footsteps followed. "I'm Special Agent Sean McGregor. This is Special Agent Terry Grant. We understand you are travelling with two young women. Are they around? This will go faster if we do this once."

"They're down the hall," Caleb said, his voice higher than normal. "I'll get 'em."

I could hear him slip past and run down the hall. "Nice room," said the other agent. "Would you mind turning off the TV?"

"Sure, no problem," Brad replied. The TV went silent soon after. "Hey, girls," he continued as the door to the room opened again.

"Oh my goodness. What's going on?" Lucy said, her voice breathy. "Is this about the robbers?"

"Did you arrest them?" Lilith asked.

"Vegas police picked them up at a roadside bar last night," said Agent McGregor. "There was a brawl of some kind. Seems they got into a quarrel with other patrons."

"Drunk as skunks, both of them," Grant chimed in.

"That's amazing," Lucy exclaimed. "I'm so relieved."

"Fuckin' A," agreed Caleb. The others muttered similar sentiments.

After they quieted, Agent Grant continued, "They confessed, after being told of the evidence against them, so you kids shouldn't need to testify. I'm sure you'll be glad of that."

"Thank you for telling us," Lucy said.

"You said you had questions, though," Brad said. "We told the sheriff everything we know."

"Well, there's one thing we are curious about, which is why we came to see you ourselves." McGregor said, hesitating. "During interrogation, they revealed that the fight was over a story they were telling. Something about being set upon by a snow monster in the desert near Lunar Crater."

"Evidently some listeners found their story laughable, and the skinny one took exception," said Agent Grant.

"Oddly enough, they stuck by this crap during interrogation," McGregor said. "They claimed you saw it, too."

No one said anything for several seconds.

"So, did you see anything like that?" Grant asked finally.

Alan snorted. "A snowman? In the desert? As if."

"Sounds nuts," Brad said.

"Yes, well," Grant began, "it's a crazy story. So crazy we're wondering why they would make it up. Now, now, I'm not saying it's true, but did you see anything that might account for their claims? A bright light of some kind, perhaps? If so, did you see which direction it went?"

A thump echoed through the bathroom unexpectedly as a wet towel hit the tub behind me, having slid and fallen off the rack. I mouthed a stream of silent curses.

"Is someone in the bathroom?" Agent Grant asked quietly.

"Uh, no," said Alan, "must be the pipes. It's a really old

building." Then, more loudly, "Hey, seriously, no one's in there, man."

Footsteps approached the bathroom door.

Chapter 8

Car Trouble

I looked around in a panic, searching for a way out. Wet towels and shampoo bottles offered no salvation until a desperate idea sprang to mind. As the door creaked open, I grabbed the damp towels from the rack, threw them over my head and reached for the Underfrost. The residual moisture in the air crystalized and grew at a rapid rate, swelling from the surface of the tub; within an instant I stood in a few inches of snow.

"Phew, cold in here," Grant said from the other side of the curtain. I plunged down into the snow. My jacket resisted, bunching up under my armpits, but I jerked downward, forcing it deeper, and reached up to ensure the terrycloth covered me. I just hoped the rattle of the ceiling fan, left running by the last bather, masked the sound of scrunching ice crystals.

The shower curtain scraped and rattled along the metal bar as it opened wide. "Humph," Grant said, his voice muffled by snow in my ears and towels above me. "Looks like a towel fell or something."

"Huh? Uh, yeah, told you," Alan said, traces of surprise in his voice. "It's just us."

"I thought I heard something," McGregor said. "Did you hear that? Turn off that fan." The fan died, and the room fell silent.

"The woman at the front mentioned one of the rooms is supposedly haunted. Maybe she wasn't kidding," Lucy said, laughing.

McGregor snorted. "Right," he said, drawing out the word. "Probably came from next door." He looked at his colleague.

"We done here, Terry?"

"It would seem so," said his partner.

Footsteps receded, and the door clicked shut. I stayed where I was, unable to hear more than muffled, unintelligible conversation from my hiding place, counted to sixty, then stood up, grabbing the towels before they could fall and betray my position again.

"Well, thanks for your time," McGregor said. "We appreciate your help. You were lucky to get away unhurt. Those two are different ends of the same piece of shit."

"Have a good trip," Grant said. "Stay out of trouble."

The door clicked shut. The bathroom door burst open seconds later as I stepped out of the tub. My companions stared at me with wide eyes and open mouths.

"How could they not have seen you?" Alan said, blinking rapidly. "No way, no way."

"Yeah," Caleb said sagely. Lilith, Lucy and Brad nodded too as everyone crowded in around me.

I shrugged. "Maybe I'll show you someday."

"Ohmigod, are we the only ones that can see you or something?" Lilith asked, wrinkling her nose, looking thoughtful. She crossed her arms, rubbing her biceps and Alan wrapped an arm around her. She leaned into him, glancing up at him briefly.

I snorted, shaking my head. "I wish." I shooed them before me. "Let's get out of here."

Brad held a finger to his lips and said in a faint voice, "I'll check the hall. Make sure they're really gone." He soon returned and gave us the all clear.

Reassured, we moved back to the main room, and the gang filled me in on what I'd missed while hiding under the towels. Before saying goodbye, the agents had asked again whether the young tourists had seen anything weird. They'd reaffirmed that they'd seen nothing like the goons described. Brad suggested the thugs were confused from blows to the head, perhaps mistaking the headlights of their truck for something supernatural.

Brad grabbed his keys and luggage. "Let's hit the road. I'll meet you downstairs by the back door. Bring the room keys and we'll check out once Shivurr's safely aboard."

"Hold up," Caleb said, grabbing his own belongings. "I'll come with you."

Ten minutes later, Brad circled the block, turning left onto Mineral Street, left onto Oddie, then left again, heading east on Erie Street, which would take us to Las Vegas. As we drove down Erie, passing the Mizpah Hotel again, I watched the old town scroll past. Waves of heat rose from the sidewalks and my feet twanged with the memory of walking on hot sand.

I felt excitement and trepidation to be leaving behind a place of relative safety, once again, for the open road.

"Hey, there are those FBI agents," Lucy said, pointing at the passenger-side mirror, as we crossed Brougher Street.

"Where's that?" Brad asked, checking the mirrors himself from the driver's seat.

"Back there. In the black car," Lucy said. As she spoke, a black sedan pulled away from the curb and drove our way. "I hope they're not going to pull us over."

"Can't see why they would," Brad said.

"Maybe they didn't buy our story," Alan said, looking nervous. "That McGregor dude seemed suspicious."

"Get a blanket to hide Shivurr in case they do," Brad ordered. "And cool it. Maybe they're just heading the same way."

The van stopped at one of the few traffic lights in Tonopah, allowing the black car to close the distance. Another vehicle, a red pickup truck, separated us. When the light changed, we moved again, the truck turned right, and for a moment, through a gap in the drawn curtains, I got my first look at the agents.

They were not FBI.

I recognized them from the Bodhi Institute. These two were part of Dixon's security team. It made sense. The Bodhi Group must have been checking with state police and sheriff's departments, looking for anything that would suggest my location. When the robbers, Simmons and Esterhazy, had been arrested, telling stories about a snowman in the desert, it would have been too unlikely a coincidence for them to pass up. Without inside knowledge of my existence, any law enforcement official would dismiss the thugs' story as ridiculous, of course, but McGregor and Grant knew that I was real.

They must not know for sure that I'm here, I thought. When the fake FBI agents hadn't found me in the hotel room, they must have decided to follow my friends, hoping that they'd lead them to me.

If they spotted me, it was a good bet that our pursuers would call in backup to try to capture me. Knowing my capabilities, they were unlikely to try to apprehend me alone. Then again, maybe they'd already called for that backup to waylay us after we were out on the secluded highway. Either way, I felt ill at the thought that my new friends might now be in danger too.

As Brad drove faster, the agents' vehicle dropped back. *Must be trying to keep a low profile*, I thought. Before long, Erie became Highway 95 as it angled south toward Las Vegas.

"Can you lose them?"

Brad ran a hand through his hair. "Shivurr, we're in the middle of a flat desert on a highway that doesn't turn for miles in a 1977 VW van." He glared at me in the rear-view mirror. "How do you suggest that I lose them?"

"Right, sorry," I said. "Damn it. Give me a second to think."

A few possibilities existed—if I could manage one of them. Neither would be easy under these conditions, but if they worked, we'd lose the tail, and no one would get hurt. The first, less dangerous, option was almost certain to confirm my presence to the agents. The second option was a bit more dangerous, though unlikely to be fatal, but less likely to reveal my involvement. *Ah well*, I thought, *might as well go for the safer choice.*

Moving to the back of the van, I peeked between the curtains and took a deep breath, closing my eyes in this reality and opening them upon the wintery maelstrom of the Underfrost. Its icy white glow, in this state of focus, coloured and illuminated all in shades of bright whites and blues—a frosty paradise superimposed over a sweltering desert hell.

I gave my head a shake and blinked, feeling woozy. Seeing two realities mingled while travelling down the highway at fifty-five miles per hour was disorienting. Like focusing on a single voice in a crowded room, I pushed aside irrelevant data in one realm while emphasizing relevant data in the other, and the nausea quickly subsided.

In the distance I could see the ghostly outline of the pursuing vehicle cutting through the blue-white ether as it accelerated and drew closer.

I held up a hand and a beam of frost energy lanced from my palm to the car's front end, too fast for my mind to perceive. I squinted my eyes and turned my head, seeing stars. If I were stationary, the beam would've quickly become visible in this reality as its cooling effects accumulated, but since we were moving, the space it passed through was continuously changing, keeping it from becoming visible to our pursuers.

"What's he doing?" Lilith said. "Why's he holding his hand like that?"

"I don't know," Alan said. "Some kind of Jedi mind trick?"

I thrust my other hand next to my head, pointing my fingers skyward.

"I think he wants us to be quiet," Lilith said, her voice low.

I closed my hand, snapping thumb to forefinger. They finally shut up.

The beam poured frost energy into the radiator, super-cooling it at the point of impact, but it kept slipping off target with every bump in the road. By the time I'd realign it, the hot fluid pumping through the engine took back the ground that I'd gained. I widened my beam, making it easier to keep it focused, then staggered. Water formed pools at my feet, and my body ached as my core temperature rose. Pursing my lips, I stood taller, pushing my hand forward as if closing an invisible drawer in slow motion.

A dozen heartbeats later—it seemed longer to me—the liquid coursing through the radiator thickened and solidified. Then a hose burst, yielding to the pressure as the pump tried to force engine coolant through the frozen block. A cloud of vapour billowed up from the hood of the car, blinding the occupants. I seized the moment to switch tactics. Holding my hands to my front, I made an upward gesture of my hands, as if urging a crowd to their feet, changing my focus to the hot asphalt flowing into the distance behind us. A half inch of snow grew upon its surface in moments, painting a wide trail of snow in our wake. The black sedan made no attempt to avoid it and slid sideways on contact with the now slick pavement. The driver counter-steered, overcompensating, and the vehicle spun a hundred and eighty degrees. It slid off the side of the road before coming to a hard stop.

I grabbed the seat in front of me, steadying myself, as Brad slowed the van to a few miles per hour. My nose brushed the back window as the vehicle rocked on its springs and he threw it into park. The three teens crowded in next to me, peering through the rear window. The sedan sat facing the wrong direction as the snow on the hot asphalt steamed, evaporating into the dry desert air.

"Oh, man, are they okay?" Lilith said. "Shouldn't we go back to help them?"

"Screw that," Caleb said. "I'm not getting disappeared by these spooks."

"Don't sweat it," Alan said. "They're all right. Look."

True to his words, the doors to the car swung open and the occupants clambered out.

"Let's go, Brad," Caleb said. "They're good."

The van lurched into motion a second later, rumbling and straining as we resumed our journey.

I turned away from the window and sank into the seat, sighing like a deflating air mattress.

"That was intense," Caleb said. "What'd you do, dude?"

I waggled my fingers. "Magic."

After the excitement, we chilled for a while. Brad and Lucy chatted quietly while Alan napped, mouth agape, a jean jacket thrown over his chest for warmth. Caleb borrowed Lilith's Walkman and read a well-worn paperback copy of *The Hobbit*, nodding slightly to the music.

"Good for you, Caleb. Reading," Lilith said. "Nobody reads anymore."

"Where'd you hear that?" he asked.

"Read it somewhere," she said, shrugging before closing her eyes and falling asleep.

I studied the passing desert, thanking whatever frost gods there might be that I wasn't out there, dragging my melting butt over its scorched surface.

"Shivurr, we'll come in for a bit. Make sure this dude's cool," Brad said as he turned onto Wilhelm's street a few hours later. "All right?"

"Sounds good, I appreciate the backup. I kind of know him but we've never met in person. This should be interesting."

Chapter 9

Dungeon Master

Wilhelm lived on the outskirts of Las Vegas in a large Mediterranean-style home with an attached three-car garage. The house sat on a large lot, landscaped with desert rocks and plants. The homes were spread far apart on a largely treeless street, the backyards of which looked out upon the desert with hills rising in the west four or five miles away. We stopped in the driveway while Alan ran to the door to announce our arrival. As the teen walked back to the van, the middle door of the garage trundled upwards in invitation.

"He said to park inside," Alan said, hopping back in through the side door of the van. Brad reversed a short distance and drove in, parking in the empty middle spot. On the left sat a black Pontiac Firebird Trans Am with a gold phoenix emblazoned on the hood. The bumper of the sports car sat inches from a Ducati motorcycle leaning on its kickstand next to stairs leading into the house.

"Does Burt Reynolds live here?" Lucy said, smiling.

The moment Brad cut the engine, the garage door rolled back down.

An interior door opened, and a man wearing a black *Star Wars* T-shirt, shorts, and sandals stepped out onto the short staircase landing leading from the house, giving a friendly wave. A large dog resembling a German shepherd walked out with him and sat obediently at his side.

A faint fog billowed from the van's cool interior into the warm garage as we got out. The doors slammed shut, and we walked to the front of the vehicle to meet the man I knew only through words displayed on a green screen. Of slight build, he looked about five-eight, mid-thirties, with dark hair, green eyes, and a black goatee. On his head he wore a pair of Ray-Ban sunglasses, pushed up his forehead to regard us like a second pair of eyes.

"So, which one of you is Cool Hand?" Wilhelm asked, glancing from face to face.

"That'd be me," I replied as I slid between Caleb and Lilith, holding up a hand.

"Well, holy shit...," Wilhelm said, taking a step back. He glanced down at the dog, eyes wide, then regarded my companions. The dog looked back calmly and the others suppressed grins.

"Now you know how we felt," Lilith said, eyes twinkling.

"You're freaking kidding me, right?" Wilhelm whispered. He leaned closer, staring me up and down. "You're real, aren't you?"

"Far as I know," I said.

"Scott tried to warn me...that I wouldn't believe...," Wilhelm said. "This is wicked."

"Are you okay?" I asked. "Sorry to freak you out, Boreas."

He shook his head, taking a breath. "No worries, Cool Hand." He thrust out his hand. "Good to finally meet the guy on the other end of the wire."

I pumped his hand in return. "Uh, it's Shivurr, actually. Call me, Shivurr."

"Well, all right, then," Wilhelm said, taking back his hand. He looked at his palm as if seeing it for the first time. "Cool hand," he said, tapping his nose and winking. "Nice."

Wilhelm turned to my companions, who were watching us with broad smiles. "And who are your friends?"

For the next few minutes, introductions were made and hands shaken. Before we could move inside, Wilhelm's canine companion gave a quick bark.

"Oh, this here's Bear," said our host. "Sorry, buddy, I didn't mean to forget about you."

"Ah, he's *beautiful*," Lilith said. "Can I pet him?"

"I'm sure he'd like that," Wilhelm said.

The girl knelt and ran her hand over the dog's black-and-white fur. She squealed as Bear licked the side of her face and threw her arms around his neck.

"Don't worry," Wilhelm said, looking at Lucy, who hid behind Brad. "He loves people."

"What about ice people?" I asked.

"Sure," Wilhelm said. "Go on. You'll see."

As Lilith stood, I took a step forward and extended my hand as if into a box of snakes. The dog cocked his head, then raised a paw in greeting.

"Awesome," Alan said as I grasped Bear's paw and shook it. "What kind of dog is he?"

"Alaskan shepherd," Wilhelm said. "One of the smartest dogs I've ever met." The dog's head turned to regard his master, who coughed. "Scratch that, *the* smartest." He tousled Bear's fur. "Let's get inside, where it's cooler; you look like you're melting." He pushed open the door into the house. "Olivia's at work, but she'll be home tonight."

"That your wife?" Alan said.

"Yep, love of my life."

Brad held the door for the rest of us. "Where does she work?"

"The Golden Nugget," Wilhelm replied. "She's a blackjack dealer."

The house was large, and almost comfortable as the air conditioning worked hard to cool it, making it like a warm day at the beach for me. Wilhelm led us to a spacious room at the back of the house. It contained a large dining room table surrounded by several chairs and a long comfy sofa off to one side. A bookcase lined the far wall, filled with books, stacks of VHS tapes, cassettes, records, and a stereo system. Next to that sat a colour TV with an Atari game system attached. Several pizza boxes, casually strewn books, pencils, and dice littered the tabletop.

"Have a seat," Wilhelm said, gesturing to the long table. "Would anyone like something to drink? I just made a pot of coffee."

"A glass of ice cubes would be great," I said.

"Coffee would be sweet," Brad said. The others, except for

Caleb, all agreed.

"Mind if I use your bathroom?" Caleb said. "We haven't stopped since Tonopah."

"Second door on the right," Wilhelm said, nodding and pointing to the hallway.

Over the next half hour, we got comfortably settled. My travel companions removed the jackets they'd worn during the trip but kept on long shirts and pants against the chill of house's superb AC. Only our host—still in a T-shirt and shorts—and I seemed unbothered by the chill.

Wilhelm brought coffee, sodas, and snacks for the group. Hungry from the road, my companions dug in eagerly and re-laxed. Mugs in hand, Brad and Lucy sat next to each other on the large sofa and sipped their coffee while Lilith examined Wil-helm's large record collection with rapt interest. It wasn't long before Caleb and Alan asked to use Wilhelm's Atari and took turns playing Pac-Man, bickering happily among themselves. Bear, the Alaskan shepherd, lay nearby, his face resting on the floor, keeping silent watch.

Wilhelm put down his coffee and pulled up a chair across the dining room table from me, as I was eating ice cubes and thumb-ing idly through one of the nearby tomes. "Scott said you're on the run from the government. That you were being held against your will."

My eyes widened. "He *told* you that?"

His head bobbed. "Didn't give him much choice. We—Olivia and me—insisted on knowing what we're getting into here." Bear raised his head and barked softly. "Correction, Olivia, Bear and me."

"And hearing *that*, you're still helping?"

"Of course. It's every citizen's duty to fight government op-pression and overreach." He looked around at the group. "Though, beats me how you all ended up travelling together."

I nodded. "It's been a crazy few days."

"I'd like to hear about it," Wilhelm said. "Scott would say only that you were special. That we wouldn't believe how, but to be prepared." He looked at his watch. "We've got time before he gets here."

"Sure," I said. "I guess you deserve to know."

For the next while, I told him the same story that I'd told my travel companions, including my amnesia but leaving out my adventures at the cavern, as I had before. Our host listened attentively, shaking his head and widening his eyes at the more spectacular parts, particularly at the fight with the thugs at Lunar Crater, our flight from Tonopah and our escape from the phony FBI agents on the road.

Wilhelm shook his head and sighed. "Secret agencies are going to be the end of this country. They're supposed to work for us, but how do we, the people, evaluate our employees if we don't know—"

"You a fan of the Who?" Lilith asked from across the room, sitting cross-legged near the wall.

"What makes you say that?" Wilhelm said, turning his head.

"Duh, your record collection," she said, holding up an album.

"I guess you could say that. I saw them at Woodstock. You?"

"Nah, I was just a baby," Lilith said, slipping the album back into its place on the shelf. "But we're going to see the Police in San Diego next month."

"Nice, should be decent," Wilhelm said, grinning. "Got a few of their albums, too."

"Woodstock, though, that's amazing," Lilith said, unwrapping a fresh piece of Hubba Bubba bubble gum. Chewing wetly, she sprang to her feet and walked over to the long table, pulled out a chair and sat down. She pushed a pizza box away and grabbed one of the books that lay scattered about the table.

"Sorry about the mess," Wilhelm said. "We had a game last night."

"What kind of game?" Lilith asked, opening the large hardcover tome. "Poker?"

"D&D," Wilhelm replied. Lilith blinked, raising an eyebrow. "Dungeons and Dragons. It's an RPG. A roleplaying game. I'm Dungeon Master." He looked at me. "Our buddy Scott's a regular party member."

"Oh, right," Brad said, grabbing the book and flipping

through the pages. "That's the game making kids go nuts and kill themselves. I heard about that."

"That's a whole lot of bullshit," Wilhelm said. "Just a bunch of religious fanatics making shit up. Can't have any other competing mythologies, especially those that acknowledge the fantasy, I guess."

Lilith snickered, pointing a thumb at me. "Says the guy hanging out with a walking, talking, living snowman."

Wilhelm's eyes widened. "Uh, yeah, I suppose you got me there." He paused, looking thoughtful. "But there's one significant difference."

"What's that?" Lilith said, eyebrows raised.

"Evidence. You just said it," he said, waving a hand in my direction. "Shivurr is standing right here as undeniable proof."

"Did it ever occur to you that you all are as weird to me as I am to you?" I said, frowning. "How are you any more likely than me, when you really think about it?"

"It's just that no one's ever seen anything—uh, anyone, like you before," Wilhelm said. "People are as common as dirt, but you're entirely unprecedented, except in cartoons and storybooks." The others nodded their agreement. "What I just can't figure out is whether you're some sort of government experiment or alien from outer space. You say you're not, but since your memory is compromised, we can only guess."

"Like I said, I remember some stuff from before the Institute." I popped another ice cube into my mouth. "I wasn't born there. I don't know. Maybe I am an alien. This place, this countryside, sure doesn't seem like home."

"Nah, you're an earthling, dude," Caleb said. He still sat on the hardwood floor next to his larger friend, guiding Pac-Man through a virtual maze on the large TV, running from monsters, clearly determined to beat Alan's high score.

"How d'you figure, Caleb?" I asked.

"Simple, dude: snowmen. Kids have been making snowmen for years, right? I don't know what it means exactly, but what are the odds they've been making snow dudes that are dead ringers for aliens for forever? Maybe you guys have been around a while.

Maybe still are, living in Canada or something. It's supposed to
be freezing there year-round."

"No, it isn't," Lucy said to the back of his head. "We get
summer. It can get up to forty degrees Celsius in summer. That's
like a hundred degrees Fahrenheit. We don't live in igloos, either." She shook her head, exasperated. "Americans."

Caleb snorted. "Yeah, well, whatever, it's cold there in winter,
right?"

"Sure, freezing. Depends where you are, though. Winnipeg
winters can be brutal. The West Coast, not so much."

"Sounds like my kind of place," I said, smiling. "Winnipeg, I
mean."

"Yeah, but it's warm there—hot, even—in summer," Lucy
said. "I suppose it could be Canada, if you stayed far enough
north, maybe near the North Pole. That's probably cold enough
year-round. That, or the South Pole. If you are from Earth—I
can't believe I just said that—that's where you'd live. Antarctica
is the coldest place on earth, all the time. We talked about it in a
geology course at university last year."

"I thought you were from California," I said.

"Nope, just for school. I'm Canadian. Brad and I shared a
geology class first year. That's how we met." She squeezed his
hand fondly. "I came back early, before school starts, for this
road trip."

"Geology, eh?" I said. "Are you a geologist? Is that why you
were out in the desert?"

"Uh-uh. Brad's the geologist. I just took the one class."

Brad held up his hands. "I'm not a geologist yet. I've been a
rockhound since I was a kid, though."

Wilhelm grabbed a hardcover book lying on the dining room
table and slid it across to Lilith and me. The cover had crude
drawings depicting a dragon, a centaur, a unicorn and other creatures. "Maybe the Monster Manual is non-fiction after all. But it
needs updating. You're not in it, Shivurr."

"Is this a D&D book?" Lilith asked, dragging her chair
closer.

Our host nodded. "One of many, but this is my favourite. I

like to dream up monsters of my own—for the game—but it serves as inspiration sometimes. This one covers the abilities and nature of various creatures. The stats are the most important for die rolls." A telephone rang somewhere in the house. "Excuse me, I'd better get that."

He rushed from the room to answer the call. Caleb cursed as his last guy died in the mouth of a pink ghost and handed the controller to Alan. The blond surfer took it eagerly and started a new game. Lilith and I paged through the Monster Manual for a few minutes before our host returned.

"That was Scott. He's been delayed. He said to hole up here for the night. He'll be here tomorrow afternoon." He looked around at the gathered group. "I called Olivia, too. She said to tell you that you're welcome to stay the night or longer, if you'd like. We've got a few extra rooms. If you don't want to double up, you can set up tents in the backyard. We've got a pool out back if you want to hang out there, too."

Everyone looked at each other but didn't immediately respond. "I'll give you a few minutes to discuss it. It's time for Bear's lunch anyway." The dog leaped to his feet and padded after Wilhelm toward the kitchen, tail wagging.

"You don't have to," I said after the two had left. "I know you guys want to get back home."

My new friends looked at each other thoughtfully. "Well, we're here already," Brad said, looking at Lucy. "I'd still like to see the city. Maybe check out a few casinos."

"Maybe you can get married at one of the quickie spots," Lilith chirped.

"Oh, right," Alan said, snorting, gulping a flashing blue ghost on the TV screen. "Our parents would freak."

Brad and Lucy avoided each other's gaze, looking uncomfortable.

"A swim would be nice," Lucy said with pink cheeks. She turned to the teenagers. "What do you guys think? Stay or go?"

"Stay," Alan and Caleb said in unison.

"Sure," Lilith said, and her eyes brightened. "The asphalt looks really smooth out front. We can go skateboarding, Alan."

Brad stood up, grabbing his keys. "All right, cool. Let's set up the tents, then check out the pool."

"You're a poet and don't even know it," Caleb snickered, smiling wider when everyone groaned.

The doorbell interrupted further conversation.

Wilhelm walked back into the room, scowling. "Wait here," he said, leaving the room. After a moment's hesitation, I followed, creeping down the hall, my feet quiet on the carpet.

Wilhelm stood at the front door, holding it half-open with one foot wedged against the base, blocking my view of the visitors. "Sorry, guys, I'm not interested in whatever you're selling."

"We're not salesmen, sir," said a man's voice. "We have come to share the word of God, if you are willing to listen."

"Which God is that?" Wilhelm asked.

"Why, the one and true God, of course."

"Not interested," Wilhelm said. "Zeus and his pantheon are the only true gods."

After a pause, the voice said, "I do believe hell awaits you, sir."

"Been there, friend," Wilhelm said. "Don't believe the hype. You have a good day now, gentlemen." The door clicked shut a moment later and Wilhelm threw the deadbolt into place.

"Oh, hey, man," Wilhelm said as he turned to face me. "Nothing to worry about. Just a couple guys selling tickets to God."

I raised a brow. "Do you really believe that? About Zeus?"

Wilhelm laughed. "Just having a bit of fun." He chuckled again, slapping me on the back. "Did you see the looks on their faces, though? Priceless."

Chapter 10

Pool Party

We spent the afternoon in Wilhelm's spacious backyard, which was enclosed by a high stone fence, shielding the area from prying eyes. At our host's urging, the Californians had set up camp and two tents now flapped in the dry desert breeze, pitched a half hour earlier. Wilhelm left for the store while they did so to get supplies for a late-afternoon barbecue.

While we waited, Brad, Alan and Caleb tossed a Nerf football in the pool, showing off. Lilith, wearing cut-off denim shorts and a halter top, watched with a smile from a nearby lounge while idly flipping through a *Teen Beat* magazine in her lap. A broad-brimmed hat and oversized sunglasses protected her fair skin from the sun's power. Lucy sunbathed next to her, wearing dark sunglasses and a pink bikini. Her skin, lightly tanned except for pale hips and thighs, glistened in the sun, coated in a thick layer of Coppertone 6 that filled the air with the smell of coconuts, attracting sidelong glances from the boys in the pool. I sat in the shade of a large umbrella with my winter coat zipped tight, out of view of the neighbours, and sipped a large glass of iced tea.

Not long after, Wilhelm returned, visible through the glass patio doors that looked out on the backyard from the kitchen, hefting armloads of groceries like they weighed nothing. He quickly stocked the fridge and cupboards, then slid the patio door aside, slipped into a pair of flip-flops on the way and came over to join us. Grabbing a beer from the red-and-white Coleman cooler sitting by the poolside, he collapsed into a nearby lounge, cracked open the can, and lay back with a sigh.

"Ahh, what a gorgeous day," Wilhelm said. "Anything happen while I was gone?"

"Not really," I said. "It got a bit hotter. I think."

"Does the winter jacket help?"

"Quite a bit."

"Hmph, I never really thought about heavy clothing working in the other direction," Wilhelm said. "If it gets too hot, go inside and cool down. I cranked up the AC."

"Thanks, I'll do that," I said. "When do you leave for work tonight?"

"I don't," Wilhelm replied. "I do most of my work from here; just need to dial up the network."

"I'm surprised you have any free phone lines, what with Olympus and all," I said.

"Olympus?" Lilith said. "Don't they make cameras?"

"They do, but Shivurr's talking about my BBS," Wilhelm said.

Lilith wrinkled her nose. "I don't understand."

"My computer bulletin board system," Wilhelm said. "People dial up my computer from wherever and post messages, play games, stuff like that."

"Why?" Lucy asked, raising her sunglasses. "That seems like a waste of time."

"To connect with like-minded people anywhere and everywhere," Wilhelm said, gesturing to the group. "To not feel alone, especially if those in our vicinity don't share our interests."

"Pretty deep, dude," Caleb said, towelling off. "I get it, though. It's like video games."

"I'm not sure I follow," Wilhelm said.

Lucy made a face. "Video games are signs of a misspent youth."

"That's exactly what I'm saying," Caleb said, pointing at her. "What's wrong with video games? What do you do with your free time that's so great? Talking on the phone for hours, drinking coffee? Shopping all weekend?"

"Easy, Caleb," Brad said.

"I'm just saying, none of that is any different. Same with watching sports. What's so great about that? My old man's always going on about how I'm wasting my life when he sits in that fucking easy chair of his watching that sports shit all day, getting fat."

"Sure, everything's a waste of time, if you're not interested in it," Wilhelm said. "I guess that's what people are really saying, without knowing it."

Caleb bobbed his head. "Exactly. But they shouldn't judge it. Let people do what they want. Don't get all high and mighty like their shit's any better."

"The key, my man, is balance," Wilhelm said. "Everything in moderation, even moderation."

"Speaking of playing games," I said, looking at Lucy, "when are you guys heading down to Fremont?"

"I'm not going," Lucy said. "I've seen it before. I'm not a big gambler. It's a waste of time," she finished, looking at Caleb, who rolled his eyes and shook his head, then grinned.

"I'm going. I want to take some pictures," Lilith said, holding up her camera, "and Alan and Caleb want to try the slots."

"They're not old enough," Lucy said. "Only Brad and I are over twenty-one." Lilith shrugged but said nothing.

"Just make sure you wait until Olivia gets home," Wilhelm said. He smiled. "She wants to meet the people wandering around her house."

"Absolutely," Brad said. "We'll go tonight, after the barbecue. It'll be better after dark anyway."

Wilhelm sat forward in his chair and leaned toward me. "Give me some time when she gets here to prepare her to meet you," he said in a quiet voice.

"Good luck with that," Lilith said, taking a sip of her iced tea. She stood up and looked west over the plain. "That's a beautiful view. What are those mountains?"

"That squat one is Turtlehead, and La Madre to the right, behind it," Wilhelm answered, pointing a finger. "It's all part of Red Rock Canyon."

"Wilhelm, why do helicopters keep flying that way?" Lucy asked, pointing at one as it flew over the desert.

"Tours. For tourists. They fly there, take you to Hoover Dam, and over the city. People love it. Olivia and I took one once, when we first moved here."

Wilhelm looked to the north, narrowed his eyes, and frowned. He walked toward the fence, making a "get down" gesture to me as he passed. The umbrella at my back blocked my view but I huddled closer to it, just in case.

"Can I help you, Gordon?" Wilhelm said.

While I couldn't see the newcomer, I heard a voice reply, "One of your 'guests' parked in front of my driveway a few nights ago."

"Yeah?" Wilhelm responded. "What makes you think they were my guests?"

"They were dressed oddly," said the neighbour. "Always with you, strange comings and goings, at all hours. What is it you do?"

"This is Las Vegas, man," Wilhelm said. "Get used to it. Just knock on my door if it happens again. Now, if you'll excuse me, I need to get back to my guests."

Wilhelm stomped back and threw himself into a chair. "Damn neighbours," he said, looking around. "Probably trying to get a look at Lucy. I could see him peeking over the fence. The perv."

I peered around the umbrella to see if we were still being watched but saw no one.

"Not friendly with your neighbours?" Brad said, eyebrows raised.

"We used to be," Wilhelm said, still looking at the fence. "Then I caught the son of a bitch cutting branches off our trees because they grew a little over onto his side of the fence." His hair tossed about as a gust of wind nearly blew my umbrella away. I grabbed it before it could be ripped from the ground.

"It's just a tree, dude," Brad said. "What's the big deal?"

"No, it isn't *just* a tree," Wilhelm said, giving the younger man a cold stare. "Trees are precious, especially in this climate. They give us shade, tame the wind, keep the soil from eroding, and produce the oxygen that you now breathe."

Brad held up his hands in surrender. "Fair enough."

"I can see why you'd be angry," Lilith said, looking around.

"This is a really nice house, and beautiful yard. I love your trees."

"Must have set you back a fair bit," Brad said, looking around.

"That it did," Wilhelm agreed, nodding.

"You don't see many trees like you have here, I bet," Lilith said. "Have you lived here long?"

"We moved in about five years ago," Wilhelm replied, leaning back in his chair and sighing as if setting down a burden. He closed his eyes a moment, then opened them to check his watch. "It's getting late. Olivia should be home soon. I'll start getting the burgers ready."

Wilhelm fired up the barbecue a short while later and started to grill the first patty as Olivia arrived home. Spotting her in the kitchen through the patio doors, Wilhelm made a down motion with his hands. "Sit tight. Let me talk with her first," he said as he walked away. He waved a hand to his wife a moment later as I kept a low profile behind the umbrella and watched their reunion.

Olivia appeared to be in her late twenties or early thirties. She had long mahogany-brown hair, braided and tied back to reveal a narrow, regal face centred on an aquiline nose. Tall for a female warm blood at about five-eight, she looked Wilhelm straight in the eyes as they spoke. Her work clothes, a white shirt and black pants, complemented her lean, athletic figure and flawless complexion.

Periodically, she'd glance toward the pool as they spoke. Her face twisted, then her eyes widened, then her head cocked like a bird's and her chin dipped as if trying to hide in her chest as she regarded her husband through one eye.

Wilhelm put a hand on her elbow, guiding her to the patio door and into the backyard and steering her over to the poolside. Seeing the gathered young people first, she smiled and said hello, welcoming them to her home with all the grace of a queen or princess welcoming guests to her castle.

"And this is Shivurr," Wilhelm said, gesturing in my direction.

"Uh, hi," I said, holding up a hand.

"Oh, Wilhelm, don't you have enough Halloween costumes

already?" Olivia said. "Scott, is that you? Take that off." Caleb snickered, then winced as Lucy pinched him.

"They're *Star Wars* costumes, Liv," Wilhelm said. "And, no, this isn't Scott. This is Shivurr. The guy Scott says needs our help. He's real, just like I tried to tell you inside."

She looked around as if searching for cameras. "What a lot of nonsense," she said, touching her outstretched hand to my face. "You're as cold as ice. Wilhelm, what's going on?"

"Let's eat," Wilhelm said. "Shivurr can tell you his story over burgers."

Chapter 11

Jackpot

Wilhelm and I played Centipede on his Atari 5200 later that night. At his suggestion, we'd moved to the living room with its larger TV and more comfortable sofa. My new friends from the desert had left a few hours earlier, eager to see the night lights of Las Vegas after an enjoyable barbecue by the poolside. A bit sunburned and having been there before with her parents, Lucy stayed behind. She and Olivia had found a common interest in fashion during dinner, and the two went off to view our hostess's wardrobe.

"You want a soda?" Wilhelm asked. His eyes drooped as he regarded me. "I need a coffee. Still need to get some work done."

"I could use a cold one," I said, dodging a spider on the TV.

"Hot coffee and cold soda, coming up," Wilhelm said, pulling himself up from the sofa. My guy died as he returned, coffee mug in one hand and soda in the other. I traded him the controller for the can and leaned back.

"Help me, Shivurr, you're my only hope," Lucy said as she walked into the room, wearing large buns of hair on the sides of her head and a white dress. "What do you think?" She stood sideways, held a large *Star Wars* blaster next to her face, and gave us a smoky stare.

"Nice, Princess Leia," Wilhelm said. "Olivia showed you the *Star Wars* costumes, I see." He looked at me. "I've been building a collection. Luke, of course. A Stormtrooper, Darth Vader, Boba Fett. Yoda. I'll show you the others later." He turned as a new figure entered the room. "Well, hello. Who are you?" he asked, as a figure in green-and-red armour appeared behind Lucy, striking a pose.

"Someone who loves you," Olivia laughed, lifting Boba Fett's green-and-red helmet from her head and shaking out her long hair.

"Classic reference, but wrong bounty hunter," Wilhelm said, chuckling. He glanced at me. "*Return of the Jedi*," he said, nodding.

"No spoilers." I hadn't seen it yet. It had come out only a few months earlier. Even Scott, with the Bodhi Group's backing, couldn't get a copy yet. Now that I was living on the run, I had no idea if I ever would, but I still hoped to do so one day.

"Why so many costumes?" I asked.

"San Diego Comic Con, and Halloween, mostly, plus some friends have a yearly winter solstice masquerade party," Wilhelm said, leaning back. Olivia joined him, snuggling up, after putting the helmet onto the coffee table. He wrapped an arm around her and squeezed. "I've been thinking about renting them. Maybe opening a shop."

"My husband the entrepreneur," Olivia said. She rested her head on his shoulder, rubbing his arm with one hand and clasping his other hand. Her eyelids closed, and she seemed to fall asleep almost as soon as the words left her mouth.

Lucy sat in a leather easy chair to my right and watched me play for a few minutes. "I wonder where those guys are," she said, looking at the clock on the wall over the TV. "They've been gone a while."

"Probably just having a good time," Wilhelm said, checking his watch. He gently eased out of Olivia's grasp, replacing himself with some nearby pillows. "This has been fun, but I need to get some work done in my office. If you want something to drink or eat, you know where the kitchen is."

"Thanks, man," I said, pausing the game.

"Yes, thank you," Lucy said. "You've both been wonderful. Thank you so much for allowing us to stay here."

"Olivia, hon, time for bed," He reached down and picked her up with a grunt. "Let's go, Boba Fett."

"I think I'll get out of this getup, too," Lucy said. "I'm going to bed as soon as they get back." She sprang from the easy chair and disappeared down the hall.

I sat back, sipped my drink, closed my eyes, and sighed. It'd be nice to just stay here, surrounded by friends, despite the heat. I shook my head. Somehow, here I sat in Wilhelm's home. Yesterday he was just a digital friend, someone I knew only through words typed on a screen. I tapped the empty soda can twice and plunked it down on the table. *Staying's not an option*, I thought. The Bodhi Group still hunted me, and they weren't about to stop. Even if they did, the nightmares and visions demanded my attention. They seemed to have stopped since leaving the desert chamber, but that had been less than forty-eight hours ago, so I had no reason to think that they'd stopped for good. If they came back, there'd be no ignoring them. *No, when Scott gets here, I need to get moving and figure things out.*

I resumed the game and shot centipedes for a few minutes before a vehicle screeched to a stop in the driveway behind me. Wilhelm, looking puzzled, walked back into the room from deeper in the house as Brad burst through the front door a moment later with Lilith on his heels.

"We've got trouble," Brad said. "Alan and Caleb are in deep shit."

"Casino security guards took them," Lilith said, her eyes wide as saucers, biting her bottom lip.

"What?" I said, tossing the game controller onto the sofa and hopping to my feet. "Why?"

"Caleb played one of those giant slot machines near the front of a casino," Lilith said, blinking back tears. "He won—a lot. He couldn't fit it all in his pockets, so Alan and I started helping him. Then security showed up asking for ID, saying he was in big trouble. Caleb got scared and ran and one of the goons grabbed him. He knocked me over trying to get to Caleb, so Alan pushed him, and another guard jumped on him, and they started fighting." Her hand rose to her face, exploring the start of a bruise under her eye.

"I missed it all," Brad said. "I was playing blackjack. Lilith came and got me after they took them to the security offices, but they refused to let us see them, so we rushed back here."

"We've got to do something," Lilith said, chewing the inside of her cheek. "Who knows what they're doing to them?"

"Why not call the cops?" Wilhelm asked, pursing his lips thoughtfully.

"If they call the police, and they find Caleb's marijuana, he'll be arrested," she said, collapsing into a nearby easy chair, burying her face in her hands. "Alan might get charged with assault. He was only defending me. It's not fair."

"What's going on?" Lucy said around a mouthful of toothpaste from the hallway. She now wore loose cotton pants and a T-shirt. "Who's going to call the police?" Lilith told her. "I don't know how those two manage to find trouble everywhere they go," Lucy mumbled. She pointed at her mouth, then held up a finger, before rushing away.

"Which casino?" Wilhelm said as she left.

"The Golden Fleece," Brad said. "I was at the Four Queens. Lilith and the guys were going to walk around and circle back to get me in an hour."

"I know of it. I've done some work for them. It's a smaller one, off the main strip, so not as popular or nice," Wilhelm said. He stroked his goatee. "I'd bet money they're not going to call the cops. It doesn't look good. It makes people nervous and distracts them from gambling. Also, the cops don't like being bothered for trivial things. If the casino calls too often, maybe they take their time showing up when there's a real problem, when they really need them. Then, there's the issue that they'd be admitting that underage gambling occurred on their watch."

"Then what will they do?" Brad asked as Lucy returned. He wrapped an arm around her waist, and she leaned against him, arms folded.

"They'll probably scare the shit out of them and let them go."

"They won't hurt them, will they?" Lucy said, looking up at Brad.

"They'd better not," he replied.

"I'll try talking to someone over there," Wilhelm said. "Let's take my car, Brad. Anyone else coming?"

Before the others could answer, the phone rang, and Wilhelm

snatched it from the receiver before the first ring died.

"Hello?" he said, glancing at the rest of us. "Uh, yeah, they're right here. Are you okay?… Uh-huh.…Uh-huh.…Okay. One sec." He held the receiver against his chest. "They let them go. They're calling from a pay phone by the Four Queens."

Fifteen minutes later, Wilhelm pulled up to the curb in front of the Four Queens as a stretch limo pulled away. Wilhelm's Trans Am couldn't seat everyone, so Lucy and Lilith had stayed behind, promising to fill Olivia in if she woke up before our return. I sat in the back and kept my head down as Brad hopped out—letting in a gust of hot desert air, cigarettes and cotton candy—and scanned the sidewalk for the boys.

The street boomed with the beeps and bops and bells and whistles of the casinos and the chatter of countless pedestrians. Hawkers handed out pamphlets to passersby under the bright neon and flashing lights, promoting shows, gambling, and quickie weddings. Costumed street performers worked the street for tips, some dressed as Elvis, others scantily clad as showgirls and costumed movie characters.

I spotted Caleb first. He stood at the edge of a crowd, smiling as tourists wrapped their arms around the slim waists of two young women dressed as showgirls. Alan emerged from the crowd a moment later and spotted Brad waving him over. Alan clapped a hand to Caleb's shoulder and the teens raced over to the car.

Caleb ducked into the back seat next to me, and Alan squeezed his larger form in beside him.

"Hey, dudes," Caleb said. "Thanks for the pickup."

"Nice ride, man," Alan said. He rubbed against me and re-coiled. "Whoa, you're freezing, dude."

Brad slammed the door shut and the car pulled away, merging with the slow-moving bumper-to-bumper traffic.

"Yeah, sweet car," Caleb said. "I like the sunroof."

"It's called a Hurst Hatch," Wilhelm replied, sticking his right hand through the opening above. "Or a T-top."

"It's a Trans Am, right?" Caleb asked.

Wilhelm nodded. "The 1977 Special Edition. I went for the

full package: custom gold decals, gold snowflake wheels—the works."

"Forget about the car, Caleb," Brad said, turning sideways in his seat to look at his brother. "What happened, Alan? Are you okay?"

Alan sneered, flaring his nostrils. "They stole our money—not just what we won, but all of it. Everything I have for the trip. Said it was a *fine* for underage gambling."

"They took all my cash too, and my stash," Caleb said, glaring. "Some fuck-knuckle sucker punched Alan."

"You're kidding," Wilhelm said, scowling at the rear-view mirror.

"Slugged me in the gut when I told them to go fuck themselves, after they robbed us," Alan said, rubbing his stomach.

"How much?" Wilhelm asked.

"Nine hundred for me," Alan said.

"Four hundred for me, not counting the five thousand for the slot machine," Caleb said.

Wilhelm whistled softly. "That's a lot of ducats."

"They can't do that," Brad said. "That's robbery and assault, pure and simple. We'll call the cops."

Caleb shook his head. "They got my stash. They said they'd have us arrested for possession."

We drove in silence for a while after that, digesting the situation. Brad was the first to speak again. "There's no proof it's yours. We can deny it," he said with a shrug. "We'll say it's theirs."

"How many guards were involved?" Wilhelm said, turning right onto his street. "Did you get their names?"

"Two of them," Alan said, looking thoughtful. "Randy—big, thick dude, taller than me, pasty white, red face, red hair. The other guy was called Shane. About Brad's height, muscled, dark hair, blue eyes."

"Nice description," I said.

"I guess I'm getting good at describing assholes that rob me," he said. "I wish I weren't."

"Where'd they take your money?" Wilhelm asked. "Were there any witnesses?"

"Nope," Caleb replied. "They took us to a room in the back."

"I was afraid of that. We can try, but I doubt calling the cops will get your money back," Wilhelm said. "It sounds like these two probably split the cash. They'll just deny they took it. It's your word against theirs. That's probably why you got punched in the stomach, not the face: less obvious bruises, no abrasions on their knuckles."

Wilhelm parked the Trans Am in the garage and cut the engine, and we piled out. Bruised and battered, Alan and Caleb followed us inside as the garage door trundled closed behind us.

Once inside, the boys received sympathetic hugs and kisses as they repeated the story for the girls' benefit. Struggling to keep their eyes open, the kids chose to go to sleep and figure out what to do in the morning. Still having work to do, Wilhelm went to his office, leaving me—too wired to sleep—to watch a movie and try to think about something else. But I couldn't let it go.

I'd met these kids only a few days ago, but I liked them a lot already. Aside from Scott, Emmett and now Wilhelm and Olivia, they were my only friends, at least that I could remember. With my memory limited to about ten years, I'd effectively been lonely my entire life. Not the loneliness of just being alone but the loneliness that comes with a lack of history. Even someone stranded on a desert island can at least console themselves with the thought that people that they know, and that know them, exist somewhere, possibly thinking of them on occasion or remembering common experiences. There's companionship in that shared history, and I'd lost that, if I'd ever had it, along with my memories, which made the few friends that I had more important to me than anything. And, for the second time in two days, they'd been terrorized by a couple of goons.

It wasn't right. I wanted justice and their money back.

The problem was I wasn't sure how to get it without grim consequences for me and possibly them. I couldn't exactly launch an assault on the casino to take the money back by force. There'd be too many cameras and witnesses. I didn't know how many guards there'd be or if I could take them all down and escape before the police arrived. Even if I did, the Bodhi Group would be alerted, and agents would be on my trail again. Halfway through *Star Wars*, I found myself staring at the Boba Fett helmet Olivia had left on the coffee table earlier that evening, and a plan started to coalesce in my mind. I leaped to my feet and flew down the hall to Wilhelm's office.

Wilhelm smiled, listening to my plan. "This may take a while, Shivurr," he said as his fingers flew across his keyboard.

"I'll let you focus," I said, making for the door. He murmured a reply. I grabbed a soda and a large glass of ice from the kitchen, threw myself back on the sofa, and hit play on the remote, resuming the movie.

About an hour later, Wilhelm strode into the room, smiling. He was holding a piece of tattered paper torn from a notepad.

"How'd it go?" I asked, muting the television.

"Jackpot," he said, winking. "Let's roll."

"Where's that leftover pizza?" I asked, following him down the hall.

Chapter 12

Pizza Guy

We sat in the Trans Am outside the home of Shane Parker. Wilhelm was dressed as Boba Fett, minus the helmet for the drive over. I wore a Stormtrooper helmet and body armour. In the dark night, the white armour blended perfectly with my snow-white complexion. It wasn't the best disguise but would have to do. Anyone that saw me would hopefully figure I was some *Star Wars* fanboy or maybe a street performer heading home. Whatever they thought, it was a sure bet they wouldn't think, "Hey, is that a living snowman?"

Wilhelm had pulled Parker's address from the casino's computer records. He'd set up their payroll and related systems a few years prior, and no one had thought to remove his remote access after the job was done. His access to employee records was restricted, but he'd used one of his automated password guessers to launch a brute force attack on the account of a human resources person and soon had the guards' full names and addresses.

We'd been waiting for an hour when someone drove up in an old Dodge Charger, parked and entered the house. The dim streetlights failed to reveal the newcomer's face, but the person's silhouette suggested a man of the build and height described by Alan.

"Remember, whatever happens, stay in the car," I said, my voice muffled by the helmet, as I got out of the sports car.

"I'll keep the car running," Wilhelm said with a nod. "Watch yourself, man."

Holding an empty pizza box, I made my way to the steps leading up to the porch. A dog barked somewhere in the distance, briefly subsuming the sounds of cicadas and other insects. A moth bashed itself repeatedly into the dim porch light as I approached. I tried the doorbell but heard no buzz or ring coming from inside, so I knocked instead.

"Yeah, who is it?" said a gruff male voice from within.

"Pizza guy," I said loudly to the door.

The door sprang open. "Wrong house. I didn't order any," said the man, icy blue eyes glaring at me. The man wore dark blue slacks and a button-up shirt open to the waist. He looked to be mid-twenties and a few inches shorter than me. "What's with the getup?" he said, looking me up and down.

"It's a work thing." I said, holding up the pizza box. "Say, you're Shane Parker, right?"

"Yeah, what of it?" he replied, ripping the box from my hands. "I didn't order…hnnnh." He doubled over as I buried my fist in his gut and followed it with a haymaker to his face, knocking him back. I pushed him inside, where he fell to the floorboards. Entering, I closed the door behind myself as Shane groaned, holding his stomach.

Wordlessly, I reached down and rifled through his pockets, finding nothing. "Where's your wallet, Shane?" I asked, looking around the entryway.

The casino security guard wheezed in reply. I spotted his wallet and keys sitting on a nearby coffee table upon which sat a half bottle of beer next to a plate of food. I pulled a wad of bills from the well-worn black leather wallet, letting the driver's license and other ID fall to the floor. I counted a few thousand dollars, mostly hundreds. *Guess they switched the coins for bills. Good thing. I don't have the pockets for that much change.*

"Put it back," Shane said, snarling. A loud crack exploded in my ears as a bat plowed into my helmet, shattering the plastic. "I didn't order any damn pizza. I'm damn sure not paying a few grand for it."

I stumbled forward, arms outstretched, seeing stars and grunting in pain, blinded by the helmet, which had been knocked over my eyes by the blow. I fell forward onto my stomach, reaching out to brace my fall a moment too late. The helmet bounced off the floor with my head still inside, lodging into the soft outer layers of my snowy face, fixing it in place.

I dropped the money, I thought through the fog of pain.

I scrabbled along the floor, trying to avoid the next blow, but it didn't come. Instead, running steps creaked across the floor as I shook my head to clear the stars from my eyes. The bat hit the hardwood with a dull clunk, followed by the distinct click-click-clack of a shotgun being loaded a few moments later.

"Get up," Shane ordered, "or I'll blow a hole through you where you lie." I pushed myself to my feet, facing the wall, the casino security guard behind me. I was still blinded by the helmet and reached up to adjust it. "Freeze, or I shoot. Turn around, fucker. Slowly."

I lowered my hands and did just that. He held the shotgun at his waist. His eyes were wide, frantic, and excited; he was clearly enjoying the situation, having the drop on me. Like other security guards I had known, this guy was a bully that longed for power over others, full of insecurities and doubts about himself, or just born with a mean streak.

"Take it off, slowly," Shane snarled as I aligned it, able to see clearly once again. The room was dimly lit by a lamp on an end table next to the sofa, and light coming from the hallway before me. "I want to see your face."

I hesitated, still hoping to get through this with my identity intact. "Do it," Shane said, brandishing his weapon at me. "Or I blow it off."

I raised my hands in apparent compliance, then my right hand flashed with a halo of energy as I ripped frost from thin air and hurled it at the guard's chest. Milliseconds later, the shotgun exploded, launching a cloud of deadly pellets at me from short range, just as my fastball reached its mark.

Shane instinctively ducked and took my projectile in the neck instead. He fell for the second time since I arrived, hitting the floor with a thump like a dropped toilet seat. He wheezed horribly, discarded the shotgun, and grabbed his throat. His face and neck were icy and moist from the impact, flash-cooled.

I wasn't doing much better. The shotgun blast had opened a

hole in my guts, spraying my lifeblood out my back in a cloud of snow, leaving a void in its place. I slumped down, wincing, as Wilhelm, wearing the Boba Fett helmet, appeared from the still-open door, peering around the edge.

"Get out of here, dude," I said, breathing through a cloud of pain, worried he might be seen.

Ignoring that, he stepped over Parker's prone form and came to my side, staring at the hole in my abdomen. "Oh, man," he said, worry in his voice. "Are you okay?"

"Uh, I'm not sure." I looked down to check the damage and fingered the edges of the gaping hole, trying not to pass out. I could feel harder areas of ice mixed in among the snow. *My bones*, I guessed. "Get the water bottle from the car, would you?"

While Wilhelm ran off to do so, I continued to assess my wound. As the initial shock faded, I decided it wasn't going to be fatal. I could see it healing already, shrinking in size as my body redistributed snow and ice to fill the void. I felt dizzy and weak, but everything vital still worked, it seemed. Having decided I would live, I scrambled for the shotgun, which lay nearby. Shane still struggled to breathe where he lay, though he seemed to be improving.

Wilhelm hurried back into the room with a green water bottle in hand and tossed it to me. I pulled the white cap to the open position and sprayed water into my mouth, restoring the liquid that I'd lost as the wound continued to close, then disappeared altogether.

"Better?" Wilhelm asked.

"I'd like to go a week without being shot by some asshole," I said, closing my eyes and nodding.

"Is he okay?" Wilhelm asked. "Should we call an ambulance?"

Shane seemed to be breathing easier. "Stay down, Shane," I said as he started to sit up. I held the shotgun in my left hand but kept it pointed at the floor to my side.

Parker eyed it cautiously from where he lay. "What'd you hit me with?" he said, wheezing. He eyed the gun. "That ain't loaded anymore."

My right hand glowed as a fresh frost ball appeared within my grasp. Tendrils of steam swirled slowly as the frost ball fluoresced in my clenched fist. Shane's gaze shifted to it and his eyes widened. He swallowed nervously. "You some kind of magician?"

"Quiet. Lie face down," I said, raising my throwing arm. He rolled over onto his stomach, taking his sweet time. "Hands behind your back." I dispelled the frost in my hand and placed the shotgun on the coffee table, then looked at Wilhelm and held a finger to my lips; I didn't want Shane to know his voice. "Can you find something to blindfold him? Tie him up?"

The Boba Fett helmet bobbed affirmatively in reply. Wilhelm began to look around the house.

"Hey, no need for that," Shane said, raising his head from the floor. "Take what you want. I won't say nothing. Just go."

We couldn't risk him calling the cops, or seeing our car, until we were long gone. The lack of sirens so far gave me hope that the lone gunshot in the middle of the night had gone unnoticed or unidentified by Shane's sleeping neighbours.

I closed the front door, keeping an eye on Shane as I slipped by him. He stayed still. I walked back into the living room and collected the money from the floor. My hat was in the back seat of Wilhelm's Trans Am, so I just clutched the bills in my hand until Wilhelm returned, holding handcuffs and a white pillowcase.

"These should work. Found them next to the bed," he said, forgetting my sign to keep quiet. "Dude likes it a bit kinky, I guess."

"They're for work," our prone captive protested as the cuffs clicked into place, keeping his hands behind his back. "Ouch! Not so tight."

"Now you know how it feels," Wilhelm said, his voice muffled by the helmet. He pulled the pillowcase over Shane's head, cinching it by tying the corners together so it wouldn't fall off. Finishing, he looked at me. "What now?"

Headlights lit the curtains as a car pulled into the driveway. Loud rock music was audible before the engine died moments later. We looked at each other, holding still, listening.

"Who's that?" I said, looking at Shane. He shrugged, or tried to, from his prone position. Either he didn't know or he wasn't going to help. I suppose I couldn't blame him.

The sound of a car door opening and closing followed as I moved like a ghost to the front door and threw the deadbolt into the locked position. Making a shush sign, dollar bills sticking out of the bottom of my hand, I grabbed Shane by an arm, motioning Wilhelm to grab the other, and we heaved the guard upright and shuffled him off to the bedroom.

"Stay quiet, Shane," I ordered. "Who's coming?"

Before he could answer, the door handle rattled. "Shane, what'd you lock the door for?" asked a loud voice through the wood. The door shook with a thunderous knock a few seconds later.

I handed the cash to Wilhelm, who stuffed it into his jeans. With my now-free hand, I conjured fresh frost and held it near Shane's ear so that he could hear it crackling through the pillowcase. I repeated the question quietly.

"Friend from work," he said through gritted teeth.

"Randy?" I asked. Shane's sharp intake of air told me that I'd guessed right before the pillowcase fluttered as he nodded. *Well,* I thought, *that saves us a trip.*

"One sec," I yelled in what I hoped was a passable imitation of the hooded hoodlum next to me as another knock shook the door. Moving like a cartoon burglar, I left the bedroom, closed the door to it, and slipped down the short hallway to the front door. Standing behind it, I unlocked the door.

Randy burst through immediately, a twelve-pack of beer in hand. He was tall and thick, a few inches over six feet, with a pale complexion, balding with thin wisps of ginger hair encircling his head.

"Holy shit," he said, saying *shit* as a two-syllable word. "It's cold as a witch's tit in here," he continued as I snuck up behind him. "Something wrong with your AC?"

"Run, Randy," Shane shouted from the bedroom, followed by a crash and sounds of a struggle and flashes of green light from beneath the closed door. Randy dropped the beer with a crash and reached for the knife he carried on his belt.

"Don't," I said softly.

The bearlike man spun around, pulling the blade as he did so. He lunged at me, stabbing with the knife, which glanced off my fake Stormtrooper armour. I grabbed his knife-hand wrist and channelled cold into him. He pulled away as if burned, dropping the weapon with a gasp of pain.

He rubbed his wrist, looking at me with confusion, then charged me like a linebacker, pushing me out the open door onto the rocky ground of the front yard.

I fell back off the edge of the steps, with Randy following me down to the ground. I felt myself compress under the impact and grunted. With me as a crash mat, Randy seemed largely un-bothered by the fall, judging by the body blows he rained down on my torso as we struggled.

Reaching up, I locked my arms around him in a fierce em-brace and pulled hard on the Underfrost. The air was dry, and I had to reach out wide to pull moisture from a larger area to ac-complish what I had in mind. No sooner had I done so, then snowflakes began to fall from the air all around us as ice crystals welled up from the warm, sandy earth below.

Feeling the bite of frost, Randy pushed me away, gasping, trying to escape. I hung on tighter. He punched me in the sides, trying to loosen my hold. I grunted but gripped harder. Within seconds, the temperature dropped twenty degrees, and Randy's struggles weakened as his blood cooled and his body spasmed and his teeth chattered.

I released my hold, regained my feet and looked around like a meerkat on watch. No one appeared to have noticed our wres-tling match, but that would change if a car came down the street or an insomniac looked out the window. For all I knew, it might have already happened, but I didn't hear sirens, so I chose to hope for the best.

I dragged Randy's limp body through the snow and back into the house by his arms as he continued to shake from the initial stages of hypothermia. *Hopefully his fat will insulate him enough to survive*, I thought, though his readiness to stab me made it hard to care. As I approached the steps, a neighbouring porch light lit up. With an explosion of energy, flush with power from the snow beneath me, I picked him up by his belt and threw him inside, then stormed in after him and closed the door behind me. Outside, the snow that I'd summoned still fell.

The door to the bedroom opened, and Wilhelm pushed Shane, still hooded, through. He pulled off the Boba Fett helmet and wiped away a small drop of blood that trickled from his nose. He looked at his hand, then wiped it on his jeans.

"What happened, man?" Wilhelm asked, looking at the shivering body lying at my feet. "Guy looks like he's freezing."

"Dude jumped me," I said. "He'll be okay. No one dies of hypothermia in the Mojave Desert."

"Happens more than you'd think," Wilhelm said as he donned the Boba Fett helmet. "Gets cold enough some nights."

"That can't be right," I said, looking sidelong at him.

"Randy, you all right?" Shane asked, facing the wall where Wilhelm pressed him, his vision blocked by the pillowcase. "What'd you do? Randy?"

"Time to jet, man," Wilhelm said, looking at the door. "Down on your knees, Shane," he ordered. "Stay where you are, and we'll be out of your hair in a jiffy."

"Get to the car. I'll finish up here," I said as I knelt and checked Randy's pockets for the rest of the cash. Wilhelm tossed me the keys to the handcuffs and ran off. The fallen security guard's shivering seemed less intense, and he mumbled to himself unintelligibly. I pulled a worn brown wallet from his back pocket. It had several thousand in large bills tucked inside. I stuffed the bills under the Stormtrooper helmet. His driver's license said he was thirty-seven years old and identified him as Randolph Paulson. I checked his other pockets and found a clear plastic bag full of Caleb's weed.

"All right, Shane. Be cool, forget we were here," I said, walking to the still-open door. "Don't make me come back."

I grabbed a heavy leather jacket from the front closet and draped it over Randy, still in a torpor, curled up on the floor, shivering.

"Wha…," he muttered, confused.

"Your buddy here can free you when he recovers," I said to Shane, placing the cuff keys on the floor next to Randy. "Make him some hot tea. He seems chilly."

"Get bent, freak," Shane spat.

I said nothing and walked out into the night, closing the door behind me. The wind had picked up, blowing cool air across my face. I smiled at the sight of the Trans Am idling out front with its windshield wipers clearing the still falling snow. I flew over the melting snow like quicksilver and jumped inside through the open window. My friend, no longer wearing his helmet, his hair sweaty and matted, stomped the accelerator and we roared off.

"Easy, dude. Slow down," I said as we screeched around the first corner. "We don't want to attract attention."

"Yeah, right. You're right," he said, easing up on the accelerator. As if summoned by my words, a police car came down the street toward us seconds later, its lights flashing, with no siren. We looked at each other, Wilhelm wide-eyed, me still wearing the black-and-white helmet. "Oh, damn."

Wilhelm's knuckles were as white as mine on the steering wheel as the police raced past without slowing down. He glanced repeatedly in the rear-view mirror. "That was too close," he said, exhaling a blast of air as he checked the side mirrors. "Breaker, breaker, we've lost the smokies."

"Nice driving, Bandit," I said, taking a deep breath. "What happened with Shane?"

Wilhelm shrugged. "He elbowed me in the face. Bloodied my nose. How's your stomach?"

I looked down at my waist. "Getting better by the second."

"That went pretty well," Wilhelm said, glancing at me. "All things considered."

"Like taking cake from a baby."

"Candy," he corrected.

"What?"

"Candy," he said. "Take candy from a baby."

"Why would I want to do that?"

"The expression is, 'take candy from a baby,'" Wilhelm said, squinting his eyes at the road.

"Uh, pretty sure it's cake."

By the time we got to Wilhelm's home, the sky was already beginning to lighten with the coming dawn. He gave me the cash that I'd handed to him at Shane's house.

"Shivurr, it's kind of late now, but let's try to talk privately tomorrow," Wilhelm said before heading up to bed. "There's something I've been meaning to talk to you about."

I took off the damaged Stormtrooper gear, redonned my winter jacket, then trudged down the hallway to the kitchen to grab a tray of ice cubes and a jug of water. Collapsing onto the sofa, I replenished lost fluids while watching TV and counting the cash. I stowed the weed in my pocket and bills in my hat for safekeeping, pulled the brim over my eyes, then fell asleep, wondering what Wilhelm could possibly want to talk about.

Chapter 13

Snow Day

I woke to the sounds of the morning weather forecast. "That's right, folks. Parts of the Las Vegas area reportedly got snow last night, in what seems to be a freak weather anomaly. Some residents called in to tell us they woke up to an unusually chilly morning and a winter wonderland in their front yards. Spontaneous snowball fights have been reported. Other residents took the opportunity to build snowmen as well. Sorry, kids, it won't be a snow day as temperatures, already at seventy-six degrees, are expected to reach ninety plus later today," said the perky weather woman with an exaggerated laugh. "Back to you, Nick."

"Bad news for those snowmen, Wendy," said the news anchor as the camera cut to him. "Amazing stuff. In other news, police were called—"

The news anchor disappeared abruptly, replaced by a cartoon centaur, as the TV switched to a new channel.

"Morning, Slim," I said affably.

"Hey, man, you're up," said Caleb from the nearby easy chair as he continued to click the remote. He had a serious case of bed-head. "I didn't think you ever slept."

"Seldom," I said. "Where's everybody?"

"Sleeping, I guess," he replied. "Lucy's taking a swim. Haven't heard from Wil yet, but I saw Olivia head into the bathroom. I just got up a half hour ago. Figured I'd come say hello." He continued to click, stopping at another cartoon, another I had never seen. A heavily muscled shirtless swordsman was facing off with a skeletal villain.

We watched TV for the next hour until Olivia, freshly

showered, poked her head in from the hallway, preceded by Bear, who flopped down next to me and put his head between his paws.

"I'm making bacon and eggs," she said. "Would you boys like some breakfast?"

We followed her to the kitchen and helped set the table while she cooked. Alan showed up, bleary-eyed and yawning, a short while later.

"Morning, Alan," Olivia said. "Be a dear and pour the orange juice." Alan nodded, walking like a zombie to the fridge. "Wilhelm is still in bed." She handed a plate piled with bacon and eggs to Caleb. The lean teen dug in voraciously. "I guess he worked late again. He was tossing and turning, a lot."

I avoided her gaze and sipped my soda. "Uh, yeah," I said as Alan moved around the table, pouring.

"Good morning, Lilith," Olivia said. "Did you sleep well?"

"All right, I guess," said Lilith. "It's getting warm out, so I couldn't sleep any longer. That and Lucy and Brad are splashing around in the pool. Those two can't keep their hands off each other."

The young girl pulled up a chair next to Alan and started drinking his juice. She wore a black T-shirt displaying a picture of a large tongue poking out of huge red lips and faded cut-off denim shorts with the white bottoms of the pockets peeking out. Her long dark hair stuck up wildly in the back.

"Do you have any coffee? Oh my gosh, thank you," she said, lurching to her feet as our hostess pointed to the automatic coffee maker.

"You're welcome," Olivia replied, continuing to cook. "I'm not myself without my first cup, either. You're a bit young, though. I didn't start until college."

"Hello, everyone," Wilhelm said, walking into the room. He gave Olivia a squeeze on the shoulder and a peck on the cheek and poured himself a cup of coffee before sitting down. He looked freshly showered, but his eyes were bloodshot and his face drawn. He closed his eyes with pleasure as he took a large swallow from the mug. Grimacing, he reached for the sugar.

"Did you work late, Wil?" Olivia asked, passing another plate to Alan. "I didn't hear you come to bed."

Wilhelm looked at me as he stirred his mug. "Shivurr and I went out to have a word with those casino security chuckle-heads," he said, quietly.

"We got your money back," I said, looking at Caleb and Alan as Wilhelm grabbed the box of Cap'n Crunch that sat in the middle of the table and began to fill a nearby bowl.

"What? You're kidding," Alan said. "How?"

"We just had a little chat and they offered it up," Wilhelm said, giving Olivia a sidelong glance. "They saw the error of their ways. They were very regretful."

I doffed my cap, rummaged around and produced the cash with a flourish. "Here you go."

"You dudes are badass," Alan said, counting his cash.

"Here's your weed too," I said to Caleb, handing him the bag.

"Omigod, that sounds so dangerous," Lilith said, gasping and shaking her head. "What if they attacked you?"

I shrugged. "Nah, it was nothing," I said, following Wilhelm's lead.

"I look forward to hearing more about it," Olivia said, staring at Wilhelm with a raised brow.

"You guys are awesome," Alan said, flashing pearly white teeth.

"Just keep it safe," Wilhelm said.

"Alan, let's skate," said Lilith. "I want to try that kick flip before it gets too hot."

"Sure, Lil," Alan said. He gave his surfer pal a playful nudge and smirked. "You coming, Caleb? Or are you still hurting from sacking it last time?"

"Yeah, right, and then you woke up," Caleb said, snorting. "Get your board."

"Well, I need to take Bear for a walk," Olivia said after they'd left. "Come on, Sir Bear, let's go. You boys have fun."

"I can do that," Wilhelm said. "Don't you leave for work soon?"

She gave him a peck on the cheek. "I switched shifts with

someone. I wanted to be here with our guests."

"Awesome," he said, watching her fondly as she left the room.

"Any word from Scott yet?" I asked after she left.

"Dunno, but let's check the board," Wilhelm replied, getting up from the table. "Come on."

I followed him across the house to his office. There was a message from Scott letting us know he should arrive that afternoon. With nothing to do but wait, we joined Brad and Lucy by the pool. Wilhelm set up a few umbrellas for shade and set out a pitcher of ice water for me. Hungry after swimming, the young couple left to get donuts and coffee for breakfast, promising to bring back a bag of ice and a six-pack of Dr Pepper for me. I'd developed a taste for it after Caleb had offered me one in Tonopah.

They returned within an hour, and we all relaxed as the warm desert wind blew and the shadows grew shorter. Lucy occupied herself by taking photos of the view of the desert and mountains to the west while Brad and Wilhelm tossed a football behind us.

Sometime later, the three youngest members of our group returned, skateboards in hand, switched to swimsuits and jumped in the pool. Lilith brought over the boom box from the van and put in a cassette.

"Now it's a party," I said. "What's the plan for today?"

"We might go see *WarGames* tonight," she answered. "Alan says it's great."

The surfer dude lifted himself out of the water with a splash and sat on the edge, dripping. "I saw it opening night. Hey, Wil, have you seen it?"

"Sure did," Wilhelm replied, sipping his beer. He'd had several throughout the afternoon but appeared unaffected. "Good flick."

"Scary," Alan said, looking grim, "knowing the world could end in fifteen minutes." He looked west at the hills in the distance, thoughtful for a moment, then shook his head. "You hack, right? Can you do that stuff?" he asked, putting his sunglasses back on as he drip-dried by the pool.

"What *stuff* is that?"

"Hack into military computers," Alan said. "Like in the movie. Is that how you can afford this place?"

"Maybe," Wilhelm said, tossing the empty and grabbing a fresh beer from the nearby cooler. "With enough time, and some social engineering. If I didn't want to go to prison as a commie spy or something. No chance I'd do it from home, though. That's asking to be caught."

"Protecting Shivurr seems just as risky," Alan observed.

"There's no law against having guests over," Wilhelm said. "Plus, they have to find him first. I'm not worried."

"What's social engineering?" Alan asked.

"Hacking people. Conning them, really, into giving you access you shouldn't have. People are the weakest link in any system. What you do is start near the bottom and work your way up. You research your target, get to know who the players are, then call someone and name-drop to build trust. Or you might say you're a tech support guy calling and need to know their password to fix their computer. People are always having trouble with computers. Then you work your way up the chain."

"Huh, that's not as cool," Alan said, looking crestfallen. "Seems like cheating."

"Some of it involves exploiting holes or backdoors," Wilhelm said. "Like the backdoor in the movie. That would work, if you had access to the system. But the easiest is if you know someone on the inside—someone that can hold the door open for you. Of course, the artificial intelligence part is make-believe."

"Why's that?" Alan asked.

"AI's nowhere close to that. Computers aren't powerful enough for one—least not yet."

"Oh, cool," Lilith said, pointing at the back of the yard. Within the branches of an oak perched a large great horned owl, regarding us with drooping eyelids.

"That's the dude that kept me up last night," Caleb said, waking from his nap and squinting toward the backyard. "He was hooting half the night."

"Oh, she's beautiful," Lucy said from the pool. She and Brad had stopped their splashing to look until the bird took off and flew to another yard.

"Nice, you don't see them often during the day," Wilhelm said. "They really like our trees. That oak's their favourite."

"There are a lot more animals here than I thought," Lilith said, fiddling with her camera—much smaller and cheaper than Lucy's high-end one. She popped the spent roll from it and popped in a new one. "I thought deserts were supposed to be empty wastelands."

"It didn't seem all that empty to me," I said, thinking of my journey.

"Very true. There's a lot more life than you see at first glance," Wilhelm said, springing to his feet. He stepped down into the pool and dunked his head before rising back out. "This world teems with life in unexpected places. It's a shame that people are going to make a desert of it all. A desert of plastic and concrete."

"Yeah," Alan said. "I heard we're losing the ozone layer now. Pretty soon we won't be able to go outside without SPF 1000 sunblock. Between that and the greenhouse effect, we're screwed. There're just too many people on the planet. Isn't there something like four and half billion of us now? How many more can the world take?"

"I wish I was born years ago, before the end of the world," Lilith said softly. "Nuclear bombs, the greenhouse effect, holes in the ozone layer, acid rain, pollution, the rainforests being cut down. It's all so depressing. I've thought about having kids one day, but…" She trailed off, blinking her eyes rapidly. "It's like the planet would be better off without us."

"That's why you got to have fun while you can," Caleb said, looking at her. "Live life to the max. Die surfing."

"Or do something about it," Wilhelm said. "There's time. Not much, but some. After billions of years, the earth isn't going down that easy. It's got friends, antibodies fighting the infection of human progress." He made quotes in the air with his fingers as he spoke the last word. "I know you kids didn't make this world. You were just born into it, but it's the only one you have."

"Careful, Wil," said Brad, climbing out of the pool. "That's commie talk."

"Is it?"

"My dad says we need growth for the good of the economy," Brad said, "or we'll be like the Soviet Union, with no reason to do anything or try to achieve anything."

"Fair point, but where does it end? This world is finite. It's just a small island in the ocean of space. A bit too large, since people can fool themselves into thinking it isn't, while they cut down all the trees and melt the polar ice caps with excessive industry, as if there's no end to it."

"Nah, we'll colonize space. Go to other planets."

He sipped his beer. "Space is far, far more hostile and unforgiving than you think. It's anathema to life. This world is rare— exceptional, even in the vastness of the universe. Even if leaving it for other planets is ever an option, what a tragedy to kill Mother Earth and all her children, save one, in doing so. What a thankless, cruel barbarism. What a lonely existence."

"You're really bumming me out, man," Caleb said. "How about some chow?"

"We just ate. Where do you put it all?" Wilhelm said, smirking.

The patio doors of the house slid aside as Olivia came out to join us. She wore a bikini and a wide-brimmed hat that shaded her shoulders. She bent to give her husband a kiss on the cheek.

"You look amazing," Lucy said.

Alan stared, his mouth falling open. Lilith rolled her eyes and smacked his shoulder with the back of her hand. He studied the ground before his eyes drifted back. Olivia, for her part, appeared not to notice and sat down on a nearby lawn chair next to her husband.

"Smoking hot," Caleb said, eyes as wide as saucers. "Most definitely." His face reddened, seeing Wilhelm's face. "Did I say that out loud?"

"I like your necklace, Lilith," I said, trying to change the subject. "What's that symbol?"

She pulled the necklace forward with her hand, looking down at it. "Oh, it's an ankh. It's Egyptian. Alan bought it for me."

"Right, it symbolizes life," he said, looking at me.

"Mortal existence *and* the afterlife, actually," Olivia said, kneeling to scrutinize the teen's necklace. "The ancient Egyptians believed life extended beyond this mortal coil to a hereafter."

"Wow, that's cool," Lilith said, looking thoughtful. "How do you know so much about ankhs?"

"I'm a bit of a history buff," Olivia said as she regained her feet. "Especially Ancient Egyptian, Greek, and Roman history."

"Hey, everybody," said a voice. Scott waved a hand from the corner of the house. He smiled broadly and wandered over. His white dress shirt hung open, in deference to the heat, and a black tie dangled loosely from his neck. He still wore black slacks, and a pager on his belt. "Hey, buddy," he said to me. "These the new friends you mentioned on the phone?" He looked around through black-rimmed eyeglasses, nodding amiably at the assembled group.

As introductions were made, Wilhelm handed Scott a beer and gave him a comradely slap on the shoulder. Scott cracked the can and took a long gulp as I related the story of how I'd met my new friends.

"Saving people while on the run?" he said, rubbing his temples. "You've got a hero complex, my friend."

"I like to think we saved each other," I said, looking around.

"I really appreciate you guys watching out for Shivurr," Scott said, taking a seat. "What happened to the assholes that robbed you?"

"The cops got them," Brad said. "At least we think so."

"FBI agents came by our hotel to tell us—" Lucy began.

"They were from the facility, Scott, not FBI," I said. "I recognized them. We can't trust what they said, but I think it was mostly true."

Scott's eyes widened. "You're kidding. How'd you get away? Could you have been followed?" He looked around as if expecting security agents to leap over the stone fence at any moment.

"They had some car trouble," I said.

Alan laughed. "Right. That's one way of putting it."

"It was amazing. Shivurr's amazing," Lilith said, touching my shoulder. I shuffled my feet, studying the ground. "He did something, somehow."

"Yeah, I don't doubt it," he replied, smiling at her. He looked at me. "It snowed in the city last night. Heard it on the radio on the drive. Know anything about that?"

"Maybe," I said, avoiding his gaze.

"Not exactly keeping a low profile," Scott said, chuckling. "Snow in Las Vegas in the summer. That's got to be a red flag to Dixon's boys, if they hear about it."

I shrugged. "I heard it was across town."

"Yeah, but they'll know you're in town now, if word gets back to him. They'll focus all their efforts here, instead of spreading them around."

"I guess I hadn't thought of that."

"Don't sweat it," he said, looking sympathetic. "Maybe they won't catch wind of it. And if they do, it's a big place. I'll get you out of town soon enough. Like I said on the phone yesterday, we've got lots to talk about. I've got something to show you at my place, too."

"Hang out a bit first," Wilhelm said. He stood up and walked over to the barbecue. "I'm just about to grill up a few more burgers."

"Sure," Scott said, putting down his beer. "I just need to go home to change."

Thirty minutes later, he reappeared wearing shorts and a T-shirt and took a burger from Wilhelm. Over dinner, conversation soon returned to my delicate situation. Scott stopped me from sharing too much detail with the rest of the group, for their protection. He warned us that the more they knew, the greater the danger they would be in if the Bodhi Group ever found them.

"No sweat," Brad said. "We're going home tomorrow."

Scott nodded. "That's good. It's safer that way. I've got plans to get Shivurr somewhere safe tomorrow anyway."

As the day wore on and the temperature cooled, I felt content, sitting among friends, but apprehensive about the future—mine and the planet's—given what we'd discussed this afternoon. Whatever the greenhouse effect was, it didn't sound good, especially to me.

Focus on the positives, I thought, *you're free, you've got friends.*

I'd made more friends in the past three days than the past decade. With Wilhelm, especially, a fast friendship had formed; it was as if we'd always been friends. Last night's adventure had just solidified it.

As the sun dipped toward the mountains in the west, Scott and I excused ourselves and left for his house, promising to return soon.

Chapter 14

Total Recall

With my hood up and hat pulled down low, I slipped out into the fading light of the day, rushed across the driveway, and hopped into the passenger seat of Scott's white-and-black 1975 Ford Mustang. I kept low in my seat as he drove the short distance down the street to his home. He backed into the single-car garage and we entered the building through an inside door without needing to go back outside.

Though it was on the same street, Scott's house and yard, the latter visible through the windows, were noticeably smaller than the Schmidts'. The house itself had fewer rooms and sat on the east side of the street, backing onto other homes instead of the empty desert. It was a well-kept but sparsely decorated home—lots of chrome, leather, and hardwood floors, with few paintings or photographs—suggesting a bachelor who wasn't frequently in residence.

He led me to his office, stooping to pick up a small black house cat with white paws who purred like an idling motorcycle, audible from several feet away. "Hey, Jane." He scratched behind the cat's ears, eliciting more utterances of joy. "My sister, Odile, must have dropped her off. I'd better get her something to eat. I'll be right back."

I leaned against the wall by the AC vent until he joined me five minutes later and sank into the only chair in the room, a well-worn reclining black leather office chair. He swivelled it back and forth as we talked while the screensaver drew designs on the monitor of the computer behind him. An old cup of coffee sat on the desk blotter, slowly evaporating, next to a Rolodex and a shiny Newton's cradle.

"What is it you wanted to show me?" I asked.

"Hang on, buddy. First tell me about what happened at the cavern. I didn't want to say too much in front of the others, but something big went down there. Lots of soldiers and attack helicopters left the base, heading in that direction. Was that you?"

"I was there, but it wasn't for me."

He looked relieved. "Good. That makes sense, but I wanted to be sure. I was pretty worried they were being sent to get you at first. Except they seemed to still be looking for you all over Nevada. It wasn't until I heard that they were talking about extending the search to Utah, Arizona, and California that I began to relax. So, what went on?"

"It was crazy," I breathed, reliving the experience. "They were conducting some kind of experiment. Firing beams of light and other things at some pulsating energy sphere floating above the ground. Something went wrong, I guess. These things—fire elementals, I guess you'd call them—appeared out of nowhere. They attacked me, everyone really. I ran; barely got out of there alive."

Scott sucked air into his lungs over clenched teeth. "That explains the choppers and truckloads of soldiers. And no one saw you?"

I shrugged. "One of the soldiers guarding the camp did. I helped him escape the fire elementals and he let me go. He said he'd keep quiet about me being there."

"I think he probably did keep quiet. Nothing I heard suggested they knew you were there. Like I said, from what I overheard, they're looking in other states now. They seemed sure that you'd been to Tonopah, though. After hearing about your adventures with the kids, I now know why."

"I don't suppose they'll just give up, will they?"

Scott shook his head and bit his lip. "No chance of that. Director Wallace was furious when they realized you were gone. He tore Dixon a new one, I heard. By my estimate, they had half the security force out looking for you. They probably still do. They've got choppers combing the desert, too. Dixon ordered us to check law enforcement databases, and to monitor police scanner frequencies for leads. That'll be how they came across the Lunar Crater robbery report. Too bad it wasn't me. I'd have quashed it."

"No doubt," I said. "I'd do it again, though. I hate bullies. Besides, I meant it when I said they saved me too."

Scott waved a hand. "I get it, man," he said. "They seem like good kids and you're here, safe. They're lucky you were there."

"Yeah, I suppose so," I said.

"What about the chamber? Did you find any answers? Anything to explain what the visions mean. Maybe figure out where you're from?"

I shook my head. "No, I didn't get the chance before everything went to hell."

"Damn, that sucks," Scott said, slumping. He took a deep breath and let it out slowly. "Maybe you can try again, once things settle down. They can't keep this up forever. Dixon already had to lift the lockdown. No one could come or go without his authorization, and a mutiny was brewing. Even the security forces were getting tired of it, wanting to go home."

"Yeah, maybe," I said. "If I live that long."

Scott smiled. "I've got some good news there. Like I said on the phone, with everyone out looking for you, I had a chance to get into the archival vault."

"Aren't there cameras in there?"

"Just at the entrance, and I looped the camera feed. It's overwritten every forty-eight hours or so. In a day, they won't even be able to find the loop."

"Smart," I said. "What did you find?"

He yawned, then rubbed his face. "You know how your memory is all messed up, right?"

"How could I forget?"

"I think I know why," Scott said. "What do you know about your biology? How your body works and operates?"

"Uh, aside from being prone to heat stroke? Not much. I know that I can do things that people might call magic."

"Okay, stupid question. Sorry. It must be weird not knowing anything about your physiology. I just realized that. I mean, humans today, we know tons about our own biology. Even the average person knows they've got a heart and kidneys and stuff like that, and the basics of how it works. We know how disease spreads, to wash our hands regularly, all that stuff. But a few hundred years ago, maybe not even that long, they knew jack shit. Even the doctors were clueless. Bleeding people with leeches was the only thing they knew, or thought they knew, to do. But today we tend to forget that and take all this knowledge for granted. But for you, you're living that now. You don't really know much about how your body works, if anything. If you have a heart, things like that. Don't look at me like that. I'm not trying to be a dick. I'm just saying, I get how lousy that must be. It just seems like it's something we should know intuitively, but why would you? How could you?"

"Sure, you could fill a library with what I don't know," I said.

"I might be able to help with that," Scott said. "I found several filing cabinets full of data in the archives. What I hacked out of the mainframe when we first met is just a fraction of what they've compiled on you. They've been studying you for years now. Doing X-rays, testing your abilities, testing your limits, and recording their findings. You know that already. What you probably don't know is they've taken samples from you as well. Removed bits with syringes and scalpels. Scraped up any residue left behind when you were melting in the heat and captured any airborne evaporate—steam and such."

"Why?" I asked, frowning. "I've been helping them with their experiments. Why do this too?"

"They did it early on. From what I learned, you were fighting them in the early days, before I came on the scene."

I nodded. "Right, once I knew that they'd lied and weren't going to help, I left."

"Yeah, well, once that happened, the kid gloves came off, and they started experimenting to find out what you're made of and how it is you can exist."

"Why don't I remember?"

"They sedated you somehow and operated on you," he said, leaning forward in his chair and pointing to my forehead. "They must have messed up your head when they did it."

I slid down the wall and sat on the floor. "You're saying they lobotomized me? And I don't even remember?"

"I'm afraid so," Scott said, hanging his head. "People justify all sorts of horrible shit, particularly if they don't think that you're human."

"Like being human is so special when they'll do this to another sentient being."

"I'm sorry, man. It's terrible," Scott said quietly. "If it helps, they'd probably do it even if you were human, if they thought that it was for the *greater good*. If it helped fight the Reds and the evils of socialism. Any crime in the name of national security, right?"

I said nothing, staring at the wall, simmering. The room grew colder as I fumed. Seeing my agitation, Scott stayed quiet for several moments, crossing his arms and hunching his shoulders against the chill, allowing me time to process the news.

Finally he spoke again. "Finding crystals composed of elements never before found on earth likely quelled any ethical concerns. The scientists have been creaming their jeans, inventing new names to describe them, like arborium, cryominium, freonium, rorubium, tekinium, polarinium, and others I can't remember. They can't wait to add them to the periodic table. The dumbasses don't realize that's not likely to ever happen. No way the Bodhi Group is going to announce this to the public if they can avoid it. And they'll do whatever it takes to ensure they don't ever have to."

"What's so great about some new elements?" I asked with a frown.

Scott's eyebrows climbed his forehead. "Are you kidding? These elements are all kinds of weird. They're still trying to figure them out, based on what I read. That's just in raw elemental form. Blended and formed into crystals, they get even stranger. It seems memory storage is one function. They're also tied to your abilities, your powers, somehow, but they don't understand a lot of that yet. It's possible you used to be able to do even *more* than you can do now."

Scott took a swallow from the old cup of coffee, looked inside, and grimaced before continuing. "These crystals, according to the files, have unique properties. They attract each other slowly across great distance, arranging themselves into larger crystals. The samples they took, placed into a water medium, formed into several crystals visible to the naked eye."

"How large?" I asked.

Scott pulled back on a ball in the Newton's cradle and let it go. "About the size of one of these balls," he declared as they clacked back and forth. "They sent several of them to labs around the country."

I shrugged. "But how does this help us?"

"I've got the locations of the labs," Scott said. "Dug them out of the mainframe. Maybe we can figure out a way to get the samples back."

"But what's the point?" I asked, raising my voice. "My memories are gone."

Scott shook his head. "No, they're not. According to the files, you can reintegrate them. Your memories should still be intact. The crystals act like non-volatile storage, sort of like a computer floppy disc. They tested this in the experiments that they did on you. They had to do it repeatedly to map out your memories, at least roughly, so they could selectively remove memories. They wanted you to forget what they'd done and keep you compliant, so this was critical to their plans."

"But there's nothing selective about my memory loss. My memory is just a black void before I came to the Institute."

Scott nodded, regarding me with a sad face. "Yeah, the selective removal came later, when they were messing with your memories formed since coming to the Bodhi Institute. I guess they either messed up early on and botched all your earlier memories or didn't want you to remember why you came in the first place, so you wouldn't try to leave again. I just don't know."

I sagged lower against the wall and stared into space.

"You get it, right?" Scott said. He got up and walked over to where I sat, crouched down, and put his hand on my shoulder. "You might be able to get all your memories back, and any powers that might go along with them. Everything."

A slow smile spread across my face as I turned to look at him. "Getting into those labs isn't going to be easy."

"True, but I took something that might help us," Scott said. He held out his hand and pulled me to my feet. "Come with me."

I followed him to the kitchen. He opened the freezer door and pulled out a small cooler.

"What's with the box?" I asked.

"The crystals need to be kept below freezing or they disappear. Don't worry, the cooler is mine. I bring my lunch in it sometimes."

He reached in like a magician performing a trick and pulled out a glass tube shimmering with an inner iridescence.

"You took some? Won't they notice?"

"Nah, I switched them with a couple of empty bottles and swapped the labels."

I reached out and took the test tube in hand, staring at the substance within. "I can't believe you did that. Thank you, Scott."

"Here's another one. Sorry I didn't bring more, but it was risky taking even these two."

"I've got to get in there somehow," I said. "Maybe you can smuggle me back in."

Scott was already shaking his head. "It won't work, not today. Security is too high. No telling when it'll settle down."

I nodded absently, pondering. He was right. Sneaking in was unlikely to work, and getting caught with Scott would risk him being arrested as my accomplice. He'd be lucky to just be fired, but more likely he'd be sent to some secret government prison for commies and other enemies of the state—or worse. He'd already taken extreme risks to help me thus far. I might be able to sneak close enough to gain the advantage of surprise and fight my way in, but not without casualties, and getting back out would be near impossible if military forces were called in.

"So, what do I do with these two?" I asked, glancing at him. "Drink them?"

Scott tossed his shoulders. "I guess so. From what I under-stand, your body should reintegrate it. Maybe just drink one for now, see how it affects you. Does that jacket have an inside pocket?"

I unzipped my jacket and felt around inside. "Yeah."

"Put one in there to keep it cold against your body." I did as he suggested and studied the other, the first that he'd given to me. Then, before I could change my mind, I popped the stopper and downed the contents in one swallow. The substance slid from the test tube into my mouth like it had a mind of its own, leaving the glass clean as if it had been scrubbed. "Now what?"

"Now we wait," Scott said, studying my face.

I resealed the test tube and handed it back to my friend. "How long—" I began before a wave of vertigo rushed over me, and I leaned against the wall for support. A rainbow of col-our flashed through my mind's eye, dazzling me with its bril-liance and washing away the room around me. The inchoate colours coalesced into locations and faces but disconnected from each other. At once I recognized faces of people, knew them to be friends and enemies, and knew their names, but in many cases without any history to go along with it.

It was like knowing Scott was my friend with absolute cer-tainty, knowing his name but not knowing anything of how we'd met or become friends—knowing only the now. In addition to faces of people, I saw vast landscapes of snow and ice stretching as far as the eye could see, followed by scenes of battle in burn-ing forests among fiends and freaks of fire, mist, spirit, wood, stone, and flesh. Lightning crackled and wind raged over it all, and roiling black smoke rose into the sky as creatures out of myth clashed and died and cried in pain and rage.

I flew over the devastation at breakneck speed, suspended above the ravaged earth on a disc of frost, encased in a bubble of energy that shielded me from harm, as I shouted a rallying cry to my allies. Moments later, balls of white frost swirled in my hand, which I bowled in all directions. Where they passed, snow burst up from the earth, dousing flames and causing some of the oncoming horde to falter. Moaning with the recollection,

I crumpled to the floor. The cavern in the Great Basin Desert, or one like it, came next, only this time it looked different. The same tholos stood there, along with the dais and sphere floating above it, but frost and ice covered the cavern walls, ceiling and floor, and I knew it to be bitterly, wonderfully cold within, much colder than it had been in recent days.

I woke sometime later with Scott kneeling over me. "Jesus, Shivurr, are you all right?"

I sat up slowly, rubbing my forehead. "Uh-huh, maybe. Yeah, I think so."

"Looks like you fainted," Scott said. He extended a hand and pulled me to my feet. "That's potent stuff. Do you remember anything?"

"Yeah, bits and pieces," I replied. I paused, thinking. "Images, mostly. Visions. Some of them from a long time ago, I think, but there are too many gaps to make sense of it all."

"Do you remember why you came here? Why you came for help?"

I shook my head. "I don't know. I saw what looked like a huge battle, fought by…well, creatures, monsters really. You wouldn't believe it. It was crazy stuff."

"What kind of monsters?" Scott asked, regarding me keenly.

"Walking trees, giants, demons," I replied.

"Demons? You're kidding? Where were you in all this?"

I smiled, raising my brows. "In the midst of it all. I seemed to be leading a charge of some kind on a huge disc of pure frost."

"Wow," Scott said. "Do you think it was real?"

"Maybe. If it was, I'm not sure if it was the past or the future. A week ago, I'd have dismissed it as a dream, but after fighting those fire elementals…I just don't know." I paused, reliving the memories. "If they're real, then maybe that's got something to do with why I came here in the first place."

"I haven't seen anything in the news about monster battles. If what you remembered actually happened, my guess is it was probably a while ago."

"Maybe what I saw wasn't Earth," I said. "I still don't

remember where I came from, so it could be, couldn't it?"

Scott nodded, slowly. "Yeah, I suppose. Maybe the frost place you always talk about. The Ever Frost."

"Underfrost."

"Right, maybe that's your planet."

I shook my head. "That's not...I don't know why, but I think this was a long time ago. Hundreds—no, thousands of years ago...maybe longer."

"Do you want to take another?"

I rubbed my face. "Not sure. I'm feeling pretty queasy."

Scott stroked the thick stubble on his chin, then bobbed his head. "Okay, let's give it a rest for now. Maybe you'll remember more in time." He looked at his watch. "For now, let's head back to the Schmidts' place. I'm sure you'll want to say goodbye. We'll leave early tomorrow for the safe house."

Chapter 15

Are Those Flames?

As the garage door opened and Scott drove out, another car pulled into his driveway, blocking the path to the street. My friend hit the brakes, stopping the vehicle just beyond the garage door. He leaned on the car's horn as I ducked beneath the dash.

"What the hell?" Scott said, leaning out the open driver's-side window, waving to the intruders. "Hello? Can I help you?"

The sound of the doors of the other vehicle opening followed. "Stay here," the computer expert whispered before exiting the Mustang. "Can I help you?" Scott repeated.

"Sorry to intrude, sir," said a voice I recognized as belonging to one of the agents from the hotel room in Tonopah. "I'm Grant. This is McGregor. I believe we've met a few times before…at work."

"Oh, right, you're both in security," Scott said. His voice grew fainter as he moved to the front of the vehicle. "What can I do for you?"

"May we come in?" Grant asked.

I crouched lower, trying to disappear under the dash. *I'm busted,* I thought. The agents had to know I was here and had come to reclaim me and return me to the Institute.

"Look, gents, as you can see, I'm heading out for the night, and I'm in a rush. I'm back at work Monday. How about we talk then?"

"I'm afraid it can't wait, sir. May we discuss this inside?"

"Not until I know what this is about," Scott said.

"I'll get right to it, then. We'd like to search the premises, if you'd be so kind," Grant said. "The security director has tasked us with searching employee homes in search of a lab animal that went missing recently. I'm sure you're aware of the incident. There's concern an employee may have been involved with the escape or may be harbouring the creature." I glared at the dash, making a gesture with my middle finger that the agents couldn't see. *Who're you calling a lab animal?* I thought.

"You can't be serious," Scott said, outrage in his tone. "Don't you need a warrant?"

"Not if you grant us access," another voice interjected. I recognized it belonged to McGregor, the other agent from Tonopah. "You can refuse, but that'd be mighty suspicious."

"The only thing *that* should make you suspicious of is that I might just be a citizen of a free country who knows his rights and who doesn't want a couple of jack-booted…uh, strangers invading his domicile."

"Now, now," Grant said. "No need to be like that."

The whup-whup of helicopter blades chopping the air drowned out further conversation.

I leaned back and peered up through the windshield and saw one of the air tour helicopters fly past. Flames and smoke trailed from its tail.

"Holy hell," Grant said, raising his voice. "Would you look at that?"

"Are those flames?" McGregor said.

Neither Scott nor Grant replied, presumably both still looking skyward at the struggling aircraft. While they were distracted, I crawled to the driver's side, scraping my stomach on the parking brake and gearshift, and crept out the still-open door, hoping the agents overlooked my bright white rear end rising above the dash as I moved.

It was risky but a gamble I had to take. I wasn't going to sit and wait to be discovered. The odds of Scott convincing the two men to go away without conducting a search weren't good.

I felt confident that I could subdue the agents if they spotted me, but it would mean big trouble for Scott. They'd know he'd helped me, and his career, freedom, and life would be on the line then. Even if I put the agents down permanently—something I wasn't willing to do—other agents would come looking for them. Either way, they'd be on my trail again, and I'd have no one to help me from here on. Alone in the desert, I wouldn't survive a week.

"Looks like they might have put down all right," Grant said as I wriggled out onto the concrete driveway. "We should get back to the matter at hand." I scurried toward the back of the car, holding my breath.

"What *is* that?" McGregor said, sounding baffled. "Over there."

They've spotted me, I thought. I plucked frost from the Underfrost, its bright glow mixing with the red of the Mustang's taillights, and prepared to fight.

"Looks like a man on fire or…," Grant said, trailing off.

"It's coming this way," Scott said a moment later. Confused, I risked a peek over the trunk. All three men were looking away from me, down the street.

"Get down," Scott shouted as a fireball hit one of the Bodhi Group security agents in the head. The man went down like a bowling pin, his hair on fire, making no attempt to break his fall.

"McGregor," Grant yelled. He pulled a gun and moved to use the black sedan as cover, glancing back to where McGregor lay, dead or unconscious. The fallen man's hair no longer burned, but the stench of sulphur mixed with that of burnt hair lingered. The surviving agent's attention was wrenched back to the street when a second fireball struck his vehicle's driver's-side window and crashed through it, illuminating the interior with firelight.

Looking down the street, I squinted my eyes as two fire elementals moved like wildfire toward us. Their heads swivelled as they scanned left and right, searching for targets. A line of flame trailed in their wake, showing that they'd come from between two nearby houses to the northwest of our position. To my relief, the street was currently empty of foot and vehicle traffic—the occupants were probably having dinner inside or barbecuing in their backyards.

Good thing or there'd be even more to worry about.

Scott retreated to his car with the whites of his eyes showing.

I waved to him as he came around the open door, and he ran to join me in a half crouch as the sound of gunfire erupted.

Grant had taken aim over the hood of the sedan and was unloading his pistol into the approaching enemies in a controlled fashion, like he was at the gun range. In reply, several more fireballs whistled through the air like tiny meteors. Some flew over Grant's head and others crashed into the vehicle's side, dying in a flash of smoke and flame, leaving deep dents. Grant's aim was good. The leader shrieked and staggered slightly with each impact but kept coming. Large flames leapt out of the shattered driver's-side window of the black car as the fire within grew in ferocity.

As the first elemental closed to thirty feet, Grant fled the dubious safety of the agents' car and rushed toward the Mustang, behind which Scott and I cowered. He made it half the distance when a fireball crashed into his shoulder, staggering him. His gun clattered onto the concrete as he changed direction, running directly away from the danger into the neighbouring yard.

Another fireball hit him in the back of the head. He stumbled to his knees, stood again, and was hit by a third fireball, going down face-first. The last one sailed through the space where his head used to be and crashed into the side of a stone fence a hundred feet away, where it briefly continued to burn and left the fence pitted and blackened at the point of impact.

That target down, the frontrunner turned to its left, seeking new prey.

The roar of the Mustang's engine filled my ears, and a cloud of exhaust washed over my face as it raced away from me. A second later, it crunched into our approaching adversary as it came up the driveway, and the beast flew through the air and bounced off the hood of the burning black sedan.

Nice one, Scott, I thought.

I pushed myself to my feet and cast a frost ball at the creature as it recovered. The orb punched it in the chest and the fiend shrank back, screeching. I moved closer, hurling frost with each step. The creature flickered with each impact as the ice and snow quenched its flames, until it guttered like a campfire soaked with a bucket of water.

Before I could revel in the victory, another fireball sizzled past my nose. My head snapped to the right, following the path of the projectile back to its source as the other humanoid inferno attacked. I dodged to the left as Scott threw the Mustang into reverse. Stumbling, I brushed against the burning black sedan's front end and shrieked as my stomach rubbed against hot metal. Recoiling, I dashed to the right, trying to get away from the scalding heat.

As I ran, I lobbed more frost at the approaching enemy. It blew up ten feet away from its target, colliding with fire coming from the other direction.

The elemental moved forward once more when a deep, sonorous growl that seemed to come from everywhere and nowhere at once filled the air. It felt like an ox sat on my chest while it blared. I covered my ears in a vain attempt to stifle the sound. To my relief, the moving fire hazard stopped in its tracks at the sound and cocked its head as if listening, then turned around and moved down the street, northward.

I moved down to the edge of the driveway and watched it flee. Scott exited the car and rushed to join me. "Where's it going?" he asked. "And what the heck was that sound?"

I shrugged, holding out my hands, palms up. "What's that light at Wilhelm's? Do you see that?" I asked, pointing. Yellow and red lights flickered and reflected off the houses in the vicinity of the Schmidts' domicile, a few hundred feet away. "Is it burning?"

Scott squinted, adjusting his glasses. "I can't tell," he said, wiping sweat from his forehead. "Maybe. It looks like that thing is heading that way."

"We've got to get back," I said, grabbing the sides of my head. "They won't stand a chance."

"Come on," Scott shouted. We turned and ran back to the Mustang.

As he tore the door open, the first Bodhi Group agent to fall groaned. "Please, help me," McGregor said.

"Damn it," Scott said, looking at me over the roof of the

Mustang. "Go. Get over there. I've got to call an ambulance for these guys."

I nodded and slammed the passenger door shut. "I'll see you there," I said over my shoulder as I ran, skating north over the hot pavement.

My opponent moved fast, now only about fifty feet from Wilhelm's house. I tossed frost as it fled, hoping to turn the creature's attention back to me. The frothing mass of white sailed to the left, missing its mark.

The target of my salvo flinched and whirled to face me as I continued to close the distance. I'd covered only a few feet when one of the doors of Wilhelm's garage started to open. The fire elemental glanced over its shoulder in response and turned back toward the house once again.

I sucked in a breath of air and yelled a snarling battle cry, trying to keep its attention on me.

It worked.

The thing turned in response to my challenge and sent more molten fire my way. I collapsed into a slide, slipping beneath the incoming projectile, then popped back to my feet. Still coming, I deked left and right, closing the gap.

The next attack came in low.

Smart, I thought as I jumped to avoid it, launching a counter-attack in mid-air.

My projectile caught the creature in the shoulder, crippling its throwing hand. Behind it, Brad's camper bus was backing out of the garage as I continued to pepper my fallen attacker until it finally collapsed and lay motionless.

"Shivurr," Brad yelled through the open driver's-side window. "Come on." He waved a hand in a come-hither motion. The rest of the gang, mouths open and eyes wide, pressed against the windows, as I neared.

"What happened?" I asked, looking inside. "Where's Wilhelm?" Olivia had left for work hours ago, so I knew she wasn't in danger.

"The house is on fire. He told us to run," Brad said, pointing at the house. "He said he'd get the dog and join us."

"How'd the fire start?"

"Not sure," Brad replied. "There was a crash, I think; like someone threw a rock through a window. Then the smoke alarm started going off."

"What was that thing?" Lucy said, looking over my shoulder.

"Don't worry about it right now," I said, backing away. "I've got to make sure Wilhelm is all right. Stay here. I'll be back."

I entered the garage through the open door and crossed the concrete floor. As I ran up the stairs to the interior door, I heard shouts from within but couldn't make out the words.

I opened the inner door to enter the house and threw an arm in front of my face as flames blew from within like dragon's breath. I stumbled back and fell down the stairs onto the concrete next to Wilhelm's Trans Am. By the time I landed, the rush of air from within blew the door shut with a bang, locking the hungry fire inside for now.

Picking myself up off the ground, I ran out the big door and around the side, giving the thumbs-up to my friends. *No problem, dudes. I've got this under control,* I thought, but I pushed down a wave of anxiety at the thought that Wilhelm and Bear might still be inside. *I just hope they're escaping through the back.*

I hopped the fence at the side of the house and raced to its rear. A few more steps and I'd enter through the patio doors and get to them or, even better, I'd find them safe in the backyard.

I skidded to a stop as I rounded the corner and stared, wrinkling my brow as I took in the scene.

Standing in the middle of the pool, thirty feet away, was a large oak tree where no oak tree had been earlier in the day. Several fire elementals surrounded it, arrayed throughout the backyard, as the tree skimmed huge branches against the surface of the water and sent great waves cascading over its nearest foes, snuffing out their light. Already several of them lay smouldering on the ground at the pool's edge.

Between me and the melee, the Californians' canvas tents burned in the wind, their flame-resistant material no match for the fireballs that must have rained down on them before I arrived.

As I crept along the back of the house to the patio doors, a fresh tidal wave took out three more adversaries on the tree's left with a single swipe. This had the added effect of dousing a few of the other, non-ambulatory trees in the Schmidts' backyard—those not wading in the pool, battling fire elementals—having, I imagined, been set alight by stray fireballs.

The surviving vanguard counter-attacked, lighting up the yard with streamers of fire, striking the tree's trunk in several places. Bellowing, the oak dunked itself under the water before coming up to splash another wave to the right. Too far to present an immediate threat, though moving this direction, more could be seen beyond the perimeter fence out on the uneven desert plain that led up to the squat hills of Red Rock Canyon.

I approached the patio doors from the side—ducking as a fireball crashed into the wall of the house above my head—and noticed that they were broken on the right side. Smoke billowed out through the opening.

When I was ten feet from the doorway, the unbroken glass on the left side shattered as a massive ball of flame careened through it from the inside, accompanied by a blast of searing wind. I hugged the wall reflexively.

The ball of fire—*another fire elemental*, I realized—skipped off the ground and into the pool. The water hissed angrily, and steam rose from its surface as the monster sank to the bottom like a stone, its flames snuffed.

Seconds later, as I began to move again, an armoured figure emerged from the blazing home. Translucent green and eight feet tall, the ethereal ghost glided over the ground on flows of air to join the oak tree, as I stared in awe.

Shaking off my astonishment, I moved cautiously forward to the now wide-open back entrance, stepping on shattered glass.

Oh, man, that's too hot, I thought, shrinking back.

The interior was ablaze. Even at this distance, I could feel my face starting to dissolve like an ice cube on a hot griddle. I wouldn't make it ten feet into that firestorm, even if I weren't made of ice and snow.

No one could survive that, I reluctantly concluded.

"Wilhelm!" I shouted into the flames, hoping against reason that he might answer. I heard no reply, so I called again.

Seeing and hearing no signs of life, I ran along the wall to the rec room where Wilhelm had entertained us when we'd first arrived. The large windows were shattered, and fire and more smoke spewed out through the window.

Sudden motion within caught my attention. Bear, the Alaskan shepherd, his fur on fire, ran from the room as I looked on in horror.

I grabbed the windowsill, intending to enter, but the hot wood burned my hand. I shouted until my throat grew sore as huge flames climbed the walls and dark smoke moved across the ceiling. "No, no, no, no," I muttered, throwing frost balls into the blaze. They hit the walls and furniture but quickly vaporized, and the fire continued to burn undiminished.

"No," I said softly one last time, backing away as the fire intensified.

I was too late. The hell the canvasser had threatened Wilhelm with the day before had come to claim him and his dog, and there was nothing I could do to change it.

Chapter 16

That Poor Dude

I turned west to face the elementals and reached for the Underfrost. The battle behind me still raged as more elementals arrived from the desert to fill the void left by the fallen ones. As they approached, their flames guttered and flashed, brushed by a gale force wind that rose up from the north. The armoured figure floated out to meet them, surrounded by a protective nimbus of greenish light that shimmered and flared as fireballs crashed against it.

The air reeked of black smoke, suffused with fire and steam rising from the downed fire elementals, making it hard to catch more than glimpses of iridescent green as the figure moved away. The newcomer's eyes gleamed emerald green, stabbing through the smoke and darkness like laser beams as it turned back and beckoned me forward. Then, with a wave of its hands, a blast of wind blew the smoke away like a stage curtain being thrust to one side. Gliding forward, the spectre pointed its fingers at the enemy. Wherever it pointed, lightning crashed from the cloudless sky, striking fire elementals and cascading to others nearby, sending them to the earth, where they lay unmoving.

I ran to the pool's edge and tossed a torrent of frost at the nearest fire elemental. It fell quickly, and I moved on to the next. Elemental after elemental fell before me. I took a few fireballs to the body; they hurt, but I brushed them aside before they could burn through my jacket, patting out the flames and continuing my attack. For each one I dropped, another appeared to replace it. I couldn't take them down fast enough. I needed to do more.

Desperate, I remembered wrestling with the big casino guard

from the night before, when I'd done something to make it snow. I'd thinned the distance between the Underfrost and this world, somehow creating a rift through which the former could rush across, guided by my will.

As I focused on that desire, snow began to fall, mixing with the wind, becoming a blizzard. All around me, elementals flickered and waned as the nascent storm needled them with countless snowflakes, misting the air as they melted.

"Shivurr," shrieked a voice, barely audible in the thunder of battle.

I looked to my right, irrationally hoping that I'd see Wilhelm with Bear at his side. Instead, Alan, his long hair blowing wildly in the wind, stood at the corner of the house looking at the carnage, mouth wide and eyes bulging. Seeing another friend in danger pulled the plug on the bathtub full of rage that until then had consumed all other considerations.

Alan darted from cover, hunched over double, heading toward me. He kept his eyes fixed on me, as if refusing to acknowledge the events occurring around him. Driven snow swirled in the fierce wind that seemed to come from all directions, and he held up his arm to shield his face against its sting. He flinched as the wading oak tree swept its limbs in another powerful sweep that knocked another enemy fifty feet across the yard, where it crashed into the fence.

As Alan approached, another fire monster jumped the north fence, directly behind him. His forehead wrinkled and face lit up as I threw a froth of churning white past his right ear with a swoosh. Ten feet behind him, it collided with an incoming fireball.

I grabbed Alan's arm and pulled him behind me, keeping my eyes on the elemental as I did so. Another fireball streaked toward me, crackling with energy. With no time to throw, I swatted the incoming projectile out of the air into the sandy ground, using a newly summoned frost ball like a makeshift ping-pong paddle. I winced as the impact shuddered down my arm, destroyed the frost, and singed my hand. I shook my injured paw frantically, then slipped it inside my jacket and rubbed it against the ice of my chest.

By now, the raging snow was taking its toll on the elemental. It steamed and guttered like a candle in the wind as the sting of thousands of snowflakes took their cumulative toll. It held up an arm to protect its face, studying the storm, then turned tail and ran, hopping the fence into the neighbour's yard, leaving a trail of fire in its wake. In the darkness, I could see the orange glow emanating from it, just above the stone barrier, as it headed west. Reaching the back of the neighbouring yard, it joined its comrades, who were now fleeing as well, making for the nearby hills over the uneven ground.

The green spectre floated after them, calling down lightning, mopping up, while the smouldering oak tree splashed itself with water from the nearly drained pool, extinguishing the small fires that burned along its branches. The battle appeared to be won, for now. It was time to go.

I swept away black ash flakes, residue of the burnt outer shell of my winter jacket, which was now mottled with scorch marks where I'd been struck, repeatedly. Light-headed, I stumbled and felt Alan grab my arm to support me. Steadying myself, I gave him a pat on the shoulder, letting him know I was okay.

"Holy shit," Alan said, his voice low. "That was badass." He swung his arm like he was serving a tennis ball. "Booyah. Here comes the smackdown."

"What are you doing here, Alan? It's not safe."

The teen shrugged. "I figured you might need help."

"Thanks, but you could have been killed," I said. Seeing his hurt expression, I added, "Look, I appreciate it, but if that fireball hit you—"

"Doesn't matter, man," Alan said, giving me a steely look. "I'm not backing down again."

I sighed and gestured toward the sidewalk that led to the front of the house in an *after you* motion. "Let's talk about it later."

The trauma of the desert robbery had clearly left wounds on the teen surfer's psyche that were making him reckless. I just hoped that coming to help me would be enough to convince him he wasn't the coward he apparently feared himself to be. I resolved to have an extended conversation with him, to do whatever I could to quell those doubts, but now wasn't the time.

Strange how everyone reacts to stressful circumstances differently, I thought.

Things seemed to roll off his best friend's back like water off a duck, whereas Alan reacted with brooding and self-doubt. Perhaps that was why while both surfed, Alan did so competitively and Caleb only recreationally. The former felt a need to prove his worth, while the latter did not.

We shuffled for the front of the house over a thin layer of fresh snowfall, which continued to accumulate. Alan glanced to the left where, in the distance, lightning continued to flash and thunder to rumble. "What's going on, dude? An alien invasion?"

"Let's talk about that later, too," I said as we rounded the corner of the burning house and hobbled down the sidewalk to the front of the garage. We stumbled into Lucy coming our way as we passed through the gate leading to the driveway.

"Wilhelm and Bear?" Lucy asked, her face pained. I shook my head, unable to look her in the eye. A hand flew to her mouth and she looked like she might be sick. I grabbed her elbow and guided her toward the van, which sat idling in the street, pointed north.

Brad cut the engine to the van and got out as we neared. Lilith and Caleb hopped out of the side doors moments later and came around the van to join us, shivering and rubbing their hands, their faces masks of concern. As we conferred, the snowfall increased in intensity and the temperature continued to drop. Even squinting, I couldn't see well farther than a few hundred feet down the street.

"Look, I… I've got…," I said, looking down. I paused, overwhelmed, thinking of last night's adventure. How could the world change so fast and so horribly, with no warning? How could the world simply go on after such a tragedy, as if nothing much had happened? How could I? "Wil, Bear…they didn't make it."

With halting words, I told them what had happened. How I

was too late. That no one could have survived. I left nothing out, including the mob of fire elementals, the ambulatory oak tree, and the emerald green spectre that had battled them. Alan nodded vigorous confirmation of the more fantastical parts of my tale. I'm not sure they really heard much after the first part. Lilith burst into tears, burying her face in Alan's shirt. His lips quivered as well, but he held it together. Caleb stared into space, blinking rapidly. Brad and Lucy hung their heads, holding back tears.

"Is this real?" Caleb asked, looking at Alan. "Seriously. I'm dreaming or high, right? Seriously."

"Yeah, it's real," Alan said softly as he comforted Lilith. "I saw it, dude. Happened just like he said."

"I'm not sure I'd believe it if I didn't see you take down that thing right in front of us," Brad said, looking at the scorched earth where the elemental's husk still lay, looking more like a hunk of volcanic rock than a molten fire monster. "A freaking walking tree? What the hell is happening?" He looked around as he said the last, asking no one and everyone at once.

"That poor dude," Caleb sighed. His lips trembled. "That's harsh…that's so totally harsh."

I looked up as Scott's Mustang roared down the street and screeched to a halt next to the van. He jumped out and ran over. Scott studied the flaming house, then looked at me. His thick-rimmed eyeglasses slid down his nose, and he pushed them back into place. "Where's Wilhelm?"

I shook my head. "I heard him shouting inside. I ran around back to try to find a way in," I said, looking down. "I tried…but the fire…"

Scott's head swivelled to regard the burning house with a pained expression on his face. He rubbed his chin a moment, then lunged forward, as if intending to enter. Brad jumped in front of him and held the taller man back. Alan rushed to help as his older brother's Nikes slid along the concrete.

"It's too late, man," Brad said, his voice cracking. "It's too late. Come on, man. It's too late."

Scott's struggles weakened at the younger man's words. He turned away and fell to one knee, his face pale and drawn. Lucy stepped forward and put a hand on his shoulder. He appeared not to notice but stood up again after a few moments. In the distance, sirens could be heard, growing louder by the second. His voice hoarse, Scott said, "Must be the ambulance I called."

"Or fire trucks," Caleb said. "Dude across the street called nine-one-one."

Scott turned away, wiping his eyes. "We need to get you out of here, Shivurr. This place is lousy with people and going to get worse." He looked south toward his house. "We can't go back to my place. More security agents may show up. I know a place we can hide out." He looked around at the others. "You should come along."

"What about the police?" Lucy asked. "Won't they want to talk to us?"

"Maybe, but what can you tell them? We need time to get our stories straight. Let the neighbours tell them what they saw first. Besides, what are you going to say? 'Well, Officer, fire-throwing monsters lit the house on fire.' They'll think you're nuts or making it up. Besides, it may not be safe here. More of those fire fuckers may be around."

"Yeah, but the police will protect us," Lilith said.

"The police can't protect you," Scott said, scowling. "Bullets don't seem to do much to them. Trust me, I know."

"I don't want to get in trouble," Lilith said, drying her eyes.

"You won't. You were just nearby. Doesn't mean you have to stay. Besides, if they talk to us later, we just tell the truth. We were scared shitless and bugged out." He rubbed the back of his head. "Look, we don't have time to argue." When they failed to immediately respond, he sighed. "All right, stay here, but Shivurr and I have got to go. Anybody got a pen and paper?" He held out his hands as, down the street, an ambulance pulled up in front of his house, lights flashing.

"I do," Lucy said, rummaging around in her purse. "Here you go."

"One sec," he said as he fiddled with his car keys. "Here's the key to my house. It's the one down there where the ambulance is, with the burned-out car in the driveway. After the cops and fire trucks get here, you can go there."

Scott took the pen and paper. He held the pad against the side of the van, writing furiously, then ripped off the page and handed it to Lucy. "Here, this is my number. If you don't make it back to my place, call and leave a message telling us where you are."

Scott walked toward his car, motioning me to follow.

"Why wouldn't we make it?" Lucy asked, brow furrowed.

"I don't know. Maybe the cops will take you in or something," Scott replied, opening the driver's-side door. "I'll call once we're safe, so listen for my voice on the machine. Only pick up if it's me, though."

"Take us in?" Lilith said in a questioning tone. "But like you said, we didn't do anything."

Scott shrugged. "You never know. Depends on the cops." He held the door open so I could climb into the back seat. Seeing her look of consternation, after a moment he added, "Don't worry. If they do, leave me a message and I'll bail you out or whatever. Don't sweat it. They'll probably just want to talk to you."

"I'm coming with you," Caleb said. He looked at Scott apprehensively. "If that's okay. I don't like cops."

"Sure," Scott agreed. "You take shotgun. This isn't a taxi. Come on, those sirens are getting closer."

"I don't know," Lucy, the group's mother hen, said as Caleb rounded the front of the car, his face a mask of relief.

"It's cool, Luce," Caleb said, getting into the front seat.

"Oh, it's cool?" she said, rolling her eyes. "Well, all right, then. Why didn't you say so?"

"I'll keep him safe," Scott assured her, revving the engine. "When you tell them what happened, leave out the stuff that sounds insane. See you all soon."

Without waiting for further discussion, Scott punched the accelerator. As we drove away, flames appeared in the windows of the neighbouring houses—set alight, I presumed, by wayward fireballs during the attack. The occupants could be seen fleeing out the front doors of their homes, distraught and dishevelled.

Across the street, more neighbours were stepping out their front doors, pointing at the burning houses in alarm.

Scott turned on the windshield wipers as we drove away, clearing the snow that had accumulated as it sat idling. He left them oscillating as the snow continued to slowly fall. Caleb held his hand out the window, catching a few flakes on his outstretched palm. "I've never seen snow before," he said, studying his hand. "Did you do this, Shivurr?"

"Yeah, I think so," I said from the back seat. Tired and thirsty after the battle and emotionally drained, I lay back in my seat and stared out the window as we drove away. As we turned east, a half block on, several fire trucks, red lights flashing and sirens blaring, passed us by going the opposite direction.

Chapter 17

Never Heard of Her

I woke standing upright in complete darkness, disoriented, surrounded by a persistent hum and flow of chilly air blowing from unseen fans that rattled somewhere close by. I stumbled forward cautiously, unable to see my hand in front of my face. Something fell over with a crash as I moved. I stumbled over it, shouting. My outstretched hands smacked hard against a cold metal surface. I kept my feet, but my nose hit the obstruction hard enough to make my eyes water. Shaking my head, I ran my hands along the surface, trying to identify it.

A door, I thought, remembering as the last vestiges of sleep washed away.

I leaned against it, but it refused to move. I pounded the stainless steel with sweaty palms, feeling flushed.

I'm locked in, I thought, biting my lip. *Easy, Shivurr, take your time; think it through.*

Taking a deep breath, I ran my hands over the surface feeling for a door handle or latch and smiled as my right hand encountered a large rubber knob. I pushed it hard and the door swung wide, revealing a small kitchen.

The kitchen was quiet, illuminated by only the light coming from the round window of a swinging door on my right. A few deep fryers sat cold and empty next to a small stove and oven. I glanced back and saw packages of frozen hamburger buns lying on the floor of the freezer that I'd just left. I picked them up and restacked them, then pushed the door shut with a click. Smacking my hands together, I strode to the nearby door, pushed it open, and walked through.

"What do you mean, you've never heard of her?" Scott was

saying as I entered. He bobbed his head at me in greeting, then looked away, stretching the long coiled cord behind him.

Fully awake now, I remembered that we were in a video arcade on the other side of town. It was closed to the public for the rest of the month. The proprietor—a friend of Scott's—had left on vacation days earlier and had entrusted him with the key. His friend did not, as Scott put it, trust his employees to not rob him blind or burn it to the ground while he was away, so he opted to shut it down instead. Apparently, it was a slow time of the year and business wouldn't pick up again for a few weeks anyway.

Most of the machines were off, as one might expect, but the computer scientist had turned on a few of them so Caleb could occupy himself. The teen was doing just that as I entered, so deeply entranced in a game of Galaga that he didn't appear to notice my arrival. Rather than disturb him, and wanting some quiet time before engaging in conversation, I shuffled over to the lounge area that lay on my right and sat down to wait.

Complete with comfy sofas and chairs and a few low-lying tables, it was presumably there to allow gamers to relax and recover between games, or to wait for their food to be ready. A row of vending machines hummed nearby, offering a variety of sodas, chocolate bars, chips and other snacks.

I picked up one of the open soda cans that lay on the low-lying table, shook it, put it down, then moved on to the next. I grinned when the third can sloshed agreeably. Tepid and flat; I drank it anyway.

When we'd first arrived, I'd grabbed armfuls of them from one of the soda machines, supplied with quarters by Scott, who'd slipped a twenty-dollar bill into one of the change machines that were distributed throughout the place. Spent from the clash with fire elementals, I'd shotgunned the first two, gulped the next, and sipped the last one before stumbling off to sleep in the walk-in cooler.

There wasn't enough room to lie down, so I'd just leaned against a stack of crates and drifted off to sleep. How long I'd been out, I wasn't sure. Usually sleep's just something I do when

I'm bored, but after days in the desert hotbox, monster fights, and taking both barrels of a shotgun to the stomach, I felt like mush. The freezer did me some serious good, though. I felt a lot better. The full body ache that I'd entered the cooler with had faded to a dull throb.

"Olivia…Schmidt," Scott said into the phone handset. "Tall, dark hair, looks like she could audition for Wonder Woman. Like I said, she's a blackjack dealer there. She's been there for years." He paused, shaking his head, listening. "Is there another Golden Nugget?… All right, thanks anyway." He hung up, furrowing his brow. "Well, that's weird," Scott said, looking at me.

"What's that?" I asked, sitting up.

"I was trying to call Olivia at work. No one seems to know who she is."

I crushed the pop can that I'd been holding. "Probably someone that just started working there."

"Yeah, maybe," Scott sighed. He jabbed the phone book with his finger. "I spoke to three different people, though. Waited on hold for twenty minutes for the pit boss. That was him just now. It doesn't make any sense."

He rubbed his face and yawned. "I'm going to have to drive over there and look for her."

"How long has she worked there?"

"Since I met them both," Scott replied. He removed his eyeglasses and began polishing them with his shirt. "They moved to the neighbourhood a few years ago…" He paused, staring into space. "Must be about five years now, I think. I remember them both stopping by to introduce themselves; same day the moving trucks showed up. Awesome people. Both of them. You don't see much of that anymore, especially not in Vegas. Most people are too caught up in their own stuff to bother being friendly. These days, you say hi to some people and they just keep walking. Ignorant, man."

He walked over to join me and took a seat on the sofa across from mine.

"Anyway, we hit it off right away, both Wil and I being computer geeks, gamers and sci-fi fans," Scott said. "I helped him set up Olympus, the bulletin board system. Even gave him some old equipment for it. Then he started having weekly D&D sessions with some friends of his from around town. One of the regulars owns this place, in fact." He waved a hand at the machines around the room. "I made a lot of friends that way."

"Sounds cool," I said.

"Yeah, and they'd throw regular parties for the neighbours, too. People liked their pool, and free booze. Man, he could drink beer all afternoon and still seem totally sober. I'd be falling on my face if I drank half what he did."

"Sounds expensive. The parties, I mean, not the booze; well, maybe the booze, too." *Is alcohol expensive?* I wondered.

"Wil always seemed to have money. He must have charged a lot for his work. He didn't seem to work often. Course, I suppose he was a bit of a night owl. Maybe that's when he got things done."

"I didn't know him all that long, but he was a good friend," I said softly. "He took a substantial risk coming with me to get back the kids' cash the other night. And the way he and Olivia welcomed us into their home, six total strangers, one looking like me…I don't think many people would have done that. I'll never forget him for that. I just wish I could have known him longer."

"I still can't believe it," Scott said. "I don't know how I'm going to tell Olivia. I'm kind of relieved I couldn't reach her."

Scott looked over at Caleb, frantically tapping the fire button and yanking the joystick of the video game. His long hair whipped the air as he threw his entire body into it, like he was surfing. "I'll try calling home. Maybe the kids are there by now, or left a message," he said, picking up the handset and punching buttons.

"Okay," I replied, heading for the vending machines. "I'm going to get another soda."

The cold can felt good in my hand, soothing. I cracked it with a hiss and took a gulp, shivering as the cool liquid bubbled down my throat. Belching softly, I wandered over to see Caleb's progress in his battle against alien forces. He had just over sixty thousand points, and a few lives left, so he was doing pretty well.

He dipped his head in greeting but remained focused on the game.

"Not bad, dude," I said. "Mind if I take next game?"

"Sure," he replied, glancing at me. "You any good?"

"Never played before," I replied, slipping a quarter onto the glass above the console.

"Oh, sure," Caleb said, giving me a sidelong glance. "Sounds like you're hustling me, dude."

"Hey, are you guys there? Pick up the phone if you're there," Scott said into the phone's handset over by the counter. "No answer," he muttered a few seconds later. He kept the receiver to his ear and stabbed the buttons on the phone base. "No messages, either." He slapped the phone back into its cradle and walked over to join us. "I'll try again in a bit. Guess they're not there yet."

We watched Caleb's game until his last starship blew up. I took over. Five minutes later, Game Over flashed on the screen.

"Okay, maybe you haven't played before," Caleb said, snickering.

I stepped back to let Scott have a turn. A solid player, he fell into an easy rhythm and played for a while before yielding the joystick. "I'm going to call again," he said, slapping Caleb on the shoulder.

The teen leaped to take his place, managing to take over without losing a life. Tired of watching, I plunked a quarter into the Ms. Pac-Man machine next to him and started chomping pellets.

"Hey, Lucy," Scott said in a stage voice. "You guys made it. Did the cops give you any trouble?…Good, that's good.…Uh-huh.…Yeah, sure, makes sense.…" He paused, listening, then said, "Well, make yourselves comfortable. Help yourselves to whatever's in the fridge, if you're hungry.…Yeah, we're all good here.…Yeah, he's having a blast. Did you see anything suspicious? Any cars on the street that shouldn't be?…Oh, they did? Cool. That's good. I figured I'd be parking on the street.…Let's talk about that when we get there.…We'll be there in a few hours; I've got to run an errand first.…Uh, sure, one sec. Caleb," Scott called. "Phone for you."

The teen looked up, then back at his game. "I've got it," I said, grabbing the joystick. He ran over to the counter, hair streaming behind him, and took the handset from Scott's outstretched hand.

"Be right back. I've got to take a whiz," Scott said, heading for the washroom down a short hall leading to the back of the building.

"Hey, Luce," Caleb said. "Yeah, it's cool....Yeah, he's good...." I soon tuned out, focusing on the game, as my last Ms. Pac-Man died next to me.

A few minutes later, Scott returned from the washroom, jingling his car keys. "I'm going to the casino to find Olivia," he said, looking like he'd just taken a bite of a lemon. "I should be back in an hour or so."

"Shouldn't we go with you?" I asked, tapping the fire button rapidly and glancing at him.

"No, safer if you guys stay here," he said over his shoulder, walking away. "Relax, stay hydrated. We'll head to my place when I get back." He waved goodbye to Caleb, still yapping on the phone, and strode toward the back exit, where he'd left the Mustang. The back door slammed, and the Mustang drove away moments later.

"What's going on? Luce? Lucy?" Caleb said. My starship exploded, but I barely noticed. I pushed back from the cabinet and rushed to the counter. Caleb lowered the phone receiver as I joined him, his face white as snow. The phone line hummed, disconnected.

Chapter 18

The Wrong House

"Something's wrong. It sounded like Lucy was fighting with someone. She was yelling, saying for them to let her go."

"The police, maybe?" I asked.

He shrugged helplessly, eyes wide. "I don't know. Maybe."

"We've got to get over there," I said.

He looked dubious. "How? Didn't Scott leave? Where'd he go, anyway?"

"He went to look for Olivia. Said he'd be back in an hour."

"That's too long." Caleb slapped the counter. "Damn it."

I rubbed my face and slapped my cheeks. *We can run over there, but I don't know the way*, I thought. *I should have stayed awake on the drive over.*

Travelling on foot would take a while even if I had a clue which way to go, and wandering the streets, even at night, was a sure way to be spotted. We could wait for Scott to get back, but that might be an hour or more, and our friends might not have that much time.

"We need transportation," I said. I looked out at the street through the large glass windows at the front of the arcade. "Can you hotwire a car?"

"Uh-uh," Caleb replied. "What about a cab?"

"Maybe," I said. "Do you have cash?"

"Sure do," Caleb said. "What you got back for us from those casino dicks." He reached for the yellow pages and began flipping through them rapidly.

"Come on, Caleb, hurry."

"Not helping, dude," Caleb said, practically ripping the pages as he flipped through them. "Give me a break. Brad and Lucy usually take care of this stuff." Finding the page he was searching for, he began dialing.

Less than ten minutes later, a cab pulled up in front of the arcade. Caleb and I ran to it from a nearby alley and hopped in. I kept my jacket zipped tight with the hood pulled forward to hide my face and used Caleb as a screen as I slipped inside. As agreed, Caleb did the talking. With no way to contact Scott, we'd left notes on the counter and stuck to the Galaga machine's screen, telling him where we'd gone.

The taxicab stopped a few houses north of the Schmidts' so that we could walk the rest of the way to Scott's and scope things out. Caleb paid the cab driver as I got out and waited at the rear of the vehicle. The street was deserted, dark except for the occasional streetlight. Only the bark of a dog a few blocks away disturbed the silence.

As the cab drove away, Caleb cupped his hands over his face and lit a marijuana cigarette. He sighed, and I coughed as he expelled a thick cloud of smoke.

"Seriously, Caleb?" I said, wrinkling my nose, edging away from him. "You need to stay alert."

"I've got to mellow out, dude," he said, taking another puff. He held out his free hand, palm down. "Look at my hands. I can't stop them from shaking."

I shook my head but said nothing. We walked in silence. Caleb continued to smoke, and I scanned ahead, moving my head like a gun turret, looking for trouble.

A short walk later, the Schmidts' residence, site of the too-fresh tragedy, lay to our right. The fire was out, as were the flames in the neighbouring buildings, and the house sat completely dark. In the dim light, it looked almost undamaged, if you ignored the broken windows, smashed front door, and blackened stucco.

I stared at it, my head hanging low, reliving the events, only a few hours old. *I should have been faster. If I'd gotten there sooner, maybe they'd still be alive.*

A flash of light in my peripheral vision drew my gaze north.

A police car pulled onto the street from the intersection a few blocks away, rolling forward like a cat on the prowl.

"Cops," I hissed. I raced up the driveway, ducking low. Reaching the Schmidts' front steps, I gripped the side of the attached garage and peered around its edge. Too late, I realized that Caleb wasn't with me.

Turning, I spotted him fifty feet farther south.

Damn, he must have kept walking when I stopped.

Finally, he turned to look back. His face shone white in the glare of the approaching headlights, a lit joint hanging precariously from his lips. He snatched it from his mouth and held it behind his back.

Don't run, I thought, *maybe they'll just drive by.*

He bolted.

The red and blue lights of the patrol car blazed to life, and the siren bleated a brief warning. "Don't you run from me," said a voice over the car's loudspeaker as it swept past my hiding spot.

I clenched my fists and banged them together like cymbals. Caleb flicked his joint to the ground and pulled up short. He raised his hands but didn't turn around.

They're going to arrest him. This is bad.

I shot from my hiding spot as if from a cannon, rushed to the end of the Schmidts' driveway and launched a frost ball at the back window of the cop car. It tore through the air, a streak of white light, and crashed into the patrol car's rear window, shattering it with a loud crash. Shouts and swears erupted from within. The vehicle's rear lights ignited as the driver threw it into reverse and squealed the tires, barrelling it in my direction.

I scurried back up the driveway. Leaping onto the landing at the top of the steps, I pushed open the broken front door and entered the ruin as the police car screeched to a halt outside.

I slid along the wall to the living room window and peered around its edge. A floodlight blazed to life at the side of the car, lighting up the front door.

"Come on out," said the same voice as before over the car's loudspeaker. "Don't make us come in after you, asshole."

Oh, very nice. Who're you calling asshole, asshole?

I looked around, taking a deep breath. The air felt moist. The floors and walls still dripped from the efforts of the firefighters. The only illumination came from outside, through the shattered living room window, casting long shadows and hiding the corners in darkness. The charred remains of furniture huddled at the edges of the room, identifiable more by their position than their appearance. The sofa was just metal springs and wiring stretched across the carbonized wooden frame. Tatters of fabric hung from it, somehow having survived the inferno.

It felt weird seeing the house in this state, so unlike the place of happiness and safety it had seemed earlier the same day. I felt like an invader, a tomb raider, entering a mausoleum, disturbing newborn ghosts.

Just great, Caleb, I thought. *This must be why they call it dope.* Our friends were still missing and now the two of us were separated, and the police had me trapped. *You'd better be hiding, kid.*

I took a deep breath, feeling the knot between my shoulders loosen. *He's a good kid. Just a bit unreliable.* I should have kept a closer eye on him, not let my grief distract me.

The passenger door of the police car swung open and a figure emerged. A police officer approached the house, his hand hovering over his hip. I pulled back from the window and stepped toward the rear of the house. My head snapped to the right, hearing one of the garage doors trundling open, muffled but audible through the walls. The rumble of a motorcycle followed.

I crept back to the window and looked out as a darkly dressed figure straddling a Ducati flew down the driveway, sending the cop scrambling to the side. The bike fishtailed as the rider turned onto the street, and its back wheel tapped the tail end of the idling cruiser before roaring away to the north.

The driver of the patrol car reversed into the driveway as his partner picked himself off the pavement and jumped into the passenger seat. Seconds later, the vehicle's sirens blared and rooftop lights blazed as the police tore away after the fleeing motorcyclist, leaving crumbs of shattered glass in their wake.

Who the hell was that?

Whoever it was had come from *inside* the Schmidts' garage. Thinking back, I remembered a Ducati parked in front of the Trans Am when we'd first arrived at the Schmidts' domicile a few days before.

Must be a motorcycle thief, fleeing the scene of the crime.

It made sense. A smart criminal watching the news about the recent fires might see a chance to loot in the aftermath, suspecting that there might be undamaged property unguarded and ripe for the taking.

Not cool, dirtbag, but thanks for leading the cops away. I hope they catch you though.

A door thumped shut somewhere in the house as I turned the doorknob to leave. I froze, clamping a hand over my mouth, stifling a yelp.

The motorcycle thief must have a partner still searching the house for plunder, or hiding while his crony fled the scene. Wilhelm's body had barely cooled, and vultures were already picking through the aftermath.

I narrowed my eyes. *You picked the wrong house, pal.*

I still had to find Caleb but figured he'd made it to Scott's by now. After a short detour to deliver a little street justice, I'd be there, and we'd either find our friends or figure out what had happened to them.

I inched the doorknob back to its default position before letting go. The sound had come from the back of the house, so I held my breath and slid along the hallway like a phantom.

Burned and charred like the rest of the home, the rec room was almost unrecognizable in the dim light entering through the broken windows. It was also unoccupied.

I shuffled around the edge, looking for signs of the intruder. A sliver of light bleeding from the floor near the room's centre drew my attention. I squinted, moving closer, then realized what I was looking at.

A trap door. What's a trap door doing in the middle of the house?

I remembered the spot. Yesterday, a large wooden table covered in D&D books and papers had sat over its position. The table's remains, broken and burned, now lay a few feet away, partially covered with charred carpeting pulled back from the floor. The fire must have burned away enough of the rug that had covered the trap door for the thief to spot it.

He must be down there.

I made my body glow and ran my finger along the trap door's thin seam. It blended so well into the surrounding floor that I'd probably have missed it if not for the light seeping through into the dark room.

This guy must have sharp eyes, I thought. *Did the Schmidts even know it was here? And where does it lead?*

Wilhelm had said they'd moved in five years ago, but the house was older than that. Scott had once told me that basements are a rarity in Las Vegas homes. In colder regions, he'd explained, house foundations need to be below the frost line, or the frost/thaw cycle pushes them out of the ground over time. The ground doesn't freeze in Vegas, though, so footings don't need to be deep, making basements an extra expense rather than a necessity. If people want extra space, they build out or up, not down.

Probably not a basement, then, I thought.

I moved to the hinge side so that the trap door would shield me from view when the burglar exited, doused my inner light, and waited.

I lingered patiently for about sixty seconds before I started to worry about Caleb. I'd convinced myself that he'd made his way to Scott's, but what if someone had waited for him there? They might have taken him too, or maybe he was hiding in a nearby yard, waiting for me to find him.

Torn between two desires, I looked around for something heavy to lay over the hatch. If I could trap the prowler inside, I'd go find the kid, and we could call the police on this guy. The ruined sofa didn't look heavy enough, but a nearby bookshelf added to it might just do the trick, if I could slide them across the floor before the crook escaped.

Shuffling over to the sofa, I prepared to lean into it when the room brightened. My eyes snapped to the source as the trap door separated from the floor. I froze, gripping the sofa's back in my hands. My whole body trembled with nervous energy.

The burglar held the trap door as he exited, keeping it from falling over and crashing to the floor. He turned to lower the door back into place while I conjured frost, reaching back like a baseball pitcher. The prowler's head turned toward me as I hurled it at him. He blurred to his right milliseconds before the bolt of frost brushed past his left shoulder. It crashed into the far wall and the trap door hammered closed a moment later.

"Shivurr, what the hell, man?" demanded the intruder. "It's me, Wilhelm."

Chapter 19

No More Secrets

"Wil?" I said, covering my mouth as my jaw dropped. "You're alive? You're alive." I rushed across the floor, lighting up my body to better see him. "I thought you were dead—that the fire got you." I grabbed him in a bear hug and pounded his back, then let him go, with my eyes still popping out of my head. "What about Bear? Is he okay? Tell me he's okay."

Wilhelm held up both hands, motioning for me to calm down. "Easy, Shivurr. He's fine. He's totally fine."

"But I saw him on fire. It was…" I paused, looking down at the floor. "Is that how you survived?" It made sense. He must have grabbed Bear and, seeing no way out through the flames, fled below.

Wilhelm looked uncomfortable, rubbing the back of his neck. "Well, not exactly. Look, let's talk about this downstairs." He pulled the trap door open again and moved to the side, motioning me in with his other hand.

Stairs led down into the depths, with rough stone walls lining either side. Instead of a simple ladder into the subfloor, it looked more like the entrance to a castle dungeon.

"Uh, I've got to find Caleb first," I said, taking a step back, eyeing the void. "He's out there somewhere."

Wilhelm paused, looking thoughtful. "Olivia's going to look for Caleb. Don't worry, she'll find him and bring him here."

"Olivia? Where is she? Was that her on the motorcycle?"

He nodded. "She's just got to lose the police first."

"It's not just Caleb that I'm worried about," I said. "Something happened at Scott's. I think the others may have been taken."

They're not tied up under the house, are they? I thought.

"What do you mean, taken?"

I told him about our decision to split up, how the gang hadn't wanted to leave the scene without first speaking to the police, then how we'd hid out at the arcade and tried to call Olivia.

"Weird thing is no one there's heard of her." Wilhelm looked uncomfortable. "You don't seem all that surprised." He shrugged but said nothing. "Anyway, after Scott took off, Caleb was talking to Lucy. She started shouting, there was a struggle, then the call disconnected. We were totally freaking out. With Scott gone to look for Olivia, we called a cab and here we are. You seem to know the rest. I guess you were watching what happened with the cops."

Wilhelm's forehead wrinkled and he rubbed his goatee. "Hmm, that's not good," he said, sighing.

"Damn right it isn't," I said. "Look, I've got a lot of questions, but I've got to get over there. I'll be back as soon as I can." I turned to leave.

"Wait," Wilhelm said. "I might be able to help. Give me a minute." Still holding the trap door with his right hand, he held up his left, extending his index finger skyward like he was testing for a breeze. He froze like a department store mannequin and stared at the floor, a faraway expression on his face, like he was looking beyond it, as if through a glass window.

After ten seconds without any word or gesture, I couldn't keep my mouth shut any longer. "Quit playing around, Wilhelm." My bearded friend didn't respond, still holding up a finger. I crept closer and extended a hand to touch him like testing a stove top to see if it's hot. "Hello?" Still no response.

I counted to ten Mississippi, then snapped my fingers by his right ear. "Hello? What is this, Wilhelm? You there?"

His hand moved like a Cobra strike and clutched mine as his head swivelled to regard me. He let go as I pulled away. I stumbled, flailing my arms as I backpedalled. Catching my balance, I reached for the Underfrost.

"Easy, buddy," Wilhelm said, holding up his hands in the

universal sign of surrender. "Caleb's fine. He's with Olivia. She's going to Scott's now to look for the rest of the gang. If they're there, she'll find them. If they aren't, she'll let us know what she finds. There's nothing more you can do now to help them."

"How do you know that? What was that? Were you using some kind of radio?"

"I can explain. There's a lot of stuff I need to tell you. Let's talk while we wait. Some of this you may not want the others to hear. I'll let you decide that." He motioned at the staircase again.

I stretched my neck and looked at the steps like a pool of piranhas swam inside. "It's me, man. Bandit," he said, referencing last night's adventure. "Trust me."

I cocked an eye at him. "Can't we just talk here?"

He looked around, smiling wryly. "Not the best place for a chat anymore," he said softly. "We'll be a lot more comfortable down there."

"You first," I said. I grabbed the trap door and made a sweeping gesture with my other hand.

Wilhelm began to descend. I followed a moment later, pulling the trap door shut behind me. The light coming from below made my own redundant, so I shut it off.

"So, why doesn't anyone at Olivia's work know who she is?"

He looked back, sheepishly. "Patience, man. I'll explain everything when we're settled."

The stairs descended twenty feet into the earth, turned a corner, ending at an open doorway.

"Welcome to our inner sanctum," Wilhelm said, stepping to the side and sweeping his arm like a circus ringmaster.

Tentatively, I stepped through the portal into the room beyond. It was a thousand square feet of comfortable living space. Immediately in front of us, plush furniture—sofas, easy chairs, and footrests—gathered around a large glass coffee table. A large TV and VCR sat near the wall closest to us, next to a well-stocked bar, filled with liquor of all varieties, and a full-size fridge. Off to the right, large speakers bookended a stereo system that included a cassette player, record player, receiver and other electronics that I didn't recognize. Stacks of albums and cassettes lined the walls to both sides. On the left, about twenty feet away, I could see a line of several arcade game cabinets nestled in a far corner. The outer walls of the space were stone, and the inner walls drywall, painted simple white. The ceiling was surprisingly high, perhaps ten feet overhead, despite giving up some room for pipes, wiring and ductwork; far higher than your usual basement—or even aboveground floors of a typical home.

"This place is huge. It must have cost a fortune."

He nodded. "I know a guy."

"Why do you have this place?" I did a full turn, taking it in. "Your house is already big."

"Privacy and security, mostly," Wilhelm said, taking a seat on a large L-shaped sofa. The BBS SysOp gestured to the bright red easy chair that sat at the edge of the sitting area before us. "Have a seat, Shivurr."

I remained standing, arms crossed, with a stern look on my face. "Who are you, man? How did you survive the fire? Why do…quit smiling. This isn't funny. I thought you were dead. I thought Bear was dead. Brad, Alan, Lucy and Lilith are missing. You've got a freaking magical tree living in your backyard and fighting alongside some green armoured ghost against fire elementals from who knows where. You're not just a computer programmer or SysOp. Is Wilhelm even your name?"

"Relax, man. I'll tell you everything," Wilhelm said. "There will be no more secrets between us."

He stood and walked over to the bar. Grabbing a crystal tumbler, he dropped in a few ice cubes from an ice bucket, poured a generous portion of a dark liquid into it, then added cola from an already opened can.

He took a sip. "Rum and Coke? No? How about just a Coke?" I inclined my head, and he grabbed a second glass, filled it to the brim with ice, then cracked a fresh cola pulled from the small fridge under the wet bar and poured it in. I took the beverage and open can from him and drank. Wilhelm did the same, then sat down. I joined him.

"To answer your last question first, Wilhelm is my name, but it's one of many. You first knew me by another name."

"Huh? What are you talking about, Wilhelm?"

"Boreas. My 'real' name is Boreas, but I've gone by Wilhelm for a while now."

"Your SysOp handle? No kidding. Of course I knew you by that first."

"Yeah, but you knew me as Boreas for a lot longer. From before you lost your memory," Wilhelm said gently. "We're friends, Shivurr. We've been so for many years."

I threw back the tumbler and drained the last of the soda, then poured in the rest of the can. I placed the empty on the glass end table next to the chair, stalling for time to think.

With my messed-up memory, I didn't know what to believe. Anything was possible. We'd always seemed to get along like old friends, even before meeting in person. And few people would have joined a raid on the casino guard's house for someone they knew only through a BBS, risking their life and freedom.

"I think I believe you. And Olivia?"

"Her too, though not as long. You knew her as Orithyia, back in the day."

"So, our meeting through the BBS—it wasn't a coincidence, was it?"

"Nope, Orithyia and I orchestrated that. After you went missing, it took us a few years to figure out where you were, then a few more to put the pieces into place to rescue you."

"Scott is in on this, isn't he? I knew him before, too."

Wilhelm shook his head. "Uh-uh. Well, not exactly. Scott is as he appears to be. He doesn't know Orithyia's or my true identity," he said, taking a sip of his drink. "When we knew where you were and who held you, we knew we had to proceed with great care. Once we located you, we started surveilling people leaving the Institute and made plans to bust you out. We identified Scott as the most likely to be helpful in our endeavour. New to the Institute at the time, he was less likely to feel much loyalty to them, so we figured out where he lived and bought a house nearby. The owner wasn't looking to sell, but our generous offer convinced him, eventually. Well, that and a few seemingly supernatural occurrences. After that, we made sure to introduce ourselves and set our plan in motion. It depended on Scott becoming friends with you, of course, which was something we managed to encourage, after getting him to confide in us."

"Seems like a bit of a dirty trick."

"I didn't feel great about it, but it was our best option. Remember, when we started out, he was just another Bodhi Group employee, imprisoning a friend of ours—against his will, we believed, and later confirmed. Scott has become a good friend, and it hasn't been easy, but I think he'd ultimately forgive us, as he's exceptionally fond of you. Anyway, at our urging, he investigated where they were holding you and found you. It was my suggestion that he set up the system to allow you to connect to the BBS, so we could converse."

I looked at the ceiling. "I guess Olympus is dead now. The computers must have burned up in the fire."

"It lives on in spirit," Wilhelm said. "But maybe I'll restore it from backup in the coming days. I've got extra hardware down here, but it would be too suspicious if it went back up right after the fire that destroyed the house. I made some good contacts through it, which I wouldn't want to lose. I'll probably log on to a few other BBSs that my members frequent and get the word out about what happened, let them know that Olympus will rise again." He took a deep breath and continued with his story. "I knew from what Scott had told me that you'd lost your memory, so when we finally met, virtually, I couldn't just explain everything. I didn't think you'd believe me, or I thought you'd say something to Scott, and I'd lose his trust. Plus, I couldn't be sure that Scott's relay system was as secure as he claimed."

I rolled an ice cube around in my mouth, sucking it slowly, as I took this in. "Scott said you moved in five years ago," I said, narrowing my eyes. "You're telling me you've spent the last five years trying to get me out? That's a long time. We must have been really good friends."

He shrugged, swirling his glass. "We're nothing if not patient. And, yes, we were and are pals."

"Okay, I can accept that. It helps explain a lot, but there are still a lot of unanswered questions. Why doesn't anyone at

Olivia's…uh, Orithyia's work know who she is?"

"Keep calling us Wilhelm and Olivia, even in private; it's too easy to slip up at the wrong time if you don't. To answer your question, that's easy. She doesn't work there; she never did," he said, grinning. "That was just our cover story. Neither of us need to work. We've got substantial resources at our disposal."

"What about Bear? Where is he?" I asked, looking around the room. "You said he was fine, right?"

"Right, he's fine, or will be."

"You're going to have to explain that one," I said, scratching my head. "Where is he now?"

"Recuperating. The battle took a toll on him," Wilhelm explained. "He got hurt, but he's tough; he'll be okay."

"I know, I saw him. He was on *fire*."

"Yeah, he was pretty agitated about that," Wilhelm said. "I was worried, so I brought him down here, then started fire-fighting."

I paused, thinking. "I didn't see you there."

"No, you saw me," Wilhelm insisted. "You just didn't know who you were looking at."

Understanding dawned, and I said, "Were you the spectre or the oak tree?"

Wilhelm winked and pointed a finger at me. He made an approving sound and said, "Now you're getting it. The oak is an old friend. Don't look so shocked, man. There's more to this world than you know, or at least than you now remember."

"And Olivia? If she wasn't at work, where was she?"

"She was on a mission and too far away when those things showed up. She didn't get back until just before you got here."

I waggled my empty glass and tilted my head toward the bar, looking at Wilhelm.

"Sure, man," he said, bobbing his head. "Help yourself. No need to ask."

I topped up the ice in my glass and popped another in my mouth for good measure before returning to the plush recliner. Wilhelm sat back and closed his eyes until I retook my seat.

"She'd just gotten home when you showed up with the police

in tow," he continued. "When it looked like the police were going to come in, she decided to lead them away."

"Why didn't you tell me who you were when we met the first
time? The other day, I mean."

Wilhelm placed his glass on the coffee table and put his feet
up next to it. "I couldn't—not with the kids there. There wasn't
really an appropriate time otherwise. I was hoping you'd start to
remember me on your own over time, the more we hung out.
You haven't, though, have you?"

I shook my head and took off my hat. "Just dreams and visions, mostly."

"Nice hat," Wilhelm noted. "Looks military. How'd you
come by it?"

"I took it from a guard at the Bodhi Institute when I escaped," I said.

"And the winter jacket?"

I looked down. "This? I stole it from a chamber in the desert." Seeing no point in keeping it to myself any longer, I told
him about the Great Basin Desert cavern, revealing what I'd held
back when we'd first met. "The Bodhi Group scientists wore
them in the chamber. It was cold in there, for them anyway." I
jiggled the jacket's zipper, pulled it down, and reached inside,
grabbing the other vial Scott had given me.

I held it up for Wilhelm to see. His eyes widened and his jaw
dropped. "Where did you get that?" He jumped from his seat
and came closer, keeping his eyes on the iridescent substance
within.

"From Scott," I said, staring at the swirl of colours and light
within. "He liberated it for me; he snuck into the restricted area
after I escaped."

"You know what that is, right?"

"Tissue samples stolen from me. Scott took this one from
the Institute." I held it to my chest. "It needs to be kept below
zero or it disappears. At least, that's what Scott said."

"He's right," Wilhelm said. "Why haven't you swallowed it
yet?"

"I drank one already, but it messed me up. I figured I'd wait before drinking this one."

"Did it help?" Wilhelm asked. "Do you remember anything new?"

"Not really. I just saw fragments of some pretty freaky stuff. It was a lot like earlier tonight, now that I think about it."

"Maybe you should drink this one too. It might help you get back more memories or your powers."

"Scott said the same thing, but what else could there be? I've *got* powers," I said, looking at him. "You saw me."

"Sure," Wilhelm said. "It's what you didn't do that interested me more. You're a caterpillar, Shivurr—waiting to turn back into a butterfly. You've either forgotten some things or maybe can't do them anymore. Maybe the Bodhi Group did it deliberately to weaken you, make it easier to keep you confined, or maybe it was an accident. We're not really sure."

"Okay, why not?" I pulled the stopper from the vial with a faint popping sound. "Here goes." I tossed my head back, up-ending the vial, and pouring its contents into my gaping mouth. I tapped the bottom of the vial and gave it a shake, coaxing the remainder out. By the count of five, I felt dizzy and slumped forward in my seat. Wilhelm lunged, putting a hand on my chest to catch me as I passed out.

Sometime later, the fog of sleep receded. I heard Wilhelm's voice calling to me.

"Oh, good," Wilhelm said. "You freaked me out there, man."

"How long was I out?"

"A few minutes, I think. Not more than five." He extended a hand. "Let me help you up. Do you want another soda?"

I nodded wearily, retaking my seat in the plush chair. I held my head, rubbing away residual bleariness. Wilhelm held out a fresh glass, filled to the brim with ice and dark soda, just the way I like it. I thanked him and gulped it down, ice and all.

"Do you feel any different?"

"Not really. It was different this time," I said. I felt better, no longer dizzy—my energy restored by the soda and ice.

Aside from that, I don't feel all that different.

Then lights started clicking on in rooms in my head that my

brain hadn't known existed. Suddenly, I knew things that I hadn't known before, fully and completely. If I hadn't already been sitting down, I'd have fallen.

I closed my eyes and grabbed the chair's armrest with my free hand as Wilhelm stooped to take the empty glass. I sank back in my chair and tried to slow my breathing like Emmett had taught me.

That's it, Shivurr. Breathe in slowly, deeply from the diaphragm, hold a moment, and let it out.

Wilhelm was right. I *was* capable of more than I knew.

Flash.

I saw myself walking, impossibly, on wisps of frost through thin air.

Flash.

I was lying prone in some laboratory, at the Institute. Masked faces leaned over me, holding nasty-looking utensils near my head, ignoring my pleas to be released.

Flash.

I was on a windswept glacier that stretched into the distance as far as the eye could see, heading for a wide crevice where the ice split in two, creating the entrance to a cave.

Flash.

I was on a sandy beach bordering a beautiful blue sea, with waves crashing on the shoreline to my right, as I channelled the pure energy of the Underfrost, shaping it into a sphere, enclosing my body in a protective shield.

Flash.

I was racing a foot above the ground atop a frozen disc of ice and snow down a thin trail through a rainforest as a deluge of rainfall pounded down in the dark of night, punctuated by occasional lightning strikes.

The flashes stopped as quickly as they started. The recovered memories slipped into place like the corner pieces of an intricate puzzle. They were a start at understanding my past, but not enough by themselves to guess at the larger picture. I put my face in my hands and rubbed and slapped my cheeks, blinking back tears.

Like a kid at Christmas, I wanted to run outside and take my new abilities for a spin.

A shield of frost energy? Holy shit! I think I can find a few uses for that.

In a way, it seemed a bit too easy, acquiring these gifts so effortlessly. One swallow and I had new abilities in their entirety. No training, no sacrifice, no painstaking study and commitment.

But, no, that's not true, I thought. *These abilities are mine by right, by birth, and by toil—stolen property, taken back from the thieves that took them.*

At some point, I had earned them through experimentation and trial and error, and dedicated effort. I might not remember the experiences now, but I'd worked for the results all the same.

I grinned. They'd broken me like a vase, and I'd just glued a few pieces back together.

Chapter 20

Signs of Struggle

"You've remembered something, haven't you?" Wilhelm asked, squinting at me.

I nodded slowly. "I think I'm a bit of a badass," I said smiling and leaning forward in my chair. I gave him a brief rundown of what I now knew I could do.

"That's great," Wilhelm said. "I've seen you do that stuff before. Anything else?"

"Anything else?" I asked. "Uh-uh. Wait, is there more?"

"Yeah, there's more. I'm not sure I knew everything you were capable of, but do you remember how to Frost Walk?"

I thought a moment, concentrating, sifting through my new-found wealth of knowledge, then shook my head. "I remember walking through the air on a carpet of frost. Is that Frost Walking?"

"I can see why you'd think so," Wilhelm said with a crooked smile. "The Frost Walking I'm talking about is something different. If you don't remember it, I'm not sure I can tell you how, but maybe knowing it's possible will be enough to help you figure out how to do it again."

"If I could do this before, why don't I remember it now, though?" I wondered, looking at the empty vial as if it held the answer.

"Didn't Scott say he saw more vials? What you drank must have been only a part of what they took from you. The rest of your memories must still be there. Maybe we can get them back with Scott's help."

"Are you kidding? He can't go back," I said. "They must suspect he helped me. Two agents showed up at his place. They were attacked by those fire elementals, maybe killed, right in his driveway. That's a bit of a red flag, don't you think?"

"Maybe that's related to what Caleb heard over the phone," Wilhelm said, stroking his chin. "We'll see what Olivia finds, then locate Scott and figure this out."

"What's Frost Walking, then? Describe it to me."

"I can only describe it as an observer, but it allowed you to pass through solid objects, like a ghost. You called it Frost Walking. You explained it as crossing partly over to the Underfrost, so that you were in both that world and this one simultaneously. It scared you, though. You said you were afraid of losing yourself to the Underfrost's pull and vanishing into it forever."

I swallowed. "I don't like the sound of that. I don't remember that, though. I've got…" I paused as I heard the trap door opening at the top of the stairs.

Wilhelm looked at the door leading to them. "That's Olivia and Caleb," he said. He stood and walked to the foot of the steps as his statuesque wife and the slight-framed teen emerged into the room. Wilhelm and Olivia embraced, kissing briefly. I gave Caleb a slap on the shoulder and shook my head at him.

He avoided my eyes. "Sorry, Shivurr," he said. "I guess I fucked up."

I cocked an eye at him. "What's with you and the police?"

"Give the kid a break," said Olivia with a smile. She held up a baggy full of green plant matter. "I'm going to keep this safe for now. Next time, try to be a bit more subtle when you see them coming."

"No promises, dude," replied Caleb. "Cops scare the shit out of me."

"Quit calling me dude," Olivia said, shaking her head. "Dude."

He looked around. "Nice digs. Can't believe you had all this extra space. Where's the bathroom? I've got to piss like a racehorse." The teen ran for the door to which Wilhelm pointed, leaving the three of us behind.

"Charming," she said, grinning. "Little shit."

"Does he know your real names?" I asked.

Olivia shook her head. "No, there was no time. I'm not sure we should tell him."

"How'd you explain Wilhelm and Bear surviving the fire?" I asked in a faint voice, holding my right hand to the side of my mouth.

"I told him that they hid down here, and that Bear is at my parents'," she said under her breath. "He bought it. Why wouldn't he, right?"

"What about the others? Were they there?" Wilhelm said nothing. I had the impression he already knew the answer, somehow.

"No, but there were signs of a struggle," Olivia said. She put her motorcycle helmet down on the coffee table. "Sit, please. Wilhelm, my sweet, would you be my hero and fix me a drink?"

"Coming right up," Wilhelm said. He made his way to the bar and got busy, not bothering to ask what she'd like.

Olivia held up a hand. "Easy, Shivurr, honey. I can see you're about to have kittens. I know you must be worried sick. I am too, but let's wait for Caleb. He'll want to hear this too."

"Doesn't he already know?"

"Uh-uh. I told him to stay outside while I went in." Wilhelm handed her a glass filled with bubbly water and a lime hooked over the rim. He collapsed onto the sofa next to her. "Oh, that's tart. I love it." She took another sip and waved, looking over my shoulder. "Would you like something to drink, kid?"

Caleb took a seat in a nearby chair. "No, thanks, du…uh, Olivia."

"Help yourself, if you change your mind," she said, pointing at the bar. "Just stay out of the alcohol. I'm not contributing to the delinquency of a minor."

"So, tell us what you saw," I said. "Was anyone there?"

"No, no one, but the van was still parked in the driveway. Someone kicked in the front door, and the walls were smashed up a bit, too. There's a huge dent in the drywall, like someone fell into it, hard. There was definitely a struggle of some kind."

"What do we do?" Caleb said, squeezing his head with the palms of his hands. He stood and paced around the room.

"We've got to do something."

Wilhelm held up a hand. "Easy, buddy. Take a breath."

"But what if they hurt them?"

"I'll turn myself in," I said softly. "If they let them all go, I'll give myself up."

"Forget that," Wilhelm said, frowning. "We didn't spend the last five years getting you out to simply hand you back over to those people."

"Wil's right," Olivia said, giving me a stern look. "There's no way that's happening."

"It's my choice, guys," I said quietly.

"Just cool your jets, man, before you go falling on your sword," Wilhelm said. "We've got other options. We'll launch a rescue operation."

I shook my head. "There's no way a full-scale assault would work. They've got weapons, attack helicopters, soldiers. I think they've even got a few flamethrowers on hand, just for me. Even if I fought my way inside, they'd still be able to hold them hostage. They might be hurt or even killed."

"Who said anything about that?" Wilhelm said. "I'm thinking about something more covert. You can sneak in."

"I'm not exactly a ninja, Boreas."

"No, but if you can remember or relearn Frost Walking, you'll be better than a ninja. We can drive you close, then you sneak in and get them out. Olivia and Caleb can wait in the getaway van, and I'll come with you to act as lookout and provide support."

"Who's Boreas?" Caleb said.

"It's my BBS handle," Wilhelm said, giving me a look.

"I told you guys that on the drive from Tonopah, Caleb." I jumped in my chair as if electrified. "Oh, man, Scott. We've got to find him—warn him. He's looking for you, Olivia. He still thinks Wilhelm and Bear are…he doesn't know you're all right."

"Shit, you're right," Wilhelm said. "We've got no way to contact him, though."

"We left a note at the arcade," Caleb said.

"What did it say?" Olivia asked.

"That something happened to the gang at his place and we went to look."

Wilhelm looked at his watch. "When was that?"

"Not sure—an hour, hour and a half?"

Wilhelm looked thoughtful for a moment. "He should be back at the arcade soon, if he isn't there already." He hopped to his feet. "I'll try calling there. Maybe I'll get lucky. Olivia, why don't you run over to Scott's and see if he's there? If not, wait there in case he shows up. We'll be there soon."

"Should I come with you, Olivia?" Caleb asked, starting to rise from his chair.

"That's all right," she said. "I'll move faster on my own. Stay here, where it's safe." Without another word, she ascended the stairs and disappeared.

"I'll go make that call," Wilhelm said. "Shivurr, give that rescue some thought. We can drive out to the Bodhi Institute after Scott gets back." He exited through a door behind the sofa, leaving Caleb and me alone. The teen got up and walked around, eventually turning on the TV, which played only static. Presumably whatever line or antenna had once fed it had been damaged in the fire, if it had ever worked.

I lay back and closed my eyes. *All right, brain, what's Frost Walking?* I squeezed my eyes together, concentrating, then stood up and paced back and forth.

The Underfrost is oceans deep, a universe unto itself—an abyss of snow and ice that knows no bounds. Since losing my memories, I'd just been wading at the edge of that water, slapping my hand along the surface to splash targets by the shoreline.

But the potions showed me that I'd once surfed that sea like a phantom of frost. That's the key to surviving it. You've got to skim along the surface. If you don't, you risk being pulled under to drown in its depths, disappearing into its cold embrace forever.

Yet disappearing is exactly what I wanted to do. That is, disappear and pass through solid objects in this world, so I realized that maybe I needed to go deeper and take a metaphorical swim. My hands trembled at the thought, but it made sense. Instead of gliding over the surface, I needed to immerse myself and swim through it, resurfacing back into this dimension at the right time.

I felt sure I could dive in, but far less confident that I could get back out. I'd have to take the chance to free my friends and hope instinct or muscle memory would take over at the right time.

If the Bodhi Group had grabbed them, which seemed almost certain, Dixon would want to question them, and I knew that he probably wouldn't be too gentle about it either. That meant that they'd probably be there at least a day before he'd either release them or ship them somewhere for further questioning or who knew what. I just didn't know which was more likely.

They were just kids, and American citizens, but the Bodhi Group protected its secrets. Instead of letting them go, or disappearing them, the Group might have them arrested on trumped-up charges, ruining or severely damaging their futures. I needed to get them out before that happened; ideally even before the Bodhi Group had a chance to question or identify them. *While I'm at it, maybe I'll make a detour to the vault, too.*

The potions Scott had pilfered had restored some new memories and abilities, but most of them seemed to be of the knowledge and skills variety rather than experiential. I still didn't remember Wilhelm and Olivia further back than a few days ago. Most of the events I did now remember seemed more fragmented—disordered and disconnected in time.

I guessed that the vials contained memories from a different part of my brain (or the equivalent for someone like me). They'd helped make me a bit more myself, but my memory was still mostly gone.

Nice fantasy, I thought. It was going to require a miracle to get in and out with my friends without adding another level of difficulty. I'd try to do both, but if it came down to getting the vials or getting my friends, I'd choose the latter.

"What did Wilhelm mean?" Caleb said, drawing me from my reverie.

"Huh? About what?"

"About spending five years to get you out. I thought you just met him too."

"I did just meet him. Well, sort of. It's complicated. You caught that, eh?"

"Sure, I may blaze up. Doesn't mean I'm stupid."

"I didn't say you were."

"People underestimate me all the time," Caleb said, studying the floor. "I got caught smoking weed with some older kids when I was thirteen. The cops showed up and grabbed me. Word got around. I was just a dumb stoner after that. Teachers started treating me differently. Everyone did."

"That's messed up," I said. "Then why keep smoking it?"

"Don't knock it until you try it, dude," Caleb said.

I shrugged. "I don't know, you might want to think about making a change before it's too late."

"Pretty sure that ship has sailed, Shivurr," Caleb said, looking at his feet. "What were those things?" He pointed at the ceiling. "You know, that started the fire."

"Elementals," Wilhelm said, walking back into the room. "Fire incarnate. Primitive beasts, uncomplicated in their goals. They're like fire itself, or animals, instinctual, unrelenting. Minions of the fire demon that spawned and shaped them from fire and crystals."

"Gnarly," said Caleb, slack-jawed. "How do you know all this stuff?"

Wilhelm smirked. "Dungeons and Dragons."

"Did you get a hold of Scott?" I asked before Caleb could respond.

"No answer. I tried several times. He's probably on his way home. If so, Olivia will find him." Wilhelm held out his hand. "Let me see your hat."

"What for?" I asked, pulling it from my head.

"Before we head over to Scott's, I thought I'd give you a few upgrades," he replied.

"What sort of upgrades?"

He frowned. "Don't make me spoil the surprise." I handed it to him, giving him a sidelong look. "Thanks, I'll be right back."

"He was kidding, right?" Caleb asked, after he'd left. "And

what's a fire demon?"

Chapter 21

Knock, Knock

Wilhelm tossed me my hat like a frisbee, grabbing the brim and giving it a spin. I snatched it from the air as it helicoptered toward me.

"Thanks," I said, looking it over. "What did you do? It doesn't look any different."

"Turn it over," he replied, smiling. "Look inside."

The interior looked unchanged. "I still don't get it, man."

"Hold it out in front of you like a basketball hoop," Wilhelm said. He strode over to the fridge and pulled out a few cans of soda. "That's it, hold it steady."

I shrank back reflexively as Wilhelm tossed one of the containers into the air toward me. I watched it, my arms outstretched, chin wedged into my right shoulder, eyes half-closed, as it arced through the air and into the hat. I tightened my grip, expecting the weight of the can to knock it from my hands, but felt nothing at all.

"Shh-wish," Wilhelm said. "Nothing but net."

I opened my eyes, retracted my arms, and looked within. *It's empty.* My jaw dropped and I held up the cap to show the interior to my friends.

"Wicked," Caleb said. "You a magician, dude?"

Wilhelm swirled his hands as if waving an invisible wand. "Reach inside." I did as he asked, regarding him with a puzzled look. "Deeper."

I kept reaching, still eyeballing him. As I did so, my hand and forearm cooled as if plunged into an ice-cold mountain river. It felt great. I gasped when, up to my elbow in the four-inch-deep hat, my fingers closed around the metal of the can. I withdrew my hand and held up the soda can like a trophy, staring at it with my mouth gaping wide.

Wilhelm beamed, flashing pearly white teeth. "It's bigger on the inside than the outside and doesn't add weight. You can store all the liquid you need in there, and it'll stay nice and frosty."

"Who *are* you, dude?" asked Caleb. "That shit's amazing. You're not a magician. You're a wizard."

He looked at Caleb as he dropped another can inside the up-turned hat. "I suppose you could call it magic, but I call it science. It's cool, though. I'll give you that."

"It doesn't look any different on the inside," I said, staring at the interior. I pushed my hand into it and watched my out-stretched fingers disappear as they reached the cloth, or where the cloth appeared to be. "It's an illusion of some kind."

"Sort of, I suppose. Technically, it's still there, but out of phase, so your hand can pass through it. I've tuned it to you personally, so unless you're touching it, anyone or anything else would hit the cloth and be unable to reach across," explained Wilhelm. "Basically, it's just a hat unless you're touching it."

"This is awesome, Wilhelm," I said, this time being careful to use his alias with Caleb around. The kid obviously knew by now that there was much more to Wilhelm than met the eye, but it seemed better that he learn the full story gradually; it was hard enough for me to digest. "Thank you. Seriously."

"Come on, load it up from the fridge. I'll get some more from storage." He returned a few minutes later with another two cases, and we loaded those in as well. "These are warm, but they'll cool down in there in no time."

"Where do they go? The cans."

"An interdimensional null space," Wilhelm said. "Don't worry, they're not hitting someone's house or anything." He dropped the last can into the hat. "Go ahead. Put it on."

I did so gingerly, half expecting to be hit in the head by a few dozen soda cans. The cap felt completely normal, not the slight-est bit heavier. The only difference seemed to be that my head felt pleasantly cool, as if I were wearing an ice pack on my head.

"Feels good, doesn't it?" Wilhelm said. He grinned. "I guess you could say it's a polar ice cap."

"Whoa, it's blue now," Caleb observed, pointing a finger at my head.

"It's like that mood ring Lilith wears," Wilhelm said, nodding. "Shows how you're doing. It reacts to your physiology and changes colour based on it."

"You're kidding?" I walked over to a large decorative mirror hanging on a nearby wall. The cap, once dark black, was now radiant with the colour of the sky on a cloudless summer day. I adjusted the cap, trying different orientations for the best look. "That's wild. Not the most discreet, though."

"Pfft, right," Wilhelm said, chuckling. "Like it's the hat people will notice when they see you."

I smiled, pulled the visor low over my eyes, and looked sideways. "What I wouldn't have done to have had this a few days ago. I don't know what to say. Thank you so much, my friend. This is truly awesome."

"Ah, shucks," Wilhelm said. "Think nothing of it. You helped develop the tech. You don't remember?" I shook my head. "It was a long time ago. I'll tell you all about it sometime."

"Okay, how long have you dudes known each other?" asked Caleb.

"I don't know," I said. "My memory ain't what it used to be."

"A long time," Wilhelm said. "No time for that now, though. Let's—" A phone rang in another room. "I'd better get that." He returned a minute later, holding a cordless phone to his head. "You're kidding? Are you all right?" Wilhelm looked at me, wide-eyed. After a moment, he let out a breath. "Can you bring them here?" He paused, listening. "What about the van?… One sec." He held the phone against his shoulder. "Caleb, do you have keys for the van?"

The teen shook his head. "No, but Brad keeps an extra taped to the spare tire, under the cover."

"Did you catch that?" Wilhelm said into the phone. "We'll have to take the chance. I'll wait by the door to open it. Cruise by. If it looks clear, drive right into the garage. . . . Right. . . . Just make sure you're not seen. . . . See you soon, beautiful." He ended the call. "Scott showed up. They're coming over…and bringing company."

"Who?" Caleb asked. "My friends?"

"I'm afraid not," Wilhelm said. He patted the teen on his shoulder. "We're going to figure this out, buddy."

"Then who?" I asked, wrinkling my brow.

Wilhelm shrugged. "A couple of dudes in suits. They caught one. They're going to bring him here. I should get up there and help."

"Isn't the garage all burned up?"

"It's not too bad, actually. The fire didn't get that far."

Wilhelm disappeared up the nearby stairs, leaving Caleb and me behind. We regarded each other with wide eyes and confused expressions.

Ten minutes later, we could hear the trap door being opened, followed by heavy footfalls and voices. We both moved to the bottom of the steps as Wilhelm emerged from the stairwell with a body over his shoulder. Olivia appeared moments after with Scott in tow. The computer expert looked around the room as if in a daze. Wilhelm unloaded his burden onto the sofa as Scott, Caleb and I hugged and shook hands. After greeting each other, we joined the Schmidts by the sofa.

"He was lying in wait," Olivia said. "I had to take him down."

"You killed him?" breathed Caleb.

Olivia made a face. "No, of course not," she said. "I wouldn't bring a dead body back here. He's just unconscious. When I got back to Scott's, two men were hiding inside. They waited until I entered, then tried to grab me. We fought; one of them hit me. I defended myself, and that was it. I mean, honestly, what kind of charmer hits a woman?" She touched her cheek. "His parents must have been so proud."

"You're awesome," Caleb said in a faint voice, staring at her.

"Agreed," Scott said. "I guess I showed up right after. I'm running all over town looking for her and there she was in my living room, standing over this guy." He rubbed his temples, sighing. "And then I find out Wil and Bear are fine, but now the kids are missing."

"Where's the other one?" I asked. "You said there were two of them."

Olivia shrugged. "Escaped."

I waved a hand at her captive. "What're we going to do with him?"

His mouth was gagged, and his hands were bound with what looked like one of Olivia's headscarves. I didn't recognize him. His head lolled over the edge of the sofa and he appeared ready to slide off at any moment. His face was unblemished, showing no sign of violence, tinted an unhealthy blue by the soft, dim light of my hat as I leaned in close. To my relief, faint warm air blew across my palm as I held it near his mouth to verify that he was still breathing.

"Question him, of course," Wilhelm answered. "We need to know who he is and what he was doing at Scott's."

"Damned if I know," muttered Scott, scratching his head. "I still can't believe you're alive, Wil. I mean, I'm really glad you are, but..." He trailed off, seemingly at a loss for words.

Olivia looked at me. "Do you recognize him, Shivurr? Is he a Bodhi Group agent?"

"No, I've never seen him before," I said. "Assuming that he is, why would he and the other guy have come back to Scott's place after grabbing our friends the first time?"

"Huh? Oh, I don't know, maybe they came back again hoping to get Scott," Olivia speculated. "It probably would've worked, if I hadn't shown up instead."

"Let's stop speculating and ask him," Wilhelm said. He pulled the unconscious man from the sofa like picking up a child. "I'll take him to my office." He turned to face Scott. "It's better if you wait here. You, too, Caleb. Grab a drink; try to relax. Play some Dig Dug or Ms. Pac-Man." He waved to the row of arcade cabinets. "The TV's not picking up a signal, but you can throw in a VHS tape if you're bored."

Scott looked uncertain. "What are you going to do?"

"Find out where our friends are," Wilhelm said, looking stern. He turned and walked away as if he were wearing a scarf rather than a full-grown man across his shoulders.

Olivia and I followed him down a short hallway to a modest-sized office in which a plush black rolling chair sat behind a wooden desk in front of floor-to-ceiling bookshelves. A computer sat on the desk, monitor glowing green. Wilhelm dumped his cargo onto the small black leather sofa that sat against the opposite wall, next to the door.

Standing erect, he held the back of his hand to the side of his mouth and in a low voice said, "Time to find out what happened to the kids." Then in a louder voice, "Olivia, if you please."

The brunette beauty stepped forward and ran her hand across the comatose man's forehead. Seconds later, his eyes started to flutter and then opened. His expression was relaxed, as if he were waking from a pleasant sleep, then changed quickly to alarmed as his eyes focused and he saw the three of us standing over him.

Wilhelm stepped forward, grabbed the guy's chin and looked him in the eyes. "I'm going to take that off. Don't bother calling for help; no one can hear you down here. Understood? Good stuff." He reached down, fumbled around for a bit, and pulled down the gag. "All right, man. What's your name?"

"I don't know who you are," the man hissed, "but you're in big trouble, pal."

Wilhelm sighed theatrically. "Come on, man. Can we skip the part where I get nasty and you answer my questions anyway? It's a simple question."

The man just glared.

"All right, I'm going to call you Sue. You look like a Sue. Where are they, Sue?"

The man mumbled something.

"What's that? Speak up, Sue."

"Phillip," said the man, red-faced and glowering. "My name's Phillip."

"Oh? Well, all right, Phillip." Wilhelm grabbed the man's chin with an iron grip and stared him in the eyes. "Where are they?"

"Who? I don't know who you're talking about."

"Don't give me that shit. Four kids, Phillip. Two gals, two

guys. A blond-haired girl, early twenties, looks like a cheerleader with a Colgate smile. Name's Lucy. She's got a big heart. Her boyfriend, Brad, a few years older, maybe. Feathered brown hair, kind of a James Dean type. Then there's Lilith. Long-haired brunette pixie, about five-five, sixteen years old, and her surfer dude boyfriend, Alan, muscular, athletic, about five-ten."

Phillip wrenched his face away and pursed his lips, making a hocking sound. Lightning fast, Wilhelm slapped the man hard. "You don't want to do that, man."

The man eyes flashed like fire; he swallowed audibly. "I don't know anything about any kids."

"Tell you what, Phil. You've lost your partner, right? Help me find my friends and I'll help you find yours."

"Get bent," Phillip said, looking away.

"Who do you work for?" I asked, stepping closer. "Are you from the Institute?"

He flinched as I moved closer, staring daggers at me.

"Are you?"

"I don't know what you're talking about," Phillip said, snarling.

"All right, fuck this," said Wilhelm. He touched a hand to the man's forehead. His fingertips appeared to glow, and a halo of light enveloped the man's skull. Phillip's eyes closed tightly, his jaw tensed and a vein at his temple started to pulse, accompanied by beads of perspiration that trickled over his cheek and down his neck. "Interesting. He's resisting, somehow."

Olivia moved closer. "Well, force your way in if you have to."

"He's stronger than he should be. I'd rather not turn this guy into a vegetable. We still might let him go." The prone man's eyes widened further at hearing Wilhelm's casually spoken words. "Oh, calm down, man. Answer our questions, and maybe you'll get out of this all right. All right?"

Olivia crossed her arms. "Very strange. Maybe he's Faction."

"Faction?" I said, looking at her. "What faction?"

"That's a lengthy conversation," Olivia said. "We'll fill you…" She trailed off at the sound of footsteps running down the hall toward us.

Caleb burst through the door moments later, his eyes like saucers. "Someone's upstairs."

Wilhelm released Phillip's head and jumped to his feet. "Probably this guy's buddy." He rushed to the doorway, muttering over his shoulder to Olivia. "Watch him. I'll be right back."

Caleb and I followed him out to the living area where Scott kneeled to the right of the stairway, listening. He held a finger over his lips and waved us over, looking tense. Before we crossed the distance, the trap door at the top of the stairs banged open with a crash, and a parade of booted feet stomped down toward us. If it was our captive's partner, he hadn't come alone.

Scott backpedalled away from the opening, and I grabbed Caleb. "Get down. Hide."

We ducked behind nearby furniture as Wilhelm sprinted and threw shut the heavy stairwell door. It had stood open to this point, so I hadn't noticed before that it was more heavily reinforced than typical for the interior of a residential home. Also unusual was the slab of wood that he slid into place to seal it shut.

Seconds later, a loud crash shook the door frame as something, or someone, bounced off the other side. Wilhelm backed away, studying the door like it was a mountain lion prowling closer. Another crash followed, sounding more like a boot than a body. Then another. Then another.

The door held.

I sighed in relief. Then it occurred to me that we were trapped down here.

"Hello in there," said a muffled voice. "This is the police. Open the door, get on the ground and put your hands behind your head."

Damn, how'd they find us? After a moment's contemplation, I concluded that someone must have seen Olivia and Scott pull into the garage and reported it. *That or the police decided to double back to investigate the house after losing her.*

Wilhelm gazed at me, raising a brow. I tossed my shoulders, holding my hands out, palms to the ceiling. I didn't see any way out of the situation. With no other route of escape, the police just had to wait us out. After a pause, he seemed to reach the same conclusion and walked to the door, making a down motion with his hands, urging me to stay out of sight.

"All right," Wilhelm said in a raised voice. "I'm opening up. Don't shoot." Wood scraped across the metal slots as he pulled the locking bar free. "This is my home," he said, pulling the door slightly inward. "What's this all about?" He peered through the opening. "Where's your uniform?" A voice mumbled something that I couldn't hear, then Wilhelm started to shove the door closed. "You're not cops."

I clamped my hands over my ears as gunfire blasted into the room and bullets tore into Wilhelm. He stumbled back a few feet, and the door banged open, kicked by his assailant. A man dressed all in black stood in the doorway holding an assault rifle, with two similarly dressed men behind him.

"You bastards," I yelled, springing out of cover, chasing the frost that I'd thrown milliseconds before.

These creeps weren't cops, and even if they were, they were going down. My projectile struck the leader in the face, knocking him back into his companions. His weapon clattered to the ground. He would have followed it, but the other gunmen held him upright, using him as a makeshift shield. One of them managed to get his weapon up, and he pulled the trigger. Bullets whizzed past me. Off balance, his aim was poor, but not all his bullets missed.

I grunted in pain, staggering as the room brightened, lit by a nimbus of intense white light coming from my right, and a gale force wind rose from nowhere, swirling around the room, knocking papers and lighter objects flying. I froze, too amazed to move, seeing Wilhelm, still alive, in the centre of the maelstrom. The invaders fired their guns at him, but the bullets stopped in midair, then fell at his feet, leaving him untouched. His hands danced through the air, conducting an invisible orchestra.

Dropping their colleague, the two men still standing resumed firing, advancing on him until Wilhelm slapped his palms together and all the air left the area in a howl, taking the three men with it. They blew back up the stairs like rag dolls, a tangle of limbs. The immediate danger past, Wilhelm took a knee, holding his abdomen. "Ouch, it's been a while since I've been shot."

Our friends emerged from their hiding places.

"What just happened?" Scott asked, coughing. "It felt like the air was sucked right out of my lungs."

Caleb nodded. "That light was harsh. What was that? I'm still seeing spots."

"I'll tell you later," Wilhelm said, pulling himself to his feet. "I've got to make sure they're down for—"

A series of clunks drew our attention to the door as a small cylindrical object bounced off the ground at the bottom of the stairs and rolled across the floor, stopping at Caleb's feet.

"Grenade!" shouted Scott, pointing, a horrified look on his face.

I didn't know much about explosives, but by my calculations Caleb and Scott, and maybe even I, were about to die. Wilhelm stood too close as well, but he'd just shrugged off a barrage of bullets; maybe he'd survive this too.

With no time for us to get clear, I lunged across the floor in the direction of the grenade, arms extended, and tripped over a hassock. I fell onto my chest as Scott and Caleb scrambled back. With my outstretched hands just inches away, the device went off.

Chapter 22

Collateral Damage

The world went white as a wave of heat seared my fingers and face, and an ear-splitting sound tore through my head. I lay there blinded and dazed, head ringing painfully, trying to recover my senses. Gloved hands grabbed mine and dragged me across the floor. My head bashed the first step of the stairs as I was tugged along. I couldn't concentrate, couldn't shape the Underfrost; I was too disoriented. My arms ached as I was yanked carelessly up onto the stairs and bumped along them like a sack of potatoes over sharp-edged speed bumps. Friends weren't dragging me.

I'm being kidnapped, I realized.

"Quickly now," said a deep baritone voice, just audible over the ringing in my ears. "Toss another flash bang. If the Anemoi recovers, we're done."

My left hand slapped against the stairs as the hand holding it let go. Another loud noise and flash of light somewhere behind me soon followed, but more distant, and far less blinding and loud.

"What about Phillip?" said a second male voice.

Strong fingers clamped onto my free hand again. I tried to pull away, unsuccessfully, and began to slide up the stairs once more.

"Nothing we can do," said the first voice. "Malcolm, we have the snowman and are ascending. Send the rest of the team to assist and cover our retreat."

Static from a radio crackled and a woman's voice replied. "Acknowledged, Vasquez and Henderson are on their way. Milton and Starling are inside already, helping with wounded. I recommend haste."

"Sheesh, this guy's heavy. Come on, pick him up."

They grabbed me under the armpits, stood me upright and hoisted me up the stairs.

"Hurry, I'm freezing my nuts off," said the voice on my right.

I fought to free myself, but my captors now held each arm with both hands. I realized my resistance was helping them carry me, so I went limp, sagging to the floor like a puppet with its strings cut. It slowed them down, but we continued to ascend. At the top of the stairs, as my vision finally started to clear, another indistinct figure threw a cloth sack over my head, obscuring my compromised vision further.

The trap door slammed shut behind us as they started to drag me toward the front of the house. I felt a flush of fear that started somewhere in my feet, rising to my head. It cleared the cobwebs. I reconnected with the Underfrost at last, wrapping myself in a shroud of frost and ice. My outer shell crackled as it flash-cooled to well below zero and sucked all the warmth from the air around me. The two men holding me pulled away as if burned, shouting in alarm. I staggered slightly as my feet took my full weight, tearing off the hood.

"Feels like I just grabbed a block of dry ice bare-handed," said one, rubbing his gloves together.

"Stop what you're doing," warned the other. He raised the assault rifle that hung from a strap on his shoulder, pointing it at me. Ignoring him, I retreated deeper into the Underfrost's chill, and the dark shadows and warmth of the world were subsumed by the bright whites and blues and coldness of the Underfrost.

I smiled a crazy smile that turned into a laugh. It felt *good* to slip into its cold embrace, washing away the effects of the explosion and healing my aches and pains. *I could get used to this*, I thought.

Something told me to be careful about sinking too deep, though; I might get lost and spend eternity trapped there or be absorbed into it, losing myself completely. Neither thought appealed. While I liked the weather, it wasn't as interesting as the warm world—the Overfrost—so I straddled the threshold between both worlds.

One of the men reached out to grab me again and touched only air. He waved his free hand through my torso, mouth gaping.

This must be Frost Walking, I realized. With that comprehension, I stepped across fully to the other side.

"Holy shit," the one nearest to me yelled. "He's gone."

The other two raised their weapons and swept them about the room. In case they decided to open fire, I stepped back, moving away from where they'd last seen me.

The floor under my feet felt spongy, flimsy even. I felt like a spider walking over the surface of a pond. Surface tension kept me from sinking, but just barely. Scared I'd be trapped inside a solid object, I treaded softly. Fortunately, I seemed to be still subject to gravity. Without it, any step I took might send me into the air, with no way to return to the ground.

I crept to the trap door and reached down to grab the recessed handle. It rose an inch before slipping through my ghostly fingers, making a clinking sound. Alerted by the noise, the armed men rotated their weapons toward me. I backed away on tiptoe but, without meaning to, phased back into the mundane world and became visible once more. My outer layer of ice, exposed to the sudden warmth of the Nevada night, hardened spontaneously.

"There he is," shouted one of the men, pointing his weapon at me. He scuttled sideways to block my escape.

I held up my hands in surrender. "Easy, dude," I said, scrunching my eyes, willing myself to sink back into the Underfrost's protective embrace.

"He's ghosting again," the gunman shouted.

His weapon spat loudly, blinding me with its muzzle flash. I froze, waiting for the gunshot wounds to register. They didn't.

Ha, you missed, asshole, I thought.

A thump sounded behind me.

"Cease fire," shouted one of the men. "God damn it, Troy. What did you do?"

"He came out of nowhere," the shooter said, lowering his weapon. He took a few steps forward, passing right through me. "Jesus, is he dead?"

Confused and curious, I turned.

Scott lay groaning, lying halfway out of the hole in the floor. The trap door lay closed upon his legs and a trickle of blood leaked from beneath his torso. As I ran over to his side, someone moaned a terrible sound, part anguish and part anger.

A moment later, I realized that it was me.

"Scott, come on," I pleaded, but I wasn't sure that he could hear me. I wasn't sure if anyone could in my ethereal state. I bent down and reached out to stop the blood with my hands, but they passed through my fallen friend like a ghost's. I struggled to rise back from the Underfrost, to rejoin the warm world, but I was too frazzled to focus. "Don't die on me, man."

I winced as a gust of wind blew from the hole in the floor, knocking ash and filth from the fire-damaged ceiling above. I reeled back to my feet, raising my hands defensively. The green spectre that I'd seen in the Schmidts' backyard rose from the depths like a wraith, glaring at the intruders.

Wilhelm's voice boomed from it. "Leave, while you still can."

He thrust his hands wide, and the air exploded. It rushed through me unhindered but threw the three intruders across the room, where they crashed against the back wall.

Bullets rattled off Wilhelm's armour, fired by two new arrivals that entered from the side.

Vasquez and Henderson, I thought.

My friend waved a hand like he was dusting crumbs off his chest, and the shooters retreated in the face of a hurricane of debris that sailed across the room like a swarm of flies. As they fled, he stooped and gently gathered Scott into his arms, raising him from the ground like he weighed nothing, before looking around the room.

"Shivurr?" Wilhelm rumbled in an otherworldly voice. "Are you here?"

I pushed the Underfrost away, and the surreal blues and whites faded, replaced by the blacks and browns of the burned-out house. "Here," I said, inhaling the dry and warm Las Vegas air once again.

Wilhelm jerked his head toward the stairs. "Let's go. Quickly, man. We've got to get Scott help."

I looked at it uncertainly, then at the fallen men. "But we'll be trapped."

"It's cool, man," Wilhelm said. "Trust me."

I slipped past him, grabbing the railing for support, and descended once more into the earth. Caleb met me at the bottom, his face a mask of fear and concern. Olivia was hovering over Phillip, standing guard. Before they could say anything, Wilhelm, just his regular self, green spectre no longer, appeared behind me. Scott, pale as a ghost, slumped in his arms, holding his abdomen. His lips moved as if to speak, but he grimaced instead, scrunching his eyes shut, sending his spectacles, already askew, sliding toward the tip of his nose.

"They shot Scott," Wilhelm said, casting his eyes downward.

Olivia swore. "Put him down here," she said, gesturing to the empty sofa. Wilhelm strode quickly over and laid his friend down with great care. Olivia knelt beside Scott, pulling his hand away from his waist. He struggled against her weakly. "Let me see. It's okay, Scotty." Reassured, he stopped struggling, allowing her to examine him.

"Time to take out the trash," Wilhelm said. He lifted the bound prisoner from the sofa like a throw pillow, carried his burden across the room and dumped him at the foot of the stairs just beyond the doorway. He slammed the door shut and slid the bar into place, securing it against further assault, before returning.

"How is it?" Wilhelm asked his wife.

She shook her head. "I've stopped the bleeding for now, but he's lost a lot of blood. There must be internal damage, too."

Caleb squinted. "But how do you know that? You just stared at it."

"He needs a hospital," Olivia said, ignoring the question.

Wilhelm made a face. "That'll draw too much attention, too many questions, and it'll take too long to get him there. Plus, they're as likely to kill him as help him."

"Come on, Wil," Olivia said, looking at him sidelong. "Medicine has come a long way this century. It's not the dark ages anymore."

"Bah!" Wilhelm said, waving a hand.

"All right, then," Olivia said, sighing. "What do you suggest?"

"We've got to take him to Axe."

Olivia raised an eyebrow. "You think she'll help? She swore she'd never—"

"She's got to," Wilhelm said, cutting her off. "This is our fault. We got him involved."

Olivia studied Scott solemnly, then nodded, taking a deep breath. "We'd better hurry."

"Everyone, sit down and hang on," Wilhelm ordered.

Caleb and I found seats on the opposite sofa as Wilhelm began to sing in an unrecognizable language. As when in green spectre form, his voice rang out in a deep baritone that thrummed against my chest. In a day of surprises, Wilhelm breaking into spontaneous song was right up there near the top as most unexpected.

"Dude, what the hell?"

"Quiet, Caleb," Wilhelm said, scowling. "Now I've got to start over." Clearing his throat, he began to sing again.

Olivia remained crouched on the sofa next to Scott with her hand over his wound. The computer programmer's eyes remained closed, as if he were merely sleeping. She smiled at us, but it didn't reach her eyes.

"If I'd known, I'd have bought a new bathing suit," she said softly. Caleb and I looked at each other with wrinkled brows.

Before long, the room appeared to shudder as if shaken by an earthquake and wavered like a TV screen during a brownout, one moment there, then replaced by blackness, then back again. The room seemed to spin. Artwork fell from the walls; the lights flickered and dimmed, then went out altogether. I luminesced, and Caleb and I regarded each other and our surroundings with wild eyes. Olivia appeared unmoved, eyes closed, resting.

As quickly as it started, it ended. The room stopped shaking and solidified, but the electricity remained off, leaving us in darkness save for the faint light cast by my hat and body.

"My ears just popped," muttered Caleb. The teenager opened his mouth wide, holding a finger to his ear.

"That'd be the elevation change," Olivia said.

Wilhelm walked to the stairwell door, slid aside the bar securing it, and opened it. The stairs that should have been there were gone, replaced by darkness.

My bearded friend sang another short tune and a light began to shine from the far side, revealing a rocky tunnel forty feet in diameter. A rough path over fallen lava rock led upward into the distance.

"Where're the stairs?" Caleb breathed.

"Gone," Wilhelm said matter-of-factly. "Liv, how's Scott?" he asked, moving to her side.

"As pale as Shivurr, Wilhelm. He's started bleeding again. We need to hurry."

"Here, I'll carry him," he said, lifting him gently from the sofa. "Come on, guys. Let's move."

We followed him out the open door into the tunnel beyond, where I stopped to take in our new surroundings. Water dripped from the ceiling above, where balls of pure light glowed and lit our way. The floor of the tunnel was heavily textured lava rock and the walls were black, mixed with iron reds, deep purples, and the yellowish white of gypsum. The tunnel was quiet and calm, hovering around room temperature, too warm for me but comfortable for my companions. It was surprisingly quiet, reminding me of the Nevada Chamber that housed the tholos; our voices were muted as well, not echoing against the walls like I'd expect, as if the rock, starved for conversation, swallowed up any sound. Nor, I realized after a moment, could I see signs of animal life. *Nothing for them to eat*, I supposed.

"What is this place?" Caleb whispered, peering from the doorway, his face pale.

Olivia grabbed his hand and coaxed him out to join us. "It's a lava tube, left behind when the volcano erupted millennia ago."

"Come on, let's go," Wilhelm said with a hurry-up face.

"Scott's dying here."

He turned and dashed away, and we followed, moving quickly to keep up. My bleeding friend's long limbs drooped down, nearly brushing the rough floor of the ancient tunnel. Occasionally, Wilhelm lifted him higher, compensating for his shorter stature, whenever he needed to step onto a large boulder. Other times, he leaped the distance between boulders with startling ease, bending his knees upon landing to cushion the impact for Scott, who made no sound of complaint, his eyes closed as if in a coma or trance. Unencumbered, I kept up without too much trouble, but I could soon hear Caleb gasping for breath behind me. Looking back, I could see Olivia trailing him, urging him on.

Wilhelm stopped and whirled about. "This is taking too long." He shifted Scott over his shoulders into a fireman's carry. "I'll run ahead and take Scott to Axe. Olivia, take our friends to the cottage. I'll meet you there later."

"Try not to jostle him too much when you run," Olivia said, her breathing easy. "The stasis matrix has its limits."

"Got it," Wilhelm replied. He turned around and walked backwards. "I've got him, Shiv. Stay, gather your strength. You're going to need it to get our friends back." He smiled. "You did it, buddy; you Frost Walked. That's going to be key." Then he whirled about and ran up the rocks, at a speed that would have been impressive even if he weren't carrying the extra weight of a tall, full-grown man, and disappeared.

For a moment, I considered following him, confident that I could keep pace, but I dismissed the thought in its infancy. Wilhelm would have known that I could keep up, but he hadn't suggested it, so he must have had a reason he hadn't had time to share. Maybe this Axe person didn't take kindly to strangers, or there were other factors of which I was unaware; maybe he wanted me to keep an eye on Caleb and Olivia. Well, Caleb, at least. I got the distinct impression Olivia could take care of herself.

Heck, after taking down that guy Phillip at Scott's house all by herself, maybe she's the one staying back to protect Caleb and me, I mused.

Absent the need to rush, we moved at a more moderate pace,

allowing Caleb to catch his breath. Olivia, knowing the way, took the lead, and I dropped back to bring up the rear. Before long, the tunnel's slope increased, and we picked our way more carefully up toward the gleam of light coming from the exit. Beautiful yet perilous, it soon outshined the light of the orbs overhead.

"I didn't know Las Vegas had lava tubes beneath it," I said as we walked.

"It doesn't, as far as I know," Olivia said. "We're not in Vegas anymore."

Caleb snorted. "Yeah, right—and then you woke up."

Olivia made no reply and just kept climbing until, moments later, we reached the exit. "Maybe you're the one still dreaming, kid," she said finally, pushing aside the huge leaves of a tropical plant with her back and holding it as we passed.

The air was warm, much warmer than the cave, and thick with humidity, like it had just rained, a sharp contrast to Las Vegas. Palm trees towered overhead, and ferns and other greenery dotted the forest floor. Birdsong filled the air. We were in a tropical rainforest, and somehow, the sun still shone.

Caleb's mouth opened and closed repeatedly as he looked up at the canopy of trees surrounding us, like a guppy feeding from the surface of a fish tank. "I don't—how? Where are we?"

A blood-curdling roar ripped through the air somewhere in the distance to our left. It sounded large enough to be a bear but had a vaguely avian aspect to it, like it was part pterodactyl or another dinosaur.

Caleb turned snow white and sidled closer to me. "Oh, shit," he said, scanning the greenery and swallowing audibly. "What the hell was that?"

Olivia, several feet ahead of us, stopped and looked back. "Don't worry about it," she said gravely. "Stay close to me and you'll be fine."

"That's not really an answer," Caleb said, frowning.

"It's better if you don't know," she said, resuming her walk.

We hiked through the tropical woodland for ten minutes before arriving at a large house. A gravel path led away from the building, and a vehicle, covered with a tarpaulin, sat in the carport next to it.

We took the stairs that ran up the right side to a deck that looked out over a beautiful ocean. In the west, the sun was beginning to sink below the horizon but still had some power to it.

"Where are we?" Caleb asked breathlessly.

"An island in the Pacific Ocean," Olivia said, grinning. "We live here sometimes."

"This is wild," the teenager said. "Is that a beach down there?"

"Yep," Olivia replied. "If we're here long enough, you can take a swim."

"How can we be here, though?" Caleb said, his voice too loud.

"Magic," Olivia answered, straight-faced. "Well, science really. Just so far beyond the science they teach you in school that you might as well just think of it as magic. It tends to ease the transition."

"I don't get it."

"Yeah, exactly," Olivia agreed. "You guys wait here a few minutes." She pointed to nearby lounges. "Relax. I've got to take care of a few things." She opened the door to the house, which didn't appear to be locked, and left us alone.

"I'm still not sure this isn't all a dream," Caleb muttered as we lay back and watched the sunset. "Maybe I'm still wasted, sleeping in the van at the edge of Lunar Crater, and Alan, Lilith, Brad and Lucy are totally fine."

"I'm afraid not, dude," I said, shaking my head.

"Yeah, I know," Caleb said, shrugging. "Still, it'd suck if you were just a figment of my mind, brah. I just hope everyone is okay. Those dudes aren't going to hurt them, right? I mean, they shot Scott."

I pursed my lips. "I think shooting Scott was an accident. They were trying to shoot me." I hesitated, pondering. "I sure hope not. They've no reason to. You guys just happened to give me a ride; it's not like you busted me out. They'll probably ask them some questions to try to find me or keep them a while— use them as bait for me."

"Yeah, but they know you exist. Won't the Bodhi Group want to keep that a secret?"

I snorted softly. "Doubt they're worried about that. Would you believe them, if you hadn't met me yourself?"

"Fuck no," Caleb said agreeably.

"Exactly."

"So, what are we going to do?" Caleb asked. He looked at our surroundings meaningfully. "How do we even get back there?"

"Beats me. Maybe the same way we came, but in reverse. Whatever brought us here should bring us back, right? Wilhelm will get us back, once Scott's in the clear."

"If he's ever in the clear," Caleb said grimly. "It didn't sound like this Axe chick's going to help."

The sun was now fully behind the horizon and the light rapidly fading to black. In that restful moment, I became aware of the incredible variety of sounds surrounding us. The ocean breeze blew through the trees, shaking the leaves as a symphony of bird calls mixed with insects clacking and chirruping erupted. Caleb, who had struggled to keep his eyes open since sitting on the lounge, closed them and seemed to drift off to sleep. Before long, the unlit torches that lined the deck flared to life on their own.

"Hey, guys, I'm making dinner," Olivia said from the nearby doorway. "Come inside and set the table."

Chapter 23

The Gods' Honest Truth

Outside, the world was inky black save for the torches lighting the deck, or lanai as Olivia called it. We sat around a large table in the dining room of the villa, eating spaghetti and meat sauce that Olivia had made from a can.

"We're not well provisioned, I'm afraid," Olivia said, laying a plate of crackers on the table. "I'd have stocked the larder with fruit, vegetables and bread if I knew we were coming. That's what we get for an emergency departure."

Caleb dug into the meal eagerly, displaying no sign of disappointment at the lack of selection. I nibbled a bit, extracting trace elements necessary to maintain my well-being, but mainly availed myself of several glasses of water and bottles of soda pop.

"Sorry, Shivurr, we're out of dark soda; just got Sprite, ginger ale, and one Mountain Dew," Olivia warned as I opened the fridge. "Just what we left behind after our last visit."

The drinks were cold, so I didn't care too much. A Dr Pepper would have been sweet, though. I thought of the stash cooling in my hat, but I hoarded them like a leprechaun's treasure; those might be the difference between life and death at some point.

Halfway through my first beverage, Caleb pointed out that the fridge had an ice maker. My mouth fell open and I raced to transfer handfuls into a glass for my drinks, then into a large bowl. Humming to myself, I sat back and gobbled the cubes like popcorn. Popping one into my mouth, I noticed Olivia watching me with a smile on her face.

"Sorry, Olivia," I said, holding an ice cube halfway to my mouth. "Do you want some too?"

She waved a hand and chuckled softly. "No, thank you. I forget how hard it is for you to be here, out of your environment, where it must be so unbearably warm, like a human living in a dry sauna all the time. I'm really glad to see how happy a simple thing like ice cubes makes you."

"You get good waves here?" Caleb asked, craning his neck as he looked outside. "Looks like ankle busters down there."

"Not much on this beach, but the windward side is another story," Olivia replied.

"Damn, wish I had my board," Caleb said, looking wistful. "Carving some waves would be bitchin'. Be nice to blow off some steam. Get my head right."

Olivia made a face. "Too dangerous."

"No sweat, Liv. I'm hard-core. I'm no Alan, but I'm no Barney either."

"Who's Barney? Friend of yours?"

"Nah, Barney's a noob."

"I'm sure he'll get better with practice."

Caleb laughed. "No, Liv. Barney's like metaphorical."

"I see," replied Olivia, raising a brow. "I wasn't worried about your surfing skills."

"Then what? Men in grey suits?"

"Are we still speaking the same language?" Olivia asked with a smirk.

"Sharks, dude."

"No, *dude*," Olivia said, flashing her eyes and smiling. "Something more dangerous than sharks, in the water *and* the forest."

"Like what we heard in the jungle?" I asked. Olivia nodded, pouring herself some wine.

"I never should have left California," Caleb moaned, slumping into his chair. "I could be hanging at Antonio's, chowing on 'za."

"Why did you?" Olivia asked, taking a sip of her wine.

"It's Lilith's fault. She wanted to see Lunar Crater. She convinced Alan and he persuaded me."

I swallowed another ice cube. "Lilith? I thought it was Brad's idea. He's the geologist."

"Yeah, true. Plus, Lucy wanted to take photos, but Lilith was the reason Alan wanted to go."

"You guys are good friends, eh?"

"He's been like a brother, dude; since we met in grade school."

"That's a rare and beautiful thing, my friend," I said, emptying another can of soda into my glass.

"I must say you all get along exceptionally well," Olivia said. "You hardly ever bicker."

Caleb tossed his shoulders. "Nah. If we did, what'd be the point of being friends? Who wants to hang out with jerks and assholes? I'd rather be alone."

I looked across the table to Olivia. "Speaking of Nevada, how do we get back there? The same way we came, right?"

Olivia looked uncomfortable. "I don't know. It's probably not safe. The house is sure to be watched closely, and you getting captured or worse won't help our friends."

"Can't you just take us somewhere else?"

She frowned. "Spatial transposition doesn't work that way."

"Spatial trans—what?" Caleb asked.

"It involves transposing two physical areas of space—trading places, really. The region of space that corresponds to our basement was switched with the same volume of space on this island, in the location where we arrived. Setting it up is not easy—the space-time manipulation is incredibly complex and energy greedy—and the two places are inextricably linked thereafter. You don't just point it somewhere else, at least not easily. Despite the hassle, we'll have to relink this end to somewhere else now that the Las Vegas house is compromised. That'll take weeks, though."

"Then how do we get back?" I asked, my voice rising. "We need to get our friends back. They can't wait that long. We must be hundreds of miles from Nevada."

"Thousands, actually," Olivia corrected. "The Pacific is huge."

"But you must have other ways back, right? Using this spatial transference."

"Transposition. The closest linked location is nowhere near. It's an option but will take longer."

"Don't suppose you've got an airplane?"

"Uh-uh."

"Then how? By boat? Won't that take days or weeks?"

"Try not to panic, Shivurr," Olivia said, holding up a hand. "Let's wait for Wilhelm to get back."

A man stood on the lanai, looking in through the screen door. In his late thirties or early forties, he was a bear of a man, six feet tall and thick like a slab of meat. He wore a tank top and bright red shorts with a floral pattern and sported massive tattoos on the brown skin of his arms, which appeared to extend beneath his shirt to his chest as well.

Olivia rushed to open the door. "*E komo mai*, Hanale," she said. He stepped inside and picked her up in an embrace.

"*Aloha*, Olivia," the big man replied in a deep, rumbling voice. She nearly disappeared as he wrapped his meaty arms around her. He released her and looked to me. "Howzit, Haukea Kane?" said the man, smiling. He bowed slightly, causing his long black hair to fall in front of his face.

I stood up to meet him. Caleb remained seated, mouth open. The newcomer stepped forward and locked me in an embrace. Large as he was, I could feel great strength in his arms and solidity in his form. I froze, then patted him on the back. I didn't want to be rude, even to an effective stranger. He released me after a moment, showing no outward signs of discomfort from the chill of my touch.

"I'm sorry," I said. "I get the impression we know each other, but my memory isn't what it used to be."

"Shivurr's got a touch of amnesia, Hanale," Olivia explained helpfully, closing the lanai door and joining us. "Thanks for coming so quickly."

"And what of Huhu Makani?"

"Gone to Aceso. One of our friends needs her help."

"Not Kolohe, I hope."

Olivia shook her head. "Bear is safe. This is a new friend. His name is Scott."

"Scott? Is he `ohana?*"

"Not in the strictest sense, no. But he is to us."

Hanale looked uncomfortable but said nothing.

"Come, join us. There's still pasta left."

We sat and Hanale loaded a plate with spaghetti and dug in, smiling. Over dinner, we learned that he lived on a neighbouring island, part of a chain of similar volcanic islands, coral reefs, and sand shoals.

"Do you live here, dude?" Caleb asked the big man.

"Hanale keeps the islands safe," Olivia said, looking at him fondly. "He's our resident guardian, protecting them against the outside world. Keeping people from finding them."

The big man nodded, chewing wetly.

"How's he do that?" Caleb asked.

Hanale swallowed. "Illusion. Weather manipulation, mostly. Sea monsters. Anyone makes it past that wish they hadn't." Seeing Caleb's face, he added, "Don't happen much, brother," pronouncing brother so it sounded like bruddah. "Most days, we live the simple life, fishing, swimming, surfing."

"We?" I prompted.

"Me and the others on the islands," the big man replied. "Not just me living here." He waved a hand at Olivia and himself.

"Hanale has help. Protecting the islands against people is the least of it," Olivia added. "There are worse dangers. And keeping the technology running smoothly takes time and maintenance."

"Who *are* you dudes?" Caleb asked, leaning forward. "The stuff I've seen this week—fire monsters, teleporting here—this is witches and warlocks shit."

Hanale guffawed. "They used to call us gods, little brother."

"Ages ago," Olivia agreed. She stood and walked to the patio doors, looking out at the ocean, lit only by starlight now. "We…they were so ignorant back then. They thought the earth was *flat* and a *few thousand years* old, if you can believe it. Even mankind's current technology would have been magic to them."

"Some people still believe that sort of thing," I said, thinking of the men that Wilhelm had sent away with talk of Zeus.

"They sure do," Olivia said. "Homo sapiens are still cave dwellers in the dark places of their minds. People want to, even need to, believe; anything to give their lives purpose and assuage the fear of death."

"How much of the myths are true, then?" Caleb asked, wide-eyed.

"It depends what you heard," Olivia said, shrugging. "Even non-mythical history textbooks are ninety percent guesswork and outright fiction. Trust me, I know that from experience."

"But you are gods?" Caleb pressed. "Like in the myths?"

Olivia waggled her head. "More or less. They got a lot of stuff wrong and embellished a lot. Most of us got several different names and backstories. Wilhelm alone is the inspiration for several of the god myths. Eventually they started using us to explain everything that happened, even when we had nothing to do with it. Of course, they had their own myths and fantasies from before we arrived. When we were starting our own religions, we leveraged those."

"Then it's all bullshit," Caleb said. "The fantastic creatures. The stories." He paused, looking thoughtful. "But that doesn't make sense. Shivurr is sitting right here. And I saw those fire things."

"Oh, I didn't say that. A lot of it is real, in a general sense. We've got inherent abilities that allow us to do extraordinary things, and we augment that with technology. But we didn't create the earth, and none of us drag the sun across the sky in a chariot. What we do is based in science, but so advanced and unobtrusive that people can't see how we do it, so they call it magic. It's not like watching a clock tick with the back cover off, where you can't help but see the cause and effect."

"But aren't you mad no one believes in you anymore?" Caleb asked, looking at Hanale. "Don't you need followers, worshipping you? Like for power and stuff?"

Hanale shrugged and blew air through his lips, flapping them noisily. "No, brother. Don't matter if people believe in me or not. I am still me."

"Only lies are a matter of belief," Olivia said. "Unfortunately, entire societies are built on lies, and the more fragile the lie, the more those that believe in it will fight and kill to protect it."

Caleb narrowed his eyes. "Then why the con? If you don't need worshippers and are so advanced…"

"Control, mainly," Olivia said. "Some of us thought we could help steer human civilization in better directions, maybe even to enlightenment eventually. Others wanted worshippers to use as tools for their own amusement."

"Doesn't that make you liars, too?" I said.

Olivia nodded and gave me a glum look. "We were as guilty as the priests, shamans and witch doctors that have manipulated people for their own gain since the earliest days of humanity. If you're a lazy ass with no skills, invent a god and make yourself his gatekeeper…or be one yourself."

"So, how old are you?" Caleb said.

Olivia raised an eyebrow at him. "A gentleman doesn't ask a lady her age."

"Not really a gentleman, du…Olivia," Caleb said, grinning.

"If all that happened, and you're still here, why isn't everyone still worshipping you guys?" I asked.

Olivia swirled a spaghetti noodle around her plate. "There was a schism among us. Some objected, morally, to the lies and exploitation—the sacrifices in our names. We wanted to stop our meddling and let humanity develop on its own, unmolested. Using a sentient species as slaves, willing though they were, bothered the more enlightened among us."

Caleb stroked his chin. "Sort of like vegetarians."

Olivia smiled, staring into the distance. "Sort of, yeah. Some wanted to share our knowledge selectively, to help ease the suffering we saw daily without making the help contingent on offerings and adoration." She filled her wineglass halfway, then looked down the neck of the wine bottle, scowling. "Many of us could not be convinced."

"The Faction," I said.

Olivia touched her nose. "You got it." She grimaced. "The problem with laying out smart ideas for others is that they filter them through the prism of their own personality, experiences and expectations and reach different conclusions."

Hanale bobbed his head. "Wrong depends on how you been raised."

"Exactly," Olivia said, pointing a finger at him. "Humans are capable of anything, if they are *raised* into it." She stared into space with haunted eyes. "Did cannibals think they were evil? What about slavers and their patrons?"

"We're not all like that," Caleb said, frowning. "Some of us are just trying to be happy. Trying to figure it all out, you know?"

"What do you mean?" Olivia asked.

Caleb tossed his shoulders. "You know. Why am I here? What does it all mean? What's the point?"

She walked to the kitchen, grabbed another bottle, and worked a bottle opener into the cork. "I should think it's obvious." Olivia looked at him expectantly. Caleb blinked but said nothing. She shook her head impatiently. "Life is its own point. Period. End of story."

Caleb blinked, looking thoughtful. "So, there's no afterlife?"

Olivia waved a hand as if shooing a fly. "Who knows? But if you don't remember this one in a future life, how's that comforting to you now?"

Caleb shrugged. "I don't know. It just kind of is."

She rubbed her face. "Look, guys. Maybe we're all just living in a giant computer simulation created by people in another universe. Without proof, anything anyone invents as an explanation for why we're all here or what happens after death is as likely as another."

Caleb snickered. "Seems like Santa Claus not believing in the Easter Bunny to me."

"Give me a hand clearing the table, smartass," she ordered, grabbing dishes.

"We don't age or die of disease," Hanale said. "Guess we never needed an afterlife."

I stacked plates near the kitchen sink. "You're immortal, then?"

Hanale pursed his lips. "But not invincible. We can be killed, but not easily."

Caleb furrowed his brow. "Then who are you to judge people for being scared of death? For making stuff up to make it easier?"

Olivia paused, looking thoughtful. "I get it. More than you know. Being afraid of death is why I'm still here. Why I chose this life."

Something clicked in my head—maybe another memory falling into place courtesy of the potions Scott had rescued from the Institute. "You're not one of them, are you?"

"She is as much one of us as any," Hanale said, shaking his head. "More so."

"Thanks, Hanale," Olivia said, eyes glistening. She looked at me. "I don't judge people for being afraid of death. I was mortal once. But wallowing in ignorance and self delusion isn't a solution. At least, not a good one."

"Yeah, well, not all of us get a chance to live forever," Caleb said, snorting.

"I'm sure it sounds great to you, kid, but it's not all wonderful." She looked haunted. "Watching everyone you know and love age and die."

"I get it," Caleb said. "Growing old scares the shit out of me."

"But you're just, what, fifteen?" Olivia said.

Caleb shrugged. "Is Shivurr one of you?"

"He was here when we came," Hanale said. "He is the oldest of us all, probably."

"This is heavy," said Caleb, blinking. "Wait, if you're gods, why do you sound American?"

"We all speak many languages," Olivia said. "Adopting an accent is no more difficult, especially if you live somewhere long enough."

"What about the others?" I asked. Olivia looked confused. "The Faction. What did they want?"

She tossed her shoulders. "They wanted to continue as we had in the past. They enjoyed the adulation. Being worshipped is its own kind of intoxication. Maybe some started to believe their own hype. These radicals wanted us to take the planet entirely for ourselves. They despised humanity and believed they would one day rise to conquer us if we didn't act first. Hanale, Wilhelm and I, and others, moved to stop them."

"Sound like a bunch of nutcases," Caleb said, flaring his nostrils.

"Zealots, all of them," Hanale agreed. "The worst of us."

Olivia nodded. "Zealots see things in binary. To them, you either agree one hundred percent or disagree completely. Anything that challenges doctrine must be crushed without mercy. They just don't get it."

"What's that?" I asked.

"It's a fuzzy world," Olivia said. "Few things are ever truly zero or one." She rubbed her temples and frowned. "And once they've decided something is a zero or one, forget about changing their minds. Even more moderate people tend to be rigid and absolute in their thinking. Sure, they'll listen to your arguments, but only so that they can tell you how you're wrong."

"That's pretty grim," Caleb said, raising his brows.

"Maybe," Olivia said, sagging in her chair. "It's just that I'm not sure that I've ever changed anyone's mind about any subject if they'd already formed an opinion on it. People's minds close rapidly."

"Is Aceso one of you?" I asked.

"Gesundheit," said Caleb, grinning.

"Ak-see-so," Olivia repeated, exaggerating the pronunciation. She smacked Caleb lightly on the back of the head before retaking her seat. He smoothed his hair, still grinning. "We call her Axe for short. And, yes, she's one of the good guys."

"Is she a doctor?" Caleb asked.

The big man wobbled his head side to side. "Kind of. Sometimes she heals those that need it."

"Does Aceso live on the islands too?" I asked.

Hanale wagged his head. "No, brother." He pointed a thick finger of his meaty hand skyward, poking holes in the air.

"But Wilhelm took Scott to see her," I said. "She's got to be around here somewhere."

Olivia shook her head. "This was just a stop on the way. He

took another trip to get to her."

"Will she help Scott?" I asked.

"I don't know. I haven't heard from him yet." Olivia said. "He's been unusually quiet. I'm hoping that's a good sign."

"Why does Wilhelm need to convince her to heal Scott?" Caleb asked.

"She swore she'd never heal another of your kind."

"My kind?" Caleb said, blinking.

"Human," Hanale said. "It's a long story."

"We knew each other before," I blurted at Hanale as a memory surfaced. "Didn't we?"

The big man nodded vigorously. "A long time, Haukea Kane."

"You called me that before," I said. "What does it mean?"

"Hanale's nickname for you, Shivurr," Olivia said, grinning. "It means 'snow-white man' in Hawaiian."

"Sounds better in Hawaiian," I said with a wry smile that faded a moment later. "How many other friends did the Bodhi Group rob me of?" I growled.

"Chill, dude," Caleb said, flashing his teeth in a broad smile.

"Really? Cold puns, dude?" I said, shaking my head slowly. "You're better than that, Slim."

He smiled wider still. "Come on, Shivurr…be ice."

I snorted, spilling cracked ice out the side of my mouth and down my chest. Hanale chortled, sloshing his wine dangerously close to the rim of his wineglass. "Good one, brother," he said, slapping the teen on the back.

"Okay, Caleb, that's enough wine for you," Olivia said with mock severity. "I never should have given you that glass."

"She's right, Caleb," I said, winking. "Underage drinking is snow laughing matter."

Olivia smirked and took another sip of wine. "You see what I'm dealing with, Hanale?" We all chuckled at that. Olivia stopped abruptly and held up her hands for silence, staring into space.

She drew a silver necklace from beneath her shirt, revealing an emerald pendant that glimmered in the artificial light. She pulled it over her head and laid it in the centre of the kitchen table. A moment later, Wilhelm's disembodied head, three feet tall, appeared in the air above it and looked around the room.

Chapter 24

No Man's Island

"Hey, guys," Wilhelm said with a tired smile. "Hanale! Glad you made it."

The big man waved hello and resumed chewing his second plate of pasta.

"Whoa," Caleb breathed, his mouth gaping. He waved a hand through the floating head. "That's too cool."

"Hey, kid," Wilhelm said with a wink.

"Is Scott okay?" I interrupted.

Wilhelm bobbed his head. "He's out of the woods, in recovery. There was a lot of internal damage, but Aceso says he should recover fully; it's just going to take time. Could have gone either way for a while. We had to synthesize a lot of blood."

I closed my eyes, smiling. "Thank the Underfrost."

"Hell, yeah," Caleb shouted. "Thank the—whatever that is."

"He'll be on bedrest for a few weeks," Wilhelm said, beaming. His expression grew serious. "Aceso is monitoring his condition closely. I'm going to be tied up here with her—part of the deal for Aceso's services. Which means I won't be able to get you back to Nevada, Shivurr. You're going to have to make the trip yourself."

"Sure, I'll start swimming now."

He snorted. "There's a better way. It'll get you back fast. There's an Allfrost Chamber on a nearby island. You can use its transporter to get back."

"Allfrost Chamber? Is that like the cavern in Nevada?"

"Right, sounds like your memory is coming back. Unfortunately, of us all, only you can make the trip. The Allfrost Transporter sends you to your destination through the Underfrost.

None but you can cross that threshold or make the journey through its icy void unscathed. You can use it to send yourself to the Allfrost Chamber in Nevada. You've been there before, so you should have no trouble finding your way from there to the Institute."

"How do I use it, though?" I asked. "What does it look like?"

"Don't worry. It'll detect your presence and respond to your desires telepathically. Just think about what you want and where you want to go, and it will send you there. The launch point is on a platform next to the tholos," Wilhelm said. "Understood?"

"Sure," I said. "That's the temple-like thing with the pillars, right? There was one in the Nevada Chamber, but it didn't react to me—not as far as I could tell."

"Right," Wilhelm said, nodding. "That's no surprise. That Allfrost Chamber is damaged—courtesy of the Bodhi Group scientists. It's incapable of sending passengers, but it can still help receive them."

He turned his head from me, appearing to look over his shoulder at the wall, then looked back, clenching his jaw. "I've got to get going soon, so let's keep this brief. Once you've entered and confirmed your destination, the launch vessel will rise from beneath you. Submerge into it, and the launch will be initiated."

"Submerge into it?"

"It's a huge snowball. Merge with it and the transporter will launch immediately."

"I don't know how to get there," I said, looking around doubtfully.

Hanale's expression became serious. "Is this why I'm here, Makani?"

"You've got it," Wilhelm said. "I need you to take Shivurr there. His memory being compromised, I figured he wouldn't remember how to find it, and getting across the water will be an issue."

"What are these chambers?" I asked the floating head. "How do you know about them, let alone have one?"

"It's tech that we collaborated on years ago; I'll explain more when we meet again. For now, just know that the Allfrost Chambers are connected by a network of transporters capable of guiding passengers to chosen destinations, providing for precise positioning and guidance within each cell in the system. You need to be launched from an Allfrost Chamber, but you don't need to land in one, just within the general vicinity—a hundred miles or so. The Nevada Allfrost Chamber will assist in getting you there safely."

"Who were those guys?" I asked. "The ones that shot Scott, I mean. They weren't from the Bodhi Group, were they?"

"No, I don't think so," Wilhelm said, looking thoughtful.

"But you know who they are, don't you?"

He nodded, looking sheepish. "It's a long story, but yeah, probably."

"Very likely they were human followers of the Faction," Olivia said. Seeing Wilhelm's eyes widen, she added, "I've provided our friends with some of our history."

Her bearded husband looked dubious. "Be sure to keep what you've heard to yourself, Caleb, once you get home. If the wrong people were to overhear, or to think they could use you to find us, it would be highly perilous for you and for us all." He turned to regard his wife. "I didn't have a chance to say so before, but when they shot Scott, I recognized one of them."

"Who was it?"

"Our neighbour, Gordon."

Olivia's jaw dropped. "Damn. Not just your typical nosy neighbours, then."

His eyes darted to the side as if distracted by something. He shook his head a moment later, muttering under his breath. "Time for me to go. You and Hanale should leave for the Allfrost Chamber soon so you arrive before the sun comes up."

I must have looked as doubtful as I felt.

"You can do this, man. Like I said, Frost Walking is going to be key. Use that to get inside without being seen. You know the layout. It'll be super risky, I know, but it's the only way to get your memories back—and the kids, if they're there."

"What do you mean, if? I thought we were sure that's what

happened."

"Maybe not," Olivia said, glancing at Wilhelm's ghostly head. "They may have been taken by the Faction. It'd make sense given their appearance at our house."

"Let's hope not," Wilhelm added. "Their chances are better if the Bodhi Group took them. They're American citizens, after all. At least you should be able to rule that out. If they're not at the Institute, we can conclude that the Faction took them, and we'll have to adapt to that."

"Damn it," I said, banging a fist on the table. Caleb looked queasy, his face pale despite his tan.

"Relax, Shivurr," Wilhelm said. "One problem at a time, one step at a time. We're going to set things right."

I pressed my lips together and nodded slowly. "All right, how do I get in touch with you guys if I get them out?"

"If you succeed in restoring your memories, you'll know where several of our safe houses are and can go there," Wilhelm said. "But a prearranged plan wouldn't hurt." He paused. "Shivurr, if it looks too risky, observe and contact us. We'll be there as soon as we can. It may take a few days, but that's preferable to you being captured again."

Wilhelm's head turned to his wife. "Do you have a modified Walkman to give him?"

She nodded and moved to the balcony door. "I'll be right back. They're in the workshop."

After she'd left, his head rotated back to me. "Okay, I've got to go now, big time. Olivia and Hanale should be able to help with the rest. Be safe, my friend."

"Bye," I said, feeling suddenly weepy. His head winked out of existence a moment later.

Olivia returned ten minutes later, holding a small blue-and-grey Walkman cassette player in one hand and orange headphones in the other. She thrust them at me. "It's got one of my mix tapes in there." She held out her other hand and dropped batteries into my outstretched palm. "It runs on regular batteries, so use it sparingly. I've put in a fresh set, but here are some spares, just in case."

"I don't understand how this helps," I said, placing the headphones on my head and hitting play.

"I've modified it to work as a communication device," she said, standing taller. "Press the buttons on the side in this sequence and it will activate it." She demonstrated, tapping out an unlikely sequence of presses. "That sequence will dial me, and we'll be able to speak. Just be sure to wear the headphones; that's how voice is picked up and transmitted."

"That's the coolest thing I've ever seen," Caleb said, staring at the Walkman with envy.

Olivia swelled and patted him on the shoulder. "It's something I've been working on, hiding our tech in everyday items. Mostly to hide it from the Faction, but it'll do the same for the Bodhi Group, if…if things don't go well. That's why it uses regular batteries. The Faction would be more likely to detect one of our power sources. I wish we could come with you, but maybe infiltrating will be easier if it's just you."

"Thanks, Olivia," I said, putting the headphones on. I had to extend them as far as they would go to fit over my ears.

She looked at her watch. "You should get going soon, before you lose the cover of darkness. It's much later in Nevada."

"When can we leave?" I asked, looking at Hanale.

He grabbed the mug of beer he'd been nursing off the kitchen table and chugged the last of it. "Right now, brother," he said, wiping his mouth with the back of his hand and thumping the mug down on the table. He slapped Olivia's shoulder. "Thanks for the grinds, Tita."

"Wait, what about me?" Caleb said, looking confused. "I want to help. They're my friends, too."

I shook my head, smiling sadly. "Appreciate the offer, Slim, but you heard Wilhelm; this isn't a trip you can make."

"Don't worry, Caleb," Olivia said, squeezing his shoulder. "We'll get you back home when Wilhelm gets back. You can relax here until then."

Hanale smiled. "It's all good, little brother. We'll surf, swim, snorkel—live the good life. Some of the waves we get here going to give you chicken skin. You won't want to leave."

Caleb looked doubtful but inclined his head after a pause.

With no time to waste, we said our goodbyes. Olivia kissed my cheek and hugged me hard enough to crack a rib, if I had any. I drew a strangled breath and smelled sandalwood mixed with garlic. The warmth of her skin lingered against my chest for several moments after she released me. I bumped knuckles with Caleb, then shook the teen's hand, and Hanale and I left through the front door.

Glancing back, I saw Caleb, looking wistful, give me a hang loose sign. I returned it, saluted, then descended the stairs at the far side, following Hanale.

We made our way down through the rainforest by the stars and moon to the shore of the bay. The water was calm; only mild waves broke against the fine sand of the beach.

We walked a short distance along the thin strip of sand under a starlit sky until we came to an outrigger canoe that sat among the trees at the forest's edge.

"Hey, brother," Hanale said. "Give me a hand getting this to the water."

I grabbed it awkwardly at first but with Hanale's direction adjusted my grip and we carried it down to the water's edge. It was surprisingly light, more cumbersome than heavy, and required little strength to move it.

The tattooed man strode into the surf without hesitation. I held back at the surf's edge, holding my end of the vessel at arm's length, not wanting to get my feet wet. Hanale gave me a puzzled look, pulling lightly on the canoe. Bracing myself, I stepped into the saltwater at last. My icy flesh reacted immediately, forming a barrier of ice that kept the water from soaking into my body.

As soon as the outrigger settled in the water, I jumped in as if I'd been walking across hot coals. Slightly dizzy and breathing like I'd just run up ten flights of stairs, I sat down in the canoe and tried to push visions of myself dissolving like a sugar cube in hot tea from my mind.

"You okay?" Hanale asked, squinting his eyes at me. He guided the canoe into deeper water, turned it about and climbed in, so that he was in the stern.

"Yeah, just give me a minute," I said. I rubbed my face, slapped my cheeks, and took a deep breath. "Saltwater's a bit rough on the undercarriage."

He stared at me. "What happened to you, Haukea Kane?"

"What do you mean?"

"You love water. Surfing, snorkelling." He handed me a paddle, grabbed another for himself, and dipped it into the water. "You don't remember?"

With several powerful strokes, we left the shore behind.

"What are you talking about?" I asked, looking back at him. "I'm made of snow and ice. This might as well be a lake of acid."

He shrugged. "Don't know. Never bothered you before."

"You're kidding," I said. "How's that possible?"

He shrugged again. "Mind over matter, I guess."

"That explains it," I replied. "I lost my mind. But I'm going to get it back." I dipped my paddle into the surf and looked back at Hanale over my shoulder. "How far do we have to go?"

He pointed to the northwest, where an island rose out of the sea. Even in the dim light of the night sky, thick green foliage could be seen covering the sides of the volcano that stood near its centre, much like the island that we'd just left behind. A layer of cloud encircled the mount like a gossamer scarf. No glow of lava could be seen, nor any steam rising from the peak, and no signs of cooled lava flows were visible either, on this side at least. *Dormant, then*, I thought.

"Pretty," I said. I inhaled deeply, smelling the fresh sea air and the wind on my face. Overhead, the sky was clear and the stars shone bright, competing with the moon for attention. The air had cooled somewhat since the sun had set. With the winter jacket providing insulation, I was almost comfortable. "I could be happy here, if it wasn't so freaking warm during the day."

"No doubt," Hanale said. "You *always* like it here."

"Always?"

"You've been here many times," Hanale said.

I stopped paddling and turned in my seat. "Are you serious? Where?"

He pointed a thick finger over my shoulder at the island to which we were heading. "That's yours, Haukea Kane. It's been many years since you been back."

I resumed paddling, studying the island with renewed interest. *My island,* I thought, *my* tropical *island.* It might have been the power of suggestion, but now that Hanale had said it, there was something familiar about it.

"You seem surprised."

"It's warmer and greener than any place I thought I'd live."

Hanale chuckled. "Roger that. Inside, the Allfrost Chamber, it's *ho`oilo.* Very *anu.*"

"*Ho`oilo,*" I said. "That means winter, right? And *anu,* that's chilly or cold."

"Your memory coming back, brother?"

"Not sure," I said.

My memory was like a partially completed puzzle. Many of the finished pieces made no sense without knowing the larger context. Being here in this familiar place added pieces that formed connections in my mind, made other parts make sense and dredged up deeply buried or long disused memories. My guess was that these weren't lost so much as in deep archival storage, brought to the surface by current events and the lack of other memories to obscure them.

"The Allfrost Chamber—it's inside the volcano." I knew it to be true even as I said it.

"There's an entrance this side of the island," Hanale said.

"Have you been inside recently?"

"No, it's blocked by ice. Frozen shut."

We paddled in silence for a while. "Are you Hawaiian, Hanale?"

"Kind of," Hanale said, chuckling. "More honorary and in spirit. I've spent a long time here, there and all over the ocean."

"But you're like Olivia and Wilhelm, right? Yet you don't speak like they do."

"We talk like people where we live," Hanale said. "We blend into our surroundings, like chameleons."

"How many others like you live here?"

"Depends," Hanale said. "Many come and go. Just me on my island, most of the time."

"Seems kind of lonely."

"I like my privacy, brother. People, they want you to behave like they think you should, live like they think you should, think like they think you should, use the words they want you to use, do what they want you to do. They take what you make, demand your time and attention. Constrict and constrain. Me, I want to do, be, what I want when I want, as much or as little as I want."

"Everyone needs someone," I said, glancing back at him.

"Humans, maybe. Most are too weak to survive alone."

"But not you?"

"No *man* is an island, but we are," Hanale said, giving another powerful stroke. "Our knowledge, abilities, and biology free us of the tyranny of the group."

"Right, but you've teamed up with Wilhelm, Olivia and Aceso."

"Against the Faction," Hanale said. "Against the Group. Against those looking to control how we and others choose to live."

"And your job is keeping people from finding this place?"

He grunted affirmatively.

"And what if someone manages to break through those wards?"

"They wish they hadn't," Hanale said. "Only animals are allowed to freely come and go from here."

I dipped the paddle into the sea once more. "Sounds like you like animals more than people."

"Depends on the person," Hanale said, waggling his head. "I like some people a whole lot, but they're the exception."

"But why give animals slack that you don't give to people?"

"Animals are innocents," Hanale said. "They're just being themselves. People they know better and do horrible things anyway."

"Or they've convinced themselves that the horrible things are actually good things," I said, thinking of the Bodhi Group. "Still, a lot of people *are* good, too. Like my friends."

"When it comes to protecting Olympus, we don't take any chances," Hanale said.

"Isn't that where the gods live? Some mountain in Greece, right?"

"Used to be, but now it's here," Hanale replied. "Well, not the mountain, but where the gods live. Least those not part of the Faction. This is New Olympus."

"And my island is part of New Olympus?"

"Yeah, brother."

I stopped paddling and turned to face him. "Do the protections you mentioned include *my* island?" I said, waving the blade of my paddle to the front of the outrigger.

Hanale nodded. "All the islands are under the same enchantment, but yours has some of its own."

"Enchantment? Olivia said you use technology, not magic."

"Just words, brother," Hanale replied.

"Anything I need to watch out for?"

He shrugged. "Don't know. Been a while since I last visited. It's your island, so not likely."

The green volcano lay nearer now. A thin strip of white sand could be seen along the shoreline, and mild waves washed toward the tree line before being clawed back by gravity. Hanale steered us parallel to the shore and we paddled a short distance southwest before heading in. We hopped out and pulled the canoe onto land, far enough that the incessant waves wouldn't disturb it. Hanale led me up the beach to the thick jungle's edge and pointed to a narrow path leading into the tangle of green. "This will take you to the entry to the Allfrost Chamber. It's about a fifteen-minute walk, mostly uphill."

"You're not coming?"

Hanale looked back out at the water. "I need to get home. I've been away too long already. You've got this, my friend."

I looked sidelong at the trees. "But how will I find the entrance?"

"The trail will take you right there. You can't miss it, brother. It's blocked by a wall of ice. Hard to overlook."

I held out my hand. "Thank you, Hanale, for getting me this

far."

"Geev'um, Shivurr," said the big man. He grabbed my hand firmly, pulled me closer, and slapped my shoulder.

"Frostspeed," I replied, the word rising from the depths of my recovering memory. I turned away, walked up the sand, and entered the forest.

Chapter 25

Homecoming

Within the trees, the world was pitch black, as the vegetation blocked out the light of the night sky. Countless birds sang overlapping songs competing with insects for volume. I luminesced my body for light. I was alone again, after days in the company of friends.

With time to think, my mind drifted, thinking about the Faction that Olivia, Wilhelm and Hanale had mentioned several times now.

Why did this Faction try to kidnap me? I thought.

I should have asked more questions, but there had been too much else going on at the time—too much information and worry over Scott and my missing friends. Olivia had described the Faction as a splinter group of their people, meaning that they must be gods too—and they wanted me for some reason. As if I didn't have enough on my plate with my memories gone, the Bodhi Group hunting me, and my friends missing, I was now apparently caught in an ancient war against hostile mythological deities pursuing an unknown agenda.

I ascended the winding path for several minutes when a monstrous roar shook the trees, silencing birds and insects alike. I froze in mid-stride, looking to my right, toward the sound. A few hundred feet in that direction, the sound of breaking branches and flapping leaves disturbed the evening's calm. The sound of running feet thundering through the underbrush, directly toward me, came next. I picked up my pace and jogged up the path.

The sounds of pursuit changed direction to match my new position. With my body aglow, I stood out like a lighthouse in the darkness. I thought about quelling my light source, but I'd be effectively blind. Besides, if the thing chasing me caught up, I wanted to see it coming. Whatever it was, I knew it must be huge, judging by the cracking of branches and heavy footfalls of its approach.

Wild boar? I wondered. Hanale said he doubted there was anything dangerous on the island. Then again, a boar probably wasn't all that dangerous to a god. I slowed my pace. My shoulders relaxed and my breathing calmed as I turned and waited for my pursuer to catch up.

Okay, I thought, shaking my head. *I may not be a god, but bring it on, boar. This is* my *island after all.*

The footsteps slowed as they approached. The thing stopped just beyond the reach of my light. I could hear it breathing—huffing like a steam engine—and imagined its eyes were studying me from the shadows.

Then again, maybe it's something else. Something truly dangerous that Hanale doesn't know about. He did say it'd been a while since he'd last visited the island.

I rushed forward several steps. "What do you want?" I yelled. "Go on. Get out of here."

Footsteps retreated a few steps deeper into the jungle. Before they did, I saw huge glowing eyes glaring at me from ten feet above the forest floor.

Damn, not a wild boar, I thought.

Moments later, it burst from cover, closing the distance on all fours with stunning speed. A telephone-pole-sized arm knocked me off my feet, and I crashed through the damp leaves of tropical plants, flying twenty feet through the air. I slid along the ground and came to rest at the base of a koa tree.

The beast reared back on its legs, standing taller, thrust its arms wide, and gave an ear-splitting howl of triumph out of a mouth that looked like it could swallow basketballs whole, leaning forward as it did so.

The thing was massive, twelve feet tall hunched over on its knuckles. Immensely muscular, greenish-skinned, with long arms. Its forearms sported dangerous-looking bony spikes, ending in hands the size of small refrigerators. Its head looked nearly the size of my entire body, with a hooked nose and pointed ears and angry cat-like eyes.

It reminded me of something from Wilhelm's Monster Manual, but a lot scarier in person in the dark forest, alone. The word *troll* surfaced from the depths of my damaged memory, accompanied by a flash of a long-ago encounter with others of my attacker's kind. But this wasn't at all like the troll in the Monster Manual. That looked frail, twisted, and small—nothing like this hulking mass of green flesh and muscle.

Spittle flew from its maw as I regained my feet and stood unsteadily.

"All right, *numbnuts*," I said under my breath, dusting myself off with my free hand. "Catch frost."

My arm blurred, and a solid line of blinding bright white vapour appeared in the gloom. The creature moved as I threw; instead of striking its nose, the gob of frost plowed into its right ear. Its hand flew to the side of its head. It grimaced and howled as I continued my attack, hitting it in the nose and eyes.

Scrunching its eyes tight, it charged toward me. I shuffled to the side, trying to get out of the way, but the monster threw its arms out wide like a net and gathered me into a crushing embrace. I slugged it in the chest and face with frost-charged hands. Sparks of white flared in the murk with each impact. The troll winced and grunted, then grabbed me around the waist, squeezing me like he was trying to get the last bit out of an empty tube of toothpaste.

Right, like this guy's ever brushed his teeth, I thought.

My body constricted, thickening its outer layer of ice to resist the crushing force. Cracking sounds, like ice breaking off a glacier emanated from my lower half, making me cringe.

Desperate to escape its crushing grasp, I routed deep cold through my body, super cooling it. The troll hollered, but instead of letting go, it leaned back and chucked me into the trees. I saw stars as I slid into a large moss-covered boulder. Dazed, I pushed myself upright, using the rock for support.

The troll waggled its fingers, then rubbed its hands like it was trying to start a fire. Cupping its meat hooks together, it blew hot breath into them and gave me the stink eye while I shook my head to clear it. Then it clapped its hands three times and went down on all fours again, kicking up earth behind it.

Here we go, I thought.

The giant lumbered toward me like a defensive end eager to sack the quarterback. I stepped back, bumping into the boulder that had stopped my trip through the jungle. Unable to retreat further, I crouched low and bellowed a challenge of my own.

"Come on," I snarled, taunting it.

Trying not to flinch, I waited until it had a full head of steam, then thrust my hands out, palms up. Snow and ice welled from the ground beneath my feet, expanding outward in a circle twenty feet in diameter.

I ran at the behemoth, shouting like a lunatic.

Its massive arms reached out, trying to grab me in another bear hug. At the last moment, I dropped into the snow and felt a rush of air as its outstretched hands swiped past, almost taking my hat with them.

The troll ducked its chin into its chest to glare at me as it sped by. It looked up and squawked, braking at the sight of the rapidly approaching boulder, but kept sliding forward on the slippery snow. Milliseconds later, a sound like meat hitting concrete reached my ears as the creature crashed into the unyielding rock.

I swam forward through the snow to the circle's edge, resurfaced and spun a hundred and eighty degrees, readying a frost ball.

The troll lay unmoving at the base of the stone. I nudged it with my foot. No reaction. I walked around to its massive head. The troll's eyes were closed, its face scrunched in a rictus of pain, its tongue lolling. I crept closer, leaned in, and held my hand in front of its mouth. Warm air blew across my outstretched hand.

I patted its huge arm. "Play with the bull, my hard-headed friend, you get the horns."

The troll's eyelids twitched, and I jerked my hand away, before retreating on tiptoe, keeping an eye out for further movement. Belatedly it occurred to me that this guy might not be alone, so I looked and listened but didn't see or hear anything else unusual or threatening. I exhaled a breath that I hadn't realized I was holding.

What are you doing here my oversized friend? And why didn't Hanale know you were here? They were good questions, but I knew that the troll wasn't going to answer them, and I certainly didn't want to wait for him to wake up so that I could ask them. I realized that I'd have to take it up with the big man when next we met.

I hurried away, following the trail of destruction back to the path and racing along it, eager to put as much distance between me and the sleeping giant as I could before it recovered. My feet ached and my chest heaved as I ascended the steep slope moving, I presumed, higher up to the dormant volcano.

A few minutes later, the trail opened into a large clearing: a rough semicircle thirty feet wide. The floor was covered in snow, glistening with wetness. The top layer looked a bit slushy, melted by the jungle heat, but thick snowfall fell from thin air ten feet above the ground, replenishing it as fast as it melted. Near the centre sat a circular platform of stone like the one in the Nevada Allfrost Chamber. Similar runes, mostly nonsense to me, decorated the innermost ring, lit by the cool blue that emanated from the material itself. Also, as at the Nevada Chamber, a pulsating globe of white energy hovered a few feet above it at the epicentre.

I moved out onto the snowy ground, stepping from a steam bath into an icebox. I glided deeper into the clearing and held up a hand to savour the cold radiating from the pulsating globe. I slipped off my jacket and turned my back to the orb, letting the cold sink deeply into my pores, massaging away aches and pains like magic. The sound of my skin crackling into icy hardness was like footsteps on crushed glass. *Beautiful.* Tossing the jacket onto the wet snow, I held out my hands, palms up, and caught snowflakes as they fell, then turned my head to the sky and opened my mouth to catch them on my tongue.

Feeling rejuvenated, I looked around. Whatever this clearing was, it wasn't the Allfrost Chamber. For one, it stood in the open air, making it hardly a chamber.

And there's no tholos, I thought. *Is this just an oasis of ice and snow for people like me—a resting ground or temporary sanctuary—or did it serve another function?* The former made sense. *Snow people like me, living in the tropics*, I reasoned, *would need to escape the heat now and then. There's just no way of knowing for sure. What I need to do is get my memories back and I'll know what this is and a lot more.*

I grabbed my jacket from the snow and put it back on. I zipped my jacket up to my neck and walked from the clearing, taking a path at the far side that continued uphill, deeper into the island. The warm air hit me like a punch in the face as I stepped from the snowfall onto the bare forest floor, but I took it in stride, re-energized from the cold oasis. Eager to get this over with, I broke into a run, racing through the tropical jungle like a lunatic, trailed by a cloud of steam, heading, I hoped, for much drier, even warmer Nevada air.

Ten minutes later, the trees fell away, presenting another clearing, larger than the last. A wall of greenery rose steeply from the other side, hiding all but a few bits of volcanic rock that peeked through intermittently. The barrier was rough and irregular, rising into the mist overhead fifty feet up the wall. A large crooked opening, fifteen feet high and thirty feet across, sat in the middle, reminding me of the troll's gaping maw.

Shadows danced within as I approached, descending into the cave. Fifty feet inside, the walls gathered close, narrowing to about arm's length, forming a tunnel that was soon blocked by a wall of solid ice.

Eyes wide, I ran my hand over the surface, savouring the sensation. The ice seemed impervious to the warm air of the tropical night, showing no signs of melting. A few tendrils of misty water vapour drifted lazily off the surface, but the cave floor where I stood was virtually dry.

This must be it, I thought. I leaned forward, pushed against it, and slipped into the hard ice as if it were mere fog.

I followed the tunnel down into the earth for several hundred feet before emerging from the ice back into open air. The walls here glowed, lit by some unknown substance or process from beneath a thin layer of ice and the air felt well below zero. I doused my inner light, relying instead on the tube's built-in illumination, and continued my descent.

Now this feels like home, I thought, sighing.

A few minutes later, the lava tube gave way to a vast roughly oval chamber, three hundred feet across, rising a hundred feet overhead. Clouds of fog filled the far spaces of the chamber and floated a foot off the floor, illuminated by a halo of bluish-white light that shone through the thick coating of ice that covered its walls and floor.

Like the Nevada Allfrost Chamber, the room contained a large tholos at one side, near the centre of a sunken amphitheatre. Unlike in the damaged Nevada Chamber, a huge ball of snow, glowing a bright blue-tinted white and emitting a powerful thrumming sound, floated up and down, floor to ceiling, at this tholos's centre. Across the room rested another raised circular dais like the one in the forest outside. This one's surface also displayed a variety of intricate runes and a pulsating ball of white energy floating five feet above it.

"Greetings, Sentinel Shivurr," said a voice as I strode down the steps toward the tholos. "Welcome home. It has been five thousand, three hundred and twenty-nine days since your last visit."

Chapter 26

Hue, Are You?

I peered into the fog, trying to locate the speaker, but didn't know which way to look; it seemed to come from everywhere, as if broadcast over a loudspeaker.

"What the—? Hello? Who is that?" I asked when I didn't see anyone. "Show yourself."

"Certainly," said the voice. A translucent humanoid figure of white light materialized in front of me, ten feet away. Its face was just a hint of a nose, two eyes, and eyebrows suggested by subtle alterations in the colour of the light that defined it. "How may I be of assistance?"

"Who are you?"

"Is this a diagnostic query, Sentinel?" asked the figure as its colour shifted, taking on a light blue tone.

"Uh, sure," I said. "Why not?"

"My name is Hue," answered the voice amiably, now tinged a faint green. "I am Allfrost Controller four zero two."

"Do you live here?"

A slight pause. "I do not so much live here as I am *of* here. Are you well, Sentinel?"

"Sure, I'm great. Just a bit of amnesia."

"Understood, Sentinel," the figure said. "How very interesting."

"I'm glad you're entertained."

"My apologies. My existence has been tedious for many years, since you left. Without you, I have been unable to fulfill my purpose."

"What purpose?"

"To safeguard and preserve the Allfrost."

"What does that involve?"

"Careful monitoring and adjustment of its systems to proactively correct problems before they require your attention. When those problems cannot be resolved, they are passed along to Sentinels such as yourself. When such situations arise, I support you and other Sentinels in resolving those issues."

"This is wicked. I lived here, then," I said, looking around. "This *is* my kind of place."

Hue shook his head. "Some of the time. Sentinels go where they are needed most. Wherever the Allfrost needs to be defended, maintained, or restored. I, and others like me, assist you in those duties, identifying and prioritizing, as well as providing a control interface to the Allfrost itself."

"And how do I do that? Defend, maintain, and restore, I mean."

"Using your gifts, you protect its nodes against any entities threatening its operation. Maintenance generally involves ensuring the Allfrost nodes remain cold enough to retain perpetual connection to the Underfrost. Restoration is the process of mending that connection when it breaks down, which sometimes occurs either through natural degradation or malfeasance."

I wandered over to the platform with the pulsating white sphere. "Sounds like a lot of responsibility. Why is the Allfrost so important? Why do we Sentinels do what we do? I mean, what is it aside from a transportation network?"

Hue stared, raising an eyebrow. "The Allfrost machine was built to create paradise on earth."

"Paradise? Paradise for whom?"

"For you, and others of your kind," replied Hue.

"You're saying this Allfrost, it makes the entire planet colder," I said. I thought of the hot Nevada desert and sultry jungle outside. "It doesn't seem to be doing the best job."

Hue's voice took on an edge. "Freezing the entire planet is beyond the Allfrost's design purpose. The original intent was to freeze the northern hemisphere from the pole to the forty-ninth parallel and the southern hemisphere from the pole to the twenty-sixth parallel, while leaving the region between unfrozen."

"Forty-ninth parallel? That's the Canada-US border. Lucy said it's cold there, but not that cold. She said it was hot there even, in summer."

"Indeed, that is expected. That is due to two main factors."

"Which are?"

"The Allfrost is operating at suboptimal efficiency."

"And the other?"

"Human habitation is creating a greenhouse effect, warming the planet. If not for the Allfrost, the globe would be much warmer than it already is."

"You're telling me that if the Allfrost was working properly, the earth would be enjoying an ice age. Is that it?"

"That is correct," said Hue. "Given the Allfrost's current state, global warming will likely delay the next ice age by several decades, possibly keeping glaciers from reaching as near the equator as in the past. However, this might be temporary should humanity's impact on the climate decline because of the ice age."

"As in the past," I said softly, staring at the snowball rising and falling within the tholos across the room. "The planet was frozen before, then?"

"Many times," Hue said.

"Yeah, but if it was frozen before, why didn't it stay that way?"

Hue cocked his head. "It is all part of the cycle. Without change, there is only stagnation. Everything has its time, then has it again."

"Yeah, if you say so," I said absently, thinking. Hue waited, saying nothing. "You said this was to create a paradise on earth for me and my kind. Do you mean Sentinels?"

"Sentinels and others of your people. Sentinels are guardians of the Allfrost, but not all your people are Sentinels."

"I see. Where are they, then?"

"Sentinels?"

"Sure."

"Unknown," Hue said in a pained tone of voice. "No

Sentinel other than yourself has been seen in several hundred years."

"And others of my kind? Those that aren't Sentinels?"

"Also unknown. The Sentinels went in search of them, and they vanished too."

I rubbed my temples and looked at him. "You're telling me I'm the last of my kind that you've seen in centuries. The last Sentinel. The last…what did we call ourselves? My people, I mean."

"You refer to yourselves as Borealans," Hue said.

"And I'm the last Borealan?"

"Apparently so," Hue said in a soft voice. "Yes."

"Borealan?" I said, stroking my chin. "Did we name ourselves after Boreas?"

"Quite the opposite. The entity Boreas chose that moniker after meeting your people."

"Huh, how about that," I said. "And how many Sentinels were there?"

"Two thousand and forty-eight at their peak."

"And I'm the last one?"

"Correct," Hue said. "The workload has been too great for a single Sentinel—hence the Allfrost's decline. Your absence these past years, coupled with the strain of global warming, has accelerated the decline." Hue's voice cheered. "However, now that you are back, your work can resume, and the degradation can be slowed, if not reversed."

I shook my head. "Not yet, Hue. First, I need to get my memory back and rescue some friends of mine." I pointed at the Allfrost Transporter. "To do that, I need to use that and get back to Nevada."

Hue studied the ceiling briefly. "The Nevada Chamber is compromised. Human invaders have infiltrated it and damaged and removed critical components. It is still on the network, but its power is nearly depleted, and its transporter is non-functional."

"But this one works, right? I can get there using it, can't I?"

"Certainly," Hue replied. "The Nevada Chamber's power

nodes have sufficient strength to assist in the transport there, but you will not be able to use that chamber to travel elsewhere. You will have to travel by other means to another Allfrost Chamber to return. The nearest is in Death Valley, which is more than two hundred miles away."

"No problem," I said. "My friends can drive. Tell me more about those power nodes that you mentioned."

"Each Allfrost Chamber is surrounded by an array of nodes," Hue said, pointing over my shoulder at the white ball hovering over the dais. "Like that one, over there. The power nodes are connected to the Underfrost, drawing energy and coldness from its limitless supply. They are also involved in the transportation process, improving accuracy, guiding the transport vessel to its destination with increased precision. They act jointly, providing redundancy and coverage. Via their Oculi, they also allow for remote viewing of their location from any Allfrost Chamber."

"Remote viewing?"

"They allow you to view the power node's location as if you are there," Hue said.

"Like watching it on TV?"

"I am afraid I do not know what that is," Hue said. "Shall I show you?"

"Please do."

"Come," Hue said. He floated over to the fountain that sat within a circle of stone at the foot of the tholos. A raised edge ran around the circle's circumference, forming a lip, as if to hold water. "Stand in front of the fountain, please. You need to select a destination so that the tholos knows where to send you."

I stepped out of the snow into the stone circle and stood next to him. I looked down at the fountain in front of me, leaning my stomach against the bowl. Half-filled with unfrozen water, two feet in diameter, it reminded me of a large bird bath. I looked at Hue—now magenta-coloured—expectantly, wincing at the glare. "Looking at your face is like staring into the sun, dude."

"My apologies, Sentinel," Hue said. "I do not have a

complete visage of my own. I am not really here at all—at least not physically." He gestured theatrically at his body, looking down at himself. "This is just a phantasm created by sophisticated manipulation of light and matter."

"You're kidding." I moved closer to Hue and reached out to poke his shoulder. My hand passed through unhindered. "So, you're a ghost." I smiled wryly. "A ghost in the Allfrost machine."

"An apt description, but technically I am an artificial intelligence with a holographic corporeal form and limited telepathic interface."

"Wait, did you say telepathic?" I made a face. "You can read my mind?"

Hue held up his hands. "Just surface thoughts and images, when you are standing on the Allfrost Transporter pad. It is invaluable in communicating where you wish to travel with maximum accuracy."

I nodded imperceptibly, looking at him where his face should be. "I get it, I think." I winced again and looked away, blinking.

"I believe I have a solution," Hue said. He covered his face with his hands, then pulled them away and looked at me with Brad's face. "Is this better?" he asked. "This is one of the faces at the forefront of your thoughts."

My jaw dropped and I stared.

"Not to your liking, I see," Hue said after a pause. He covered his face again. Brad's short hair lengthened, growing long and wavy. When he took his hands away, Lucy stood before me. "Would you prefer this one?"

"Whoa, you're freaking me out, Hue. I'm not going snow-blind anymore, but I'm getting a bit creeped out; it's like my friends are haunting me."

"Oh, are these friends dead?"

"*No*, they aren't dead," I said, too loudly. Taking a breath, I continued in a softer voice. "They are *not* dead."

"These friends—they are those you are intending to rescue," Hue said. It wasn't a question. He looked thoughtful. "Oh, I see. I understand now. Your memories…stolen…outrageous. How dare they? Thank you, Sentinel. I believe I understand your mission parameters now. Thoughts are so much faster than words."

I scowled and took a step back. "Get out of my head, Hue."

The AI, still wearing Lucy's face, looked affronted. "Forgive me if I have intruded, Sentinel. These thoughts are very palpable. I could not help but perceive them while you are standing on the departure platform."

"All right," I said. "Just forget about it. Please go back to looking like a ghost or something. You're still weirding me out." A moment later, the ghostly apparition reappeared. I took a step forward to stand in front of the fountain. "So how does this thing work?"

"To begin, think about what you would like to see. Just visualize it in your mind."

I thought back to my time in the Allfrost Chamber in Nevada, watching the scientists conducting their reckless experiments, when the fire elementals had appeared out of thin air. Moments later, an image of that chamber appeared before me on an oval viewscreen three feet wide and six feet tall, suspended a few feet off the ground. The vision was so clear, it was as if I were looking at it through a doorway to another room. The Nevada Chamber was mostly dark, with a few figures moving around within.

Thinking of my flight from the chamber, the exterior camp appeared as if viewed from a distance, then zoomed to a closer vantage point. It teemed with people. Many more than before. Trucks moved in and out and soldiers moved about, armed and alert.

"Unbelievable," I said. "How is it I can see outside when the node is inside the cavern?"

"The Oculi permit viewing within a limited range; the vantage point can be moved within a sphere surrounding it to a range of several thousand feet for a fully-activated node."

"It looks kind of busy there," I said. "Not the best place to arrive."

I thought of the Schmidts' home, but the screen faded to black.

"That location is beyond the reach of the closest Allfrost node," Hue said, answering my unspoken question.

"Got it," I said, frowning. "How many nodes are associated with the Nevada Chamber?"

"One thousand and twenty-eight, minimum, but often more depending on location. They are typically arranged in loosely concentric circles, radiating outward."

"Is that required, technically?"

"No, it is more to maximize coverage with the minimum number of nodes, by distributing them evenly. This is frequently not possible for reasons of practicality and security, in which case the nodes are moved to the nearest feasible location."

"Is there a way to go through all the locations in sequence?" Hue's glowing amorphous head bobbed affirmatively. "Great. Please cycle through them, Hue. Show me every area for one second each."

For the next minute, desert scenes lit by the night sky materialized on the screen before me. There was little to distinguish one from the other in the dim light. Bushes, rocks and hills changed position but otherwise the locations looked nearly identical. Then a streak of reddish-orange fire appeared, distant but unmistakable, before the view switched to another poorly lit visual.

"Wait, go back!" I said, leaning forward, resting my hands on the stone basin. The viewscreen flickered, and the fire returned. "Can we get closer to that? To the fire," I said, pointing a finger.

A gang of fire elementals jumped into view, perhaps twenty feet from the camera's viewpoint. They were moving across the desert in loose formation, travelling a straight line to somewhere, leaving a trail of scorched and burning earth in their wake. "Looks like they're on the march," I muttered. "But to where?"

"Unknown," Hue answered, now coloured deep purple. "They are heading southwest. Would you like to see a top-down view of the region?" Before I could answer, another viewscreen appeared to the left of the first one. It looked like a star map at first, with numerous white dots distributed in roughly concentric rings with a larger dot of light at the centre. *The Allfrost power nodes*, I realized. A dot of red light moved near the lower left. "The red dot represents the fire entities."

"Thanks, but without landmarks, I'm not sure that helps," I said. A moment later, additional icons with lettering next to them appeared. One in the southeast read "Las Vegas." To the upper-left, Tonopah was marked; on the right, Lunar Crater; and above it, the damaged Allfrost Chamber. Seconds later, another icon appeared along the fire elementals' path of travel. Then more text appeared, identifying it as the Bodhi Institute.

"More mind reading," I said, glancing at Hue sidelong. He said nothing, shrugging. I returned to studying the map. I pointed a finger, dragging it from the fire elementals to the Bodhi Institute. "It's almost as if they're heading straight there."

"They are still a few miles away. It is possible that the facility merely lies along their path."

"Yeah, maybe. At least we've found a node that's reasonably close to where I need to go. Though I don't want to tangle with those things again, if I can help it." I studied the image of the fire elementals, still blazing a trail toward the Institute. "Please continue to cycle through the locations. I want to see if there's a better option. Maybe something closer."

The slideshow restarted, showing more nondescript locations. Then the screen went entirely black. "Wait, hold it there," I commanded. I leaned in and squinted, studying the view intently. "Is there something wrong with the view? Why is it black? I should be able to see something. It's not *that* dark."

Hue sounded puzzled. "The node's location must be enclosed within something that lacks a light source."

"Can you move the viewpoint? Try to find a lighted area within range of it?"

"Of course," Hue said. "One moment." The view remained black. Several minutes passed.

"Are you doing it? It's still dark."

"Indeed, the region to cover is quite large, and moving the Oculus through the entire area is taking some time," Hue said in a patient voice. "The node must be located deep underground."

"Well, keep—" A flash of light appeared on the screen, then

disappeared. "Did you see that? Go back." The view brightened again as the camera reverted, displaying a lab room. Beakers and flasks sat on long tables next to Bunsen burners. Counters and sinks lined the walls. The room's overhead lights were off, presumably due to the late hour, but illumination entering through large windows that lined one wall cast enough light by which to see.

"Move the view to the hallway, Hue. Let's walk around and try to figure out where this is."

"Just envision where you'd like the view to go and it will follow your desires," Hue suggested.

"Neat," I replied, moving it a few feet. "How does that work?"

"I'm acting as an interface between you and the Oculus," Hue explained, "passing your wishes along in real time."

"I'm starting to see telepathy's appeal."

I moved the view through the windows and raced it along the hallway, passing doorways labelled with numbers but no names. Doors and signs rushed past as I searched for clues, something, anything, that might help me figure out where I was.

I turned a corner and gasped, stepping back from the viewscreen. A uniformed security guard, black baton hanging from his belt, turned a key, locking a door down the hall. He rotated to his right and walked down the hall away from me a moment later.

"Can people on the other side see anything? See me?"

"No, not at all," Hue said. "The Oculus is undetectable without the proper equipment. Equipment that humans do not as yet possess."

Comforted by that knowledge, I jumped the camera ahead of the guard and turned to face him. Seeing his name tag and uniform up close, I realized where I was. I'd seen that same grey-and-black uniform on other guards too many times before.

This was the Bodhi Institute.

"This is the facility where I was held," I said aloud. I looked at the left-most screen, still showing the icons identifying the Allfrost nodes. "There's no node marker at the Institute, though.

Is the Bodhi Institute marker covering it?"

"One moment," Hue replied, holding up a hand. The security guard walked through the camera, out of sight. After a pause, he continued. "That is Node Six. It is not where it is supposed to be."

"Node Six? Where is it supposed to be?" A light started blinking near the damaged Allfrost Chamber. "That's pretty close to the chamber. The Bodhi Group must have found it and moved it to the Institute."

At my command, the view started moving again. I caught up with the guard as he stepped onto an elevator a short distance away. I moved the Oculus into the car and watched as he pressed a button on the control panel. The elevator rose fast. The doors dinged open on the top aboveground floor and the guard got out.

I followed.

He turned right and walked over to a nearby bank of vending machines. As he fumbled with his change, I slipped past him and roamed the halls of the floor, searching for my friends. I found a lot of offices and storage rooms and small kitchens with eating areas for the employees on that level but no sign of my friends, so I moved on to the lower level.

I found more of the same until I moved the Oculus to the building's entrance, a foyer that looked out on a mostly empty asphalt parking lot. The foyer ceiling towered twenty-five feet above, with one side lined by a balcony, next to which offices and conference rooms could be seen.

I took the stairs that led up to it at one side of the cavernous room. Reaching the top, I saw that the balcony continued to my left as a two-sided hallway. As I turned in that direction, the same guard that I'd seen earlier leaned over to lock another door sixty feet in that direction, then strode toward the viewscreen.

With a thought, the view drifted forward, heading for the door that the security guard had just locked. I moved it through the frosted glass that formed the room's outer wall.

Lucy and Brad sat at a table in the centre of a spacious conference room, snuggled against each other in rolling office chairs, looking tired and dishevelled, holding hands. Several plastic trays lay on the table, holding bottles of Coke and partially eaten sandwiches. Against the wall to the right, Lilith slept in Alan's arms on a black leather sofa, both apparently asleep.

I had found them. The Bodhi Group had them after all.

Chapter 27

Return of the Snowman

It made sense keeping them in one of the conference rooms on the main aboveground floors; the facility wasn't well-equipped to hold a group of young civilians anywhere else. Subfloor fifteen had holding facilities, but they were spartan to say the least. Plus, keeping them there would reveal more of the Institute to them than would be desirable to the secret organization. No, to the Bodhi Group, it made far more sense to keep them in the more public areas, keeping the existence of the much larger underground levels secret. It was a good omen, indicating that Dixon didn't plan on making their stay permanent, at least not yet. If they were kept in the lower levels, it would be like a bank robber removing his mask—not a good sign.

Everyone looked tired and tense but otherwise okay. Judging by the food on the long mahogany conference table, they'd been fed at some point, too. I couldn't tell if they'd been interrogated yet or not. *Maybe Dixon's letting them sweat first, softening them up for questioning.*

If they were okay, it didn't matter to me what the kids told him; it would just waste his time. They didn't even know the location of the arcade where Scott, Caleb and I had hidden out in Las Vegas when we'd fled the Schmidts' place. *Good luck finding me in the middle of the Pacific Ocean*, I thought, smirking.

My friends located, I kept exploring the compound, visiting areas that I'd been barred from entering during my captivity. The hallways and rooms were mostly quiet. Some early risers were starting to move about in their quarters while security guards roamed the building checking doors, looking bored. I moved quickly; I didn't have time to search the entire facility. I didn't know how long I had before the gang would be questioned again or moved. Parts of it lay outside the Oculus's range anyway.

Thirty minutes later, I had worked out that the Institute lay mostly underground, beneath a two-storey aboveground office building. The latter contained several conferences rooms like the one holding my friends, a large cafeteria, vending machines, waiting areas and washrooms. The northwest corner of the ground-level building also contained an indoor parking lot, protecting employee vehicles from bleaching in the merciless Nevada sun. The parkade looked about a quarter full currently. *The lot outside must be mainly reserved for visitors*, I thought.

Banks of elevators were positioned throughout each level to take personnel to the lower levels. There were stairs too, but they were locked from the stairwell side, requiring a key card to get through. Only the aboveground stairwell doors appeared to lack card readers, suggesting that they were unlocked by default. If you took the stairs on a lower level, you'd better have access, or you'd have to walk to the top to get out. The deepest, those eleven storeys and below, which included the archival vault, were restricted access, requiring a key card to get to by elevator as well.

Fifteen floors down lay the large cave-like room where I'd spent most of the past few years. It looked warm; the layer of ice that had covered its walls during my incarceration had melted away, but my entertainment devices, books, and paraphernalia remained.

I guess they're saving power, I thought, moving along.

I could now see that it was one of several habitats on that level, apparently there to hold other experimental subjects. Most were empty, but one of those habitats housed a group of fire elementals like those that I had fought a number of times in recent days. They circled the room like fireflies trapped in a bottle, throwing the occasional incendiary at the concrete walls, leaving scorch marks but causing no meaningful damage.

The image wavered slightly as I shifted the viewing perspective inside.

"What's with the image, Hue?" I asked as it continued to waver. "Am I going out of range?"

"Negative, Sentinel. Thermal interference is degrading image quality."

"All right. Must be the heat those things are throwing."

I pulled the camera's viewpoint out of the holding cell and continued exploring. Near the centre of the same level sat a large cavernous room, three storeys high, with stairs leading up to balconies that overlooked the floor in the middle. At the epicentre, within a large refrigerated box of transparent glass, sat the unmistakable bulk of an Allfrost node, standing on its side—Node Six, I presumed. Photographic and electronic equipment surrounded it. I'd seen some of the same items in the Nevada Allfrost Chamber, but many were completely unfamiliar to me. I did, however, recognize the tools of geology and archaeology that lay resting on and nearby the platform.

Other levels contained kitchens, offices, auditoriums, washrooms, and supply closets. There were also sleeping quarters, both temporary and long-term. The former, I guessed, were for personnel working long hours, judging by the lack of personal items. The latter clearly belonged to those assigned full-time to protect the facility, as made clear by the nearby weapons lockers and the look of the occupants. There were even a few gymnasiums and an indoor pool that included attached showers and locker rooms.

I found the archival vault—where Scott had snatched the memory vials that he had given to me at his house—on a lower level, near the end of my search. The vault lay inside a large cave carved out of the earth and sealed by a thick circular vault door eight feet across. A woman wearing a lab coat and carrying a clipboard was leaving as I arrived, passing through an outer gate that allowed passage through a wall of thick bars.

"Will the transporter get me there?"

Hue hesitated before answering. "The cave within the vault should be a large enough arrival zone, yes. However, arrival points fluctuate with a small error rate. This is increased when transporting to underground destinations. Given the location, the transport vessel may try to rematerialize a few feet off, in solid matter."

"Doesn't sound good. Guess I'd be annihilated, right?"

"Nothing so severe. However, your final arrival point in such cases is indeterminate."

I turned my head to squint at him. "What does that mean?"

"You will rematerialize at a random unoccupied location," Hue said.

"Okay, but I'll still be close by, right?" I said, looking back at the screen. "What's the concern?"

"Probabilistically speaking, yes," Hue said. "However, that is not guaranteed. You may also arrive a hundred miles away, four thousand feet above the earth, or at some other undesirable position. The likelihood of any given location becoming your alternate arrival point declines the farther away that point is from your desired landing zone, but improbable things do occur on occasion. The worse the attempted arrival location, the greater the probability of a severe, catastrophic correction."

"Why does going underground matter?" I asked.

"Energy and matter in *this* reality have a presence and effect in the Underfrost," Hue said. "Temperature variations along the route of travel, as well as the density of the matter and energy through which you travel, can have unpredictable side effects."

I stroked my chin, staring into space. "All right, I get it." I paused, thinking. "I'll have to take that chance. Getting there from ground level has to be at least as dangerous." I leaned my hands on the edge of the stone fountain and looked at my reflection in the water within. "How do I operate this thing?"

"It is simple," Hue said. "Now that you have chosen a destination, you just need to activate the tholos by dropping frost into the fountain before you. Snow will rise from the platform on which you stand. When it does, submerge yourself, and you will be propelled through the Underfrost to your destination."

"What will it be like?"

"I do not know," Hue said. "But you have done this many times before and never voiced any complaints about the experience."

"Well, I'd better get going, then," I said, producing a frost ball. "Thanks, Hue. I hope we meet again."

"As do I, Sentinel."

Without further discussion, I dropped the frost into the liquid of the fountain before me. Immediately upon contact with the water, snow welled up from beneath my feet, lifting me up. I sank into the snow and, moments later, was on my way. There was no sensation of motion as the snowball passed through the floor of the tholos, exited through its ceiling, and shot out of the Allfrost Transporter into the Underfrost, an icy missile, headed for the continent.

Time passed like a dream before I popped up from the snowball and gaped at my surroundings; I'd returned to the Bodhi Institute, albeit to a part of it that I'd never been to before. Less than a week had passed since I'd escaped through a side door of the surface-level building, but it seemed more like a month.

My chosen destination—the archival vault—was still deserted. It was still early enough to be called late, but the circular door that sealed the vault like a massive metal plug, eighteen inches thick, stood wide open. Beyond its bulk, a wall of metal bars provided a first line of defense.

It must be open for early risers getting a jump on the day or night owls pulling an all-nighter, I thought. *Too slow to open and close every time someone comes and goes. Which means someone might show up at any moment. I need to hurry.*

Nearby, an array of freezers and refrigerated cabinets sat next to each other in rows, like bookshelves in a library. I strode up and down the aisles, reading labels on the doors and shelves and containers within. I grimaced. To my dismay, many were marked with codes rather than plain English labels.

I pulled open the doors. *Not locked*, I thought. *Guess they figure if you made it this far, you must be authorized.* Glad of that at least, I started searching.

The first few contained test tubes of blood samples and other substances that I couldn't identify. I returned one to the shelf as the metal gate through the outer bars slid aside behind me, a hundred feet away. I ducked low and gently closed the glass door that I'd just opened, with an audible but muted sucking sound as the rubber liner resealed itself. Two sets of footsteps entered the room, their owners engaged in amiable conversation. I scuttled to the end of the aisle as the footfalls neared.

"I don't know," said a woman's voice as she slid open a drawer. "Marcus has been pushing the whole team for results. I don't have time to date anyone."

"You've got to eat sometime," said the second woman in a higher, louder voice. A freezer door opened with a pop, followed by the clink of bottles being rearranged. "We'll be there to break the ice." Several seconds of silence followed, then the same speaker said, "Come on, he's really cute."

"So was the last guy," said the other woman. I held my breath as they moved closer still. "And he knew it. He spent the entire dinner talking about himself and his work."

"It's not like you can talk about your secret research in an underground facility," said her companion. "Hey, what's this water doing here?"

"What water?"

"The floor's wet here," said the other woman.

My palm sparkled as I reached for frost.

"Oh, yeah. Condensation, maybe?"

"Yeah, I suppose so. I'll let maintenance know."

Another glass door opened, more bottles moved about, then the door slammed shut. I expelled the lungful of air that I'd been holding and sighed, hearing their footsteps growing fainter.

I peeked around the corner and watched as they exited the room, still chatting. I counted to five, then crept back along the cabinets, picking up where I'd left off. *Got to be systematic.*

I found what I was looking for two rows over. A tray of test tubes, glowing colourfully like radioactive sherbet, rested on the middle shelf. I grabbed a bottle. The label read "WB-19790605-HX0012." Beneath the serial number, it read "Rorubium 0.03%, Polarium, 0.026%," written with black marker in someone's careful hand. Like the other potions, the contents fluoresced as I held it in my hand, reacting to me in some way.

Should I drink them now? I wondered. I shook my head. *No, better not. The last two knocked me for a loop. Got to get out of here first.*

I slapped my hands over my ears and dropped the bottle as

an alarm blared to life. I stooped to grab the test tube as it fell, but it hit the concrete floor and shattered, spilling its contents across the floor like blood from a wound, but thicker and more viscous; it oozed wider in slow motion, rather than running wild like water.

Fuck a dirty duck, I mouthed silently. Having no hair to tear out, I banged my fists against my temples instead.

Red lights flashed in the hallway beyond the vault door, and it began to swing shut. *They know I'm here*, I thought. *The researchers must have seen me and played it cool.*

I didn't have time to wonder. I had to move. I dropped flat, put my mouth to the cold concrete and sucked up the broken vial's spilled contents, along with a lot of the glass shards.

I hope they keep these floors clean, I thought, spitting out fragments of glass.

I hopped to my feet, wiped my mouth, pulled my hat from my head, and started shovelling the other bottles into it.

I squinted one eye and put a hand over my mouth. *Is that stuff hitting me already?*

Dropping the last one into my cap, I plunked it on my head and raced for the vault door.

Only a three-foot gap remained. *Not enough*. I sprinted full bore toward it, cursing my luck.

I'm done. I walked right into their hands.

I rammed the door, throwing all my weight against it. My feet slid on the smooth concrete floor, and the door continued to swing closed, albeit slower than before. I sidestepped as the gap narrowed and channelled snow and ice into the breach, spreading it a few feet into the vault and out the door to the other side, then submerged into it and swam. Popping out the other side, I leaned against the wall, panting and wide-eyed. The vault door sealed itself a few seconds later, compressing and displacing the snow before steel bars locked it into place.

Got to keep moving. Bodhi Group security must be on their way.

I staggered for the outer gate, then rubbed my temples, snarling as a sharp pain stabbed through my head. I stumbled a few feet from the outer cage bars, reaching out to grab them before

I could fall, pressing my face against the cool metal.

That's potent stuff, I thought.

I pulled the unlocked gate aside and smiled through the pain, thankful getting out didn't require a pass card. I lurched through it, stooped over, then fell onto my hands a few steps later, jarring my wrists, and passed out.

Chapter 28

Emergency Exit

The alarm still rang when I woke. I pulled myself to my feet and teetered down the hall.

Dixon's team must be losing a step, I thought. *They should be here by now.*

As I ran, memories of Wilhelm and Olivia bubbled to the forefront of my thoughts, except that I thought of them by different names. *Their real names*, I realized; *Boreas and Orithyia.*

Orithyia wore a leather skirt and top that exposed a flat, muscular stomach and strong arms and legs. She held an ornately carved staff at her side that rose a foot past her head. Boreas looked as he had when battling fire elementals over the pool in his backyard—an eight-foot tall armoured green spectre held together by flows of air, light and unknown forces.

The stone walls of a castle keep surrounded us.

"Why won't they listen?" I asked, shaking my head.

Boreas's voice boomed, echoing against the stone of the hall. "We create. We watch. We manipulate. They're addicted to it. They won't give it up easily."

The scene changed to another part of the same castle—the interior of one of the massive towers that stood sentry at each corner of the large fortress; information that I knew intuitively in my waking dream state. Torches high on the walls lit the cylindrical room, leaving much of the area in shadow.

From the edge of the space, a humanoid thing of flesh, bone and sinew stared daggers at Boreas and me with an eyeless face. Its two arms ended in long fingers that sported vicious claws resembling the talons of a bird of prey.

"What is that thing?" I asked, making a face.

"Thing?" Boreas said, sounding offended. "Ouch, you wound me, Shivurrous. This is something I've been working on for a while. To help in the fight."

"Why does it look like that?"

He shrugged. "It's unfinished—a work in progress."

The patter of footsteps washed the vision away, forcing my mind back to the present.

Focus, Shivurr, I thought. *Take a walk down memory lane when you're not behind enemy lines.*

Back in the present, I huddled against the wall and moved ahead to a turn in the hallway and peered around the corner. Bodhi Group security forces, armed to the teeth, stood waiting by a bank of elevators. The doors of one dinged open a few seconds later. Seven men jumped on, and the doors closed.

I stepped from my hiding spot and approached. Numbers over the doors showed the lift rising rapidly toward the surface. I crashed through the doors to the left of the elevators, setting off an alarm, but the buzzing stopped as the spring-loaded door slammed shut and I bounded up the stairs.

No one's going to be coming to check it anytime soon. At least that's what I told myself.

Large numbers painted on the doors, three feet high, marked each level as I ran past, huffing and puffing. I winced, remembering that the archival vault was fifteen floors below ground and my friends were trapped on the second aboveground floor.

At subfloor five, I stopped, holding the railing for support. I tried to slow my breathing, listening for sounds of pursuit, and heard nothing but the still-ringing alarm. I resumed my ascent, continuing past ground level until I reached the second-floor exit. Unlike on the subterranean floors, this level's door did not appear to have an alarm.

Cracking it open a sliver, I peered out into the hallway. To the right, a hallway ran deeper into the facility. Ten feet to the left lay the balcony that I'd seen through the Oculus. I knew from my explorations that it overlooked the first-floor foyer and ran north toward the conference rooms and my friends. Seeing no one about, I slipped out the door and used my hand to inch it closed with a dull click.

"Attention, all non-security personnel, the facility is under attack. Proceed to your quarters or designated panic rooms and lock the doors until the situation is resolved. Security forces are working to resolve the situation as we speak," said a man's voice over a nearby loudspeaker. *I know that voice*, I realized. *It's Bodhi Institute Executive Director Wallace.*

I crept to the balcony's edge and looked down. A security force member stood by the wall, speaking into a red phone while two others wrestled with a fire hose pulled from a nearby cabinet and looked apprehensively toward the building's entrance and the sounds of gunfire beyond.

I crouched and hugged the far wall. Keeping back from the edge, out of their sight, I tiptoed along the balcony, heading for the conference rooms.

The phone clattered as the soldier returned it to the hook and shouted to the others. "Reinforcements are twenty minutes away. We've got to hold out until then."

A blond soldier with short hair stepped into my view, looking north. "What about the parking garage?"

"Don't sweat it. That's Jimenez and his team's problem."

"But why are they here?" asked a short soldier with curly black hair.

"It's obvious, isn't it?" spat the first. "They're here for the others. Use your head."

"Didn't think they were that smart," a soldier muttered as I moved out of earshot.

I left the balcony on the other side, entering a hallway of glass. Conference rooms lined both sides. I raced down the hallway to the room where I'd last seen my friends and swore under my breath. They were nowhere to be seen. They'd been taken—relocated when the attack had started, no doubt.

I turned to retreat and stopped, spotting them huddled under the conference table, looking at me with wide eyes and pale, drawn faces.

My eyes locked with Lucy's. She stared a moment, then a smile spread across her face. Her lips moved and the others turned to regard me as well. I smiled in return and waved, pointing to the door. I ran to it and gave it a push. The door refused to budge. *Oh, well, it was worth a shot.*

I scanned the hallway, looking for other options.

I flinched, throwing my hands up as the conference room door thumped loudly and an office chair crashed to the floor on the far side. The glass door appeared unscathed by the assault. Alan grabbed his makeshift battering ram as it settled against the floor, raising it high. I waved my hands like a base umpire signalling a runner as safe and shook my head. The teen cocked an eyebrow but lowered his arms.

I held up a finger on my right hand, then placed my left hand on the door, splaying my fingers wide. Taking a deep breath, I channeled cold into the glass. The door frosted over in seconds, making faint cracking sounds as it contracted and grew brittle. Wisps of vapour floated across the surface as the intense cold interacted with the warmer air of the hallway.

I continued to pour cold into it and watched the ice spread beyond the door's edge to the larger windows at either side. Hearing the glass crunch and crack, I reached back, clenched my hand into a fist and hammered the door. The glass spiderwebbed but failed to shatter.

I shook my hand and flexed my fingers, checking that everything still worked, as Alan waved me to the side and raised the chair. I stepped back, rubbing away the pain in my knuckles, as he smashed the chair's base into the weakened door sending pieces of glass and ice to the carpet at my feet.

I grinned and pumped my fist.

Alan used the chair to clear the opening, knocking the remaining debris out of the way. Lilith burst through a second later and wrapped her arms around my neck. The others soon followed, patting me on the back and shaking my uninjured hand.

"I knew you'd come for us," Lilith said, beaming.

"What's going on, Shivurr?" Brad asked. He pointed to a ringing alarm bell. "Is that because of you?"

I shook my head.

"Is Caleb okay?" Alan asked.

"Yeah, he's safe," I said. "Worried about you all, but totally safe."

Lucy grabbed my hand, studying it. "How's your hand? Does it hurt?" I nodded and she rubbed it lightly. It felt good. In a weird way, the warmth of her grip was soothing. "I wasn't sure you felt pain like we do."

"That'd be awesome," I said with a crooked smile, "but no such luck."

"Better put some ice on it," Alan said with a wink.

"Right," I said, snorting. "That'll work actually." I looked at Brad. "They don't know I'm here. They're under attack. By what I'm not sure."

"What's the plan?" Brad asked.

"We escape the same way I did before," I said. "There's an emergency exit. Scott disabled the cameras watching it."

"How do you know they're still disabled?" Lucy asked. "You've been gone for days now."

I shrugged. "There's not much choice. They've got better things to do than watch that camera right now, I'm guessing."

Brad was shaking his head. "Maybe, but then what? Where do we go? Back to Las Vegas?"

"That's where the van is," I said. "In the Schmidts' garage. You'll need it to get home, back to California, right?"

Lucy bit her bottom lip. "That's got to be a hundred miles from here. We can't walk that far across the desert." She looked down at her shoes, lifting a foot to display the raised heel. "My feet are killing me already."

"What about the parking garage?" Alan said. "It was full of cars when they brought us in. We could hotwire one."

Brad stared at him. "Do you know how?"

Alan looked at the floor. "I did it to Otto once, for kicks. Just need to find the ignition, battery, and starter wires, twist the first two together, then spark the starter wire."

Brad glared. "You hotwired my van?" He shook his head. "My brother the car thief, everyone."

"I don't know," I said. "I think there may be fighting in the garage, or at least soldiers patrolling the area."

"What do you think, Lucy?" Brad asked, looking at her. "Without supplies and a compass, we might die hiking across the desert."

"I'd rather not get bitten by a rattlesnake," Lucy said. She looked down the hall. "Can we at least try to sneak into the garage and take a car? If we have to, we can take the emergency exit instead."

The garage was a more immediate risk, but the sun was coming up. I probably had enough soda pop stashed in my hat for me, but not enough for all of us. "Okay, let's go for it," I said. "Follow me. Quietly."

I led them down the hall, followed by Lucy, Lilith, and Alan, with Brad bringing up the rear, to a set of stairs that led down to the first floor. Reaching the lower level, we followed the first-floor hallway in single file to the edge of the foyer where the Bodhi Group soldiers, armed with the fire hose and extinguisher, stood guard.

The foyer burned, set alight by a fire elemental that was hurling fireballs at the three soldiers, who squirted the hose and extinguisher at it and the growing blaze. The glass doors leading into the building were shattered, letting in the desert wind to fan the flames, as more fire elementals entered through the breach. The soldier with the extinguisher screamed and went down, holding his burned arm, as sprinklers burst to life overhead, spraying the interior with water. The lead fire elementals howled and retreated from the deluge, shrouded in steam.

Outside, beyond the ruined doors, vehicles burned on a battlefield of fire and smoke. Bodhi Group soldiers approached from the left, shooting assault rifles from the cover of parked cars, ducking molten meteors thrown by an opposing mob of more fiery wraiths.

I herded my companions into the stairwell. With everyone safe on the other side, I slipped to the head of our procession and down a short flight of steps to another door, which I knew from my earlier reconnaissance opened into the parkade itself.

I peered through the thick wire-mesh-reinforced rectangular window upon a second battlefield. Two hundred feet away, soldiers unloaded assault rifles into a line of fire elementals as they descended an entry ramp, using cars and concrete pillars for cover.

We snuck out the door and scuttled to the left, stooped over, moving from car to car until we were three rows over, out of sight of the combatants. As we ducked behind an old Studebaker, sprinklers overhead came on, showering us with water. Shrieks and howls echoed through the garage from the direction of the firefight, followed by cheers.

I beckoned Alan to my side. "Okay, dude, which car do we take?"

Alan rose up from his crouch, scanning the garage. "Over there," he said softly, pointing.

"Lead the way," I whispered.

We scurried up the slope thirty feet and crouched next to a large desert-gold two-door coupe. Chrome lettering identified it as a Buick Wildcat. Alan tried the driver's-side door while the rest of us huddled by the trunk and sides. He shook his head, releasing the handle.

I started to follow as he moved on to check another car.

"Wait," Lilith said in a hushed voice. "Look." Still crouched by the trunk, she held up a small rectangular box—a magnetic key holder—and pulled out the spare key inside. She smiled widely. "I found this under the bumper."

We duck-walked back over to her as she slid the key into the passenger-side door, unlocked it and jumped inside. She reached across and pulled up the button on the driver's side. Alan hopped into the driver's seat a moment later, while Brad, Lucy and I squeezed into the back, pressing Lilith into the dash as we did so.

The teen twisted the key and the old car turned over with a growl, then rumbled to life. We all sighed and smiled, soaking wet but elated at our good fortune.

"Nice one, Lil," Alan said, kissing her on the cheek. He slipped the car into gear, backed out slowly, and turned toward the exit.

"Go slow, Alan," Brad said. "Try to get as close to the exit as you can before we're seen. If we're spotted, gun it."

Alan bobbed his head in silent agreement, peering through the windshield like a hawk looking for a mouse. We ascended the slope, heading for the exit, then rounded the corner as the deluge from the fire sprinklers diminished, then stopped completely. I held my breath as the car rounded the turn, and let it go.

The exit was deserted.

Alan swung the automobile to the left, taking us outside. Just beyond the exit, soldiers chased smouldering fire elementals as they withdrew to regroup with their approaching allies. The new arrivals lobbed fire at the Bodhi Group soldiers, over the heads of their fellows.

As we appeared, one of the soldiers cried out, clutching at his chest as he caught fire. A nearby squad mate tackled him, smacking at the flames like he was digging a hole, then dragged the fallen man behind the sparse cover of the nearby entry gate, while those soldiers still standing laid down covering fire.

I stared out the side window of the car, mesmerized by the fire monsters that, in the building's shadow, drew the eye like campfires on a moonless night. I squinted and frowned, spotting something peculiar in their midst. Behind the vanguard, walking at the centre of a new cohort of fire elementals like a shepherd among sheep, strode a muscular humanoid, seven feet tall, with crimson skin and horns that glowed like hot coal—a devilish man with skin awash in flames.

As he advanced, the demon moved his hands like he was conducting an orchestra, and half his honour guard raced ahead, splitting off to reinforce their comrades on both fronts: that near the parking garage and the one raging by the building's main entrance a few hundred feet away.

"Get us out of here, Alan," Brad hissed from the back seat. His kid brother nodded and stomped the gas pedal. I fell back in my seat as the Buick lunged forward. Alan wrenched the wheel nearly hitting a soldier, but the trooper ignored us, continuing to fire controlled bursts from his weapon at the approaching enemy.

"Easy, dude," Brad said, grabbing his brother's shoulder. "Easy. Don't wreck us."

Alan narrowed his eyes at the road ahead but made no reply. Lilith screamed as another of the monsters jumped into our path. The teen driver tugged the steering wheel, slaloming by the obstacle like a race car driver on a closed course. In reaction to the movement, the near-roadkill whirled and bounced a fireball off the back window sending Brad, Lucy and me down in our seats.

I popped my head back up and watched as the fire demon, the apparent leader of the attack, waved his hands and three of his minions altered course to intercept us. More fireballs streaked through the air like mini comets; one hit the windshield, spreading cracks across the surface.

Alan turned on the wipers, spraying fluid over the cracked glass. The wipers skipped across the fractures, smearing ash and dirt, reducing visibility further.

"Hang on," Alan said. He twisted the wheel to the right, tapped the brake, then stomped the accelerator.

"Alan, what are you doing?" Lucy shouted as I was thrown against her.

"Getting us out of here," he said grimly. "That's the road out. They'll move."

More fire elementals changed direction, moving to block our exit, raising trails of fire on the black asphalt in their wake. Several more incendiaries sailed toward us, knocking out a headlight and banging off the side of the car, leaving a residue that continued to burn as we drove.

They're trying to take out the engine, I realized. We still had a hundred feet to cover before breaking through to the other side. *We're not going to make it.*

Alan jerked the wheel to the left as a new barrage sailed our way, so that most of the incoming projectiles hit the car's passenger-side door, just below the window. The vehicle fishtailed slightly as it left the tarmac and its wheels dug into the softer desert soil until the teen coaxed it back onto the pavement. We were still moving but heading the wrong way, back to the

Institute, with fire elementals to the front of us and more behind.

I took a deep breath as my mind raced. There were way too many to fight. I could raise snow to slow them down and use for cover, but that wouldn't help my companions. Larry, the soldier that I'd helped on my way out of the Allfrost Chamber a few days earlier, had suffered serious burns despite a heavy winter jacket. From a single fireball. My friends didn't have even that much protection.

Damn it, I should have left them where they were, I thought. *At least inside the Institute, they'd have a chance.*

"Look," Lucy said, pointing out the back window. To the south, armoured vehicles were heading this way. *Reinforcements*, I thought. They were still far away, though, and the Bodhi Group defenders, pressed hard by the lead monsters, were retreating into the Institute, hounded by their attackers.

I pressed my eyes shut, wishing my friends and I could just disappear. *That's it*, I thought.

"Alan, turn the car around," I said. He looked at me in the rear-view mirror like I'd lost my mind. "Trust me. I've got an idea."

"Do it, Alan," Brad said.

The teen turned the wheel again, reversing our course.

"That's it," I said, patting his shoulder. "Now gun it, full bore. Run them down if necessary. Just don't stop, whatever happens."

Alan swallowed and shook his head. "I hope you know what you're doing, dude."

So do I, I thought.

I made a cage with my hands, touching fingertips to fingertips, took a deep breath, and began to concentrate, as I had at Wilhelm's when the Faction had tried to kidnap me. Only this time, instead of just imagining myself slipping into the Underfrost, I envisioned a perfect bubble of space expanding around me, encompassing my entire body, then concentrated on making it larger, growing it rapidly outward until it engulfed my friends and the entire vehicle around us.

"Sh-sh-shivurrr, what…are…you…d-d-doing?" Alan asked

as his teeth chattered. My friends gasped and huffed, hyperventilating at the sudden cold that filled the car. Their hair and clothes, still wet from the parking garage, grew stiff as the moisture froze. Lucy, Brad, and Lilith hugged themselves and shivered uncontrollably as Alan struggled to keep the car on course. Visions of my friends freezing to death because of me filled my head. I pushed down a swell of panic before it could break my concentration. This was our only chance.

The car, travelling over sixty miles per hour, continued to barrel forward, passing through the onslaught of fireballs and elementals that stood in its path like they were mere tricks of the light. The Buick shook and shuddered halfway through the mob of monsters, cooling fast and threatening to stall. I felt a wave of panic, feeling myself sinking too far into the depths of the Underfrost. I pushed my hands together like I was crushing a drink can, collapsing the imaginary bubble back down to the size of a pea in my mind, then smaller still, and then closed it off completely.

The car continued to roll forward, but the engine still shuddered. I checked the rear window. Two hundred feet behind us, the nearest fire elemental slowed and turned away, returning to the battle at the Institute.

Brad's teeth chattered next to my ears. "Did we lose them?"

"Alan, roll down the windows. Let warm air inside." *I never thought I'd say that*, I thought.

Alan looked at me, teeth chattering. "Huh?"

I leaned into the front, resting my belly on the seatback. Steadying myself with my left hand, I reached across and pushed the button to open Lilith's window with my right, thankful the car windows weren't crank-operated. Warm desert air flowed into the car. I slumped back in my seat and snugged the zipper of my jacket to my chin. Moments later, the engine revved back to life as it finally recovered from the deep freeze.

I looked behind us again. "They're not following," I said, taking a deep breath and letting it out like a balloon with a slow leak.

"Guess we're not a threat anymore," Lucy said in a quavering voice.

I could see an increase in muzzle flashes as the reinforcements arrived. Then we were too far away to see much of anything. When we were a few miles away, a column of dark smoke rose into the sky where I judged the Institute should be.

Alan stopped the car, and we got out to allow everyone to warm up and look back at the distant fire. When we hopped back into the car a few minutes later, I switched seats with Brad so he and Lucy could cozy up and share body heat. I closed my eyes and fell asleep moments after.

Just over an hour later, we pulled into a gas station on the edge of Tonopah. The car was running on fumes and my fellow travellers were hungry and thirsty. I sat slunk down low in the back with the hood of my winter jacket drawn forward to hide my face.

"Let's be quick, people," Brad said as Alan cut the engine. "The longer we're here, the more likely someone notices the cracked windshield."

"Not to mention the busted headlight and scorch marks," Alan said with a smirk.

Lilith breathed into her cupped hands. "Oh my God. I need to brush my teeth before someone gets hurt," she said before thrusting the passenger door open and heading in to use the washroom.

Brad finished pumping gas and went in to pay, passing Lilith returning the other way as a green Plymouth Satellite pulled in behind us. I ducked low in the back seat as the driver got out and started to fill up.

The Satellite's driver looked to be a late twenties, early thirties male with chestnut-brown hair. He was dressed casually in a white T-shirt, jeans, and work boots. A pack of cigarettes was visible on his shoulder, twisted into the sleeve of his short-sleeve shirt. He held an unlit cigarette between his lips and looked around idly as the numbers on the pump rolled by. His gaze passed over us, then moved back abruptly.

"Oh, boy," Lilith said as he studied our car with interest. "Is he looking at the char marks?"

"Yeah, I think so," I replied.

Lilith got out as the man finished pumping and approached us.

"Morning, miss," he said, slipping off his sunglasses. "This your car?"

Lilith shook her head. "No, sir. It's my boyfriend's."

"My buddy has one just like it," the man said. He leaned to the side, looking at the Buick's rear end. "Yours is in rougher shape, mind you. You drive it through a forest fire?"

Lilith wagged her head. "He bought it that way. He's going to fix it up."

The stranger stared a moment, raising a brow. "Huh. Well, all right, then. Hope it gets you where you're going. You got far to go?"

Lilith shrugged. "Reno."

"Figured you weren't from around here," the man replied, slipping his sunglasses back into place. "Safe travels."

He stepped between the pumps and went inside as Alan appeared with grocery bags in hand.

"What'd that dude want?" Alan asked as he slipped into the back seat next to Lilith.

"Just some guy. He noticed the burn marks," Lilith said. "Aren't you going to drive?"

"Lucy's going to take over," Alan said. "I'm wiped out. I didn't sleep a wink last night."

Brad and Lucy jumped into the car a half minute later, carrying bags of snacks for the road. The young woman started the car, pulled out onto the street, and drove us toward US Route 95, which would take us to Las Vegas.

By the time we reached the highway, Alan had fallen asleep. Lilith leaned against him, resting her head on his shoulder, and moments later nodded off too. Ten minutes later, Brad joined the young couple, resting his head against the side window, mouth slightly ajar.

Pushing the car and everyone in it across to the Underfrost, and not having slept in days except for a short nap in the freezer at the arcade, I, too, found myself struggling to stay awake. I chatted with Lucy for a while to keep her company, but before long, the gentle rocking of the car combined with the air conditioning lulled me to sleep.

Chapter 29

Shoshone

I woke sometime later to the sound of music playing on the radio. Alan and Brad still dozed while Lilith looked out the window at the passing countryside.

The teenage girl looked over at me. "Déjà vu all over again," she said. "At least no one's following us this time."

"Wouldn't matter," Brad said with a yawn. He rubbed his eyes. "Shivurr would just mess them up—use his magic on them."

"It's not magic," I said.

"Come *on*, dude. We flew *through* those fire things like phantoms. This entire car. I saw it."

"Fire elementals," I said. "I call them fire elementals."

"Whatever. Point is, you ghosted us and brought us back. A couple days ago, you stopped a car just by waving your hands at it."

"And Alan told us what he saw in Wil's backyard, during the fire," Lilith added.

"Exactly," Brad said. "Magic. Tell him, Lucy."

"Science or magic, you're amazing, Shivurr," Lucy said, looking at me in the rear-view mirror.

"Ah, I'm blushing."

Lucy laughed. "I'll take your word for it."

"How much farther, Lucy?" Brad asked.

"A few more hours, I think."

Brad looked at me. "Where do we pick up Caleb?"

"Uh, you can't. At least not without a boat." I removed my hat and shoved my hand inside, pulling out an ice-cold soda.

"Hold this, would you?" I said to Lilith. She took it

wordlessly, and I reached in again. This time, I pulled out Olivia's Walkman.

"Is that my Walkman?" Lilith asked. "I thought I left it at Scott's place."

"Uh-uh. Orithyia—I mean Olivia gave it to me."

"Olivia?" Lucy asked. "Oh my God, Shivurr, she must be devastated. Does she know about Wilhelm and Bear?"

"Oh, right…about that," I said. "We better wake up Alan for this. Lilith, crack that can for me, will you? I'm parched."

For the next thirty minutes, I told them all about Wilhelm and Bear being alive and well, the secret level under the Schmidts' house, about Scott getting shot, our escape to the mystical tropical islands, my fight with the troll, and my trip back to rescue them using the Allfrost's tholos. Their expressions alternated between amazed, horrified, concerned, and amazed again. They peppered me with questions, and I did my best to answer them, holding nothing back. They deserved honesty after all they'd sacrificed for me and the dangers that they'd faced because of me.

"Olivia and Wil are gods?" Brad said, wide-eyed. "That's wicked. Crazy, but wicked."

"No way anyone's going to believe this," Lucy said, shaking her head.

"Why the frown, Alan?" Lilith asked her boyfriend.

Alan smiled. "Just thinking, Caleb's probably surfing fresh waves right now, and I'm missing it."

I held up the cassette player. "I'd better call Olivia."

I pulled the headphones over my head and began pushing buttons in the unlikely sequence that Olivia had taught me. Pressing the final button, I waited. I didn't have to wait long before Olivia's sleepy voice sounded through the headphones.

"Shivurr, honey, are you okay?" she asked. "Are the kids safe?"

"They're okay," I said, glancing at my friends. "Olivia says hi," I told them before passing their greetings back to her. That out of the way, I filled her in on everything that had happened since Hanale had dropped me on the shore of my New Olympus island.

When I got to the troll, she interrupted. "Oh, *that's* where he's gotten to. He escaped the Miraculeum weeks ago. I'll let Hanale know. He's been worried."

"The Miraculeum?"

"Yeah, I'll give you a tour when you get back," Olivia replied. "Anyway, please, go on. What happened after you left him?"

For the next fifteen minutes, I told her about Hue and the Allfrost Chamber and my visit to the Bodhi Institute's archival vault, concluding with our narrow escape through the legion of fire elementals.

Olivia whistled. "Wow, phasing and dephasing the entire car and everyone in it is impressive. You're starting to remember—becoming yourself again."

"I guess so, but just bits and pieces—flashes and visions. But they're still jumbled." I paused, studying the carpet beneath my feet. "I think some of them were from a long, long time ago." I studied my hat thoughtfully. "I've got more vials, though."

"Don't take them yet," Olivia said in a serious tone. "Wait until we get you home. We can't be sure that they won't have negative effects, at least in the short term. The last one you took knocked you out cold. You don't want to be vulnerable out in the field. At least, not more than you already are."

"All right," I replied. The truth was I was in no hurry. Life was good—the past few days an adventure—and I might not like what I'd remember. "I'll wait until I know everyone's safe; me included."

Alan waved a hand in front of my face. "Ask her how Caleb's doing," he said. "Did he go surfing yet?"

"He's still asleep; the sun isn't up here yet," she answered before I could pass along the question. As if reading my mind, she added, "Scott's fine too; still recuperating."

Everyone smiled as I relayed the good news. "We're going to get their van so they can go home."

"The one in our garage?" Olivia asked. "Are you sure that's a good idea? Someone may be watching."

"Yeah, but we're driving a stolen car," I replied. "The sooner we ditch it, the better."

"Plus, we've got stuff at Scott's," Lilith added, holding her ear next to mine to listen in. "Like my Walkman."

Olivia said nothing for several seconds. "Hello?" I said finally. "Hello?"

"I'm here," Olivia said. "You're about an hour and a half from Vegas, right?"

"Yeah."

"All right," Olivia said. "Call me back in twenty minutes. I've got a few calls to make."

After saying a quick goodbye, I pressed stop on the player, severing the connection, and fielded questions for the next ten minutes, filling everyone in. After that, we drove in silence, each of us lost in thought, until Brad tapped his watch and gave me a nod. Again, I pushed buttons on the cassette player and reconnected with Olivia.

"Okay, Shivurr," Olivia began, "I've made some arrangements. Don't go to our house. Do you have a pen and paper?"

"Anyone got a pen?" I asked. No one did.

"Check the glove compartment," Lucy suggested.

Brad rummaged in it noisily before producing a yellow plastic pen and an Arizona map. "How's this?" he said, handing it to me.

"Thanks," I said, taking it from him. "Got it, Olivia."

"You're on the 95, right? Keep going until you get to 373, turn right and go south. You're going to go south to Shoshone." I printed the name in a blank corner of the map as she spoke. "There's a cemetery on the west side, just off the road. Drive there and wait. Someone will meet you with the van and the kids' stuff. I don't know how long it will take, so if they're not there when you arrive, wait until it gets there. You're looking at three hours minimum before the meet, so you've got time. After you've switched vehicles, use the Walkman and call me back."

"Understood," I said. "How about Caleb? How does he get home?"

"We can figure that out when you get back," she replied.

I rubbed my face. "But how do I get to you? Hue said the

Allfrost Chamber here is busted—at least the tholos—the transporter—is."

"Don't worry," Olivia said. "There's a chamber near Shoshone."

"Oh, right. Hue mentioned it, but how do you know that?"

"We helped build the Allfrost," she said. "We know where they are."

"You're the best, Olivia."

"Don't forget it," she said, laughing. "Have a great drive. Give my love to the others. See you soon."

I slipped the cassette player and headphones back into my hat, returned the cap to my head, and sat back to relax and enjoy the scenery.

We stopped for gas and a meal in Shoshone at a modest roadside café. Lucy parked the Buick far away from the restaurant, away from prying eyes.

Turning off the car, she rubbed her eyes and yawned. "Sorry to leave you out here, Shivurr," she said. "We'll try to be quick."

"They don't serve your kind here," Alan said, smirking. "You'll have to wait outside."

"God, you and your *Star Wars*," Lilith said as she stepped outside.

"What? It's funny," Alan said as he followed her. "Shivurr gets it."

The teenager slammed the door shut and I stayed behind, hunched down in the back seat. The car, warmed by the rush of air from outside, soon cooled again as I poured a bit of the Underfrost across the threshold. I soon drifted off to sleep.

I sat up, throwing my arms in the air, as something rapped hard against the side window where I'd leaned my head.

Lilith held up a white paper bag. "Ha, you should see your face," she said, snickering. "We got a burger and fries for you."

"Hop in," I said, pointing to the door.

Hot dry air flowed into the vehicle as she got into the front passenger seat and handed me the bag.

"Oh my God. It's freezing in here," Lilith said as she climbed over the seat to join me. "They're just paying. Should be here soon."

I grabbed the bag, ripped it open, and started to eat. The warm burger cooled as I chewed, burning my mouth before sliding down my throat.

"Wow, look at you go," Lilith said, grinning.

"Give me a break. I'm hungry," I said around a mouthful of burger. "Stop watching me eat."

"Sorry, I'm just kind of surprised you eat food at all. I get the sodas and water, but food? It's just weird."

"Why? 'Cause I'm a *snowman*?"

"Yeah."

"I'm a living being. Different from you, but my body has chemical needs that liquids don't always cover. Doesn't have to be food as you think of it, though."

"What do you mean?" Lilith asked, wrinkling her brow.

"I can consume non-organic matter to meet my needs. Stuff that would make you sick or worse," I said.

"Like what?"

"Plastic, glass, rocks. Whatever has the elements my body requires. What my body doesn't use gets expelled."

Lilith made a face. "Geez, that sounds awful."

"Fries *are* tastier," I agreed, popping another into my mouth.

"There they are," Lilith said, looking out the window.

Moments later, the car doors opened, and the other members of our fellowship jumped inside. Brad started the car with a rumble and pulled out of the parking lot, back onto the road.

"Olivia said it should be on the west side," I reminded him as we reached the edge of town. "Keep your eyes peeled."

Lucy pointed. "There. Is that it?"

"Where?" Brad said, turning the wheel, taking us off the road to the right.

"There, by the bushes and trees."

Brad steered the Buick off the road and drove about six hundred feet over the dusty gravel, parking by a path leading up to the trees.

Lucy jumped out, ran up the short hill to a stone wall, and ran back, nodding her head. "This is it," she said, slamming the passenger door shut.

Brad backed up and turned the car to face the highway so we could see anyone approaching.

"No sign of Otto," Brad said, looking around. "Guess we're early." He turned off the car. "Shivurr, can you keep it cool in here so I don't have to run the car?"

"Of course."

"Just try not to freeze us to death," Lilith said, bumping me with her elbow.

"I still can't believe Wilhelm and Olivia are *gods*!" Brad said as we sat waiting.

"Myths," Lucy corrected. "Not real gods."

"Right," Alan said. "Except with magical powers like freaking gods."

Lucy crossed her arms. "But they're not gods, not really. They're just incredibly powerful. This just proves there's no such thing."

"Or the opposite," Lilith said. "Doesn't this mean anything's possible? That God is real?"

Alan shook his head. "Right, like there's some dude that created the entire universe and cares what people do. No way. Do you care if an ant believes in you, or if it prays to you? We'd be jack shit to something that could create this planet, let alone the universe."

"This all had to start from something, Alan," Lilith said, crossing her arms and scowling. "People can't be an accident. Something must have created us."

Alan rolled his eyes and sighed. "Fine, then where'd God come from?"

"Not this again, guys," Brad said. "Give it a rest. Who gives a shit? We're here, that's all we know."

We waited in silence for a while after that, watching the occasional car drive past the remote location. About an hour later, a light blue Volkswagen van pulled off the highway and rolled toward us, followed by a cloud of dust.

"There's Otto," Brad said, sitting up in his seat.

The 1977 Volkswagen camper bus, nicknamed Otto, pulled

up next to the Buick Wildcat, driver's door to driver's door. The van's driver, a black-and-grey-haired man in his late fifties wearing a short-sleeved button-up shirt, rolled down his window. Brad did the same, while I kept a low profile behind Alan.

"You kids Olivia's friends?" asked the man in a quiet voice.

"Yes, sir," Brad replied. "I'm Brad. You must be—"

"Kurt. Call me Kurt," said the man. "That Shivurr back there?"

I leaned forward and waved but said nothing.

"Let's do this quickly," Kurt said. "I've got to get back. Wait there."

A moment later, the van reversed. Kurt drove it to the other side of the Buick, got out and opened the large side door of the camper bus.

Chapter 30

Dublin Gulch

Bear, the Alaskan shepherd, leaped through the open cargo door with his tail wagging furiously. I stroked his head and gave him a good scratch behind the ears before he brushed past me and greeted the others. To my surprise, the dog showed no signs of injury, no burned fur, no pain as he moved.

Talk about a rapid recovery, I thought.

Alan stooped to pet him, earning a lick on the face before the big dog moved on to the next person.

"Who's a good boy?" Brad asked rhetorically, rubbing the dog's flanks. "I was worried about you. Yes, I was."

I looked at Kurt. "Why's Bear here? Are you taking care of him for Wilhelm and Olivia?"

Kurt scratched his head. "I don't know. He was sitting in the van when I got it. I tried letting him out, but he wouldn't leave. Guess he wanted to go for a ride."

"Oh, you brought our stuff," Lilith squealed, peering inside the van.

My companions' belongings, some of them, at least, sat in the back: purses, skateboards, and other small items of value in Adidas gym bags and a few brown paper grocery bags.

"I guess our tents and stuff are toast," Brad said, looking inside.

"Literally," Alan said, frowning.

Smiling, Lilith pulled her Walkman from one of the bags and started fiddling with it. "Thanks, mister."

"Don't mention it," Kurt said. "Olivia said to check the house down the street. This stuff was sitting in the front hallway, so I figured it must be yours. Didn't think a guy named Scott would have a lot of purses. That's all of them, right? If something isn't yours, let me know and I'll take it with me for safe-keeping until this Scott fellow comes home."

A few minutes going through the items confirmed that everything belonged to them. Kurt, or whoever had piled the luggage by Scott's front door for him to find, had done a fantastic job.

A vicious growl ending in a bark made me jump. I braced myself against the hot metal of the Buick as Bear brushed me aside, racing up the hill toward the cemetery. A large black bird with a red featherless head, roosting among the cemetery trees, flew skyward at his approach, hissing as it spread its wings to their full six-foot span. Still thirty feet away, Bear barked a few more times before turning around. Tongue lolling from the exertion and heat, he took a seat at my feet as I stood between the two vehicles, leaning against me, enjoying the chill.

"My God," Lucy said, holding a hand to her chest. "He scared me."

"Turkey vulture," Kurt noted. "Ugly things. I guess Bear's not a fan either. You showed him, sir."

"Well, I guess we should get going," Brad said, holding out his hand for Kurt to shake.

Kurt shook the younger man's hand, and they exchanged car keys.

"She's all gassed up," Kurt said. "Just did it in town. How's the Buick set for fuel?"

"All topped up," Brad replied as he slid into the van's front seat.

"Good man," Kurt said. "Look, why don't you all get settled for a minute? If you don't mind, I need to have a private word with Shivurr here."

Kurt guided me by the shoulder to the front of the van, where we were out of sight of the road and had some privacy. He looked at me. "Olivia said you might not remember me."

"I'm sorry, I don't," I said. "Do we know each other?"

"We do, but don't worry about it," Kurt replied. He ran his

fingers through his thick salt-and-pepper hair, studying himself in the reflection of the van's window. "It was a long time ago." He reached into the front pocket of his pants. "Anyway, Olivia wanted me to give these to you. Hold out your hands."

He dropped several roughly spherical reddish-orange gems, each the size of a marble, into my cupped hands. Heavier than they looked, they gleamed in the sunlight and, perhaps warmed by Kurt's body heat, were warm to the touch.

"What are these?" I asked.

"Not sure," Kurt said, shrugging. "Might be all that's left of whatever burned their house down. They were all over the back-yard."

"How did you know to even look for them?"

"Wasn't me that did the looking," Kurt explained. "There's been more than just me involved in this here operation. I'm just the driver and collector of purses," he added with a smile. "Oh, can't forget this," he continued, pulling forth a white gemstone about twice the size of the red marbles.

"One sec," I said, dropping the fire marbles into my hat for safekeeping before taking the white gem in hand. "Pretty. What's this for?"

"You'll have to ask Olivia," Kurt said. He looked to his left as a car drove past a few hundred feet away, heading south on the highway. "All right, I'd better move. This car ain't going to disappear itself."

Kurt walked between the cars as I dropped the white gem-stone into my hat. Joining him as he said his goodbyes to my friends, I shook his hand a final time and climbed into the van. Bear followed me in and sat down next to me.

"Whoa, there, boy," I said. "This isn't your ride now. You're going with Kurt." The dog looked back at me, then laid his head between his paws.

"Looks like he wants to stay," Kurt observed. "Why don't you all keep him with you? I'm sure Olivia or Wilhelm will come get him when they can."

"Awesome," Alan said, patting Bear's back. "Captain will love that."

"Who's Captain?" I asked.

"My dog," Alan answered.

"But how will they know where to find us?" Lilith said, wrinkling her brow.

"They just will," Kurt said. "Trust me."

"Well, all right, then," Brad said from the driver's seat. He smiled, a twinkle in his eye. "Looks like we've got a replacement for Caleb."

"Y'all drive careful," Kurt said. We waved goodbye as he got into our stolen getaway car and, with a nod of his head, drove off. I pulled the cargo door shut before a cloud of dust could get inside.

"Nice guy," Brad said. "So, what next?"

I pulled my hat from my head and reached in for the Walkman. I held up the headphones. "Now, I call Olivia."

Olivia answered on the first ring, sounding more alert this time. I brought her up to speed. We were at the Shoshone Cemetery, as ordered. We now had the VW van. Kurt had taken the Buick Wildcat and left us Bear.

"Good, that's good," Olivia said. "Bear's going to be your guide. The Allfrost Chamber that I mentioned is a few miles to the west. It's offline but still functional. You'll need to restart it. You're going to make a detour first, though."

"A detour to where?"

"There's an old settlement called Dublin Gulch, west of your position. It's a ghost town now. Miners carved caves and tunnels into the sides of the cliffs there. You can hole up there until dark."

"Why not just stay in the van?"

"The gang should get going for home, as soon as possible. The sooner they're far away from the Bodhi Institute, the better."

"All right, but isn't waiting dangerous for me too?"

"Not as dangerous as travelling during the day," Olivia said. "It's called Death Valley for a reason. It's the hottest, driest place on the planet. It's got to be over forty-three degrees Celsius right now with relative humidity of ten percent. You don't want to be out in that any longer than necessary, so get to the gulch, find a cave out of the sun and call me back as soon as it's dark."

"What about these gems that Kurt gave me?"

"Which ones?"

"He gave me red ones and one larger white one."

"The white one is to activate an Allfrost power node," Olivia replied. "The chamber you're heading to doesn't have enough power, so most of its functions are offline. We want to study the red ones. They're all that's left of the fire elementals. You're the courier. I hope you don't mind."

"Sure, no problem."

"Okay, Shivurr, you should get going right away. Remember, call me back at dusk."

"I can keep the line open."

"That'll burn through the batteries too quickly. You've still got the spares, right?"

"Yep."

"Good. That should be enough, I think, but we should end the call now just to be safe. The gulch is about a half mile away from your position. There's a dirt road leading there, so you should have no trouble finding it."

A sheriff's car drove past down the highway as I pressed the stop button on the cassette player. I needed to move.

Stowing the Walkman, I filled my companions in on Olivia's side of the call.

"We're supposed to just leave you here?" Brad asked. "Not sure I like that."

"It's the only way," I replied. "You can't use the tholos. Besides, you need to get home and stay safe."

"Okay, but we're driving you to Dublin Gulch," Brad insisted. "That's non-negotiable."

Brad started the van and puttered us along the faint path over the dusty taupe-coloured terrain, taking us between the cliffs that miners had once called home.

Staying within the comfort of the van, we said our goodbyes.

"Try to get Caleb home soon," Lucy said, kissing my cheek. "Or his parents will be asking questions."

"Not likely," Brad muttered, looking doubtful.

I hugged each of my new friends in turn, leaning awkwardly into the front seat to reach the two eldest members of the group. Bear got a pat from all, even a tentative one from Lucy. I grabbed the door handle and prepared to fling it wide.

"Shivurr, wait," Lilith said, causing me to turn. She held out the paperback that I'd seen her reading the day that we met. "Here, something to read when you're bored."

Bored sounds good right now, I thought. "But you're not finished," I said, pointing to the bookmark.

She waved a hand. "Silly. I've read it before. Besides, you can give it back when you visit us, when you bring Caleb home."

"Thanks, Lil," I said, giving her a wink.

Alan held out a flashlight and a refillable bottle of water. "Take this too. So you can read when it's dark. And water, just in case."

"I'm touched, you guys. You're the best. I wish I had something to give you."

"Don't sweat it, dude," Alan said. "Least we can do. Hang loose, brother."

I looked at each of them, memorizing their faces. "Drive careful, Brad. I'll see you guys. Soon, I hope."

Packing my gifts away, I pulled open the cargo door and drew the hood of my jacket over my head as hot dry wind bit into my face. Bear jumped out right after me and sat at my side as I drew the door shut with a thump.

The van's engine rumbled and Brad steered it back toward the highway. I watched it go, gave Bear a pat on the head and started walking south toward the cliffs, past a huge pile of rusty cans—garbage left behind by the former residents, I presumed.

Just you and me now, bud, I thought.

The cliffsides, composed of caliche clay—gravel, sand, clay and silt—were not tall, varying in height from ten to twenty feet. Holes had been carved at intervals into the sides, some of which were sealed with padlocked doors, denying entry. The walls sported a cladding of stone bricks pillaged from the surroundings and shaped to interlock with each other.

I wandered up and down, searching for an opening as the desert wind sucked the moisture and coolness from my body. I was about to give up and head to the north when I found an unsealed entryway supported by thick wooden beams. I entered and followed a short hallway down a slight grade about fifteen feet to a single room, the floor of which sloped toward the back wall. A nook had been carved into the far wall, forming a rudimentary fireplace. I could see a hole cut into the ceiling over it to allow smoke to escape. Enough light from the exterior made its way into the space that I could see well enough after a moment, so I left my newly acquired flashlight off for the time being.

I set up camp against a wall and pulled out the bottle of water that Alan had given to me. Taking a sip, I held the open end to Bear's face. His long tongue licked drops from the nipple as I tilted it. Half of it fell to the parched earth and disappeared; the other half he swallowed. Satisfied, my faithful canine companion got comfortable next to me, seemingly welcoming the coolness radiating from me, while I drew out another can of ice-cold soda. It opened with a tantalizing crack and hiss. I smiled in anticipation for all of two seconds before slaking my thirst.

The primitive domicile was considerably cooler than outside, though still warmer than my comfort zone, but out of the sun with a cold drink in hand, I felt almost content. Maybe, after days spent in these harshest conditions, I was getting used to it—toughened beyond what I would have imagined possible, beyond what I thought I could endure.

I pulled out the potions that I'd recovered from the Institute and laid them on the ground in front of me. I counted twenty-two in total. I picked one up and fingered the stopper. *Do I take another now?* I shook my head. *No, Olivia's right. Wait until New Olympus.* I put the potion back in my hat and did the same for the others before they got too warm.

My treasures safely stowed, I dug out Lilith's book and, holding Alan's flashlight beneath my chin, began to read. Soon, Bear closed his eyes and slept. A few chapters into the book, tired from my adventures, I, too, drifted off to sleep.

I dreamed, once again, of that terrible battle that I had witnessed after taking the first potion at Scott's the other day, the one where I rode the frost disc, protected by a bubble of blue-white energy. It was the same as before: monstrous beings locked in combat; ambulatory trees, fifty feet tall, throwing boulders past my head at the onrushing enemy as giants and worse rushed toward us. Words came unbidden to mind as I dreamed.

Scorched earth, ball of flame
Old gods on fields of battle
Allfrost over all

Again and again, the same scene ran through my head until, slowly, along with it came the realization that I *knew* how to do what I saw myself doing in that war of so long ago. I knew how to draw, manipulate and shape the Underfrost to create and propel the frost disc forward, how to draw frost energy around me to cloak myself in a protective bubble to shield myself from harm, and how to send it outward to pull snow and ice from dry ground and thin air. As with my other abilities, I knew all of this intuitively in an unconscious, visceral way.

I marvelled in my dream state that I could ever have lost the memory of something that I knew so well—like realizing you'd forgotten how to breathe, only after having remembered how to do so.

Since my time at the Bodhi Institute, I'd been only a ghost of my true self, I realized. I began to thrash and growl at the approaching fiends, and they gradually faded into blackness as I woke.

Chapter 31

Tiger by the Tail

The room was near pitch-black. I could just make out Bear as he stood next to me facing the exit, growling low and ominously.

"Easy, buddy," I said in soothing tones. "Probably just another turkey vulture…" I stroked his back, and he settled down, still rumbling a warning and staring at the way out.

I cocked my head, hearing a faint scurrying sound somewhere in the dark. I fumbled around, knocking the flashlight with my hand. I held it before me and thumbed the switch, but the button didn't move, and the room stayed dark.

Well, just freaking great, I thought, realizing that I'd left the hand torch on, and the batteries were now dead.

I stood and illuminated myself, squinting at the sudden glare, then backpedalled as a rattlesnake slid from view down the tunnel. Bear barked like a lunatic but stayed at my side.

The Schmidts trained you well, I thought, *or you're smart enough to know better.*

"Okay, boy, excitement's over," I said. "Time to call Olivia." I pulled out the Walkman and made the call.

"Shivurr? Where have you been?" she said, sounding worried. "Sunset was an hour ago."

"Sorry, Liv, I fell asleep; guess I slept in," I said, looking down the tunnel. "Bear just woke me up. Saved me from a rattlesnake bite. I thought he was going to chase it like the turkey vulture."

"What? Bear chased a turkey vulture? When was—" Her voice cut out without warning.

"Hello?" I studied the Walkman and gave it a light smack. "Hello?"

More dead batteries, I realized. Crouching, I doffed my cap, grabbed the spares and snapped them into place.

A minute later, Olivia answered again. "There you are."

"Sorry, the batteries died."

"Glad I gave you spares," she said. "What was that about a turkey vulture?" I filled her in briefly. "Oh, that's concerning."

"It's no big deal," I said, walking around the room. "He didn't even get close."

"That's not it," she said. "He doesn't chase things, unless they're a threat. He's an exceptionally smart dog."

"I don't know. It's a turkey vulture. How much of a threat could it be? Maybe he's a bit on edge after the fire the other day."

"Yeah, maybe," Olivia said, but she didn't sound convinced. "It could also be a Faction creature. You'd better get moving either way. Put the headphones over Bear's ears. I need to speak to him."

"Beg your pardon?"

She chuckled. "You heard me."

"All right," I said, kneeling. Bear sat calmly as I held the headphone pads near his ears. Half a minute later, the Alaskan shepherd wiped them off with a paw and I returned them to my head. "Olivia, you there?"

"Yes, I'm here. Okay, Bear will lead you to the Allfrost Chamber. You'll need to find and activate at least one nearby power node. You'll need to bring the temperature in the area below freezing; that's another reason I wanted you to wait until nightfall. Burying it in snow should do it. Can you manage that?"

I thought of my recent dream. "Yeah, I think so."

"Good. If you couldn't, you were going to have to drink those other potions until you could. Once the node is cold enough, that should bring the dais across and raise the sphere. Place the white gem into the sphere to activate it and keep it from reverting back into the Underfrost."

"Is that the glowing ball of white light?"

"That's the one," Olivia said. She hesitated before continuing. "You should know, the Allfrost Chamber might be guarded. Don't worry. It might not be, but the Faction has a habit of tracking them down and leaving their monsters behind. I guess they're hoping to catch any Allfrost Sentinels that might return."

"I thought I was the last Allfrost Sentinel."

"Yeah, but they may not know that, or they do and they're still trying to get you too."

"Is that why we're all missing?"

"I don't know…maybe."

"Okay, so what kind of monster are we talking about?" I asked.

"I don't know that either. It could be one of many or something that I've never seen before. Something new."

"Like that troll that attacked me?" I asked, thinking of the fight after Hanale dropped me off on my way back to Nevada.

"Probably something worse," Olivia said. "And he wasn't supposed to be there. He's been recaptured, by the way."

"Got it, something worse," I replied, frowning at the Walkman. "Are you sure this is the best way back?"

"Definitely. The Bodhi Group and the Faction are both actively searching for you, we must assume, so we've got to get you out of there right now. Try not to worry about it. There might not be anything there anyway. They haven't located all the chambers yet; far from it. You've got just one last desert trek, then you'll be safe, back here."

"What about Bear? He can't make the trip. Can he?"

"Bear can take care of himself," Olivia said. "Powerful foes aren't hunting for him. He'll be fine."

"Okay, let's get this over with. Thanks, Olivia. I'll see you soon."

"Frostspeed, Shivurr," Olivia replied before cutting the connection.

I packed away the book and flashlight, keeping the headphones on in case I needed to call Olivia again in a rush. Then I shotgunned five cans of soda, hyper-hydrating.

I guess it'll be mainly Sprite and Mountain Dew for me back on the islands, I thought.

I drew the visor of my cap low over my eyes and pulled the hood of my jacket forward to protect my face as the sugar rushed to my head. "Okay, Bear, let's rock."

The strong afternoon wind had calmed to a light breeze, and the dry air had cooled enough that I didn't want to immediately run back into the cliffside. I tilted my head skyward, gaping at the beauty of the clear night sky that shone brightly overhead, lit by the dazzling stars of the Milky Way.

I guess I won't need the flashlight after all, I thought, smiling. *Good thing, since I don't have batteries for it.*

"All right, Bear. Which way?"

Bear glanced at me, then started walking, turning left to the west, and I followed.

A few steps later, a skittering sound came from the cliffs above us. Bear's ears flattened and his lips pulled back, but he made no sound.

I turned my head to look and saw the shadowy silhouette of something big moving along the ridge, heading southwest, perhaps twenty feet back from the edge. As it turned, starlight reflected off of it and I could see it better. From where I stood, it looked like the middle finger of a giant hand curling back on itself, with a long, thorny nail at the tip that pointed to the earth. Whatever was moving up there was bigger than anything that should be walking around the desert.

I raced over to hug the wall on tiptoe, holding my breath. My furry companion joined me a moment later, looking upward, hackles still raised. My head swivelled right as metal clattered to the east. A second silhouette, this one closer than the first, scuttled across the pile of rusty cans that I'd passed earlier in the day. It was a scorpion, but too large—larger even than Brad's van. A segmented tail with a vicious-looking stinger rocked like a cradle above its back as it moved toward the first hole in the clay wall, clacking massive pincers. Glancing to my left, I could see another large arachnid moving along the north wall, as if searching for something.

I shuffled along the edge of the wall, heading west, quiet as an ice ninja. I took shelter behind a nearby freestanding outhouse, then peered around the corner. The scorpion on the south side, my side, was systematically moving along the wall, peering into doorways, feeling with whatever senses these arachnids had at their disposal.

An air horn sounded to the east, beyond the gulch, where several large semi-trailers were idling in front of the cemetery where we'd waited for Kurt earlier in the day. Squinting, I could see that the trailer doors that faced me were gaping wide, and the engines faced east as if they'd been backed in. The silhouettes of a few people were visible moving nearby, but the scorpions ignored them as they prowled the area.

I scanned the desert to the west and let out a breath.

No giant scorpions, I thought. *Good.*

Unfortunately, while apparently clear of monsters, it looked like two miles of open ground with nowhere to hide until I reached the hills. The peaks to the northwest were a bit out of the way but lay closer and would provide more cover, if I could cross the dirt road that bisected the gulch without being seen.

My recent dream flashed through my mind, giving me an idea. Slinking back behind the outhouse, I swirled my hands like I was rubbing an invisible ball, conjuring a ball of white-cold frost energy. When it was the size of a basketball, I tossed it lightly into the air, moved my hands like a pizza maker twirling dough to give it some spin, and let it drop to the ground. Stopping mere inches from the dirt, it spread outward like quicksilver, forming a disc of ice and snow. Still linked to it in a way that I didn't consciously understand, I sculpted and spun it until it was four feet wide and six inches thick. It floated there, waiting, steaming like dry ice, just like in my dreams.

The disc dipped and wobbled slightly as I jumped onto it, then stabilized. I looked at Bear. "Come on, boy, get on," I whispered. The Alaskan shepherd looked at the disc, then at me, then climbed aboard. The disc was crowded with two of us but would have to do.

With a thought, I propelled the platform forward. It sprang ahead as if shot from a gun. I probably would have fallen off, but the frost disc felt like a part of me, as attached as any limb. As it was, I had to grab Bear by the scruff to keep him from falling off. Rocky though the start was, we were on our way, racing over the desert floor, heading west-northwest, for the hills.

I didn't look back. I needed to concentrate. If the scorpions were watching, there was nothing I could do about it. If they did see me, I'd have to lose them in the hills somehow, or fight them. The latter didn't appeal. There were at least three that I'd seen, but there might be more. They were huge, many times my size, with vicious pincers and stingers dripping undoubtedly poisonous venom. Normally venom wouldn't worry me, but these things weren't natural, so who knew what that poison would do to me? Not to mention I had Bear to watch out for. He was a big, tough Alaskan shepherd, but he might as well be a Chihuahua compared to these monsters.

They must be here for me, I thought. *No chance these things just happened to be in the neighbourhood.*

The air blew hard across my face as we rocketed through the night. I brought the platform to a stop as we reached the hills and looked back. The southern scorpion was nearing the last doorway on that side of the gulch, still searching. The scorpion probing the north cliff wasn't visible from my vantage point, but I took it as a good sign that it wasn't racing across the ground in my direction. To all appearances, I had eluded them, at least for the time being.

Rather than taking a chance on the open plain, I moved the platform to the north into the hills, intending to circle around and return to the lowlands farther to the west, where I'd hopefully be too far away to be seen.

A half mile to the north, my right foot slipped off the frost disc's edge. Bear sidled closer to me, trying to keep all four of his feet on board. Since I'd first created it, the disc had shrunk to half its original diameter; the warm, dry air was taking its toll. I pulled to a stop and hopped off, followed by Bear, as the frost disc faded from view.

I didn't bother to create a new one. I needed Bear to lead me to the Allfrost Chamber, and he couldn't do that riding next to me on the frost disc.

I rubbed his head. "Okay, boy. Lead the way."

He started walking, and I followed. He snuffled the ground for several steps, then broke into a trot, and I ran to keep up. We travelled north about a quarter mile, then turned west for a quarter mile before heading southwest, downhill to the plain where we'd last seen the scorpions. As we neared the flat valley floor, a shrill grating sound behind us drew my attention. A giant scorpion ran down the hill toward us, scuttling side to side, zeroing in on our location.

Bear rushed in front of me, hackles raised, teeth bared, and snarled. The creature slowed its approach but kept coming.

"Bear, get back," I shouted, feeling sick to my stomach. He ignored me and continued to run at the monster ten or more times his size. "Damn it."

I threw frost at the scorpion, but the arachnid swatted it aside with a swipe of its claw. As the Alaskan shepherd neared, the scorpion's tail snapped forward like a harpoon. I covered my eyes with my hands, sure I'd see the brave dog skewered by the stinger, but he'd dodged it somehow. He continued to circle the monster, barking.

The scorpion turned to cut him off, and my arms whirled like helicopter blades, sending a stream of frost strikes into its side. The monster shrieked, flinching as they hit its legs and abdomen, and it scuttled to face me. Screaming like a maniac, I ran toward it, throwing several more strikes at its head. It lashed out with its stinger as I neared. I fell to my back, sliding under the venom-tipped spear, and wrapped my arms around the segmented tail in a bear hug. The tail, thick as a tree trunk, snapped back, pulling me through the air like a child on a teeter-totter. I slid down the tail toward the tip and squeezed as hard as I could while channelling ice and frost into it.

Sensing the danger, the scorpion moved its tail forward, bringing me within reach of its pincers. I cried out and grimaced as one snapped closed on my body. Cracking sounds, like someone chewing ice, came from my lower half. I snarled in agony and my grip loosened.

Freeze, damn it, I thought.

I tugged my hands toward my guts, reinforcing my hold,

gasping for breath, trying to touch each hand to the opposite shoulder. The pressure from the scorpion's pincers grew fainter, and finally they dropped away, leaving six-inch-deep gouges in my waist and bits of insulation hanging from my jacket. The arachnid took a few hesitant steps to the side, then settled to the ground as its tail froze and frost spread to its core. I counted to sixty after it collapsed to the ground, keeping my death grip until the entire thing was covered in a layer of frost from stinger to claws before finally letting go.

I rolled away and lay still, breathing heavily, eyes closed. A wet tongue licked the side of my head. "All right, boy, I'm all right," I assured Bear, sitting up slowly.

My torso ached and I could barely lift my arms. Wincing, I looked sidelong down at my body. Large cracks spiderwebbed across the surface ice that protected my insides. A few chunks had broken away but were already filling in as I regenerated. I staggered to my feet, shaking out the aches in my forearms and biceps, and looked around. Ten feet away, I spotted a few large pieces of ice that had cracked and broken off. I grabbed them and held them to my wounds, reabsorbing water and other elements.

"Let's go, boy," I said, waving a hand to the west. Bear sprang to his feet and jogged ahead.

As I shuffled after him, I tore my hat from my head and rustled around inside. *The doctor will see you now,* I thought as the can hissed and bubbled. I wiped my mouth, tossed the empty into the air and caught it on the way down with my upturned hat, then ran to catch up with Bear.

We were halfway across the valley plain when Bear's head twitched to the left and he barked a warning. From the east, about a half mile away, three giant scorpions scurried toward us.

I figured that I could outrace them on a frost disc but even if I did, I still had to find the chamber and activate it, which was going to be difficult to do if these things followed me into the hills. Maybe it was the soda talking, but I'd been running for days, hunted by government agents, chased by fire elementals, assaulted by Faction zealots, my friends kidnapped and one shot;

a freaking *troll* had knocked me silly, and now scorpions the size of Mack trucks were out to get me. Everyone wanted to catch me and use or kill me.

All right, I thought. *You want to catch me? Catch frost.* I pointed west. "Bear, go, wait over there. I don't want you getting hurt. This is my fight."

I didn't wait to see if he obeyed. My enemies were coming fast; it was time to lay out the welcome mat. Recalling my dream, I summoned a ball of frost and bowled it along the ground. In the ball's wake rose a white carpet of thick snow forty feet long. I did this several more times in different directions, creating a huge area of snow: an arena for the coming fight. Three against one was hardly fair, but I hoped that this would even the odds.

The first scorpion hit the snow at full bore. It lost traction after a few steps, tried to brake, and careened toward me, carving a path in the snow with its face and claws. I dodged to my left, sliding over the snow like quicksilver. I'm fast at the worst of times; on snow, I move like a lightning strike. Before the scorpion could recover, I slammed several balls of pure frost energy off its head, stunning it. The second monster skittered to a stop at the edge of the snow, while the third scuttled to my right.

The fallen arachnid twitched. *Oh, no, you don't*, I thought. I leaped onto its back, landing near the base of its tail, and ran toward the head, streaming frost balls into its exoskeleton. Something sharp pierced my back and I screamed as pain radiated like wildfire from the impact point.

I fell to my stomach and the stinger came loose. I sprang back to my feet and grabbed the scorpion where I thought its eyes must be and opened the floodgates to the Underfrost. The thing shrieked as the cold penetrated, freezing its internal fluids. It stabbed me a few more times before falling still.

A surviving scorpion screeched, drawing my eye to the right in time to see it run its claws through the slushy snow, then start to creep over it toward me.

Where's your buddy? I thought. My head swivelled, looking to my rear. A segmented tail whipped by my shoulder as I rolled to the side. *There you are.* The stinger hit its downed comrade near the head, penetrating the thick carapace and sticking. The corpse wobbled and slid away from me as the attacking scorpion struggled to retract its trapped tail.

Snow slushed behind me, drawing my attention. I turned to see the other scorpion still barrelling toward me with outstretched pincers. With no time to do anything else, I sank into the snow out of its reach as its claws snapped together like garden shears overhead. Ducking deep, I swam to its rear and burst from the snow to pepper it with frost balls, escaping back into slush as it turned. I repeated the same maneuver and the scorpion staggered like a punch-drunk boxer but refused to go down. *This is taking too long,* I thought, huffing with exhaustion.

Shrieking, the stuck scorpion finally wrenched its tail free and turned toward me. I ducked under the snow again, moving behind its weakening pal, and leaped onto its back. I stayed near the creature's tail this time so that the stinger couldn't reach me and threw more frost into its head. Its ally closed the distance and lashed out at me, brushing its tail by my ear with a whoosh. I reeled back and fell, hitting the ground, as my former ride collapsed beside me, dead or out cold.

I felt light-headed and a bit hazy; the venom was messing with my system, slowing the healing process. To catch my breath, I slipped under the snow and stayed submerged, dodging to the side as the last scorpion dug at the snow with its claws, running them before it like shovels, trying to unearth me.

My vision was getting hazy; I needed to end this soon.

I rose from the snow until my eyes were clear. The scorpion's rear, fuzzy and indistinct, faced me as it plowed a furrow in the melting snow twenty feet away. Rising fully out of the snow, I glided like greased lightning toward it and jumped, extending my arms wide.

I sailed through the air and hugged the arachnid's tail. This time, my grip was closer to the base; it couldn't fling me around as easily or reach me with its pincers. It thrashed and twitched, trying to throw me off, but I stuck to it like a wood tick, streaming cold through my body into it. Finally, the scorpion's struggles weakened, and a few steps later, it stopped moving altogether.

I staggered over the snow, wiping at my eyes. *I can't see*, I thought. *What's wrong with my eyes?*

Spent and blind from the battle, I sank into the snow and drifted.

Chapter 32

Enemy of My Enemy

I scrunched my eyes tight as warm air blew across my face and something warm and wet licked my eyelids. Cracking them a sliver, I saw a black nose an inch from mine as a long pink tongue licked my chin and cheeks.

I grimaced and sat up. "Okay, buddy," I said, wrapping an arm around Bear's head. "I'm up. I'm okay." I wiped my mouth with my free hand. "I think you gave me a bit of tongue." He tilted his head at me quizzically. "It's okay, but let's never speak of it again." I clambered to my feet. "Whatever happens in Vegas, right?" He tilted his head to the northeast and barked. "Yeah, I know we're not in Vegas, but you're from there, so it counts."

I pulled a soda from my hat, downed it, and looked around. The corners of my mouth rose. *I can see.* My head throbbed and everything looked a bit fuzzy, but my vision was returning.

The snow circle was melting fast, with small patches of the desert floor peeking through. I toed the thin layer of slush at my feet. *Must have melted and spat me out,* I thought.

My back still felt like I had a curling iron wedged between my shoulder blades. I closed my eyes as cold liquid, caffeine and sugar spread through my limbs, boosting my energy as my body fought to neutralize whatever toxins the scorpion had injected me with.

A whup-whup sound drew my attention to the north. A helicopter flew east just above the hills, bathing the ground with a spotlight on its front.

I crushed the empty can and packed it away. "Time to go, Bear. It's getting crowded around here."

I kept checking my shoulder as we trekked west. The helicopter appeared to be hovering low over Dublin Gulch but didn't land.

Walking helped clear my head, and by the time we entered the hills, I felt a lot better. We followed the low valley that led into them. A few steps in, something roared a challenge on the hills above and to the left. About five hundred feet away, a massive boulder thundered down the slope.

No, not a boulder, I thought. *What is that?*

It wasn't a giant scorpion. It didn't scuttle on eight legs. It ran more like a gorilla that I'd seen on TV at the Bodhi Institute, or maybe the troll that I'd encountered back on Allfrost Island.

It reached the valley floor and changed direction, coming right at me.

Even hunched over on all fours, it towered impossibly high. It was even bigger than the troll, maybe twenty feet tall, with hands the size of small cars. Bony spikes a foot and a half long covered its forearms and back. Its skin was coloured like the rock surrounding us—as best I could tell by starlight—dark and leathery, like a reptile's. Eyes the size of my head burned red and orange like fire, and spots of light shone from its neck as if illuminated from within.

Pulling to a stop a hundred feet from me, it stood upright, standing nearly thirty feet tall, and bellowed again. Light from deep within its throat revealed a mouth full of foot-long razor-sharp teeth.

You've got to be kidding me, I thought as my jaw dropped.

"Get back," I shouted to Bear. "Come on!" I turned and bolted.

My canine companion's paws kicked up dust thirty feet ahead. *Smart dog*, I thought as I rushed to catch up.

The behemoth thundered after us like an elephant stampede. I ran at top speed, heading for the snowy battlefield where the giant scorpions still lay, dead and thawing.

Reaching the now-slushy snow, Bear ran wide around it while I hit it straight on, accelerated and spun about. My adversary decelerated as it neared the snow. It pawed at the edge of the slush and withdrew its hand as if burned.

"Don't like the cold, huh?" I said. The monster banged its fists, shaking the earth. I conjured a frost ball, spinning it on my fingertip like a basketball player. "You're in my way, dude."

It recoiled, squinting. A hundred feet above the ground, over my shoulder, the helicopter that I'd seen by Dublin Gulch hovered, shining its spotlight into the creature's face.

Reeling back, the colossus opened its mouth and spat. A ball of fire the size of a boulder flew skyward, deflecting off the top half of the cockpit before crashing into the rotor blades. The aircraft dropped and spun wildly, smoke and flames showering down ahead of its fall. It crashed hard a few hundred feet away.

As the helicopter settled, the brute fell to all fours and blew fire thirty feet before it like a flamethrower, oscillating its head back and forth to cover a wide swath. I shrieked as fire licked across my face, plunging into the snow beneath me and rubbing feeling back into my cheeks. I swam to my right several feet and resurfaced as I hit the far edge of the drift.

The heat of the beast's fire was turning the snow to water, raising a curtain of steam that made it hard to see the dark-skinned monster on the far side. I shot a flurry of frost at it, striking its thick hide. It turned to face me like I'd tapped it on the shoulder and breathed a fireball at me.

Stooped over, I couldn't dodge it in time, so I winced and threw my hands in front of my face. By some long-buried instinct, I surrounded myself in a bubble of pure frost energy, just as I'd seen in my dreams. The projectile stopped a foot from my face, exploding on contact. I staggered as my shield collapsed beneath the assault. I shook my head, suddenly exhausted.

That's some serious dragon breath for an ogre, I thought. *Wait, not an ogre. A Drogre.*

I hobbled away and sank into the surviving snow as more fire passed overhead. Blinking at the glare, I resurfaced seconds later as the last of the snow melted. Heavy footsteps pounded behind me.

I spun around and flinched as the Drogre's fists came up and hammered down. Snow and dirt splashed wide and the ground shook. Only a quick dodge to the right at the last instant had saved me from being pulverized. Before I could get away, the beast's hand shot out and wrapped around my waist. I felt myself leaving the ground as it raised me like an empty soda can and squeezed. My body hardened, making ominous fracturing sounds under the pressure.

As I neared the Drogre's face, I raked my nails of ice across the soft sponginess of one of its fiery red eyes. It howled, opening its mouth wide, and I hurled a fusillade of frost down the monster's gullet. Its gaping maw slammed shut like a portcullis, and its free hand flew to its throat as it coughed and pounded its chest.

Giving me a nasty glare, the Drogre pulled back its arm and tossed me like a football. I landed fifty feet from the fallen helicopter with a deep thump and slid to a stop ten feet from the point of impact. I stumbled to my feet like a drunk picking himself up from the floor after a New Year's Eve party and rubbed my aching back as I turned to face my opponent.

The Drogre hadn't moved. It crouched, still coughing, as the glow at the sides of its throat dimmed and faded. Our eyes met as it looked up. The monster scowled, then pounded the ground.

Its eyes narrowed to slits and it opened its mouth. I raised my hands, creating another frost shield, but no fireball came.

"What are you waiting for?" I muttered as the shield flickered. "Come on."

It stayed where it was, eyeing me, waiting. Tiring, I dropped my hands, collapsing the bubble.

The monster charged a half second later. I raised snow drifts at my feet as it neared, preparing to duck.

As it closed to twenty feet, the sound of gunfire erupted behind me. Bullets zipped past my shoulder—some hitting *me*—before striking the charging Drogre. I dropped into the snow up to my eyes, out of the line of fire, and turned to face the new threat.

Flashes of gunfire continued to flare inside the downed chopper as the brute passed over my head. It hit the fuselage like a linebacker sacking a quarterback, pushing it several feet. Bursts of gunfire continued to sound as the beast pounded on the metal, leaving huge dents with each blow. The monster reached inside and snatched its hand back a second later, shaking drops of blood onto the desert floor.

I popped from the snow and clambered up the monster's back, using the spikes on its hide as handholds. The Drogre shook the chopper as if trying to dislodge a bag of chips from a vending machine as I climbed.

I took a deep breath and threw myself onto the spikes over its neck. I gasped and grimaced as they sank into my abdomen, impaling me.

This better work, I thought.

Feeling faint, I slapped my hands where I guessed the Drogre's ears must be and started streaming cold and frost into its head. The Drogre stood tall, forgetting the helicopter, and pawed at its neck. I felt myself tugged, pulled, and pummelled, but the monster's own spikes held me in place like fuzz stuck to a Velcro fastener as the sound of gunfire resumed.

It staggered away from the onslaught, raining blows down on my back and head. My grip weakened and stars exploded in my eyes as a huge fist bashed me in the head, driving me into the Drogre's thick hide. I blinked, struggling to stay conscious, still sending cold into it. The next blow didn't come as the creature staggered forward and crumpled. As before, I kept up my attack, counting to thirty and watching as a thin layer of frost spread from its head down to its torso.

I lay atop its back, groaning and confused. I did a push-up, lifting myself free of the spikes that impaled me, and cried out. I ached all over. I ached from stab wounds, loss of vital fluids, the heat, and the strain of working the Underfrost. I staggered down the beast's back and fell off, landing face first in the dry, rocky soil. I lay there for several seconds, then stood as Bear ran to my side.

"Hello?" called a voice from the helicopter. "Help, please."

The gunman, I thought.

"Stay back, Bear." He sat on his hind legs. "Good dog."

I stepped around the Drogre's hulking body and looked

inside the chopper. The smell of fuel permeated the air. Two men were inside. One, wearing large headphones and a flight suit, sat strapped into the front seat, his head lolling to the side at an unnatural angle—unnatural for anyone alive, at least. The other held an automatic rifle, pointed loosely in my direction. He pressed a hand to his bleeding forehead, grimacing as he regarded me.

"Hello, Winterboy," said the silver-haired man.

I know that voice, I thought.

"What are you doing here, Harland?" I asked, using Security Director Dixon's first name.

"Rescuing you, by the looks of it."

I pressed my lips together and blew air through them. "Yeah, right, I had it under control."

"Well, sure, I suppose you did at that," he said, wincing. "Nice trick, that. You've got some memories back." It wasn't a question.

I shrugged. "Maybe." I looked at the gun. "I'm not going back. Shoot me if you want. See how that works out for you."

Dixon glanced down at the weapon, then threw it out the open side door and onto the ground at my feet. "Take it. It's empty. What on earth *was* that thing?"

"How'd you find me?" I asked, ignoring the question.

Dixon sucked in air through clenched teeth as he repositioned himself. "Tracking device, in one of the test tubes. I planted one, just in case. Limited range, though, so it took us some time to find you when we finally realized that you'd taken them. For some reason, we only picked it up for a few minutes recently, but it gave us a vector to follow."

"Where's the tracker?" I demanded, tearing the hat from my head. "Which tube?" He recited a serial number. The fourth bottle I grabbed matched. I popped the stopper, sniffing the contents. I dipped a finger into the bottle and touched it to my tongue. *What is this, Kool-Aid?* I held it up, eyeing the liquid inside. *Whatever it is, it's not like the others.* I poured it out over my hand. Something hard and beige landed in my palm.

"That's it," Harland said, nodding.

I crushed it in my hand and threw the pieces at him.

"I'm going now, Harland," I said quietly, staring him in the eyes. "Don't follow me."

"Can't do that, Winterboy."

"Why the hell not? What's your beef with me?"

"No beef," he said, making a dismissive gesture. "But we need you."

"Right," I said, rolling my eyes. "For freedom. For the fight against the Reds. The commies. Nuclear annihilation. We've had this conversation before, and you use that as an excuse for everything. You're a paranoid freaking loon."

Dixon's eyes flashed. "No, I'm a patriot." He shifted his weight, groaning. "I wish I was paranoid, but the threat of socialism is real."

"Come on. What's so wrong with sharing? With everyone having a job and a place to sleep?"

Dixon made a rude sound. "Don't be a naïve fool. Yes, it sounds great *in theory*. But this is the real world, Winterboy. Socialists want to steal the labour and assets of the able-bodied and able-minded for their own so that the more pathetic and useless thrive, cared for by those who actually contribute to society."

I shook my head. "What about those that can't help themselves?"

"Sure," Dixon said, throwing up his hands. "Help those who stumble and need a hand up. Even help those who will never be anything but a burden, if it makes you feel better. But don't you dare try to enslave *everyone else* to your ideals. If it were just the needy, we'd be all right, but it's not." He paused, wincing again. "Don't you see? Most people are lazy, worthless parasites; they'll happily prey upon generosity, take without gratitude, deluding themselves that it is their *right* because they are weak, while trying to convince everyone else of the same. They're criminals…without the work ethic."

"That's pretty harsh," I replied. "Even for you."

"Look, the bottom line is, society owes you nothing beyond the right to compete. Period. You think the Soviets are happy? Of course not—they're all equal in their misery, except for the

Politburo pricks. Why strive for anything in a society where parasites feed off your hard work? It's happening already. Mark my words, if we keep going this way, one day we'll be a nation of entitled whiners."

"Whatever," I said, making a face. I stabbed a finger at him. "You drafted me into your ideological war. You talk about being enslaved by the ideals of others, but you did the same thing to me, you hypocrite."

"You'd do the same. If you could, you'd compel us to help you with your global warming catastrophe. But we're warm-blooded beings, Winterboy. We *like* the heat. No one's got any complaints, except a few tree-hugging alarmists and you. We certainly aren't going to help you bring about a new ice age, if such a thing is even possible."

"I don't remember that, but it sounds like I *asked* for your help. And you kidnapped me, and messed with my mind, stole my memories."

"No, we didn't steal them. Wait…of course…you haven't swallowed the samples yet, have you? You *asked* us to do it."

"What are you talking about? No, I didn't. Why would I?"

"Well, we did go beyond the original agreement when we realized the potential of the elements that you're composed of, but you walked us through the process the first time. There was something you wanted to forget. A tragedy, maybe, or a secret of some kind, perhaps. You wouldn't say. I've got to say, I've got some things I wouldn't mind forgetting myself. If you drink those, you'll get back the bad with the good. Think about that before you do."

"You're lying," I said, looking away. "You can't fool me. I've got a hat full of samples. Once I drink them, I'll know you're just messing with my head…again."

"No, it isn't over. That wasn't all of them. We sent samples to other Bodhi Group labs. If you come back, I'll help you get them back, too. Help you avoid the memories you don't want."

"Why would I believe a word you say?"

"Because we don't need them anymore. Don't ask why."

The radio chattered with static. "You bastard. You've called for help, haven't you? You've been keeping me talking, stalling for time, going on about socialism as usual."

Dixon chuckled, then winced. "Of course I did. I told you; we need you—now more than ever. The shit I've seen to-day…monsters out of myth. Demons. Come back with us. You can have your memories back. Just tell us everything that you know, so we can fight these things."

"Go melt yourself," I said, raising my arms.

"Are there more coming, Shivurr?" I ignored him and walked around the aircraft, raising snow drifts ten feet high. *I can't have you seeing where we go.* He continued to shout in a shrill voice. "Are there? Are there more?"

I called Bear over and we left Dixon behind, still calling to me.

Chapter 33

Can't Bear to Go

I checked the skies behind us for another chopper coming to Dixon's rescue. Seeing none, I exhaled and looked east. The headlights of several vehicles, a few miles off, were moving our way. *Must be the Bodhi Group, or whoever's trucks were parked at the cemetery*, I thought. Whether to rescue Dixon, investigate the crash, or recover the monsters, I didn't know.

I began jogging. Bear increased his pace to match, and we retraced our steps into the hills. I tensed my shoulders as we entered the valley for the second time, half expecting another Drogre to appear. Once inside, Bear led me about a quarter mile into them before we angled to the southwest. We jogged through a low point between two peaks, then turned west. The terrain grew rougher. A rocky hill rose before us a quarter mile off, running north-south, looking like the backbone of some sleeping leviathan. As we got closer, steep cliffs formed a wall. Bear turned right, head down, sniffing the ground as he moved. A short while later, he stopped, lay down, barked and looked back at me.

"What is it, buddy?" I asked, looking around. I saw only rocks and boulders and dark shadows. He stood up and walked in a large circle, then barked again. "This is it? This is the place?" He barked again.

I scratched the back of my head, studying the ground. There was no dais. It just looked like more of the rough, rugged terrain that we'd been walking over for the last while.

It must be hidden under the rock, I thought.

It made sense. Remote as the location was, travellers—prospectors or hikers—would have noticed it by now if it were just sitting out in the open.

I scraped away some of the gravel and found nothing but more of it below. Then I remembered that Olivia had said that I needed to bring the temperature below freezing. *Maybe she meant so that I could see it*, I thought.

"Watch out, Bear," I said, waving him to the side.

He hopped to his feet and padded over to my side as I rolled balls of snow over the ground. Within seconds, mounds of snow bloomed across the area. Then we waited.

It began as a pinpoint of white-and-blue light that snapped to a fifty-foot sphere an instant later. I stepped back as a semi-translucent Allfrost node phased into existence and solidified. A sphere of white light rose from its centre, pulsating with energy. I rolled a few more snowballs over its surface and walked up to the sphere, pulling my hat from my head. Standing next to the energy node, I held the white gem Kurt had given me up to the starlight and looked at Bear.

"Well, here goes," I said, holding the crystal over the sphere and letting it fall. The gem sank into the orb and didn't fall out the other side. I held my breath until it grew larger and started to pulsate. I smiled as the white snow at my feet rose higher still, the air cooled, and snowflakes began to fall. *Just like the cold oasis on Allfrost Island*, I thought. "Is that it, buddy?"

He barked a reply, got to his feet and began walking, which I took to be a good sign. I followed him a short distance to the northwest, uphill, then down into the shadow of the tall, steep cliffs on the other side. Deep within, we approached a wall of rock and he stopped. He barked at it, staring fixedly at a collection of rocks and boulders, residue of a long-ago rockslide, that lay before a small split in the earth.

I moved closer to inspect the gap. It wasn't large enough for me to squeeze through, but in the dim light, I noticed a slight blue-white glow inside. I leaned in and stuck my hand as deep as I could reach. Cooler air caressed my fingertips.

"This must be the place," I said, pulling my hand back and looking at Bear, who sat on his haunches nearby, watching with interest. "You did it, buddy."

I leaned back into the opening, extended my hand, and began filling the crack with snow. I didn't have the strength to Frost Walk, and it looked like a tight fit. When snow burst out of the rift onto the ground at my feet, I stepped back and knelt next to my canine companion. He tilted his head and looked at me, panting, as I ran a hand over his fur.

"All right, Bear. This is where we part ways, I guess. Olivia said you would take care of yourself. After tonight, I suppose she was right. I'll see you soon, I hope." I fed him the last of my water and gave him a hug, and he raised a foreleg to hug me back.

It didn't seem right leaving him unprotected. I called Olivia again on the modified cassette player. "Are you sure it's okay to leave him?" I asked after catching her up on recent events.

"Let me talk to him," she replied. I held the headphone speakers to the dog's ears. He barked several times after a moment, then pulled away. "He'll be fine. Now get moving before they catch up."

I hugged him again, gave his head a scratch and then, feeling inexplicably lonely, slipped into the crevice. Ten feet in, the crack broadened. I could no longer touch both sides at the same time, and cool air enveloped me. A thin film of frost had already formed on the smooth walls of the passageway.

Looks like the power node is doing its thing, I thought.

I strode down the hall, deeper into the earth, until it opened out into a larger cavity much like the other two Allfrost Chambers that I'd seen in recent days.

"Greetings, Sentinel Shivurr," said Hue's familiar voice. "I have been awaiting your arrival since I felt this chamber come back online. Did you succeed in your quest?"

"Hey, Hue," I said, glad to hear a friendly voice. I paused before continuing. "Yeah, more or less. I'll tell you all about it later. For now, I just want to get home. I'm beat."

"Of course," Hue replied in a cheerful voice. "This Allfrost Chamber is currently underpowered, but energy levels are sufficient to enable your return to New Olympus. Do you wish to leave immediately?"

"Yes, please," I said, stepping up to the fountain before the tholos. I rubbed my face and scowled, thinking about the active power node outside. "Hue, are you able to shut down power nodes?"

The AI materialized next to me. "Of course."

"Once I've made it back, can you turn off the one outside? Will that make it vanish again?"

"Most certainly. However, that will take this Allfrost Chamber's transporter and other functions offline once again. You will not be able to use it to return to this location."

I nodded, frowning. "I don't suppose there's a standby mode of some kind. Something less obvious than a pulsating globe of energy and mound of snow in the desert."

"Indeed, there is a low-energy conservation mode. It may still be detected as a pocket of unusually chilly air but will not be visible to the naked eye. I could place it into that state once you have returned. I will be able to reactivate it in this state, if the need arises. Of course, it will then be hard to miss during that time."

"That'd be perfect," I said. "Will you be able to monitor the area in the low-power state? Using its Oculus?"

"The range will be limited to just the immediate vicinity of that particular node, but yes," Hue said. "To what end, if I may inquire?"

"To know if you need to shut it down completely, if people show up and start snooping around. Can you do that?"

"Yes, I believe so."

"Then please do so," I said. "I don't want this chamber found."

"Of course, as you wish. Is there anything else?"

"Is Bear—the dog that was with me—still outside?"

"Negative. The canine began heading west a few minutes ago."

"Anyone else?"

"There are no living creatures larger than an insect in range of this chamber's currently functioning Oculi at this point in time."

"What about scorpions the size of a bus?" I muttered.

"I beg your pardon?" Hue said, sounding baffled.

"Read my thoughts," I said, calling up the battles in my mind.

"Oh, yes, I see now. That is quite remarkable. Most likely they are creatures of the Faction. Nothing of the kind is visible currently, but this chamber's current visibility range is severely limited at present."

"Fair enough." I took a breath and held a hand over the fountain. "Either way, it's time for me to go." I pictured the island in my mind, activating the transporter, and a huge ball of snow rose to engulf me. I was on my way home, at last.

Chapter 34

Lucky to Be Here

A few days later, I held an iced tea in hand and lounged in a lawn chair, looking out at the frothing waters of the Pacific Ocean. Caleb and Hanale sat atop their surfboards offshore, laughing and talking as they waited for another good wave to ride.

Large clouds sat on the horizon as the sun climbed higher overhead. I sighed and inhaled deep breaths of air, enthralled by the amazing view, so much more interesting than the plains of ice and snow that I saw in my dreams.

Olivia baked in the sun nearby while I kept to the shade, still drained by my odyssey.

Wilhelm had not yet returned. Tonight, Olivia promised. Then we would get Caleb back home. Then I would drink the potions for which I had struggled so hard and finally, I hoped, reclaim myself. Then we would figure out where to go next.

Olivia raised her sunglasses and looked at me from beneath a broad-brimmed hat. "What are you thinking about, Shivurr?"

"That I'm lucky to be here. Lucky to be alive, especially after Dublin Gulch."

"I knew that you'd be fine."

"Why's that?"

Olivia shrugged. "Bear was with you."

"He's a fighter, but—wait, you sent him to protect me, not just to guide me?"

She smiled. "You didn't need him, though."

"Well, he sure did try," I said, thinking of how he'd charged the giant scorpion. "I just hope he's all right. I didn't like leaving him behind."

"Don't worry about it," Olivia said. "He'll be fine. He's a special dog."

An Alaskan shepherd wandering Death Valley would have to be pretty special to stand a chance of surviving, I thought. Still, since Olivia wasn't worried, I tried to do as she asked. I had enough to do; there was no need to go looking for things to add to my list of concerns.

The Faction was still out there scheming, and the Bodhi Group still searched for me. And there was still the forgotten crisis that had led me to go to Nevada in the first place. The Allfrost was failing and it was needed now more than ever. *As an Allfrost Sentinel, it's my responsibility to restore it, right?*

I shook my head as if to clear those thoughts away. *All that can wait for another day. Today, I'm with friends in paradise.*

I took a sip of my drink and leaned back in my chair, studying the clouds overhead.

I just wish that I could freeze moments like this.

Author's Note

Thanks for reading *Phantom Frost*. I hope you've enjoyed it. Shivurr's adventures will continue in the next novel in the series, which is in progress as of this writing. You will also soon be able to play as Shivurr in the upcoming Wurreal Games video game coming to PC, Mac, and Linux.

Subscribe to my mailing list to get news, updates and more at: www.alfredwurr.com/subscribe.

Acknowledgements

Special thanks to my beta readers for taking the time to read the book and provide invaluable feedback.

Lorelei Pierce
Christopher Cordray
Mark Gabriel
David Kuik

Book cover by Damonza.com.
Editing by Clio Editing Services.

About the Author

Since he was ten years old, Alfred has wanted to write and publish a science fiction/fantasy novel. In the years between, he has been an Olympic freestyle wrestler (winning national and international championships), a computer scientist (M.Sc.), a software developer and consultant, and a video game developer.

He lives with his wife, Lorelei, in Canada, where staying frosty comes easy half the year.

Subscribe to Alfred's mailing list to get news, updates, and more at: www.alfredwurr.com/subscribe. You may also contact the author at: www.alfredwurr.com/contact-page.

Twitter: @alfredwurr
Facebook: www.facebook.com/alfredwurrauthor